Mr. Important

A Honeybridge Novel

Lucy Lennox

May Archer

Cover design: Natasha Snow
Cover Photo: Michelle Lancaster @lanefotograf
Beta Reading and Editing: One Love Editing
Proofreading: Jodi Duggan and Victoria Rothenberg

Mr. Important

One New Year's masquerade. One anonymous hookup. One billionaire-sized mistake.

Once upon a time, someone looked at my scrawny, impetuous eight-year-old self and nicknamed me Mr. Important... and I believed them.

That was my first mistake.

Two decades, a dozen failed careers, and a thousand meaningless hookups later, I've made more mistakes than I can count. My parents have decided I'm purely decorative, my brother thinks I need pep talks, and the gorgeous billionaire who hired me as a favor to my dad? He's forgotten I exist.

So I'm done with mistakes.

Call it my New Year's resolution. From now on, I'm going after what I want... starting with the mysterious silver fox in the Roman warrior mask who approached me at the charity gala and offered me a scorching, anonymous one-night stand.

Unfortunately, when our masks come off I realize mistakes are not done with me.

Because the bossy guy who blew my mind? He'd thought I was someone else. Worse than that, he's my father's friend. A supposedly-straight workaholic. The person I'm stuck on a road trip with for the next two weeks. And, oh yeah, my actual boss.

The farther we get from New York, the closer we become, and the harder it is to pretend I'm not falling for him. But I can't see how someone as brilliant, controlled, and successful as Thatcher Pennington would risk everything to be with someone like me... even if he makes me feel like I'm finally *Mr. Important*.

While *Mr. Important* is set in the Honeybridge world, it can be easily enjoyed on its own.

Chapter One

Reagan

"Mask stays on. Clothes come off," a deep, male voice rumbled in my ear. "You're going to be good for me tonight, aren't you?"

The man's indecent proposal sent a trail of goose bumps washing over my skin, and I froze in shock.

Before he'd spoken, I'd been watching various couples twirl across the floor at the masked charity ball, wondering what the hell I was doing there on New Year's Eve when there were so many other, more fun, places I could be. When I'd moved out of my parents' house in tiny Honeybridge, Maine, I'd left my designer tuxedo hanging in the closet for a reason: glad-handing at society galas wasn't supposed to be on my agenda anymore. But I'd underestimated how hard it was to break the habits of a lifetime—namely, my parents' habit of thinking they ran my social calendar and my habit of letting them. Just a couple of months into what should have been my personal renaissance, there I was, doing my best impression of a politician's silent, smiling second son while the cameras flashed, wearing a black feathered mask atop a stifling mask of bland politeness and praying someone (not me this time) would do something interesting before midnight to save me from death by boredom.

Fortunately, the Universe had heard my plea.

*Un*fortunately, it had sent excitement in the form of a creepy whisperer... which was really on brand for the Reagan Wellbridge Renaissance Era, whose tagline seemed to be "be careful what you wish for."

Under other circumstances, being approached by a creepy whisperer might have been outrageous in a fun way. A hilarious tale to trot out to my friends at parties, or maybe even a story for my Instagram followers. But the last few months had been... well, difficult.

When I'd moved to New York, I'd vowed to be a new Reagan. A different Reagan. Not an immature twenty-something socialite whose parents controlled his bank account or a pretty, wholesome-looking doll who posed at campaign rallies.

But nothing had quite worked out the way I'd planned, and New Reagan was frustrated as fuck.

All the career disappointments I'd been pushing down for weeks, all the snarky retorts I'd choked back while making my way around the party tonight, sat in my chest like a heap of dry kindling, and the creepy whisperer was the spark.

I turned around to spew all of my anger and resentment in a verbal torrent sharp enough to flay this rude, outrageous man's flesh from his bones...

And then choked on my own saliva.

Rude and outrageous he might be, but the creepy whis-perer was... *built.*

He was tall—well over six feet—and his perfectly tailored black tuxedo lovingly cupped his broad shoulders and chest. Dark hair swept cleanly back from his brow. Though I couldn't make out his eyes behind the burnished gold of his Roman warrior mask, especially in the "atmospheric" faux candlelight of the ballroom, I could feel the intensity of his gaze as he watched me.

Not creepy but *sexy*. Sexy enough to shoot a bolt of lust down my spine that left me shivering in the overheated ballroom. And so very much my type.

Maybe the Universe had done me a solid after all.

"Pardon me?" My words came out husky and flirtatious. "Do I know you?"

One black brow lifted over the top of the man's mask, and his plush lips set in a firm, unsmiling line that made my pulse race with arousal... and then with a sudden fear as I remembered exactly where and *who* I was.

Think, Reagan. How likely was it that a man who resembled a Roman warrior even without his mask was trolling for an anonymous hookup with another man at a stuffy event like this one, where every third guest was a politician, a reporter, or a society gossip? More than likely, I'd misunderstood, or—

"Not interested in games," he growled, leaning closer. A muscle ticked in his perfectly smooth jaw.

—or maybe I'd understood perfectly. I blinked. How the hell did his voice feel like it was wrapping directly around my balls, firm as a physical touch?

His earlier words seared through my brain like a flash fire, burning away all other thoughts: *Mask stays on. Clothes come off.*

Well, shit.

Back when my father had been on the cusp of his political career—which was, sadly, right around the time I'd begun transforming from a sweet child into a snarky, opinionated teenager who Needed to Be Managed—my mother had signed me up for formal etiquette lessons. I'd loathed them, of course, but they'd come in handy over the years. These days, I could chat with anyone, from a sultan at a polo match to nice, elderly ladies in retirement homes, and most of the time, I even enjoyed it. I was never, ever at a loss for words.

Until now.

"I, uh..." I stammered, face on fire. "That is... When you say...? Are you asking me to...?"

It wasn't the offer of sex, or sex with a man, or even sex at a society function that flustered me. Been there, done that, *plenty*. My mother might choose to believe I was one purity ring away from heterosexual virginity—and god knew I'd never cared to spell the truth out for her—but in the past ten years, I'd been with men, women, and nonbinary folx in all sorts of configurations across four separate continents. My DMs were always open. In fact, my brother, JT, joked that I was "try-sexual" because I'd try anything once.

But *this*—the Roman warrior's erotic vibe of control, his expectation that I'd be good for him, the way my gut wasn't screaming *hell no* but, shockingly, rolling over and panting *yes*? All of that was brand-new. I'd always sort of thought the whole "dark, mysterious, and dominant" schtick was a patriarchal cliché I was too smart to fall for. Yet here I was... falling.

"Room 4187, thirty minutes," the man said roughly, ignoring my hesitation. With two long, sure fingers, he slid a key card into the breast pocket of my tuxedo jacket, then leaned forward until I was wrapped in the scent of his cologne—something smoky and mysterious and familiar. "If you're late, I'll find another plaything."

Plaything? My whole body broke out in a cold sweat. *Sweet fucking Christ, why was that so hot?*

"Y-yes, sir," I whispered.

Those two magic words seemed to seal the deal. The man nodded once, turned, and disappeared into the crowd.

I shuddered out a breath and pushed up my mask in an attempt to provide my lungs with oxygen. Thirty minutes, he'd said? My phone showed it was 11:04 p.m., less than an hour until the champagne corks popped, and suddenly, I was very okay with my plans for ringing in the New Year.

I opened my phone, adjusted the settings, pulled my mask back down, and posted a quick, unedited selfie—wild grin, skewed bow tie, and all. *Remember, NYE sets the tone for the year!* I captioned as my body tingled with anxious anticipation. *So be BOLD! *heart-hands emoji**

I'd barely hit Post when a cloud of Chanel No. 5 swirled around me, and before I could adequately brace myself, Patricia Wellbridge appeared before me like the ghost of New Year's Past, fanning herself with her mask.

"Reagan, my darling! I sent you to fetch drinks for Lindy and me hours ago." My mother's face froze in a wide-eyed expression that might have conveyed disapproval had the Botox allowed it. "I'm absolutely parched."

I squeezed my eyes shut for an instant, but when I opened them, she was very much still there, in full jeweled-and-feathered regalia, blocking my escape. *Damn it.*

"Mother." I slid my hands into my pockets and tried very hard to shrug like a dutiful son... and not like a man who had a perfect stranger's room key burning a hole in his pocket. "So sorry. I was waylaid by a reporter who wanted to know Dad's views on Maine's strategic petroleum reserves," I lied. "The hazards of attending a press gala, right?"

"The reporter asked *you*?" she demanded, making a *tsk-*ing noise. "Was it that vulture who did the *hit piece* on your father last summer? Mr. Acton?"

I managed not to roll my eyes. The previous summer, my father had flubbed an interview badly, and the reporter had capitalized on the opportunity, but that was his job... and I would have said that even if I *hadn't* shared an unwise onetime hookup with the reporter in question—a tidbit that did *not* make it into the article, thank you—before I committed to being a more mature, professional me.

Thankfully, I was saved from having to reply when my mother promptly launched into a whispered tirade about vulture journalists. The rant might have seemed highly ironic at a gala to raise money in support of the free press... unless you understood that we weren't actually here in support of the cause but in support of my father's political ambitions and my mother's burning desire to marry me off to a "nice young lady" like Lindy, who had impeccable social connections.

After letting Mother rant for a few precious moments of my thirty-minute countdown, I interrupted. "There's no need to get worked up. I'm twenty-eight years old, and I've been doing this for years. I can handle a few questions from reporters."

My mother's face contorted into something like a pained smile, and the reek of doubt coming off her was stronger than her Chanel. "Remember the time they asked you about the changes to the state's school curriculum and you said you supported them?"

"I was seventeen," I countered, cheeks hot beneath my mask. "And I *do* support sex education, including LGBTQ topics."

"But your father hadn't committed one way or the other,

Reagan, and they weren't really asking about *your* views. When you're in public, you're a reflection of us. Your father and me."

I set my jaw.

"And then there was the time you were *inebriated*," she sighed, "and allowed yourself to be filmed singing and dancing to that vile song in public—"

"It was karaoke. For charity. Years ago. And it wasn't vile—"

My mother dismissed my protests with a wave, as she did with most unpleasant things, and patted my chest affectionately. "Your father has professional campaign staffers and lets them schedule interviews for a reason, dear. I know you'd hate to harm your father's campaign, even by accident. It's best for everyone if you just relax and smile. Jonathan learned that quite early on," she reminded me.

"Right." I managed not to sound bitter—barely—at this mention of my beloved, golden boy older brother, JT, a man I would have absolutely *hated*... if he hadn't been so damn decent and generous and annoyingly lovable.

Mother nodded serenely at a nearby woman in an elaborately decorated red mask. "Now, then. Have you taken a picture of yourself looking handsome for your internet friends?"

"Yes, Mother." It didn't matter how many paid sponsorships I'd gotten or how many social media accounts I managed, my mother insisted on seeing my *one million* internet friends as a sort of hobby. I pulled away from her fussing hands.

"Now, darling, I've been meaning to talk to you about your schedule for the next few months. You know I don't begrudge you a chance to sow your wild oats in the big city, but the governor's race is heating up back home. I know you're having fun at this little job of yours, but perhaps once Thatcher's back from his holiday beach trip, I'll speak to him about giving you some time off—"

"Do *not* speak to Thatcher," I said, so fiercely that she blinked. "Under no circumstances."

"But he's a friend of your father's—"

"I haven't forgotten." More bitterness leaked out. "And I know that's most of the reason he offered me this position. But he's not my direct boss. I don't even see him very much." *Or at all. Ever.* "And I'm not going to ask for special treatment. Besides, I offered to be part of Dad's campaign staff and was turned down. I'm concentrating on my career."

"Oh, Reagan." The look she gave me was a perfect mixture of parental fondness and crushing parental doubt. "It's not that we don't want you to be part of the campaign. Of course we do—"

"In front of the camera, as long as I keep my mouth shut. Behind the scenes, stuffing envelopes as an unpaid volunteer."

"You make it sound so... *menial.*" Mother shook her head. "It's a position that gives you lots of flexibility, remember? And if you'd like to jet off to Corfu with some lucky young woman or perhaps spend some time on the West Coast like you did a few years ago, we're happy to treat you to those things—"

"I don't want to do either of those things. I'm a social media manager—"

She patted my arm. "Of course you are. Just like you were a finance expert when your father got you that job with Buck Stanley. And the public speaking internship with Tish Cooper's firm. Oh, and the design job with Martin, Heller, Bramovich... I think you lasted nearly two months with that one! I'm sure you're doing great things at Pennington Industries, but really... how long will that last, sweetheart?"

The hardest part about hearing her recite my list of failed career opportunities was that I couldn't argue with any of it. I'd tried—genuinely tried, I thought—at all of them. But the only talent I'd demonstrated was quitting... once, after just two weeks. I wouldn't embarrass either of us by insisting, yet again, that this time was different... though it really was.

Late last summer, after JT had come home to Honeybridge and fallen for Flynn, I'd done a lot of soul-searching about what I really wanted (and didn't want) out of life. I needed a purpose. I'd realized that the things I was *already* doing—namely, successfully managing social media for myself and several wealthy friends—was making me enough money for a man to live on, if that man was willing to forego certain luxuries. What's more, I was passionate about social media. I was *good* at it. And best of all, I could continue to help my father's campaign while also building my resume by simply taking over as social media strategist for the Trent Wellbridge for Governor campaign. It would be, I'd told my parents, a win-win for everyone.

My father had literally laughed out loud.

Despite my experience overhauling my friends' images online, despite having over a million Instagram followers, despite the utter lack of social media vision in my father's campaign, despite the *decade* I'd spent attending political rallies and public events, he'd told me there was no way he'd consider me for the job.

Unreliable, he'd called me. *Untrustworthy. Undisciplined.*

I'd been angry. Hurt. But more than that, I'd been

freaking determined to prove that I meant what I said. So, I'd decided to rehabilitate my own image. To make sure I was never again seen as a slacker or a nepo baby. To make myself so valued, so in demand that my father would *beg* me to work for him.

When my father's friend Thatcher—thick-bearded, kind-eyed, straight-as-an-arrow, first-guy-I'd-ever-crushed-on Thatcher Pennington—had offered me an entry-level PR job as an olive branch to the family after his son had behaved badly in Honeybridge last summer, it had seemed like a sign. If I could impress *him*, my parents' opinion of me would rise like the tide, and the campaign job would be mine. The fact that I'd get to work with Thatcher—joke over long lunches with Thatcher, drool over the suit-porn eye candy of Thatcher, discreetly sniff the goodness of Thatcher the way I'd dreamed of doing since the first time I'd met him (and his lovely second wife) when I was fifteen —would be a delightful side benefit.

I wasn't sure whether to laugh or cry at how foolishly optimistic I'd been.

I hadn't asked any follow-up questions, like what exactly the work would entail. I hadn't considered just how little Thatcher would think of my abilities after hearing stories from my father all these years. And I'd found myself stuck working in a tiny cubicle all the way in the back corner of the PR department at PennCo Fiber, one of twelve smaller Pennington *subsidiaries*, not even in the same building as the eye candy I needed to impress. Being a public relations associate for a textile company was akin to being a security guard at a nunnery since nothing of note ever happened.

And none of that frustration meant I was going to quit—

not this time, no way—but it also meant that I was due for some good karma.

Preferably in the form of a sexy, mysterious Roman warrior who smelled like sage and woodsmoke.

"Please think about it," my mother said when I went too long without replying. "We really do miss you, Reagan."

I forced a smile. One of these days, I'd really like to be missed by someone for all the *right* reasons. Because they wanted me, *specifically* me. But in the meantime... there was a man waiting for me who'd chosen me out of a crowded ballroom without knowing a damn thing about my parents. Who'd wanted to fuck me—for me to be his *good boy*—without even seeing my camera-ready face. And that was more than enough for tonight.

"Of course," I lied. "But in the meantime, I have to go. Safe travels back to Maine." I leaned in to kiss her cheek. "And wish Dad good luck on the new legislative session."

Before she could argue, I headed through the crowd toward the nearest exit. The cool quiet of the hotel lobby was a relief after the ballroom packed with story-hungry reporters and deep-pocketed political donors, but I didn't slow down to appreciate it. I jabbed the Up button and stared at my blurry reflection in the copper-colored elevator doors, tapping my toe impatiently.

I'd been eager to get upstairs before, but now I couldn't wait another second to see my mystery man. With just a few words, the man had set off a spark in me so hot it might burn me from the inside out if I didn't let him quench it. And if the Universe was finally giving me a gift, a moment of clarity and brightness where I didn't need to prove anything to anyone, I was ready to accept.

So I stepped inside the elevator and, a few moments

later, stepped out onto a deserted hallway that I followed down to Room 4187.

I'd learned over the years that life could be full of disappointment. The trick was to keep trying… and take your moments of happiness where you could find them.

A low ding from the elevator down the hall made me realize how long I'd stood outside the hotel room, immobile. But before I could tap the lock to open the door, I realized a man had gotten out of the elevator and was heading my way, watching me steadily.

Not just any man. My Roman warrior.

It was possibly the most Instagram-worthy moment of my life, but I had no urge to take a picture and share this with the world. This night was just for me.

"You're late," he said as he approached.

In this light, I noticed all sorts of things I hadn't seen downstairs. The hint of salt and pepper at his temple, the utter assurance of his posture as he walked. This was a man who'd probably never heard the word no, who didn't understand the *concept* of failure, and for some reason, that drew me to him like a magnet.

"I've been standing here for several minutes, just… thinking," I admitted, feeling stupid.

"Is that so?" His firm mouth twitched at the corner. "Having second thoughts now that you're here?"

"No," I said honestly. "I tried, but they wouldn't stick. I rarely have second thoughts until *after* I've done something."

He rewarded me with another lip twitch and gestured toward the doorknob. "After you, then."

I let myself in the room, and he trailed me, following closely enough for me to get another hit of his woodsy scent. As soon as the door closed behind us and I slipped the key card back into my pocket, he moved even closer until his nose brushed the back of my ear and his warm breath hit the skin below.

"I expected you to be waiting for me, naked," he murmured before running the tip of his tongue along the edge of my ear. "But you know what they say. If you want something done right..." My heart hammered as the man's hands slid down my shoulders to my lapels and yanked my tuxedo jacket off.

I made a breathless sound of approval as he dropped the jacket and moved his hands back to untie the bow tie. "Mmm. An actual bow tie. The man has taste." He tugged one end, loosening the knot, then kept pulling until the tie slid away from my collar. All the while, his lips continued to tease the skin on the back of my neck with hot, open-mouthed kisses that sent electric shivers all the way to my toes.

I was so lost to sensation already that I barely noticed when he pushed me up against the door and began removing my shirt with excruciating slowness, one stud at a time.

He didn't speak but made deep noises of approval in his throat as he pulled my shirt open and leaned in to kiss my chest. The sensation of my shirt being pulled out of my pants by his sure hands was enough to send blood flowing just as surely into my dick. His confidence was sexy as fuck, and I found myself relaxing into it, letting myself surrender to him—to this thing between us—in a way I'd never truly done before.

At first, I thought it was just the novelty of the situation that was making me so compliant, the idea of letting go of control when I was normally the one to take charge. But as he moved my body in various positions to continue peeling my clothes away, I realized there was something about it... something about *him*... that made me want to please him on a deeper level.

Maybe it was the age difference. Even if I couldn't tell by the hints of gray in his hair and his large, veiny hands that he was older, I'd know it from the way he moved with certainty and decisiveness, like he was used to being obeyed. Like he'd been born to take charge.

I wanted to ask him questions—to know who he was and what he wanted—but my mouth stayed stubbornly closed. If I said something stupid, I would most likely shatter the delicious tension building between us.

When he turned me around again so his mouth could begin a trail of hungry kisses down the center of my back, I sucked in a breath and reached for my cock.

His hand quickly grabbed my wrist and pulled it away before holding it hostage against the small of my back. "Mine," he murmured, biting my shoulder. I squeezed my eyes closed and tilted my head back against him with a groan. His fingers came up to clasp the front of my throat before his lips moved behind my ear, licking and sucking.

It was both too much and not enough. I reached up with both hands to grasp the back of his head, needing to anchor myself. Needing to make this *personal* somehow.

The kiss was like a flash-bang. It shocked and disoriented me without warning. His lips were warm and soft, but his response to my kiss was aggressive and all-consuming. He clasped the sides of my head and held me in place, caught between the door and the firm press of his lips until even the very air I breathed seemed to come only from him.

It was exactly what I hadn't known I needed. The best kiss I'd ever had, in a lifetime of kisses. And for the first time in... shit, maybe ever?... I felt like the reality of this hookup was living up to its promise.

By the time he moved one hand down to brush my desperate cock through my pants, I was so dizzy and starved for more that an embarrassingly high-pitched *"Please"* escaped me.

"I've got you, baby," he growled, pressing his forehead against my neck.

I opened my eyes and tilted my head back against the door, suddenly needing to see him. Needing to know this was really happening. Needing to know he was as lust-drowned and wrecked as I was.

So when I reached down to pull his face up to me and felt the edge of his mask biting into my wrist, I yanked it off and sent it sailing across the room along with my own before tugging his face closer for another kiss.

But when a pair of warm, brown eyes met mine, I gasped, not with excitement but with something more like horror.

I knew those eyes. Had daydreamed about them, in fact.

I knew that face, too, though I couldn't remember ever seeing it without a full beard before.

Because the stranger I was hooking up with... the man who'd already done a fair job of bringing me to my knees in wretched supplication... was none other than Thatcher Pennington.

My father's friend.

The CEO of the Pennington Industries.

My boss.

Chapter Two

Thatcher

Look, I never claimed to be a saint.

The media had crafted a certain narrative about *the* Thatcher Pennington, and I'd let them run with it. They called me a self-made billionaire who lived a life of leisure. They said I loved social events and never missed a philanthropic gala. They decided I was a devoted father who'd been twice unlucky in love and that I must secretly pine for the woman who'd "heal" my "broken heart" and become the third Mrs. Pennington.

I'd let them run with these stories because I knew the truth... and it was nobody else's business.

It was no one's business that I was actively bisexual or that I'd rather slather myself in flesh-eating bacteria than ever get married again since at least the bacteria wouldn't contest a prenup and try to take part of my company. It was no one's business that my adult son was so determined to avoid me that he'd canceled our Christmas vacation.

It was no one's business that I'd planned to distract myself from the end of yet another year in which my career was the most stable thing in my life by spending

New Year's Eve at home... or that I'd felt so restless and dissatisfied, I'd changed my plans at the last minute, spontaneously shaved the beard I'd worn for years, and arranged a hookup with a guy whose profile on the hookup app promised total anonymity and absolute submission.

And it was sure as fuck no one's business that the guy had turned out to be so damn perfect—both taller and younger than I'd expected, with sun-streaked hair that reminded me of summer in the depths of a New York winter, skin so tender he moaned at the lightest touch, and a heady mix of submissive and defiant vibes that made my dick hard and my balls ache—that I'd found myself calling him *baby* and wondering how many times he'd let me take him before the night was over.

No, I was damn sure no one would ever find out about any of that.

Because for this one night, I was going to slake my lust on the handsome, pliant man in my arms, unleash every sordid fantasy I'd ever dreamed up, and tomorrow, no one would be the wiser about what the *real* Thatcher Pennington craved.

But then the man in my arms pulled back, opened his magnificent eyes for the first time without the concealing shadows of his blue-feathered mask in place... and gasped in horror. And with an icy-cold shock of recognition, I realized that my very secret, very anonymous hookup was actually neither.

"Reagan?" I breathed.

Jesus Christ.

Of all the fucking people fate could have sent to torment me... Reagan fucking Wellbridge?

Trent and Patricia's son? Brantleigh's friend? My

goddamn *employee*, since I'd rashly offered the kid a low-level position as a *mea culpa* last August?

This was so disastrous on so many levels my mind scrambled to latch onto one. Warnings tumbled through my head like falling rocks: *Danger! Steep drop ahead! Turn back!*

My hands gripped his hip and his shoulder, wanting to shove him as far from me as possible... but I was so stunned I couldn't even do that properly. With our lower bodies still entwined, all I did was set him off-balance so his shoulders hit the door and his cock pressed against the hard heat of my thigh, making us both gasp in unison.

Aquamarine eyes lifted to mine, glassy with lust, and for a crucial moment, I hesitated.

Fuck, those eyes did things to me.

They were the color of sea glass at the beach. Of precious stones. They shifted hue with the light and Reagan's mood, revealing tantalizing glimpses of secrets in their depths.

I'd done a piss-poor job of ignoring those eyes last summer when I'd visited his parents in Honeybridge. For the first time in all the years since our families had become friendly, I'd caught myself staring at them—in the moments when I could force my gaze away from his perfectly rounded ass, his well-developed pecs, his prominent Adam's apple, and his ever-present sexy smirk—and I'd gone out of my way to avoid talking to the man precisely to avoid a situation like this one.

I'd avoided doing all the things I'd have done for any other son-of-a-friend I'd employed, too—no offer of a spare room in my huge penthouse, no friendly lunches, no cushy job in the Executive Office—because I'd known those eyes were a temptation I couldn't resist, though every tenet of friendship and several pertinent employment laws required me to.

And staring at them now, filled with heat and longing and the slightest bit of hesitation, even with the truth of our identities sitting like a bloated elephant between us, I couldn't look away. I was frozen with indecision when I most needed to act. Captivated by their depths when I most needed to be rational.

Move away, I instructed myself firmly. *Tell him to get his clothes on. Kick him out. Show some fucking control. Don't be a fool. Disaster ahead.*

I opened my mouth to put a stop to this, but before I could say a word, a low sound of need escaped his throat. And just like that, my decision was made.

Mentally cursing both of us, I lunged at him, gripping Reagan's shoulders and shoving him onto the bed before following him down and covering his gasp of surprise with my mouth.

Fuck control. Fuck doing the right thing. And fuck Reagan fucking Wellbridge for putting me in this position in the first fucking place.

It didn't occur to me until later that evening, when I could spare enough blood to work my brain, that the man on the hookup app had *brown* eyes. That the identifying pic he'd sent me earlier in the evening had shown an aquiline nose beneath his blue-feathered mask, not at all like Reagan's perfect freckled one. That I'd intended to meet someone else entirely, and none of this should have happened.

At that moment, I was too far gone to think. For the first time in as long as I could remember, I pushed aside all thought of the future and took what I wanted. And what I wanted was my dick inside Reagan Wellbridge, my hands all over his fit body, and the sound of his pleas in my ears.

One night only, I told myself. A time out of time in which we exchanged orgasms and then went our separate ways, never to speak of it again. And I would make it count.

I shoved his hands above his head and held both wrists in one grip.

"Stay still," I warned him between nips of his jaw and chin.

His breath hitched in a way that went straight to my balls.

He was so fucking responsive, so perfectly willing to let go and let me be in charge. I wanted to take advantage of whatever time I had with him to see exactly how good the sex could be between us.

I shoved a knee between his legs and pressed into his erection with my hip, rolling up and down his hard length and relishing the feel of him through our pants.

Reagan threw his head back with a groan. "Stop fucking teasing me."

He might as well have waved a red flag in front of me. Now, all I wanted to do was tease him, edge the hell out of him until his cock leaked and his eyes watered.

I moved my mouth down his neck to his chest and sucked on one of his nipples, tweaking the other between my fingers, all the while not letting up with the roll of my hip against his dick. He tilted his hips up into me, seeking more friction, but every time he came close, I pulled back and weakened the press of our bodies.

His breath came in shallow pants, and both of his hands twisted into my hair and tugged. His legs finally wrapped around my back as he arched up into me again.

I reached down to open his pants before shoving my

hand inside to feel his long, thick shaft. The fabric of his boxer briefs was damp with precum, which turned me the fuck on even more than discovering the size of his package or feeling the heat of him in my hand.

"You wet for me?" I grumbled as I moved my mouth down his chest to his happy trail. "Leaking all over yourself, hmm? That's good. I like that. Show me how much you want this."

"*Fuck.*" Reagan's breathing was hoarse, and his hands trembled when he grabbed at my arm. How long had it been since this man had been in bed with someone else? I couldn't remember the last time I'd seen someone so desperate for release. "Please, Mr.— I mean, Tha— I mean, *mmpfh.*"

His attempts to figure out what to call me made me want to laugh despite the need swamping me because I understood his frustration. Despite being very much *not* a kid anymore, he'd always called me Mr. Pennington— maybe his own way of keeping distance between us—but that felt silly in this moment. Calling me Thatcher, though, made this encounter a little too real.

I did him a solid by making sure he didn't have to speak in full sentences at all.

I ran the tip of my tongue down through the rough hair of Reagan's lower belly, admiring the tight, sculpted, youthful abs and inhaling the musky scent of his groin. His pants and underwear came down slowly, only enough to unveil his cock to me little by little so I could tease him with my tongue along the way.

"Fucking *fuck,*" he muttered under his breath. "Masochist. Asshole. *Christ.*"

I smiled darkly. Looked like Reagan had solved his little name problem.

"Give me... please... just... oh god..."

He writhed on the bed, still running his fingers through my hair. The slight scratch of his nails on my scalp made my skin prickle.

I took his thick cock into my mouth and ran my tongue around it hungrily, enjoying the sound of him choking as he nearly swallowed his tongue. He shouted a deep curse into the room and cupped my head to gently hold it in place.

Good boy.

I gazed up at him and drank in the sight of his open mouth, the divots between his eyebrows as he stared down at me, and the impossibly intense gaze from those fucking incredible eyes.

One night won't be enough.

The words rushed unspoken through my head as I surrounded myself with the taste and smell and sound of him.

Too bad, I told myself firmly, shoving those thoughts back into whatever dark recess of my brain they'd escaped from. *One night is all there is.*

Even if it were possible to ignore Reagan's age, he was my friend's son... and, admittedly to a lesser extent these days, my son's friend. He was my employee. He was spoiled and immature, flighty and attention-seeking—or, as Patricia called it, "a bit... temperamental, you understand." Reagan Wellbridge was the dictionary definition of a bad idea, even if I hadn't sworn off entanglements altogether...

And I had.

"Fuck me, please," Reagan begged in a broken voice, drawing me out of my thoughts and right back into a vortex of passion. "Need it. Need this. Need..."

The *you* was unspoken, but I heard it, and my dick throbbed instinctively.

I sucked him off until he spilled hot and sticky into my throat, and without giving him time to recover—or giving myself time to overthink—I proceeded to tease and finger his sweet ass until he was ready for more.

The rest of our clothes ended up on the floor, and there was nothing left between us but sweaty skin, breathless curses, and pleas. Our hands and mouths searched out every inch and crevice of skin to enflame and devour. I dragged rough fingers over his nipples and sucked a bruise just below the enormous phoenix tattoo on his thigh, marking him... at least temporarily.

In some ways, this was familiar to me: hard cocks, low grunts and moans, seeking release with my tongue in another person's mouth. But in so many other ways, it was strangely different.

Reagan was tall and muscular, masculine and hard, but he let me move his body exactly where I wanted it. He let me command him, but I also had the sense he wasn't about to obey me blindly. It was almost like a game, like he was testing the very idea of letting me tell him what to do. At any minute, he could bark out a laugh and throw me over onto my back before becoming the aggressive pursuer.

That excited me in a way that was unexpected. My dick ached for him, for completion inside his tight body. I imagined shoving him onto his stomach and fucking him from behind, feeling the impossible clench of him around me while I came deep inside him. My brain boiled, consumed with the image, but I couldn't stop kissing him long enough to flip him over.

We ended up frotting frantically, my hips forcing our shafts to slide against each other until I had to fumble in the bag on my nightstand for lube just to ease the way.

The feeling of his hands on me, the little sounds

emerging from his throat, the heat of his mouth as he licked at my chin, my earlobe, my neck, my fingers, any part of me he could reach, brought me to the brink faster than I'd thought possible. So much for entering him and making the most of our one and only night together. I couldn't wait. I gripped us both in a fist and shuttled my hand up and down while continuing to kiss him until my lips were raw from his stubble.

"Come for me," I growled. "Now."

And he did, gloriously, his head bowing back into the mattress as he screamed.

When my orgasm hit, I vaguely noted the hot scent of it in my nose, the wet heat spilling over my hand, and the tortured groan leaving his throat and entering mine, but I was gasping so hard that black spots painted the edges of my vision. Almost like I was still wearing my damn mask. A happy, humming noise swelled in my brain, and it took several seconds for me to realize that the sound wasn't coming from inside me but from merrymakers singing in the hall and possibly from cheering on the street far below us.

The old year was over. A new one had begun.

I stared down at Reagan Wellbridge as I fought to catch my breath. His eyes were blown wide with shock, the aquamarine clear and warm as the Caribbean. His hair was a damp, tangled mess, and his fingertips still bit into my back and shoulders where he gripped me. "Oh." His words came out on a shuddering breath. "Oh, fuck."

I'm not done with him yet, I decided immediately. *Not yet.* I'd already breached the rules of propriety and professionalism to have this one night, and while the year might have ended, technically, the night was far from over, which meant...

Which meant *nothing*, damn it. Having a full-on argument with myself was a new low, especially when I knew the truth, regardless of my base desires.

This shouldn't have happened.

I didn't say the words out loud—I wasn't that much of an asshole—but Reagan seemed to read them on my face. His eyelids closed for a beat, shutting the aquamarine away from view, and when he opened them again, their warmth was gone. He threw me a bright, careless grin. "One and done, eh? Dude, I get it. This was fun, but... *eesh*." He nudged me off him and scrambled to sit at the edge of the bed, so all I could see was his muscular back. "Jesus. Brantleigh's dad. Fuck me," he murmured with a forced chuckle.

What the actual fuck?

"It's weird because of *my son?*"

"Among other things." Reagan didn't turn to face me but reached down to pluck his boxer briefs from the pile of discarded clothing on the floor. His voice was low but firm. "So, as far as I'm concerned, this never happened."

It should not have made me so irrationally angry to hear him echo my own thoughts, but something about his dismissive tone got under my skin, and I found myself saying, "Like hell it didn't. My cum is still all over you. It happened, Reagan. This. *Happened*."

For fuck's sake, Thatcher, why not just flat-out ask for a sexual harassment suit?

"Nope. Sorry to break it to you, but there are some things in life you don't control, and you don't get to have a tantrum about them." Reagan wiped his abs with a corner of the sheet, then stood and slid his underwear over his perfect pale ass... an ass I still ached to get my hands on. "I recall nothing. Therefore, nothing happened."

Jesus Christ, he was provoking. I opened my mouth to

argue with him (*obviously*, there were things in life I couldn't control, or else we wouldn't fucking be in this predicament) or possibly kiss him into submission (because apparently, I wasn't done being stupid on any level), but my phone chose that moment to ring. Very few people had this number: Brantleigh and his mother, my driver, and my most trusted lieutenants at Pennington Industries. None of them would be calling after midnight on New Year's Eve for anything less than a grave emergency.

"Don't move," I growled, reaching for my phone and accepting the call. Regardless of who was on the line, Reagan and I needed to get a few things settled. "What?" I barked into the phone.

January's voice came over the line, and I could tell right away she wasn't happy at having her night interrupted. "Thatcher, we have a problem. Nova Davidson crashed her car into a tree after leaving a New Year's Eve party—"

"Who? One of our employees?" I demanded.

"No. Sorry. I forgot you don't follow pop culture." January took a breath. "Nova Davidson is an up-and-coming musician with a large social media following," she explained. "Paparazzi videotaped her crash and subsequent arrest for driving under the influence a couple of hours ago, and it's already gone viral." She hesitated. "In it, she's wearing an Elustre T-shirt."

"How?" Elustre was a brand-new fabric conceived by PennCo Fiber, one of Pennington Industries' subsidiaries. After years of research and development, the PennCo Fiber team had found a way to manufacture a soft, durable material entirely of recycled plant material, with a true four-way stretch that made it unique among the sustainable fabrics currently on the market.

Compared to the other Pennington Industries'

subsidiaries, PennCo Fiber was relatively small. More of a plodding workhorse than a powerhouse of innovation. But I'd sat in on enough meetings to know Elustre had the potential to change all of that. Once it was released to the public, it would quickly become a household name, much the way spandex had decades before. Five years from now, everyone's workout gear would be made of Elustre.

But for now, the entire concept was a secret known only to PennCo and our partners. So how the hell had a celebrity gotten hold of it?

"I don't know yet," January admitted. "Layla's going to pull together the PennCo team and get working on crisis response. I just wanted to make sure you heard about it before you see it on social media or the news."

"I don't see how that's possible when it's not public yet, thus not recognizable in a photo," I said, trying not to be distracted by the way Reagan buttoned his tuxedo shirt while the dim light picked out golden glints in his hair.

She sighed. "Because somehow, it has a giant slogan on the front that says 'Elustre: Sponsor of Your New Year's Resolutions' along with our brand logo. And the entire world has seen it, Thatcher. Which means that now, instead of associating Elustre with working out and crushing your goals, people will associate it with seriously poor choices. It's a public relations nightmare."

"Fuck," I muttered, running a hand over my jaw and missing the rasp of my beard. "*Fuck*. Explain to me how this happened."

Reagan finished pulling on his tuxedo pants and narrowed his eyes at me in concern. I turned away.

"I think you should be in Layla's meeting, Thatcher," January advised. "You'll need to take an active leadership role in the company's response."

"Agreed," I muttered. "I'll be there."

After ending the call, I turned back to Reagan, but he held up a hand before I could speak. "Look, I have no idea what's going on, but you've got shit to do, so—"

I wanted to argue, but he was right. Pennington Industries was my priority, always. I couldn't afford a distraction with a gorgeous body and disarmingly blue eyes. I should have been glad that he was willing to see himself out so I didn't have to. And yet...

"Not so fast. I have things to say to you." I had to end this night properly. With no hard feelings or recriminations but also no doubt that *it had happened*—I wanted to see the flash of awareness in those brilliant eyes as I pressed this point. With no question that we'd be keeping it confidential and also no expectations of a repeat.

But first, I needed a minute to fucking *think*.

I grabbed my discarded tux and pointed a finger at him. "*Stay*," I said before stepping into the bathroom for the world's quickest shower.

But when I stepped back into the room a moment later, Reagan Wellbridge was gone.

Chapter Three

Reagan

He'd told me to *stay*.

I kicked an abandoned noisemaker in the middle of the sidewalk and dodged a pair of drunken revelers.

Stay. Like I was a freaking dog.

They say "never meet your heroes," but the expression should really be "never fuck the gorgeous man who clued you in to your pansexuality back in high school" because, let me tell you, the fallout was fucking awful.

Yes, sex with Thatcher Pennington had been volcanic, obliterating all my previous fantasies in a fiery rush—and birthing a few new ones involving a growly, dominant partner, besides—but those weren't the only casualties.

So much for getting people to take you seriously, Reagan. Angry tears sprang to my eyes, making the streetlights blur before I blinked them away. *How's your grand plan of shedding that slacker, nepo-baby image going? Think Thatcher will be telling your dad about your impressive skills when the only things you've shown him so far are your incredibly short refractory period and your ability to come on command?*

I was so angry my stomach hurt. Angry at the Universe for gifting me an uncomplicated hookup with a gorgeous Roman warrior only to say *just kidding* the minute the masks came off. Angry at myself for spoiling things yet again, like I was exactly the kind of fuckup everyone thought I was. Angry at Thatcher for knowing my identity when he pushed me on the bed yet giving me *horror eyes* before our cum had cooled, proving beyond a doubt that tonight had been a discount-sushi-before-an all-day-sea-fishing-expedition-level mistake.

The kind of mistake that could result in me being trapped in yet another horrifying shitshow of my own making if I let it...

So I would *not* let it.

I let myself into my tiny apartment in Midtown, which made up for its prime location by being measured in square inches rather than square feet, and immediately sprawled on my bed.

Thank god I'd gotten the hell out of that hotel room while Thatcher was in the shower, before he'd had a chance to lecture or, worse, fire me. Hopefully by the time he'd finished dealing with whatever emergency his phone call had been about, he'd go back to forgetting about my existence. Because as fun as parts of the evening had been, fucking my boss ran counter to every single thing I hoped to achieve, so it would never—*could* never—happen again.

Case closed, lesson learned, I told myself as I shut my tired eyes, pulled the covers over my head, and prepared to sleep my holiday away.

Three hours later, I awoke in the pitch-darkness to find my phone blowing up with missed calls and messages from my boss.

Bossman Stephen: *Reagan, are you there? It's me, Stephen Price.*
Bossman Stephen: *Reagan, we have a problem. Please respond.*
Bossman Stephen: *Reagan, I need you to be in the office at 8:00. It's an emergency.*
Bossman Stephen: *Reagan?*

Jesus Christ.

I blinked my eyes and tried to focus on the screen, trying to make the messages make sense. Stephen Price was a highly anxious thirty-something with an endless supply of identical brown suits, an array of Perfect Attendance plaques proudly displayed on his office walls, and an annoying habit of using my name in every sentence, which he'd probably picked up from reading *Team Management for Dummies.* He was a nice enough guy, but he'd never messaged me before, and I sincerely wished he hadn't now.

I slapped the phone down on the mattress and groaned at the ceiling. The only silver lining of my boring job was that fiber companies didn't *have* public relations emergencies, which meant I was never asked to stay late or come in on a weekend. Why did today of all days have to be the exception?

But I'd blown my shot at getting Thatcher to notice me for the right reasons, and I wasn't walking away from this job, so I was just going to have to work harder, do *better,* if I wanted to prove myself. And that meant showing up, even on a holiday, even when your supervisor gave you forty minutes' notice to haul your ass to the office.

Besides which, if I spent the day alone in my cubbyhole apartment, I'd probably end up jerking off to memories of my hot asshole boss, and... no. I refused.

I threw off the covers, sent Stephen a message that I was on my way, and quickly got ready before hustling the ten blocks to the smaller office building adjacent to Pennington Industries' headquarters.

When security let me in, the lobby was so deserted it was almost spooky. But that changed instantly when I got off the elevator on my floor. It seemed like the entire department was present, all racing around and giving the office a sense of competent but time-sensitive industry.

I paused at the cubicle next to mine, which belonged to one of PennCo's marketing copy editors. "Nataly? What's going on?"

She glanced up from her maniacal typing, and her shoulders slumped when she saw me. "Oh, Reagan, thank god. Everyone's been waiting for you. Nova Fucking Davidson, huh?"

"Nova Davidson... what?" I demanded.

Nataly's eyes widened. "How can you not know? I thought you were Mr. Social Media." She twisted in her seat, making her dark curls bounce. "You know who she is, right?"

"Obviously," I scoffed. I'd followed Nova on all the socials from the moment she started making a name for herself, which meant I'd watched her go from an up-and-coming singer to an impending train wreck over the past year or so. She was a talented musician and a classic example of what *not* to do in terms of solid social media branding. "I haven't been online yet. I was asleep until..." I glanced at my phone. "...forty-three minutes ago."

"Wellllll." She leaned toward me, speaking quickly. "Apparently, Nova left Janna Keefe's Bangers on the Beach New Year's party early because of some romantic drama. She was already drunk off her ass, though, and crashed her little pink sports car into a tree—I *know*," she agreed when I gasped. "Fucking awful. Fortunately, no one was hurt." Nataly's lips twisted as she added, "But the paparazzi were on the scene even before the police were, and they got video of her stumbling out of the wreck—"

"Oh, shit."

"Right? Get on TikTok later and see the carnage for yourself. She was screaming obscenities, talking shit about Janna, singing parts of her new single totally off-key—"

"Jesus." I took my phone from my coat pocket and opened TikTok.

Nataly's hand shot out, blocking my screen. "You haven't heard the relevant part. She did all of this while wearing a T-shirt that said 'Elustre: Sponsor of Your New Year's Resolutions.'"

"What?" I glanced up, truly horrified, my phone forgotten. "Where'd she get that? From us? Or someone at Apex Athletics? Because this is going to be bad—"

"It wasn't anyone here," Nataly said confidently, "but it's *already* bad." She waved her hand to indicate the flurry of activity around us. "Speaking of which... get your butt in the conference room. The leadership meeting is about to start, and they've been waiting on you. Scoot!"

"*Leadership* meeting? Waiting on *me*?" I snorted at the very idea. "You mean waiting for Stephen."

"Reagan, Stephen's out sick. Didn't he tell you?"

"He... no. His text just said to come in."

"He's probably not thinking clearly, the poor guy." Nataly stood with a sigh and straightened her skirt. "You know how he's been sniffling for days but insisted it was allergies because he refused to lose his perfect attendance award? Doctor says it's flu. High fever, cough, the works. And since Megan and Arvand are out of town for the holidays, you're the last man standing from the PR department. *You* are representing PR in the leadership meeting," she added, poking me lightly in the chest when I continued to stare at her, dumbstruck.

"I..." My heart rate picked up. "Are you sure?"

"Judging by the fact that Layla had me wait out here for you and keeps asking if you've arrived yet? Very." She grinned. "Eight hours into the new year, and your 'dreams' are coming true. Now, *move*. I'll meet you in there."

"Yeah." My pulse rushed in my ears. "Okay. I can do this. I can... represent."

I hurried next door to my cubicle, where I shucked my coat and grabbed my tablet. My brain was still sluggish from too little sleep and too much overthinking, which was good since otherwise I might panic-flail.

This was my shot. *Fucking finally.* They'd have to listen to my ideas. Because while I wouldn't wish a PR nightmare like this on anyone, I could help mitigate it... and prove my worth at the same time.

I practically sprinted down the hall to the tiny conference room where Layla was holding court with all the team leaders and key personnel at PennCo Fiber. The room was more crowded than I'd ever seen it, and I paused for a second at the door to catch my breath and find an available seat to slip into.

Layla glanced toward the door almost immediately and clocked me there. With a small, businesslike smile, she nodded toward an empty chair halfway down the conference table right next to Nataly. "Reagan, thanks for coming in. Have a seat. We're just about to get started."

I nodded and swallowed hard, trying to project professionalism as I walked around the table.

Layla James, the VP of Pennington Industries and head

of the PennCo Fiber subsidiary, was maybe forty and had excellent taste, as evidenced by her neat twist of auburn hair, her cream wool power suit, and her flawless Louboutin heels. Though she wasn't my type, she was undeniably attractive. More than that, she seemed intelligent and competent.

She wasn't my direct boss, but I'd met her several times in the weeks I'd worked at PennCo. Stephen had even arranged a meeting for the three of us so I could try to sell her on some of the social media campaigns I'd brainstormed. Although she hadn't (yet) given the go-ahead to any of my ideas, she'd listened courteously while I'd outlined all my ideas and even asked some intelligent questions before eventually saying no. She seemed open-minded and willing to take me seriously... which was more than I'd gotten from certain incredibly sexy boss people I refused to think about by name.

When we were all settled and turned our attention to her, Layla outlined the situation in precise, no-nonsense terms. Nova had been arrested at the scene of the accident. Now that her lawyers were involved, she'd clammed up, but the damage had already been done. Images of Nova stumbling out of her wrecked car, all smeared makeup and wild eyes with the "Elustre: Sponsor of your New Year's Resolutions" motto stretched across her ample chest, had become an instant meme. One that was currently being shared by every New Year's reveler who'd woken up hungover and regretful this morning... which was a *lot* of people.

"We're still investigating where she got the shirt," Layla said. "I've addressed the issue with our security team, and the folks at Apex Athletics are conducting their own internal review—"

"It had to be them," someone further down the table interrupted. "No one here would do such a thing."

"You may be correct, Stewart." Layla's voice sounded strained, and she cleared her throat. "But pointing fingers at our largest fashion brand partner is a waste of time and energy. What we need to focus on now is how we're going to fix this and move forward. We've already developed a targeted, multipronged approach." She folded her hands on the table in front of her. "Step one: PennCo Fiber releases a statement to the press disavowing any connection to Ms. Davidson—"

"But they'll want to know why she was wearing a piece of Elustre clothing."

Everyone looked around to see who'd interrupted, and I was horrified to find that it was *me*. I swallowed and straightened in my chair. "I... I'm sorry to interrupt. I... I only meant that the video shows there *is* a connection between Elustre and Nova Davidson, and they're going to want an explanation, whether we disavow it or not. We don't have one yet. So... maybe in the meantime, we could use this opportunity, this media exposure, to showcase the good things the company's doing? Like, I've written several posts about sustainability in manufacturing and how we pay our workers a living wage, and..." Layla's expression didn't change even a fraction, and it became even harder to push the words out with confidence. "...maybe that's some information we could include when we draft the statement, that's all."

When I finally shut my mouth, the room went dead silent, and everyone looked to Layla for a reaction before offering their own.

"Thank you, Reagan." Layla forced a smile despite

clearly being stressed. "I'm sure the communications team values your thoughtful analysis. Rest assured, though, I—*we*—have things well in hand."

Someone on the far side of the table chuckled under their breath, and my cheeks went as hot as if she'd said the words *"please don't mansplain my job to me"* out loud. I nodded, pressing my lips together to prevent any further wayward outbursts.

Layla cleared her throat again and took a sip of her steaming coffee. "The social media focus on this story is troublesome," she went on. "But the *real* concern is that the story has been picked up by several credible news organizations. *Global Pulse* has already asked for a comment."

"Them again," someone scoffed. "They should know better. We handed them their asses last time they took us on."

Layla sighed. "Yes, they've been looking for a way to smear Pennington's reputation ever since I insisted on suing them for their last fictitious story, but maybe this is an opportunity to convince them we're the good guys. They've written an article questioning whether Nova Davidson is our new 'brand ambassador,' which we can— Oh!" Layla glanced over my head, and her professional smile transformed into something warm and genuine. "There you are! Just in time."

The murmured greetings of the department heads were drowned out by the roaring of blood in my ears as Thatcher Pennington, CEO of Pennington Industries and owner of several body parts I'd recently had in my mouth, straightened from where he'd been propped against the doorjamb and moved to take the remaining empty seat next to Layla.

Mother of god.

After a brief glance that went no higher than his neck—yep, that was the torso I'd been intimately acquainted with, alright—I resolutely looked away and resisted the urge to tug at my collar, which was suddenly a size too tight.

After weeks of zero contact at work, it hadn't occurred to me that I'd see Thatcher again so soon—that his emergency and mine were one and the same. And despite experience with dozens of different morning-after scenarios, this was a new one for me. How the hell was I supposed to sit across a conference table from my hookup while pretending that the heater wasn't wafting his tantalizing cologne across the table and that my entire body wasn't flushing hot-cold-hot-cold like a neon sign announcing *Reagan Wellbridge fucked his boss?*

I could barely hear Layla as she went on. "...I was just saying that the media is using this incident as clickbait with us as the target. We'll implement a multipronged strategy. The first step will be crafting a press release. The second and more important step..." She paused for another sip of coffee. "...needs to be an in-person, multicity PR tour, headlined by both of us."

Her words were like a record scratch, cutting through all the lust and confusion in my brain.

A PR tour? Had we traveled back to 1855 and nobody told me?

Without my consent, my gaze flicked to Thatcher to gauge his reaction and found him looking as stupefied as I felt.

I was no PR expert—social media was only one tiny facet of public relations, after all—but an in-person whistle-stop tour seemed unnecessary and... frankly, useless. Why would Pennington cater to the traditional news media when the outlets that seemed to be covering the story seemed to have a grudge against the company? Why go to all that effort and expense so we could reach a few dozen people when there was a free way to reach millions of people with just a few clicks? If the issue was the story going viral on social media, wasn't the best place to handle it... social media?

I took a breath and opened my mouth to voice these thoughts... and immediately remembered that my unsolicited comments were not welcome, so I clenched my hands together under the table instead. Everyone else at the table was nodding, like this seemed utterly rational to them. Nataly didn't appear surprised, like maybe she'd gotten a memo I'd missed.

"I would have spoken to you privately about this beforehand, Thatcher, but I—*we*—only brainstormed the concept a few hours ago and fleshed it out based on your availability according to your online calendar," Layla went on. She gave Thatcher a wry smile. "You said you were committed to doing whatever it took to mitigate the damage, so I'm taking you at your word."

Thatcher frowned. "I am committed. But this—"

"Is vitally important to the response strategy," she said. "I wouldn't ask it of you if it wasn't. Now, you and I were already planning to attend the Textile Symposium in Kansas City tomorrow afternoon—"

"I'm leaving tonight," Thatcher confirmed. "You're flying out tomorrow."

"Yes, but now I think it makes more sense to travel with you so we can continue to strategize. Also, I feel strongly that we should extend that trip for a total of..." She coughed lightly. "Two weeks?"

"Two—? Layla..." Thatcher took a deep breath and let it out. "I truly appreciate the work you're doing on this, but I'm sure this isn't necessary. Last time the media wrote an unflattering piece about PennCo, you got the legal team involved, and that was incredibly effective—"

Layla's cheeks colored. "Thank you, Thatcher."

"—so I'm not sure why we can't go that route now. Wait for the media focus to settle down, like it always does."

She nodded like she'd expected this. "We *could* get Legal involved, certainly, and we will, but..." She tilted her head. "I think you may be underestimating the seriousness of the situation. This crisis has come at the worst possible time for the launch. Our partners are rightfully concerned about our company's reputation taking a hit. We can't take a wait-and-see approach. Not on this. We show everyone in our industry that PennCo's leadership is rock-steady. Remind them that we're a game-changer in the market. Make sure the media has sound bites that reflect our talking points. And we need to do it *now*."

Thatcher nodded slowly. "That makes sense, in theory. But you're the face of PennCo, Layla—"

"I am. But to be blunt, Thatcher, I need your help. I know everything there is to know about PennCo Fiber, but *you* are the face of Pennington Industries. Your reputation and instincts are unimpeachable. And you make people believe what you're saying." She grinned. "Remember that time we were pitching to Dudley Partners, back when PennCo was just getting started? Someone in their office blew a fuse, shorted out the power to the conference room—"

"And we had to do the presentation in the dark." Thatcher shook his head, remembering. "No projection screen, no nothing. And they wouldn't postpone..."

"So you did an interpretive dance!" Laughing, Layla leaned over and grabbed Thatcher's forearm. "While I held the flashlight."

"Not quite," Thatcher said dryly. His eyes flicked down the table toward me, then away. "I merely... gestured a bit to illustrate key points on the data tables—"

"You sold it, Thatcher. Everyone at the meeting thought, 'A guy like that is someone I want to partner with.' And that's exactly the energy that we need to deal with this PR crisis. Together, we can do a better job than either of us could alone. We're a good team. Trust me."

Thatcher sighed. "It's not a question of trust but timing. Two weeks is..." He rubbed his thumb over his lips thoughtfully as if deciding how to finish that sentence, and now that I was looking at the man, I found I couldn't look away. He seemed tired. A little unhappy, a little resigned, but mostly just full-on exhausted, like he hadn't seen a bed since—*the soft hotel mattress, the frantic slick-slick-slick as our sweaty bodies undulated together, the feel of his large hand wrapped oh-so-deliciously tight around my cock.* The vision was so fucking powerful I sucked in a breath.

The sound wasn't loud—no one else seemed to notice— but Thatcher's penetrating gaze swung toward me like he alone had heard it. His gaze focused on my mouth for a fraction of a second, and then he turned away.

He cleared his throat. "You know, the more I think about it, two weeks sounds perfect." He gave Layla a firm nod and managed a tired smile. "I trust your judgment."

Layla's answering smile was beyond relieved. More like *thrilled.* "I'd hope so," she teased. "Considering I've been your friend and chief flashlight holder for... how long now?" The hand still resting on his arm squeezed the muscle there.

It was a simple gesture. Friendly. No one, including

Thatcher, seemed to notice. But it sent a tidal wave of unwanted, unexpected jealousy washing through me, so forceful I had to slide my hands under my thighs against the urge to walk over, forcibly remove those squeezy fingers, and declare, "*Mine!*" in front of everyone.

Not *mine*, I told myself firmly. *In no realm. Not even a little.*

"For as long as anyone can remember." Thatcher gave Layla a soft smile, then sobered. "It's going to be a logistical nightmare, though, coordinating this kind of travel on short notice," he warned. "Winter storms will make it even more complex—"

"Leave that to me and my people." Layla swept her free hand down the table. "We'll have everything ready by the end of the day, and I've already cleared my schedule."

"That's not necessary," Thatcher insisted. "You said it's my presence that counts most and that you're at a critical stage with the launch. With so much to coordinate, surely we shouldn't both be out of the office—"

"Nonsense." *Squeeze, squeeze.* "Team effort, remember? I'll be on hand to help write your speeches and make sure you've got a background on everyone you meet at the events so you can focus on doing your own work and handling your meetings remotely. Let me take care of everything else."

"Okay." Thatcher gave a firm nod.

"It might even be fun." Layla shook him lightly. "Just like the good old days."

Thatcher huffed out a laugh. "You might be overselling it a bit, but we'll make it work. It won't be the first time I've worked from the bus."

The bus?

My confusion must have shown because Nataly leaned over to whisper in my ear. "Thatcher doesn't fly. That's his *thing.*" She shrugged. "He only travels a few times a year, and when he does, he travels in a tour bus like a rock star. Apparently, it's super luxurious."

Oh.

I chanced another glance at Thatcher, who was engrossed in a discussion of his itinerary with Layla. He didn't fly? Since when? And *why?* How was I just learning this?

I'd always assumed the Penningtons had taken a helicopter to visit my family in Maine like most of my parents' friends. Had Thatcher really been driving hours roundtrip to New York each time? Was it possible that someone as steadfast and calm and *dominant* as Thatcher was... scared? How many other details about him had I missed? And why did this only make him more fascinating—?

I wrenched my gaze away and focused firmly on my tablet. *Not fascinating. He was a jerk this morning, and we don't waste our fascination on jerks.*

Layla coughed again before continuing. "Alright, then, people. We're going to need all of our sales, marketing, and communications folks to pull together and assist PR with this..."

As she droned on, I stifled a groan of frustration. Layla was strong on corporate-speak and weak on details. One thing I did note was the decided lack of any social media component to their "multipronged" strategy, which still seemed like a total oversight.

I hesitated but decided I couldn't stay silent any longer. This time, instead of interrupting, I raised my hand like I was in elementary school and waited for Layla to acknowledge me, which didn't happen until several people had already begun collecting their belongings and preparing to leave.

"Reagan?" she said at last.

"Who's responsible for creating the social media response?" I asked. "If you'd like, I'd be happy to take the lead on that—"

Layla inhaled as if gathering her patience. "Once again, Reagan, I appreciate your... enthusiasm. But as I believe we've discussed, the textile industry is old-school, and none of the major players are active on social media. That's not where our partners will be expecting to hear from us, so putting our energy there would be unproductive."

"I hear you, but athleisure-wear *consumers* are talking about Nova Davidson on social media, so I thought..." I glanced up and down the table, but every face seemed carefully blank. No one met my eyes. No one spoke.

Thatcher watched me, too, and though I couldn't read his expression, I imagined him waiting for me to argue and whine like the entitled kid he'd probably heard about from my father. My confidence shrank like a deflated balloon.

Layla was wrong, but I was not going to tank my future prospects over this.

Not even if I was tired.

Not even if I was in the throes of a highly inappropriate reaction to my boss.

Not even if Layla's hand lingering on Thatcher's arm like it belonged there was driving me demented.

"Never mind," I said shortly. I even made myself smile. "I can see you've already got the plan laid out."

Fortunately, the meeting broke up a few minutes later. I escaped to my cubicle, where I sprawled in my chair, defeated.

So much for proving myself.

The moment I sat down, Nataly's head popped over the wall. "Hey," she whispered. "I just want you to know you're on the right track. The rest of us agree with you about social media, and I think you're doing an amazing job."

Then why didn't anyone say so? I wanted to ask.

"And you probably got some credit for suggesting a new take in front of Mr. Pennington," she went on. "He was really focused on you when you were talking, and he looked intrigued... at least until Layla said no and you backed off. You're *too* nice sometimes, you know?"

In a lifetime of criticisms, this was one I'd never heard... which only went to show how hard I'd been trying to turn over a new leaf.

I forced a smile. "You're sweet. But if Mr. Pennington thought there was anything compelling in my idea, he'd have spoken up. He kept quiet... just like everyone else," I couldn't help adding. "How's it possible the marketing team doesn't believe in social media? Or the sales people? Am I that far off base here? Has PennCo tried it and failed? I don't understand."

Nataly sighed and tapped a chipped fingernail against the metal frame at the top of the cubicle. "You're definitely not the first person who's brought this up. Remember Terrance, the marketing guy who left right around the time you got here?"

"The one whose position never got filled, even though lots of other people would have loved to step up?"

"That's him," Nataly said, apparently not hearing the irony in my tone. "He told me on the down-low that Layla let him get as far as storyboarding a whole social media campaign before she thought better of it. He was really frustrated—felt like he'd wasted his time and effort, you know?"

"I totally know. That's probably why he quit," I muttered.

Nataly shrugged. "The thing is, Layla's a great boss.

You'll see when you've been here a little longer. What she doesn't know about textiles isn't worth knowing. She's been recruited by a bunch of bigger, flashier companies—Alena, her PA, told me that in confidence—but Layla says no every time because she's loyal to us, so no wonder we're all loyal to her, too, right? Like family, kinda. So if Layla says it's our corporate policy to leave social media activity to fashion brands…" She shrugged again.

"I get that you like her. I like her, too." Or I *had*, until the arm-squeezing incident, which I really needed to get over. "But this policy is really shortsighted, and we both know Layla will have to change her tune eventually. Social media's not going away."

"True." Nataly's fingernails clicked on the frame again. "Have *you* thought about putting together a presentation—"

"To convince her? Already tried that. I pulled together a metric ton of data on the power of a social media marketing campaign and pitched it to her. I thought she was listening, maybe changing her mind, so I've been working on a new pitch with even more data, but now…"

Nataly nodded in understanding. "Even a great boss has blind spots. This is Layla's."

"I guess." The wasted potential was staggering. "Anyway, I should probably get started 'supporting the PR tour' now. Whatever that means."

"Just remember, no matter how bad that meeting was, you're still having a better day than Nova Davidson. Or poor Mr. Pennington and Layla, going on a two-week road trip in winter." She gave an exaggerated shudder before her head disappeared.

I pondered this for a second—spending way too long thinking about the *and Layla* part, if I were being honest—

then stood to poke *my* head over the wall. "Hey, so what's the deal with Thatcher not flying?"

Nataly glanced up. "You mean, why does he hate it? I dunno, officially. There are rumors he lost someone important in 9/11, but I figure it's one of those phobias that doesn't have a trigger, like chromatophobia. You know, fear of colors?" she explained when I looked at her blankly. She shrugged. "Anyway, what I *do* know for sure is that he has a driver named McGee, who is *scrumptious*. You've probably seen him around—tall guy, killer ink, looks like he could bench-press a super yacht, goes everywhere Mr. Pennington goes?"

I made a noncommittal noise. Not *everywhere*, I thought, remembering the hotel room last night.

But I did recall a guy like that arriving with Thatcher at my parents' place. He'd looked more like a bodyguard than a driver, with tattoos crawling up his thick forearms to curve over his collarbone and a dangerous, I-could-maim-you-but-I-won't vibe that would have turned my brain to mush if he hadn't been standing directly next to the shining perfection of Thatcher. And now that I knew Thatcher wasn't straight, I found myself wondering whether *he* thought McGee was scrumptious.

I rolled my eyes at myself. *What are you doing, Reagan?*

I sat down and opened my email in hopes there would already be enough work to distract me, and there was. Layla might have been shortsighted when it came to social media, but I had to grudgingly admit that she was good at her job and dedicated as fuck. She and her staff must've worked through the night in order to put a tentative itinerary together as quickly as they had.

As the day progressed, emails flooded in, and I didn't move from my desk except to grab a slice of pizza the company ordered. I learned that Thatcher's first speaking engagement would be at the Midwestern Textile Symposium in Kansas City. According to an email Layla's assistant sent out, my job was to create branded media kits specific to local outlets in the Kansas City area and deliver them to McGee—hot, tattooed McGee—at the building's loading dock by six o'clock tonight. After that, I needed to begin preparing similar kits for the event in Wichita that would take place the following day. Those could be overnighted if they weren't ready to go on the bus.

It turned out Nataly was right—Thatcher did have a tricked-out ride on standby. When I finally made my way to the loading dock with three markets' worth of media kits boxed up and labeled, a sleek maroon tour bus had already pulled up to the door, and Thatcher's driver was transferring suitcases out of a Mercedes sedan into the cargo area.

"McGee?"

"Yep," he said without turning around. His inked fingers absently carded through wavy blond hair as he examined the stuff he'd already loaded. One clear bin was filled with snack foods like granola bars and cans of nuts.

"I have some marketing materials for Th—*uh*... Mr. Pennington."

"Set 'em down. I'll load 'em in."

I stared at McGee's back, realizing I'd been low-key hoping to catch sight of Thatcher on the loading dock to make sure he was doing okay and wasn't looking as tired and worried as he had in the meeting.

Disgusting. Like you haven't seen enough? Now you're a groupie, hanging out by the stage door, all concerned about him?

But as I stood there like a dumbass, I heard myself say, "Guess you're leaving soon, huh?"

"Soon as the boss arrives." McGee rearranged boxes with a little grunt.

"And Layla, too," I reminded him. "Layla James."

At this, McGee turned and looked—really looked—at me. His face was devoid of any expression, which made me squirm, but when I really focused on his eyes, I could see he was younger than I'd thought beneath his tough-guy swagger and weathered face. Younger, even, than me. And his pierced eyebrow gave him all kinds of ruthless, bad-boy sex appeal.

This did nothing to dispel my not-jealousy.

"And you guys will be driving through the night?" I went on.

McGee inclined his head.

I hesitated, then finally blurted, "If you or, uh, Mr. Pennington had a rough night last night—" *Good job, Reagan. Could you be more obvious?* "I'm not saying you did. I mean, how would I even know? But *if* someone had a sleepless night, and a long day, too, and needed a coffee, there's a cafe on Third with these amazing espresso shots, and..." I clenched my jaw to stop my babbling. "Anyway. Safe travels."

I left McGee staring at me in bemusement as I scuttled back upstairs, two minutes too late to avoid making a fool of myself. What business was it of mine if Thatcher *Horror-Eyes* Pennington was tired? Literally *none*. Since when was I this guy?

I punched the elevator button for my floor with excessive force. Thank fuck Thatcher would be gone for two weeks. In fact, he couldn't leave fast enough. I was ready to go back to him forgetting my existence.

The elevator door opened, and I stomped out into the lobby.

"Being stubborn about this isn't going to work," a woman's voice insisted, stopping me in my tracks.

A crowd of employees had gathered in the lobby, and the air was thick with tension. I sidled over to Nataly to find out what was going on and quickly realized what had caught everyone's attention. A young woman in a pantsuit and a surgical mask with her arms folded across her chest appeared to be guarding the elevator from Layla James... or a version of Layla, anyway.

The woman who'd been so put together that morning looked like she'd been trampled by horses at some point during the day. Sweaty tendrils of hair had fallen out of her bun to straggle limply against her face and neck. Her nose glowed like a warning beacon beneath glassy eyes, and she clung to the handle of a rolling suitcase like it was the only thing keeping her wobbly knees from buckling.

"You—" Layla's cultured voice had become a bullfrog croak. "—might be Thatcher's assistant, January, but you are not in charge here. Thatcher needs me. Please step aside."

The woman in the mask shook her head resolutely. "You're sick, Layla. If you've caught the same flu that Stephen and a bunch of other employees have gotten, it's extremely contagious, and if you get on that bus, you'll get Thatcher sick, too. What good would that do?"

"Non—" Layla broke off in a weak cough but raised her chin stubbornly. "Nonsense. My immune system is bullet-proof. I haven't had the flu in a decade. I'm simply tired, and I probably have something trivial."

"Trivial like a zombie apocalypse," Nataly said under her breath. "The poor thing."

Nataly wasn't wrong. Beneath her red nose and cheeks, Layla's skin had a distinct, pasty-gray *Walking Dead* look.

"I suggest you take a flu test," January said matter-offactly. "If you don't have the flu, I'll leave the decision to Thatcher."

"But I'm the head of PennCo Fiber. The trip was my idea." Sickness made Layla sound whiny. "Thatcher can't go alone."

January squared her shoulders. "Then choose someone else to go. Perhaps someone from PR can assist Thatcher for the first leg of the trip, then you can join him when you're feeling better."

"But there's no one left in PR." Layla openly slumped against her suitcase handle now. "Everyone is sick or on vacation."

At any other time, under any other circumstance, I would have stepped forward, raised my hand, and seized this opportunity to make a good impression. Instead, I took a slow step back into the crowd...

A second too late.

"There's Reagan!" Nataly cried. She grabbed my arm and raised it like a trophy. "He's in PR."

January's head swung in my direction.

I pulled my hand down. "Oh, no. *No.* I mean... I'd love to help, but I'm so new to the company... I'm not sure I'm the best choice." *Especially since I know what the CEO looks like when he orgasms.*

"*I'm* sure!" Nataly cried. "Reagan is brilliant and innovative and hardworking. We all think so." She was laying it on thick, probably trying to make up for not supporting me in the meeting earlier. I tried to sign *quit it* with my eyes, but she ignored me. "He's formatting and printing all the media kits, too, so he's very familiar with the tour stops and can make sure Mr. Pennington has the information he needs."

January nodded, relieved. "Perfect. Thanks for volunteering, Reagan."

"But I..."

"Your willingness to step up on short notice will be noted in your employee file."

I shut my mouth. What the hell was I supposed to say to that? How was I supposed to tell her I was the last person Thatcher would want to share a tour bus with? If I refused to go, would *that* be noted in my employee file instead?

This situation had not been covered in my teenage etiquette lessons, damn it.

"Maybe you should check with Thatcher before deciding?" I suggested, knowing full well Thatcher would never agree. "A bus is a small space to share with another person."

January waved this away. "Thatcher's easygoing. He won't even notice you're there as long as you stay out of his way. But I appreciate you trying to keep his comfort in mind."

I huffed out a breath that might have been a chuckle if I'd been capable of feeling humor in that moment. "I'm really, *really* trying," I told her. "Maybe you can note that in my employee file as well?"

January laughed like I'd been joking. "It's settled, then. You can meet the bus downstairs, and I'll ask McGee to stop by your place so you can get your stuff. And Layla..." She gave the older woman a sympathetic smile. "I'll get a driver to take you home."

"I..." Layla sniffled. "I just don't understand how everything went so wrong. I had a plan."

I sympathized completely. Except Layla was bemoaning a press tour plan she'd created a few hours ago, and I was thinking about my *life*.

January glanced down at her phone. "Reagan? McGee says Thatcher will be ready to go in twenty."

My stomach swooped into my shoes. "Okay. I guess I'll just... grab my stuff and get downstairs, then?"

She gave me a reassuring smile. "Everything'll be fine."

I nodded. "Of course," I agreed.

But I knew without a doubt that *fine* was not what it would be.

Chapter Four

Thatcher

I SHOVED the last few necessities from my desk into my travel bag and took a final glance around my office. It would be two weeks before I stood here again. Two weeks of drowning in small talk, speaking at conferences, and sharing barely drinkable coffee with textile executives across middle America.

Not my ideal way to usher in the new year.

I'd planned to spend this week at my beach house, attempting to repair my relationship with my son, but after Brantleigh had blown me off with a last-minute text about an "unmissable opportunity"—probably a tanned and muscular "opportunity" with a fast car and a sparse acting resume, if I knew my son—it had proved impossible to stay away from my office.

January had reminded me with a disappointed sigh that even if I filled my days with "fun work" like checking on my personal real estate investments and researching new project ideas between my increasingly frequent attempts to pin Brant down for a conversation, being here wasn't "an actual vacation, boss," but I didn't care. I was an unapologetic workaholic, and my office was my safe haven. Here, I trusted my instincts. Here, I had a proven track record of success. Here, I could turn ideas into reality. Here, I was firmly in control.

Outside of work, on the other hand... Well, just look at the fallout from last night's clusterfuck.

As of today, Pennington Industries was no longer the safe haven it usually was. Not while Reagan Wellbridge, his distracting breathy gasps, and his sexy, hidden tattoo were on the premises. It hadn't taken more than two minutes of him blushing and frowning and *existing* across a conference table for me to realize that the one-night stand we'd shared had only made my crazy, inappropriate attraction to him flare hotter.

The temptation of yanking him out of his chair, pushing him against the wall, and demanding to know why he'd disappeared while I was in the shower had been nearly overpowering. I'd wanted to punish him for the astonishing, live-wire jolt that paralyzed my lungs in the brief moment our eyes met and the way his casual comment—*Sorry to break it to you, but there are some things in life you don't control, and you don't get to have a tantrum about them*—had been replaying in my head nonstop. I'd wanted to kiss him until I understood why his frigid indifference—not even deigning to *look* at me when I spoke, as if he hadn't sobbed his cries of release into my hot skin and begged with those gorgeous eyes for me to fuck him—had made me irrationally angry when I should have been glad.

It was no secret that I liked control. Craved it. Yet my control had been missing since the moment I'd spotted those eyes beneath a mask the night before. I had two weeks to go and find it again.

I yanked the zipper on my bag closed, threw on my coat,

and, after a pause, grabbed the box of natural supplements I'd allowed January to foist on me. I'd made the mistake of telling her I had a headache earlier, and she'd gone into a full-on flu-fighting frenzy. I hadn't argued because I'd rather gag down the witch's brew tinctures she'd provided than explain the truth—*No, January, it's not the flu. I have a headache because I spent last night fucking an employee who also happens to be the son of an influential politician. Yes, I said* son. *Because I'm bisexual. Surprise!*

Once I made it into the elevator, I closed my eyes and leaned against the mirrored elevator wall.

This goodwill trip felt like overkill, especially given my aversion to flying, but I employed a team of talented people for a reason, and it wasn't my habit to question their expertise—especially not someone like Layla, who'd been in my life longer than my second ex-wife, for Christ's sake, and had earned my trust a dozen times over.

Putting a thousand miles of road between me and a certain pair of aquamarine eyes had clinched the deal.

At least Layla's team was responding to the crisis like a well-oiled machine, so I had no doubt that the tour would run equally smoothly. And sharing the bus with Layla wouldn't be difficult. We'd known each other long enough to respect each other's privacy and boundaries, which was why we'd remained friendly through multiple project launches, our combined *three* divorces, her drunken attempt to make a pass at me a few years back, and my gentle-but-firm rejection on the grounds that I had no interest in dating anyone... especially an employee.

A policy I told myself I was still upholding since what Reagan and I had done was nothing as tame as dating.

Thankfully, Layla knew me well enough to know that interpersonal relationships were not my forte. She wouldn't hold it against me when I wasn't in the mood to socialize or chat about non-work topics.

All in all, this was probably the closest thing to an *actual* vacation I was going to get, at least until Brant returned my calls. January would be proud.

My phone rang as I stepped out into the cold winter darkness behind the building.

"January," I said after accepting the call.

"Sir, I'm down in PennCo accounting. I'm afraid we've had another *three* flu cases." Her voice was more harried than usual. "They're dropping like flies."

While I was fighting sleep deprivation, I was grateful not to have any flu symptoms. Leaving town was looking better and better. "Check with the Facilities people. If they think it's safer to close the office and let folks work from home for a few days, I'm fine with that."

McGee waited by the door of the bus and lifted a hand in greeting. "Boss," he said quietly. "Baggage is loaded, and your guest is on board. We're good to go when you're ready."

I nodded. "January, we're about to pull out, but keep me in the loop when you hear back from Facilities, okay?" I said as I climbed the steps into the bus's interior. McGee had already ensured that the space was warm and the interior lights were on, and I knew without checking that my things would already have been unpacked in the back bedroom.

Just a few of the advantages of being in control.

"Wait, Thatcher," January said before I could disconnect. "I'm calling because one of the sick employees is Layla. I practically had to forcibly restrain her, but it's simply not safe for her to go with you."

I frowned. Hadn't McGee said that my "guest" was

already on board? "If Layla's not coming, then—?" I demanded.

A small movement in my peripheral vision caught my attention, and I spun in place. Beyond the full-sized black leather couches in the lounge was the kitchen area, including the table with booth seats where I usually took my morning coffee. And there, pressed into the corner of one of the benches, looking wary and uncertain and like he was very much hoping not to be noticed, was the man I couldn't *help* noticing.

Aquamarine eyes met mine and held.

The headache in the center of my forehead throbbed.

In my ear, my assistant continued her very rational explanation for this turn of events. "—Layla didn't want you to go alone, and the rest of the PR team is either sick or on vacation, but I've been getting regular reports on Reagan from Stephen, just like you asked, and Stephen says the guy's really bright and hardworking. And since you've known him for years, I figured there'd be no problem—" I barely heard any of it.

"January." My voice sounded strange to my own ears. Calm and pleasant when I felt neither. "I need to go now."

"Oh." A suspicious pause. "Boss, are you feeling sick? You took your supplements, right?"

"I'll be in touch later," I said in lieu of an answer. Without taking my eyes off the man who'd turned my whole damn life on its head in less than a day, I disconnected the call.

Reagan and I stared at each other for a long moment as I slid my phone back into my pocket. I was dimly aware of McGee clambering onto the bus behind me, the *shush* as he closed the curtain that separated the driver's area from the living area, the *click click click* of him fiddling with something on the dashboard before we departed. I knew he was probably waiting for me to take my seat since it wasn't safe to stand while the bus was in motion, but I couldn't make my body move. Half of me was ready to climb back down the steps and call this whole thing off.

Reagan straightened in his seat and lifted his chin in the air defiantly. "I don't bite unless provoked."

I narrowed my eyes at him. "Pardon?"

"You look terrified." His wary expression shifted into a smirk. "Like you expected to find a cute little bunny waiting for you in the bus and instead found a rabid beaver who might tear you limb from limb. I thought it might help if I reassured you that I only bite if provoked." He smiled slyly. "Or if asked really, *really* nicely."

So many things were absurd about this statement—a *rabid beaver?*—I couldn't decide where to begin. Most egregious first, I decided.

"Terrified? Of you? Hardly." I tossed my coat and other belongings onto the sofa and casually slid into the booth opposite him to prove my point. "I'm pissed off."

His mouth twisted. "So you *weren't* about to run back into the building, Mr. Pennington?"

"Not at all," I lied. I folded my hands together on the tabletop, knitting my fingers together against the urge to touch him. "I was just thinking you're making quite a habit of turning up when I expect to find someone else, *Mr. Wellbridge.*"

His eyes widened in surprise, and for a brief moment, I felt like I'd scored a point in whatever strange game we were playing.

But then his voice, saccharine-sweet now, spoke again, evening the score. "Who, *me?* I just do as I'm told... *sir.* Like, if my boss's assistant tells me to get on the bus, I get on the bus. And if a sexy stranger in a Roman mask tells me to come to his room and get naked, I—"

"Stop. Talking." I glared at him, my breath coming too quickly. With just a few words, he'd taken me back to last night. To the ballroom, and the dancers, and the moment I'd spotted a pair of pouty lips beneath what I'd wrongly assumed was a *distinctive* feathered mask and had pictured them wrapped around my dick. "That's... inappropriate."

Reagan leaned back against the padded bench, those changeable eyes sizing me up from beneath half-closed lids. "You know, I sort of expected to be fired by now," he said too casually. "Isn't fraternizing against the rules?"

"Pennington Industries rules? No." I'd confirmed it earlier today, just to be sure. "My rules? Yes. But if you think I'd fire someone for a consensual... occurrence... like the one we had last night, you don't know me very well. And hell, even if I *did* want to, and even if there *was* a policy you'd violated, I'd hardly fire you when you could turn around and make a sexual harassment claim that could sue my company out of existence." I gave a humorless laugh. "Congratulations. No employee at Pennington has job security like you do at this moment, including me." I ran a hand over my jaw and the day's worth of stubble I hadn't bothered to shave. At the moment, I deeply regretted shaving my beard in the first place. "Frankly, *I* was expecting to get an angry call from your father or paperwork from his attorney today—"

"Ew." Reagan's lip curled. "If you think I'd tell my father... Jesus, literally anything ever, let alone the sordid details of our *occurrence*... then you don't know *me* at all. I'm not planning to sue anyone. I just want to keep doing my job, even if it means embarking on the world's least-scenic road trip as your boy Friday."

The last bit was thrown out in challenge, like he assumed I was already mentally making plans to kick him off the bus.

He was absolutely right.

"Reagan, you must see that you can't... *we* can't, especially after..." I shook my head, annoyed at myself. "You're not going," I bit out. "There's no way."

He folded his arms over his chest. "You need a support person on this trip to coordinate with the PennCo PR team while you're busy doing CEO stuff—or at least everyone seems to think you do—and I'm the most logical choice since I'm actually *on* the PennCo PR team, even if I happen to be at the very bottom of the food chain. If you pick someone from another subsidiary to replace me or, worse, say you'd rather go alone, people are going to wonder what's wrong with me." He lifted his chin. "They're going to think I can't do the work, which is bullshit because I absolutely can, or that you don't like me, which is ridiculous because I'm a fucking delight. I want my Pennington employee file to show that I'm a dedicated employee and a team player, thank you very much."

"Because you care that deeply about a low-level position in the PR department of a textile company." I raised an eyebrow. "*Why?*"

He opened his mouth to say something, then thought better of it and shrugged. "Why not?"

Why not, indeed. I folded my arms and leaned back, too, mirroring his position, and we watched each other with the twitchy focus of a pair of Old West gunslingers at high noon. The bus lurched slightly as McGee pulled us out onto the street.

I wanted to think up a perfectly acceptable, work-appropriate reason why Reagan should not come on this trip—

surely there were *hundreds*—but damned if I could think of a single one while he was watching me like that. I couldn't imagine why he'd want to be here, but it seemed he did. Denying him the opportunity—and potentially damaging his reputation in the process—simply because we'd slept together was the very definition of not-okay.

So... it appeared I was stuck. This was not a condition I often found myself in these days, and I couldn't say I enjoyed the feeling of powerlessness. But I was a grown man capable of resisting temptation even in forced proximity—I'd managed to get through an entire Honeybridge vacation last summer without laying a hand on Trent and Patricia's son, after all. So I could handle this.

"Fine, then." I clenched my back teeth together. "Stay."

Reagan's suspicious gaze scanned my face, looking for a catch. "Really."

"Until Layla's feeling better, yes. Truce?"

"Truce." His lip twitched, and his eyes lit with humor. "Were we at war?"

"Weren't we? You compared yourself to a feral beaver. That sounded rather aggressive."

"A *rabid* beaver," he corrected. "And you're right. If you'd seen the colony of rabid beavers that took over Lake Wellbridge when I was twelve, you'd know just how aggressive they can be. I was petrified to swim for a whole summer, convinced they'd gnaw my dick off."

I did not want to be thinking about Reagan's dick *or* about the way he'd looked when he was swimming—back muscles rippling as he dove beneath the surface, face creased with joy when he emerged a moment later shaking rainbow droplets from his hair. "You seem to have gotten over that fear."

"I was *told* I was over it," he corrected. "Which is different. The beavers might've been part of a Honeycutt plot to take over the lake, you see, so Mother insisted JT and I swim daily. Show your enemies no fear, whether they're beavers or Honeycutts."

I snorted. "I know your mother's competitive, but was she really willing to risk your... body parts... to make sure the Honeycutts didn't win?" I only wished this were as unbelievable as it sounded.

Reagan's grin appeared and disappeared, fast as lightning and just as breathtaking. "You have *met* Patricia Wellbridge, yes?"

I stared at him, wishing I could peer into his head. The man was a contrary mix of submission and snark, adorable blushes and cutting comments. But which Reagan was the real one?

Doesn't matter, I told myself firmly. *He's not yours to figure out.*

Far too quickly, the bus stopped, double-parked in Midtown, and McGee pulled back the privacy curtain to stand by the sofa. "First stop. We've got maybe twenty minutes 'til we get a ticket, so get your bags quick, kid—" He looked up and down at Reagan's perfect hair and stylish suit and revised his mental calculations. "Or quick as you can, anyway."

"I'll take far less than twenty minutes," Reagan promised. But clearly, he'd caught the hint of disdain beneath my driver's scrupulously polite tone because when he pushed to his feet, he returned McGee's up-down look and cocked his head. "Just to say, I'm twenty-eight, and you're, what, twenty-six? *Kid?*"

McGee narrowed his eyes. "How'd you guess my age? My own mom thinks I'm thirty."

Reagan waved a hand. "Spend enough time on social

media and you learn to spot the person behind the filter... or behind the hot-as-fuck tattoos and the early onset eye wrinkles, as the case may be."

"The..." McGee lifted a hand to rub the skin above his eyebrow ring, and his frown deepened. "Hey! I'm not *wrinkled.*"

"No, of course you're not." Reagan patted McGee's inked forearm comfortingly. "But if you'd ever like to talk about your skincare regime, let me know." He grabbed his coat from the sofa and dug his keys out of his pocket. "Okay, be right back."

McGee stared at the door long after it closed behind Reagan. Then, unexpectedly, he burst out laughing. "Jesus Christ. You know, I might actually like that guy? I've only ever seen him from a distance over the years, and I had an idea that he was like a younger version of his parents, but now I'm thinking he might be okay."

"Because he insulted your skincare regime?" I rolled my eyes and felt my headache grow. "You have incredibly strange standards."

He turned toward me with an easy smile. "He caught that I was giving him attitude, and he gave it right back. You know I love a fighter."

I'd known McGee since he, himself, had been a rough-and-tumble sixteen-year-old held together by pride and a bad attitude, so this statement earned him another eye roll.

"He was nice to me earlier today, too." McGee shrugged. "Just saying, he might be a decent guy under the designer duds."

I made a noncommittal noise and sank back in my seat. The band around my head was getting tighter by the minute. "Can we not talk about this anymore?"

McGee leaned against the wall, studying me. "You don't like him?"

"I didn't say that." I kneaded the back of my neck. "I don't feel any particular way about Reagan Wellbridge." Just like I didn't feel any particular way about him noticing McGee's "hot-as-fuck" tattoos and then *touching* them. No discernible feelings at all. "He's an employee. Moreover, he's Trent and Patricia's son," I reminded both of us. "He and Brantleigh went to school together."

"Yep." McGee shrugged again. "But he's pretty cute despite all that."

"Did you not hear everything I just said?" I demanded. "Don't get any bright ideas. He's off limits." *To both of us.*

"Come on, boss." McGee shot me a wounded look. "I told you, I'm done with hookups for a while. And you know he's not my type. I like 'em small enough to pick up with one hand." He lifted an enormous paw in demonstration. "Like Alden, who runs the salon up in Honeybridge. Hot *damn.* That man has an ass like—"

"Way, way too much information." I held up a hand to cut him off. "McGee, how long have you worked for me?"

"Hmm. Driver for eight years, odd jobs for a while before that..." He scratched his cheek thoughtfully with one tattooed finger. "About ten years altogether. Why?"

"In all that time, how often have I asked for the details of your sex life? How often have I shared the details of mine?"

He grinned, unrepentant. "Just showing you it's okay to be open about what—and *who*—you want, that's all."

"I'm not closeted," I reminded him for maybe the hundredth time in the years since he'd defiantly informed me that he was gay and I'd shared my own sexuality as a way to help him feel safe and comfortable. "I'm discreet.

There's a difference. I don't broadcast my attractions, no matter who I'm attracted to, because the gossip and tabloid headlines would last longer than the attraction itself. But I have no problem being open about it with certain... friends."

By *friends*, I primarily meant *men I hooked up with*, and McGee knew it.

Which was why I was shocked to hear him say, "You know, I think Reagan could be your friend. If you wanted him to be."

"McGee," I warned.

He mimed zipping his mouth shut.

Surprisingly, Reagan was true to his word. He emerged from his building—one high-end enough I had to imagine Trent and Patricia were subsidizing his rent—in just twelve minutes, carting a rolling suitcase, a duffel, an enormous pillow, and a reusable grocery bag bulging with food.

When McGee ran down to help with the luggage, Reagan thanked him profusely, and McGee gave him a "No problem, man. You were faster than I thought," which might not have sounded like a compliment to the average person but was more respect than McGee usually gave people he barely knew.

"Fast packing's my superpower," Reagan explained with a grin. "I've been sent on last-minute trips for my dad's campaigns a lot." He stood by the sofa, pillow under his arm, and glanced down the narrow corridor of the bus, all the way to my bedroom at the back. "So. I guess I should have asked before, but... where am I sleeping?"

It was an innocent enough question, but it caused images of Reagan—naked, aroused, with his head thrown back on a very different pillow—to flash through my brain in time with the throbbing of my headache. Coupled with the easy, friendly smile he'd given McGee—McGee, who was nearly Reagan's age and was not *his boss*—it was enough to make my temper flare.

"You're looking at it." I pointed at the racks of single beds that lined the hall between the kitchen area and the bedroom. There were four narrow bunks in total, two on either side of the hall, and each had a curtain to provide some level of privacy. "I'm sure it's not the spacious accommodations you're used to, but the only bedroom on this bus is mine." My tone made it clear I wasn't sharing. "You can store your stuff on one of the other bunks, or McGee can stow it in the cargo area. Your choice."

I sounded far more surly than I should have, given that *I* was the one who'd called a "truce." Knowing this didn't improve my mood or my headache. Neither did the way Reagan's lush mouth pursed and he instantly straightened his shoulders, matching my energy.

"Inside, I think." Reagan pulled back one of the curtains and contemplated the bed before tossing down his pillow. "This will be just like summer camp. Of course, I was a bit shorter then."

"You'll be fine," I said flatly.

McGee didn't say a word, but his entire body radiated disapproval as he hefted Reagan's luggage onto one of the other bunks, and that only made me *more* annoyed.

What did McGee expect me to do? Offer to share my king-sized bed? Give it up entirely? Why should Reagan be comfortable while I would be anything *but* for as long as we were stuck together?

Reagan emptied his sack of groceries into the refrigerator—a giant bottle of oat milk, three coconut milk yogurts, several cans of sparkling water, some apples, and a six-pack of mead, not that I was watching closely—then turned to me with a look of exaggerated dismay. "Oh, darn, I should have asked permission before I put my things away! Is it okay for me to store my oat milk in your refrigerator, Mr. Pennington? Or should McGee put it in the cargo hold instead?"

McGee—the traitor—snickered as he headed back to the driver's seat.

"Stow your damn groceries, Wellbridge," I said sourly. "And be silent, please. I have work to do."

I stood to retrieve my laptop from my bag, but the moment I sat back down, Reagan slid into the seat opposite me. "You know, maybe you'd feel better if we discussed what happened."

"Nope." I opened my computer as McGee pulled out into traffic.

"Are you sure?" he taunted. "Before I left the hotel last night, you seemed to want to—"

I gave him a look that could have melted asbestos. "Reagan."

He held up both hands with overblown innocence, like he knew exactly how close I was to losing my cool entirely and he *enjoyed* it, the provoking little shit.

All the things I'd wanted to clarify last night—that it had been a mistake, never to be repeated—seemed patently obvious to both of us already, and talking about sex, even in the past tense, while Reagan was *right there*, all aquamarine eyes and flushed cheeks, was asking for trouble.

When my phone rang again, I answered my assistant's call with the desperation of a drowning man grabbing a life preserver. "January, perfect timing. Have we gotten an update on the Munich project—?"

"Thatcher," January cut me off. "Thalia called."

Just when I thought my headache couldn't get worse.

My first ex-wife and I had started out as good friends with common goals. Even after our divorce and her remarriage to a Hollywood producer, we'd remained friendly. But there was only one reason Thalia ever called these days. Which meant...

"Brantleigh's in trouble," January confirmed.

I straightened in my seat, ignoring Reagan's frown of concern. "What kind of trouble?" There was a tremor of fear in my voice as visions of Nova Davidson's paparazzi photos swam across my brain. "Tell me he didn't wreck another car, January. Or crash that stupid little plane of his—"

"No," January said firmly and apologetically. "Sorry, Thatcher. I should have led with that. He's not sick or injured."

"Okay." I blew out a breath. I could deal with anything else.

"You know how Thalia is. When I told her you weren't in the office, she just started relaying all the information to *me*, like she didn't have time to hang up and call your cell phone—"

"I get it. Stop apologizing and tell me what she said."

"Apparently, Brantleigh got personally involved with an actor starring in one of his stepfather's movies—"

I'd foreseen this, but I felt no joy at being proved correct. "Again?"

"Yeah. Brantleigh has been working as a production assistant for his stepfather under the strict condition that he, and I quote, *keep it in his pants* while he's on set, but unfortunately... he didn't." She sighed. "I don't get why anyone would risk their career *and* their family for a guy, no matter how hot he is."

My eyes met Reagan's for a brief moment before I looked away. "The facts, January."

"Right. Sorry. Anyway, their relationship imploded,

and the actor actually threatened to quit the movie. Thalia and her husband are over it. So, Thalia packed Brantleigh off for a yoga retreat as punishment. She hopes that practicing mindfulness and drinking wheatgrass juice for the next ten days will help *center* him." January hesitated. "Do we think Thalia knows what punishment means?"

I slumped in my seat and squeezed my eyes shut like I could block out the world. "What the hell is that going to do? He's twenty-eight, for fuck's sake."

You couldn't force maturity on a person, could you? Clearly, I was no parenting expert.

"When he gets back," she went on, "Thalia's forcing him to move out, and she'd like you to use your influence on him to, quote, *help him find his path.*"

"My influence. Right." Any influence I might have had on my son had faded by the time he was a teenager. I'd tried to stay active in his life, to show him my business or, when he proved uninterested in that, to help him figure out what else he wanted to do. But time and again, he'd brushed me off, spending most of his time on the West Coast. I'd been busy with my second marriage, my ever-expanding business, my second divorce, and now... "I'll take care of it," I said wearily, though I didn't have any more bright ideas about how to accomplish that than I'd ever had. "Anything else I should be aware of?"

"Not really. Layla's admin emailed about getting a list of campgrounds where you plan to stop for scheduled overnights, but I refused. I envisioned her packing a suitcase and randomly showing up to meet you. *Knock, knock, Thatcher. I brought you some germs.*"

Across from me, Reagan laughed softly, and though I kept my eyes closed, my gut tightened in response. I understood all too well how you could risk your career for a guy. But unlike my son, I would not repeat my missteps.

"I'm sure they just want to arrange her travel so she can meet me when she's feeling better," I said.

January sniffed. "Well, company policy says she can't travel until she's symptom-free for forty-eight hours, and I can guarantee that won't be happening for at least a week. I will come down there to douse her with hand sanitizer and banish her like a demon if she tries to meet you sooner."

My lips twitched. "I already have a mother, January."

"And you could learn a lot from her. Your mom wouldn't go within ten feet of a germ, especially now that she's recovering from her latest cosmetic procedure."

"I'm glad one of us keeps up with her procedures," I said dryly.

"Only because she called earlier, too. She said you haven't RSVP'd for her birthday party."

I sighed, still not opening my eyes. "My mother's birthday is in October, and I already attended her party."

"That was her *Hamptons* party. The one next week is with her Palm Springs friends. But you're going to be in Colorado the day before, so I'm not sure how you'd get there..."

She didn't say "...unless you flew," but we both knew she was thinking it.

It wasn't like I never flew. In my position, sometimes it was unavoidable, especially when handling complex international negotiations that required a personal touch. The question was whether a particular situation was worth enduring the abject terror and/or nausea that being that high above the earth would cause. When it was, I popped a high-octane sleeping pill before takeoff, sprawled on my bed in the corporate jet, and paid Robert, an ex-SEAL airline pilot with an unblemished safety record, an exorbitant amount of money to get me there and wake me up after landing. Usually, I made it off the plane before the medication made me vomit.

I shifted in my seat. "Tell her I won't be able to attend, January, but please send her flowers. Gardenias are her favorite."

"Got it." She paused for a moment. "You still have that headache, don't you? I can tell from your voice. Take more supplements, boss."

"Will do."

She snorted. "Which means you definitely won't. But at least get a nap," she said gently. "Everything will look better after you've rested."

I highly doubted this. Sleep eluded me at the best of times, and nothing that had happened in the last twelve hours was going to improve my chances of catching it. But after disconnecting, I sat for another moment with my eyes closed, hoping I looked like I was deep in thought.

Christ, I really was tired. I didn't want to open my eyes to the glaring overhead lights or go another three rounds with Reagan. The more provoking he was, the harder it was to remember why I couldn't shut him up with my mouth on his, and I couldn't afford to let him distract me.

On this thought, I cracked open my eyes at last, ready to put Reagan Wellbridge in his place once and for all...

But instead, I found myself blinking at the changes that occurred in the few minutes I'd been zoned out.

The bright overhead lights were off, replaced with the soft glow from the LED strips on the floor and the reflected glare from Reagan's tablet. The challenging, sassy man I'd been expecting was gone, too; Reagan stared at his screen with total absorption, his body swaying slightly as the bus glided through highway traffic.

I cleared my throat.

Reagan glanced up and removed a pair of earbuds. "Hey. I was just checking my email. Layla asked me to brief you on your talking points for the speaking event at the Midwestern Textile Symposium. She also has a reporter who wants to shadow us at some point on the tour, and she's hoping he'll give us a featured article, but—" He broke off, his aquamarine eyes clouding with concern. "If you're too tired for this, I can brief you in the morning."

This seemed to be yet another version of Reagan—not the sexy submissive or the sassy, challenging opponent, but calm Reagan. *Kind* Reagan. Unfortunately, this version was just as compelling as the others.

How the hell was I supposed to keep my distance from the man when he kept changing the rules and ruining my plans for handling him?

"I don't need or want your pity," I informed him, waving a hand in the air to indicate him and the lights, the whole... mood shift he'd initiated. "Don't be nice now if you're just going to be a pain in the ass again later."

Reagan's cheeks colored. "A pain in the—? Are you—? *No.*" His hands clenched his tablet so hard his knuckles whitened. "I don't care how tempting it is to take advantage of my platinum-level job security; I am *not* going to tell you exactly how much of an ass you're being, or just how unnecessarily shitty that comment was, or how *someone* needs a refresher in how to have a truce. It's not pity, okay? I'm a nice person, and I saw that you were tired. That's all."

His eyes blazed with anger—honest, righteous—and I felt like the ass I was. Reagan was eighteen years my junior, but I was the one being childish.

I blew out a breath and rubbed at the center of my forehead. "You're right. That *was* shitty. It's no excuse, but I have a killer headache right now."

"I know." Reagan's face flushed darker. "I'd know even if I couldn't see it all over your face because... well, your phone volume is quite high, and my hearing is impeccable."

Meaning he'd heard my entire call, including everything about Brant.

And instead of taking the opportunity to make barbed comments and score points... he'd done me a service.

"Noted," I said. Then, in a softer voice added, "Thank you."

He nodded warily. "You're welcome."

I nodded, too, and thought vaguely that if McGee walked in right now, he'd think we looked like a pair of giant bobbleheads. Or like a pair of rabid beavers attempting to be civilized.

When I thought of Reagan Wellbridge, I thought of the kid who'd turned heads with hot pink flamingo-print swim trunks at the Wellbridge's annual Fourth of July Patriots' Picnic. The prankster who'd taken several boxes of leftover sparklers and used them to spell out a bawdy joke on the lawn at the Honeybridge yacht club the next day despite what had to be a killer hangover. The party boy Peter Pan whose parents alternately spoiled and despaired of him. The man with the sinfully sexy smirk who'd forged a permanent link in my brain between the color aquamarine and the feeling of overwhelming temptation.

And he *was* all those things... but maybe he was other things besides.

"Seriously, why *did* you take the job at Pennington Industries?" I demanded, suddenly needing to know.

He chewed his lip for a moment, then gave me a bright

grin. "Would you believe it's because I long to help spread the word of athleisure textile innovation one blog post at a time?"

The snarky answer bothered me more than it should have, but what had I expected? A thoughtful answer from a man whose father claimed he took nothing seriously? A deep confession to a man who couldn't maintain a single close relationship, even with his own son?

He was right to want to keep things shallow. Cordial. *Distant.* No provoking, no flirtation. It was better that way.

"Finish briefing me now," I said, pulling my laptop in front of me. "The more we focus, the sooner this goodwill tour will be over, and the sooner we can put the New Year's Eve debacle behind us for good. Right?"

I wasn't sure if I was talking about Nova Davidson's wild ride or the wild night Reagan and I had spent together, but at that moment, I was almost sure I believed it.

Chapter Five

Reagan

"Reagan Wellbridge, you are a stupid fucker," I whispered under my breath the moment Thatcher disappeared into his bedroom at the back of the bus and closed the sliding door with a *snick*.

From the moment I'd arrived at a hotel room for an anonymous hookup and come face-to-face (and dick-to-dick) with my longtime crush, I'd felt the threads of my life plan unraveling and slipping from my grasp. Even so, the way I'd acted with Thatcher earlier was ridiculous.

I wanted him to take me seriously as a professional. To stop thinking of me as his friend's kid or, worse, the one-night indiscretion he regretted. So why had I goaded him when I could have made peace? Why had I let my frustration out when I could have either kept my mouth shut or fought back with a stealthy stinging retort, the way I had with McGee?

What made Thatcher so different?

Because Christ, if there was one thing I knew how to do, it was be polite. I'd been smiling placidly while choking back my real feelings for a freaking *decade* on the campaign trail and, heck, even at PennCo. Smoothing things over with charm came as easy as breathing to me. I even enjoyed it.

But apparently, not when it came to Thatcher.

God, this was annoying. *He* was annoying. The way I'd veered all the way from frustrated to soft-hearted when Thatcher had seemed tired and sad was annoying. I took a deep breath, found the lingering scent of Thatcher's spicy cologne on the air, and groaned at how quickly my stomach clenched and my heart rate increased—the way I couldn't get my mind out of the gutter with him was annoying, too.

"Stupid, *stupid* fucker," I whispered again, thunking my head against the back of the seat.

That would be my new nickname, I decided. Because it was a hell of a lot more accurate than "Mr. Important" had ever been.

Of course, I'd been a different person back when Pop Honeycutt had given me that nickname. I'd been a soft, sunshiny kid back then, thrilled with the world and my place in it. For years, I'd watched Pop give a nickname— some funny, some sweet, some deep and meaningful—to every local kid who wandered into the General Store, then listened as my friends and even my big brother used their nicknames like a badge of pride... at least when my mother wasn't around to insist that no firstborn son of hers would answer to the name *Frog*. When my turn hadn't come, I'd been confident this was an oversight, so I'd taken myself off to town one summer afternoon, politely tugged on Pop's sleeve, and asked him.

God, I couldn't imagine what he must've thought of me, all messy white-blond hair, big eyes, and pre-Invisalign teeth, but the man hadn't hesitated. He'd knelt down, grinned, and said, "Why, don't you know, kiddo? You're Mr.

Important." He'd tweaked my snub nose. "Knew it from the minute you were born. And don't you forget it."

I'd carried that name in my heart for longer than I'd ever admit. So what if my brother was Honeybridge's golden boy? Who cared that I could never quite stand up straight enough to please anyone, or that I laughed too loud, or talked too much? I was Mr. Important, *and don't you forget it.*

Much like when I took the PennCo job, though, I thought wryly, it might have been good if I'd asked some clarifying questions. Important to *who?* Important for *what?* And, crucially, important *when?* Because one would think it might have kicked in before I became a twenty-eight-year-old whose crowning achievements included being caught on camera doing Beyoncé's "Single Ladies" dance at a Red Sox game during the national anthem and taking home the Honeybridge Swimming Marathon award for Team Well-bridge the summer the feral beavers had made everyone else too scared to swim.

Now, *that* might have been an Instagram-worthy moment, had I known about social media back then.

On that thought, I dug out my phone and opened the app. I hadn't posted since last night, which wasn't out of the ordinary, but I found I missed it when I went too long. I knew some people felt that curating their posts and spinning things to the positive was "fake" and created pressure to maintain a standard of perfection. For me, it was the opposite. In reframing my own life for public consumption, I reminded myself that things weren't as bad as they sometimes seemed.

I ruffled a hand through my hair, positioned myself in front of the darkened window, adjusted my settings for a long exposure, and snapped a few pictures. In the images, I looked deliberately rumpled rather than bone-weary and sleep-deprived. The bright lights of the seedy truck stop we'd passed blurred into a beautiful neon streak in the background. *Perfect.*

"Turning business into a road trip! So ready for all the twists and turns the new year will bring," I told my followers in the caption. "Where's this year going to take YOU? #businessnomad #DrivingTowardSuccess #FocusontheRoadAhead"

Focusing was exactly what I needed to do.

While the view outside changed from city lights and truck stops to unrelenting darkness, I grabbed a seltzer from the refrigerator and dug into my assignment. I took the industry talking points Layla had provided and expounded on all of them, providing facts and figures to substantiate each one. I also drew up a fact sheet, a sort of layperson's guide to sustainable textiles, that Thatcher could refer to when talking to reporters who wanted the scoop on Nova Davidson and might not understand industry jargon. And then I went a step further and started drafting some feel-good press statements to help out the communications people, which meant educating myself on PennCo Fiber's history, our corporate mission, and the innovations we'd pioneered, especially since Layla had taken the helm. Though her contributions were often overshadowed by the moneymaker subsidiaries of Pennington Industries, there was no denying that research and development had flourished under her leadership, just as Nataly had said. I almost felt guilty for being annoyed with her at the meeting earlier.

Almost.

Because what I also learned, as I slogged through the pages-long sagas that PennCo had published as "press releases" in the past, was that this company had no idea what they were doing when it came to communicating their message to the world. Layla claimed the textile business was old-school, and she was right, but PennCo's school was so old we were practically chiseling our marketing copy on stone tablets.

And it didn't have to be that way.

PennCo was a company built on innovation, so why was Layla so against innovating our approach to public relations with social media? And maybe it wasn't fair to lay all the blame at her feet—maybe that was my lingering bitterness and jealousy from the meeting talking—but even Nataly, who adored Layla, had admitted this was a blind spot.

The more I thought about it, the more keyed up I got, so that by the time six hours had passed and McGee pulled into a truck stop to take a driving break around midnight, I was so overtired and so unreasonably, *incandescently* bitter I was ready to storm off into the West Virginia night and call an Uber back to Manhattan. If this was what a career in public relations was all about, then maybe spending my life in front of the cameras as Trent Wellbridge's dim but photogenic son was a viable option.

Of course it was at *this* moment that Thatcher poked his head out of what I could only imagine was his luxurious bedroom suite, probably woken by the sudden lack of road noise.

"Hey," he croaked, running a hand over his face. "What's going on?"

Professional, I reminded myself. *Polite. Distant.*

"McGee's taking a break, and I've been working on the notes for your speech and some press stuff. I have some... concerns—" I glanced up. Thatcher had changed out of his suit and into a cashmere sweater and comfortable pants. He looked sleepy. Warm. Utterly lickable.

My dick throbbed.

I stood so fast I bumped my knee against the table, grabbed my phone and jacket, and headed for the door. "I'm concerned that I really need to stretch my legs," I called over my shoulder as I ran down the stairs.

"*Fuck,*" I said into the dark abyss as I stomped across the parking lot despite my bruised knee, fueled by frustration and unwanted lust. My breath fogged in the freezing air like tiny storm clouds that disintegrated into the night air as quickly as they formed, and I wasn't sure if I wanted to laugh or cry.

The buzz of my phone in my pocket startled me, and I immediately pulled it out. Only my family bothered calling instead of messaging, and I could use the distraction.

"Reagan! I feel like I haven't talked to you all year!" my brother exclaimed, then dissolved into laughter at his own joke. "Get it? 'Cause it's January first—"

I groaned. This was *not* the distraction I needed. "Yeah, I get it," I said shortly, stomping past the edge of the parking lot lights, hopefully out of earshot of the bus. "Unfortunately."

"Uh... pardon me," JT said after a long pause. "I must have the wrong number. I was looking for my brother, Reagan Wellbridge. Perhaps you've heard of him? Short guy, ridiculous eyes, uncanny ability to pretend nothing fazes him? Who's this?"

I rolled my "ridiculous" eyes. "Fuck off," I said without heat. "No one over six feet is 'short.' You're just too tall." I refused to explain that my ability to appear unfazed was proving unreliable when Thatcher was around. "Shouldn't you be annoying your boyfriend at this hour?"

"Already done," he said proudly. "In fact, I did it so well that just a minute ago, Flynn said, 'Frog, my darling, you're so annoyingly sexy I can't concentrate on closing the tavern. Why don't you wait for me at home?'"

"Bullshit," I said, amused in spite of myself. "You forget I've known Firecracker nearly as long as you have. He said, 'Frog, stop distracting me and go away,' didn't he?"

JT laughed. "Possibly. But he was kissing me when he said it, so I knew how to interpret his grumpiness. Love's all about interpretation," he said sagely.

I snorted again and kept stomping.

"What the hell are you doing right now?" JT demanded. "It sounds like you're hiking up a mountain. Or possibly bullfighting. Or... rappelling down the Brooklyn Bridge in the wind." He hesitated. "You're not dangling from a bridge, are you? I'm imagining some New Year's resolution about nighttime adventure sports to delight your followers?"

I huffed out a laugh that sent more white vapor billowing. "Definitely not. Though that might be preferable to what I'm actually doing. I'm in rural West Virginia, and I'm walking around a truck stop parking lot so I don't freeze."

"Dear god, why?"

"Why am I in West Virginia? On a quote-unquote business trip. And I'm on a business trip because... did you hear about the Nova Davidson debacle?"

"The what? Who's Nova?" he demanded, sounding just like someone's crotchety grandma.

I filled him in on everything that had happened last night—to Nova, at least—and the plans for PennCo's goodwill tour I got roped into. "Since she was wearing that shirt made from PennCo Fiber's new fabric, we need to do damage control, hence the impromptu trip," I explained.

"PennCo decided the best way to get their message out was... going door to door, meeting industry reps?" JT's familiar laughter helped the muscles of my shoulders loosen.

"More or less," I agreed sourly. "I tried to explain the concept of social media—even offered to handle the campaign myself—but nooope. Bus tour it is."

"Ooof. Don't believe a word they say about how backwards textile companies are, you guys! They're sophisticated as *fuck*. Why, just today, my brother told me about an exciting opportunity that's taking him through... checks notes... rural West Virginia." He paused, then added gleefully, "I bet the folks there are gonna love your Balenciaga smoking jacket and Swarovski-encrusted Crocs."

"Please. I don't own a Balenciaga smoking jacket," I said with an affected sniff. I kicked a hardened chunk of ice into the darkness. "And those Crocs were a *gift*, which I obviously did not pack. I've been doing campaign tours for years, JT. Longer than you ever did. I'm not totally incompetent, thank you very much."

JT's voice immediately lost its teasing tone. "Whoa, where'd that come from? I know you're not. What's going on, Rea?"

Leave it to a sibling to cut through the bullshit and leave you naked and exposed. "You mean besides being stuck on the press tour from hell with the boss from hell on the *bus ride* from hell because everyone else in the office was too sick to go?"

"Yes, besides all that. Because you're right—you *have* been on a billion of Dad's campaign tours. You've probably spent time in places a lot colder and less exciting than wherever you are now. And I thought you liked Mr. Pennington?"

JT's reference to the man by his honorific instead of using his first name was a reminder that we primarily knew the man as a friend of our parents—as someone we'd called "Mr." during our teenage years—which only served to remind me of how wrong it had been to hook up with him last night... something I would never in a million years admit to doing, especially to my perfect, flawless, beloved-by-the-world brother.

"It doesn't matter if I like him because *he* doesn't like *me*. Actually, correction: he doesn't care about me one way or the other. In all the weeks I've been in New York, he hasn't come by my cubicle once to say hello or ask how I'm settling in, he ignored my ideas at the team meeting earlier today, and he's made it very clear he doesn't want me on this trip with him. His bus driver's been friendlier to me than he has. It's like he's trying to pretend I'm invisible."

Except last night, of course. When I was naked in his bed, Thatcher had most definitely been paying attention. Which only made me feel worse about myself. I was valuable as a sexual partner but not as a professional contributor to his corporate team? The thought hurt. Badly enough to fuel my anger.

"I should tell him where to shove his shitty-ass PR campaign," I muttered.

"Sure. Because acting like a bratty teenager and mouthing off has worked so well for you in the past," JT agreed.

"I wouldn't *actually*," I said defensively. "I don't do that anymore." I remembered my confrontation with Thatcher earlier and winced. "Not on purpose anyway. Sometimes I get frustrated, and things just... come out."

"Uh-huh. But when you lash out, *you* end up getting

hurt. So you need to find a different way to be heard. A better way."

I knew JT was trying to be sympathetic and big-brotherly, and I appreciated it. But he made it all sound so damn easy when it wasn't.

"Better *how?*" I demanded. "I've been trying at work, JT. Really trying. And I thought this time would be different, but I can't get anyone to take me seriously—"

"*Yet,*" JT interrupted. "You'll convince them. I mean, since when does Reagan Wellbridge take no for an answer? Remember the time Ashley Waitrose refused to let you race her mother's Lamborghini, so you put on your tightest swim trunks, went up to Mrs. Waitrose herself at the club pool, and offered her double-shot mojitos until she begged you to take her for a ride in her car?"

I winced. "That, uh... might not be the best example of doing *better*, Frog."

I remembered the woman's hot mouth on my dick later that afternoon and the sun beating down on my bare back as I slid my hand into her bikini bottoms. I also remembered the cold sting of vodka in my eyes from the drink Ashley threw in my face when I came back to the club later with her mother's lipstick on my neck.

My brother must not have known that part of the story. I sort of wished I could forget it, too, along with all the other bad choices I'd made over the years. All the things that had led to this moment, when it seemed like no one in the world had any faith in me anymore...

Including, sometimes, myself.

"I'm just saying, do the same thing with Mr. Pennington that you did with Mrs. Waitrose. Be tenacious."

The dry winter air clogged my throat, making me sputter and choke. "Er... thanks, but no," I wheezed. "I'm not taking my *tenacity* anywhere near Thatcher Pennington." Not again.

"Well, you can't give up. Deep down—like *way* deep, beneath the fuck-off calm, beneath the attitude, beneath all the stuff you think you have to do and be to protect yourself—you are the sweetest person I know. You deserve to be happy. And fuck anyone who keeps you from creating the life you want, whether it's our parents or your boss or your own bad habits. You can succeed, Rea. You already are."

His words made tears prick behind my eyes. God, how unfair was it when your "perfect" big brother was actually *perfect?*

So, naturally, I made a retching noise to hide how genuinely touched I was. "*Ugh.* When the hell did you become so in touch with your emotions, *Jonathan Turner Wellbridge, The-Fucking-Third?* Our tight-assed Puritan ancestors are *rolling* right now. Mother's going to excommunicate you from the family. And are you telling me Flynn chooses to have this kind of toxic positivity in his life? I'm starting him a GoFundMe. Hashtag-Free-Flynn."

JT's laughter exploded through the speaker. "Our ancestors can fuck right off. So can Mother, for that matter. And Flynn *loves* my positivity," he said with all the smug confidence of a man who knew he'd found his soul mate. "He might even like my unsolicited advice... sometimes."

I laughed, too, though it might have been a bit watery. "You know, that man's so fucking gone for you, I bet he probably does. But I do *not* appreciate sound, well-meaning advice from kind, intelligent people." I kicked another frozen chunk of dirt and snow. "Especially when following that advice might result in failure of never-before-experienced levels."

"You're so dramatic," JT groaned. "It's true what they say about middle children."

"Seriously? For the last time, Katharine Hepburn is not our sibling," I insisted, as I always did when JT tried to claim our mother's spoiled bichon frise was her third child.

"Tell me she's not Mother's baby. Tell me Mother doesn't like her better than either of us. I dare you."

McGee's forced cough came from several yards behind me, and I glanced over my shoulder to see him give a firm nod toward the bus. "We've got a relief driver waiting for us in Dayton," he called across the desolate space between us.

"Okay. Two minutes," I yelled back.

"What you're holding is a *mobile* phone," he insisted. "You can talk *on* the bus."

"And yet, the reception's better here, so... *two minutes*," I repeated, saccharine sweet but not yielding.

McGee gave me the world's most sweeping eye roll as he stepped up into the coach.

"See?" JT said excitedly. "There you go. You know how to handle yourself, Reagan. Just keep doing it."

That was precisely the problem, though. I knew what I needed to do—ignore my sexy boss, kill everyone at PennCo with kindness and stun them with my intelligence, prove myself as many times as necessary until I got the job on my dad's campaign—and I *could* do it.

So why was I having so much trouble remembering that when Thatcher was around?

Still, it gave me a boost to know that JT had confidence in me. That he recognized my tenacity when other people— namely our parents—seemed to view me as a running list of things I'd tried and quit.

"JT, I gotta go," I said. "Thanks for calling. I feel... marginally better."

"Good. Chin up, buttercup. And if you're feeling down, just channel Patricia Wellbridge at the Box Day competition: *Failure is impossible, therefore, anyone who says differently is a fool unworthy of your notice.*"

I ended the call with a laugh despite my sour mood and stepped onto the bus, grateful to get out of the freezing wind. But when I went to close the door, McGee stopped me with a head shake and a gruff "Don't bother. Still waiting on the boss."

I narrowed my eyes. "You rushed me back here when Thatcher wasn't on board yet?"

"Yep." He made himself comfortable on the sofa and raised an eyebrow in challenge. "We wait on him; he doesn't wait on us. I figured, better to let you wait here than have you chasing us down the frozen highway in your douchey loafers."

I clenched my hands into fists. "You know," I said sweetly. "I don't care what people say. I think lines give a person's face character." I traced the skin above my own eye in the exact spot where McGee's eyebrow-pop had formed a deep crease on his forehead. "Growing old gracefully is a brave choice."

McGee clapped a hand to his face and scowled. "I told you, I'm not *wrinkly.*"

"What? No, of course not. I was just speaking hypothetically." I turned to hide my triumphant smile and busied myself finding alcohol in the galley kitchen. I could almost swear I heard McGee snort behind me, but I refused to turn and check.

JT was right. I knew how to handle myself.

In addition to a can of raspberry hard seltzer, I found a plastic-wrapped charcuterie tray in the fridge. I yanked both out and popped a bunch of fresh grapes on the platter before setting it on the dining table and sliding into the booth.

The instant Thatcher boarded the bus a few minutes later, it felt like all the oxygen in the space was suddenly sucked in his direction, including the molecules I'd been using to breathe, but I kept my attention resolutely focused on my snack.

He paused beside the table. "Hungry? I could have bought you a slice of suspicious pizza inside."

"And risk despoiling your luxury lavatory?" I smiled. "I think not. Besides, a Wellbridge has certain culinary standards." See how calm I could be? I could handle this. Tenacity, baby.

"I once saw your father take half a cookie from a baby's mouth and eat it," Thatcher said with a straight face.

I snickered, almost choking on a grape. "Ten bucks says it was the child of a voting constituent and he was doing it for a photo op."

He shook his head, clearly trying to hide a smirk. "I wouldn't take that bet."

"I'm not my father, you know." I hadn't intended the words to come out sounding so damn serious, but it was too late to pull them back. Instead, I shoved a roll of thin salami into my mouth to keep from following it with even more unnecessary honesty.

"No," he said softly. "Definitely not."

I wanted to ask him what the hell that had meant—whether it was a compliment or an insult—but it was probably better that I didn't know.

No taunting. No challenging. No schmoop.

Thatcher slid into his seat—was two hours of proximity

too soon for me to have assigned us each seats? *Definitely*—and McGee got the bus underway again, cruising us smoothly back onto the highway.

"So..." Thatcher cleared his throat, looking suddenly awkward. "I know this trip was even more unplanned for you than it was for me. I hope you didn't have to cancel any plans to be here."

"Not really. And don't feel like you need to make small talk to entertain me if you'd rather not," I said politely. I kept my gaze on the cracker selection. "We're going to be on this bus for days, after all. I'm fine being left alone."

After several beats of silence, I worried I'd offended him —figured I'd do it unintentionally—and found his dark eyes watching me even more intensely than they had the night before through the narrow slits of his mask.

"You're used to being left alone."

It wasn't a question. Thatcher said the words with a certain sympathetic finality. As if he knew more than I did about my personal life. As if he had some insight into my psyche that even I lacked. As if he pitied me.

It made my stomach churn.

"Nonsense," I said lightly. "I'm *never* alone. I have more friends than anyone I know—more than I want, half the time—and plenty of people to warm my bed every night. I think you might be projecting."

His eyes never left me, and he took his time responding. Meanwhile, I chewed a grape into teeny, tiny pieces and told myself that I would *not* get pissed off, no matter what personal, provoking thing he said next.

But what came out of his mouth was, "You're right. We're going to be on the bus for days. So *you* shouldn't feel like you need to hold back. If you have something to say to me about work or... or *whatever*... then say it. Speak freely."

Thatcher's tone wasn't condescending or patronizing. He was... sincere.

Oh, god, the man had no idea what he was asking for.

I opened my mouth to tell him—*politely*—that he should mind his own damned business and stay out of mine, but my tongue had a mind of its own around this man. "Okay, then. I want to know why someone as smart and successful as you doesn't have a social media strategy for any of his holdings."

"Beg pardon?" Thatcher blinked at me, so comically surprised that I would have laughed if I wasn't trying to keep my emotions in check. He'd given me permission to speak freely about "work or whatever" and seemed shocked that I hadn't wanted to talk about our... *whatever*. But I wasn't touching non-work topics with a ten-foot pole.

I gestured wildly with the cracker in my hand. "While you were napping, I was researching PennCo's recent history. You run a multibillion-dollar corporation with a massive global presence, yet PennCo Fiber is stuck in the fucking dark ages, even compared to the other players in the industry. Why? And why won't you—or Layla—at least allow someone to try bringing the company into the new millennium? I could maybe understand if the company was run by a decrepit octogenarian, but you're..." I tried to block out the images of his sexy, fit body. "Not," I finished lamely.

His eyebrows scrunched together. "We do have social media accounts. They're printed on all of our marketing materials and on our websites."

I threw up my hands, my restraint burning away. "It's not about having an account, Thatcher; it's about having a *strategy*. What's your brand about? What's the story you want to tell? How do you want to make people *feel*? My dad's campaign has better branding than you, and he has the worst-run social media platform I've ever seen. Hell, Willow Honeycutt—you know, the woman who runs the Artists' Retreat and Centering Center back in Honeybridge?—has a better strategy than PennCo, and her entire feed is pictures of her doing a *very* bendy downward dog in front of the same tree, week after week after week. At least I know what her business is about. It's criminal how wasteful this is. Even if you never had another PR crisis like the Nova incident, you still—"

"Okay," he said calmly.

"—need to have a basic... wait, what?"

Thatcher shrugged, his cashmere sweater shifting across his wide shoulders with the movement. "If you say we don't have a social media strategy, I believe you. Come up with one. Pitch it to Layla. She'll hear you out."

I wanted to throw the charcuterie tray across the bus like a Frisbee. "If you recall, I brought it up in this morning's meeting as a potential part of her *multipronged approach*, and she spoke to me like a child."

Thatcher lifted one shoulder. "Well, she wasn't at her best today. She was getting sick, even if she didn't know it yet, and had a sleepless, stressful night."

Jealousy came like a sweet, sharp stab to my chest. Sure, it was great that JT believed in me, but what would it be like to have someone like Thatcher believe in you? To have his loyalty and know he'd give you the benefit of the doubt? For damn sure, I'd never know.

"She *didn't* hear me out. This wasn't the first time I pitched her the idea. We had a meeting a couple of weeks ago—Layla, Stephen Price, and me—and I explained everything. A whole slide deck. Layla said, 'Not yet.'"

Thatcher stroked his stubbled cheek with one blunt

fingertip, and my eyes tracked the movement. I wondered why he'd decided to shave his beard and whether it had been a spontaneous thing—

"I'm sure she gave you her reason," Thatcher prompted.

I startled and quickly looked away. "She says the company's policy is to let the fashion brands handle social media. I strongly disagree—for all the reasons I mentioned and more besides. First of all, the fashion brands don't care about creating Elustre brand recognition. *Our* product isn't their marketing priority; *theirs* is. Second—"

He held up a hand to stop me. "Show me your pitch tomorrow morning, and I'll try to find out why the policy is the way it is. Sound fair?"

It... did. In fact, it was so reasonable it took the wind out of my sails. So I nodded and answered without thinking. "Yes, sir."

Thatcher's eyes darkened, remembering the last time I'd spoken those words to him, and he drew in a breath so deep his chest visibly expanded.

"I need you to go get some sleep," he said. His voice was a low, commanding rumble.

When McGee tried to give me orders earlier, I'd gotten angry. But Thatcher's bossy voice provoked an entirely different reaction. It curled around my balls, sent a shiver up my spine, and stole the moisture from my mouth. I nearly choked on my cracker.

"We'll be taking on a replacement driver in a few hours," Thatcher went on, not looking at me now. "And McGee will take one of the spare bunks. Get some rest, and we'll tackle the rest of this tomorrow."

I didn't trust myself to respond without offering the man my ass, so I simply nodded and stood, doing my best to ignore the tightness in my pants and the faint scent of pine trees and woodsmoke as I passed Thatcher on the way to my bunk.

But it was a long, long while before I could calm myself enough to sleep. And when I did, Thatcher's voice followed me into my dreams.

Chapter Six

Thatcher

I woke up somewhere in Missouri with weak morning light crawling over my face and groaned at the ceiling. We weren't scheduled to arrive in Kansas City until midday, which meant I'd have to share the small common area of the bus with Reagan for *hours*.

Hours of sitting across from him at the table in the kitchenette while his aquamarine eyes watched me. Hours of ignoring the way his even teeth sank into his soft lower lip. Hours of learning about the sharp intellect, the passion, and all the many intriguing "Reagans" hiding beneath his smirking, sexy face. Hours of willing myself not to get hard for my employee.

More time alone with Reagan Wellbridge was the last fucking thing I needed.

Yesterday evening, after Reagan overheard my conversation with January, I'd managed to work with the man for only a few minutes before excusing myself, making a vague excuse about sleeping off my headache. In truth, my throbbing head had only been part of the problem. The larger, more compelling issue had been my constant arousal, which had only grown worse every moment I was in his presence.

When I'd finally made it to the privacy of my room, I'd tried not to fantasize about Reagan's hard body as I furtively stroked myself off... but then I'd remembered the way his eyes had rolled back in his head when I'd clasped a hand around his throat in my hotel room, and that was all it had taken to bring my orgasm screaming on. I'd thought, in that fucked-out instant, that I could simply revisit that one mental snapshot in the future anytime I needed an incredibly quick release.

Not that I *would*, I'd quickly amended. I was a better man than that. More in control than that.

But later that night, after visiting the truck stop in West Virginia, I'd stayed at the table long after ordering Reagan to bed, trying to ignore the gravitational pull of the man in the bunk several feet behind me. I'd gotten another snack. Then a drink. I'd pulled up financial projections and sent out a couple of emails. I'd taken some of January's ginseng and turmeric supplements. I'd checked in with McGee. And finally, after a couple of hours, I'd called a halt to my pretense of productivity.

The strange restlessness that compelled me to change my New Year's plans had come over me again, and when I finally made it to my bedroom, I immediately took my cock out.

As it turned out, I was *not* a better man.

Fortunately, my second intense orgasm helped me sleep deeply through the night as the bus continued west. But now it was morning, and my restlessness was back with a vengeance.

After showering and dressing, I made my way out to the kitchenette. Reagan was already at the table, eating breakfast while scrolling on his phone, and I wondered what sort of mood he was in today.

"Morning," I said, rifling through the box of coffee pods to find the one I wanted. "Sleep okay?"

"Not really. McGee snores like a piece of rusty farm equipment with no muffler. I considered tossing him out onto the highway, but I figured that might be the one thing that would jeopardize my platinum job security."

McGee's deep grumble came from behind a bunk curtain. "You're not so quiet either, princess."

I tucked my chin to hide my amusement. "Good call," I told Reagan. "Homicide is a hard limit. For legal reasons."

"Always have to check the fine print, even on platinum job security." Reagan sighed forlornly. "Fine. No murder."

Charming, wry Reagan was not going to make it any easier to keep my wayward lust under control.

I finished doctoring my coffee but remained by the counter, reluctant to take the empty seat at the table precisely because I wanted to so badly. But the sway of the bus made it impossible to drink standing either.

You're being ridiculous, Thatcher.

I slid into the seat facing the front of the bus, steeling myself against the sucker punch of his blue eyes, but Reagan didn't look up. I found my gaze straying out the window instead to the flash of snow-dotted fields in cold winter sunshine that sped past the window at top speed as the steady rumble of the bus vibrated up through the floor.

"There's something meditative about being on a road trip," I found myself saying. I wasn't usually one to share stuff like that out loud, but I blamed it on not being fully awake yet.

Reagan didn't seem to find my observation unusual. He glanced up from his breakfast to look out the window, also, and nodded pensively. "Mmm. Nice being away from the daily routine. You can ignore your messages and blame cell service."

"That's trickier when your boss is on the bus and the bus has satellite," I said dryly. "But you're right about the routine. I know January can't come barging in and change the direction of my day, and Merriweather from Finance can't pop in with a quick question. There are no business lunch commitments or evening social events to attend."

Reagan tapped the laptop he'd pushed to one side of the table. "Hate to break it to you, but there are definitely business lunch commitments and evening social events you're going to have to attend on this trip."

"I know." I sipped my coffee. "But it's not the same. I can't say I enjoy industry events. Small talk's never been my thing. But I do enjoy meeting people in different places. It reminds me New York isn't the entire world the way we sometimes think it is."

Reagan looked at me curiously, and as expected, the aquamarine had my gut clenching with want. But with his eyes on me, I also felt like I could draw a deep breath for the first time all morning. It was a strange push-pull, wanting to be near him and wishing I was anywhere else.

"I assumed you'd prefer the city." Reagan licked yogurt off his spoon, and I tried not to focus on the way his tongue licked greedily at the lucky utensil. "You were on edge in Honeybridge last summer, but you seemed to be in your element at the... uh. The other night."

He glanced back out the window at the reference to the gala, and a faint tint of pink crawled up his neck.

"I do enjoy the city," I agreed, distracted by that blush. "But being in my element that night wasn't about the location, Reagan."

Reagan's startled face turned back to me, the pink flush deepening, and I snapped back to reality.

What the fuck was I doing? One distracting blush should not be able to loosen my tongue that badly.

I cleared my throat. "I meant that I feel comfortable in many places. The Hamptons. Stowe. My beach house in Hilton Head. Honeybridge, too. It's beautiful there." If I'd been on edge last summer, it had nothing to do with the town and everything to do with one distracting resident. "It's always nice visiting your parents," I added deliberately.

Reagan closed his eyes for a moment and nodded. "My *parents*. Right." He plopped his spoon into his half-empty yogurt container and pushed it aside before pulling his laptop in front of him. "So. Work time. You promised you'd listen to my social media strategy, right?"

With just a few key clicks, he pulled up a slide deck, and I told myself I wasn't disappointed. No matter how interesting Reagan was to talk to or how unexpectedly easy it was to let down my guard and be myself with him, we weren't friends. He was my employee. My friend's son. And my son's friend, too... at least until last summer.

"Did Brant ever apologize?" I demanded before Reagan could launch into his presentation. "For trying to screw things up between your brother and Flynn Honeycutt?"

Reagan frowned at this topic change. "Yes. It wasn't particularly sincere, from what I've heard, but he did it. You knew that, though. I was under the impression you made him apologize."

"To JT and Flynn, yes. But has he apologized to you? He put you in a difficult position as a friend."

"Thatcher..." Reagan rolled his eyes like I was hopelessly naive. "No, and I..." He shook his head and pressed his lips together like he was making a physical effort to hold back. "I didn't expect him to. Now, the presentation—"

"Speak freely," I instructed. "Like last night."

Reagan sighed. "Fine, then. Brantleigh and I know some of the same people, so I can't help seeing him socially, but we're not friends. The last time he messaged me, back in October, he wanted me to use my social media platform to help him get a lucrative sponsorship he'd done nothing to earn, as though he didn't even remember what he'd done to JT." His lip curled in disgust. "Speaking frankly? Brantleigh's an entitled ass."

A muffled sound of agreement came from the bunk behind me, reminding me McGee was listening... and that he, too, was not a fan of my son's behavior.

I probably should have been offended on my son's behalf, but unfortunately, this was all too easy to believe. "I'm sorry," I said. "Sorry that happened. Sorry for... how he turned out."

Reagan's gaze snapped to mine, and his eyes narrowed. "Ouch. Does my father say the same thing about me? Do you all trade stories about your parental failures over cigars at the country club?"

"First of all, *no*. Secondly, why would he? You're bright and competent."

He seemed flustered by my compliment, which made me want to do it again.

I refrained.

Reagan's eyebrows drew together. "Why do you think *you're* responsible for the way Brantleigh is?"

Wasn't it obvious? "Because I'm his father. Thalia and I, we raised him."

"So?"

"So... we took a wrong turn somewhere and fucked up.

It turns out I make a better CEO than parent. I can fix a complex global supply chain issue, but I can't fix my kid."

I snapped my jaw shut, shocked I'd exposed so much of myself to him after vowing to keep him at a professional arm's length.

"Have you considered maybe giving yourself a break? Letting him fix himself? A twenty-eight-year-old is capable of that, you know," he said softly. I wasn't sure if he was talking about himself or Brant. "I told you before, there are some things in life you can't control..."

I lowered my chin and glared at him. "I'm not. I'm just trying to give him what he needs."

He laughed ruefully. "It's funny how parents say that but never seem to get that what their kid needs is independence and respect."

I frowned. "Reagan, do your parents—? I mean, I know Patricia and Trent can be—"

In an instant, his face closed off, his eyes going flat and hard. "Oh, hard no." He held up a hand. "Too weird. I'm not talking about my mommy and daddy issues with *their* friend who's also *my* boss."

He was right. About all of that. *Fuck.* Talking to him was so easy my control kept slipping.

"Back to work." Reagan squared his shoulders and grabbed his computer. "Before we arrive in Kansas City and you get too distracted to pay attention to me."

God. I sincerely hoped something in Kansas City would make me too distracted to pay attention to Reagan. I was beginning to doubt whether such a thing existed.

"Give me a minute," I told him, digging my phone out of my pocket so I could let Brant know I was thinking about him.

Talking about my son had made me want to get in touch

with him that much more. I'd heard what Reagan said, and I appreciated his compassion, but I couldn't let it go. Maybe now that Brant was at his yoga retreat, away from his usual environment, he'd be more likely to reach out.

Me: *Hey, how's it going?*

Like I didn't already know? I deleted the message and restarted.

Me: *Hope you're enjoying the retreat. I'm here if you want to talk.*

And if he didn't want to talk? I deleted the message again.

Me: *Hope you're enjoying the retreat. Please reply and let me know you're okay. We can chat about some career ideas when you're ready. I love you.*

I noticed Reagan watching me over the top of his laptop with way too much sympathy in his gaze and realized he could probably see Brant's name on the top of the screen. I forced myself to hit Send before overthinking further.

"You okay?" he asked.

"Yeah." I slid my phone back into my pocket and focused on Reagan's laptop. "What've you got?"

"Right. So..." Reagan sank his teeth into his bottom lip, and my cock throbbed at the nervous gesture. But the moment he began speaking, his excitement about the topic overtook his nerves, and I found myself every bit as captivated by what was being said as by the man saying it.

Admittedly, I was expecting something less professional, more abstract, and certainly with less understanding of PennCo's business needs. When Reagan immediately began explaining the specific requirements of a social media strategy for textile manufacturing, along with some of the challenges inherent in an industry that still struggled with modernizing in many ways, I scrambled to adjust my expectations.

"Social media is pervasive," he said. "Obviously. We all know that. But it took corporations a long time to realize that by creating parasocial relationships with their brands, they could impact brand loyalty, expand subversive consumer education, and tee up the younger generation before their own consumer habits have been truly established. The opportunity here is tremendous. Let me show you some conversion data from a campaign that Spandex did a few months ago."

As he clicked through several slides of charts and graphs, explaining the graphs while highlighting the nuances of the various social media posts that triggered each outcome, I could tell just how much time and effort had gone into this pitch.

"And you showed this to Layla weeks ago," I interrupted. "This exact presentation?"

"Yeah. At first, she seemed really impressed. Asked loads of questions about all my ideas. She said no, but I was hoping she'd change her mind once she got to know me a little better. That she'd trust me a bit more. But... well, you heard her at the meeting yesterday." Reagan scrunched his nose. "Nataly told me afterward that the last marketing director quit because he was so frustrated about this same issue, so... fuck. I don't know anymore." He scrubbed a hand through his hair. "And it really *sucks*, if you want to know the truth, because social media could legit save the day with this Elustre situation, and I have data that backs that up. Meanwhile, Layla's side-eyeing me like she's a fucking flat-earther who thinks I'm showing her doctored pictures from outer space, and..." He cut himself off. "Sorry. I shouldn't have said that. I swear, I usually do a better job at being professional—"

I huffed out a laugh.

"—and I know you and Layla are..." Reagan ran his tongue over his front teeth and glared at my forearm like it had personally offended him. "...close," he finished.

I nodded. It would be entirely inappropriate—and, yes, unprofessional—for me to discuss Layla's management decisions or our relationship with Reagan. But I also understood his frustration.

"Well, I'm impressed," I said. "By your hard work and passion. But..."

He smiled tightly. "There's always a *but*."

"*But*," I emphasized, "I need you to explain what a potential social media campaign for PennCo and Elustre would look like because, I'll be honest, this Nova Davidson business is showing me the ass-end of social media's impact on a brand. Before I can agree to move in this direction, I'm going to need more specific information."

Reagan's brows knitted together, and I could almost see him replaying my words in his head, like he was looking for the catch and unable to find it.

He cleared his throat. "Well... you're right," he said slowly. "The power of social media can be used for good or for evil. The Instagram giveth, and the Instagram taketh away, as we've just seen. But..." Excitement kindled in his eyes. "When you have an experienced social media strategist—and I've been running my own accounts *and* my friends' for a while now—you'll find that you can get back what was taken away *and more*. There is no better way to direct a narrative and shape or rebuild a reputation than a positive social media campaign."

I made a mental note to search for whatever personal social media accounts he might have been referring to. In the meantime, I wanted to hear more.

"So what would you do if you were in charge?" I asked.

"I mean, it's pretty obvious. We need to make sure that the negative posts aren't the only thing the public sees about Elustre or PennCo, you know?"

I nodded.

"So in addition to the regular social media strategy we should be running, I would recommend—and honestly, any PR crisis company would tell you the same—a campaign specifically targeted to overcoming this particular gaffe. Like..."

I listened intently while he went through the kinds of accounts, posts, and influencer agreements he would include. He explained the reasoning behind every decision and gave examples of PR disasters in the past that had used similar techniques—including some he'd managed for his friends. It made me realize just how much worse our situation could have been than it was, but I still liked the idea of fighting fire with fire.

"So how do we start?" I eventually asked.

"Start?" Reagan repeated.

I pointed to the screen. "One of the examples you gave was a simple set of posts showing regular good news the company was involved in. We can post about this tour. Do a post for each event explaining a facet of why Elustre is such a game-changer in the performance fiber industry. We might even be able to get some of our industry connections to help us."

"Well... *yes*." He cocked his head. "But the posts need to be a little more engaging than, like, 'Here are three long, science-y paragraphs about fibers.'"

"People in the textile industry would enjoy—"

He reached toward me like he was going to lay his hand on my forearm but stopped himself. "We're not talking about just reaching textile people. We're talking about reaching non-textile people, too."

My skin tingled where he would have touched me. "Non-textile people don't care about textiles."

"They do if we *make* them care." The excitement in his eyes was contagious. "We want everyone to fall in love with Elustre. Period. We want the industry to fall in love, yes. Definitely. But we also want the soccer mom to know why she loves the new uniform shorts. We want the yoga instructor to recommend us to her students. We want the coolest kids in school to put a word on their favorite new fabric so that they can set a trend that's defined by it. We want to reach *consumers*."

He was right, of course. It seemed like we'd set a priority a while back of marketing and selling to manufacturers, and it had landed us in the situation we were in now, without a robust consumer marketing program in place. I was confident that Layla had excellent reasons for not jumping into the social media fray earlier, but if she was concerned enough about the fate of the Elustre launch to throw together an impromptu road trip, surely this was the time to try new things.

"Let me talk to Layla before we create any Elustre-specific posts," I said. "She's in charge of PennCo Fiber, and I don't want her to feel like I'm countermanding her orders, especially when there might be a solid reason for her hesitation that I'm unaware of, like a conflict with some part of our launch strategy with Apex Athletics—"

"Yeah." Reagan's disappointed sigh felt like a cloud blocking the sun.

"—but I don't see why we can't take advantage of this trip to create some good general content about PennCo," I concluded.

His eyes met mine. "Wait, really? You're giving me the go-ahead?"

"Yes. It makes good business sense." The words were a reminder to both of us that this was about more than the way my own heart galloped when Reagan's eyes sparkled with hope. "It can't hurt to try, and it won't cost anything. If the posts don't move the needle after a while, we can conclude that Layla's right, it's really not a good fit for this industry. I'll have January get Layla on a call so we can decide about the Elustre-specific content and get the credentials for you to have access to those accounts—"

Reagan winced. "Layla's sick, remember? Should she be doing calls?"

"Good point." I ran my hand over my jaw, still surprised to find stubble instead of my usual beard. "Who has the login information for our accounts?"

"Nataly could get them. I'll shoot her an email." He turned his laptop toward himself and began typing.

"Perfect." I stood and lifted my arms to the ceiling, stretching my back. Somehow, the morning had flown by, and it hadn't been nearly as torturous as I'd expected. In fact, spending time with Reagan had been surprisingly easy.

At least until I noticed that his eyes had locked onto the strip of bare skin at my waist where my shirt rode up.

His gaze slammed into mine, drowning me in blue, and my cock stirred.

One of the bunk curtains slid back noisily, and McGee's feet dropped to the floor of the bus with a thud. "Oh, man, I needed that," he groaned. "Bus sleep is the best sleep."

I dropped my arms to my sides, and Reagan focused on his laptop screen like his email was a matter of life or death.

McGee wandered into the kitchenette, rubbing his eyes blearily with tattooed fingers. His face was covered in pillow creases. "Morning, boss. Morning, princess." He looked back and forth between us. "All good?"

"Yep," I agreed. "We got a lot done this morning."

McGee nodded. "Good, 'cause we'll be in Kansas City in twenty." He reached for a coffee mug with a yawn. "I was planning to wake up a while ago, but listening to you two talk was like having one of those white noise machines on, and I zonked out again. *Whrrrr... algorithm targeting... whrrrr... click ratios... whrrrrr...* I should've recorded it as a public service for people with insomnia."

"It's good that you take sleep seriously," Reagan said without glancing up. "Just a single sleepless night can make a person's skin cells age faster and lose elasticity."

McGee ran his tongue over his teeth, clearly amused. "Still not wrinkly, princess."

"Hmm?" Reagan glanced up, all innocence. "Oh, no, of course not. *Yet.* Though, gosh, what would happen to your tattoos if you did get wrinkles? Would they wrinkle, too? Huh." He shrugged and gave McGee a beatific smile.

I pushed McGee's shoulder before he could retort and directed him toward the back of the bus. "Do me a favor and check my suit while I freshen up. See if it needs a steam."

"Yeah," he grumbled. But I noticed that he paused to check his reflection in the mirrored door to the bathroom as we passed and ran a hand over his tattooed arm as if checking for elasticity. And when I shot him an amused glance, he ducked his head and grinned.

I was dressed by the time the bus pulled to a stop at the convention center, and I hustled back to the kitchenette. "Reagan, you have my notes, right?"

"Yep. Right here." Reagan tapped his work tablet. "Nataly also sent me three different logins already for our accounts..." He trailed off as he assessed my outfit. "Nice suit, but are you sure that's how you want to play this? You're speaking to textile executives in Missouri, not Wall Street power players."

"Executives wear suits, Reagan," I explained patiently.

He pursed his lips as if he was going to argue but then held up his hands. "Okay. I'm sure you know better than I do. Carry on."

It turned out... I did *not* know better than he did. When we entered the convention center, it was filled with more pairs of cotton khaki pants than I'd ever seen outside of a Dockers commercial. I stuck out like a sore thumb.

It had been a while since I'd been at an industry event outside of a large city like New York, Boston, or Chicago. Apparently, things were different in Kansas City. I couldn't even imagine how much more so it would be in Des Moines or Wichita.

As I was being introduced as the next speaker in one of the sessions, I pulled my arms back and tugged off my jacket before rolling up my sleeves and loosening my tie. Reagan chose this moment to lean over and whisper in my ear, "Don't worry. McGee is zipping over to Walmart to get you some less embarrassing pants before our next stop. I'm so sorry. I feel like it's my fault. I really should have *said something.*"

I stretched my neck from side to side, fighting off the

effects of his warm breath on my skin. I was tempted to remind him that nobody liked a know-it-all... except I wasn't sure that was true. Certain parts of me liked Reagan far too much.

The speech went better than I'd expected. After a luncheon with several of the other presenters and local industry executives, we walked through the vendor area and stopped to speak to several key contacts. And I meant *we*.

I'd mentioned to Reagan earlier that I hated small talk, and he stuck by my side the whole time, effortlessly smoothing my way without ever talking over me or trying to make himself the center of attention. He was charming and informative, polite and gracious. He even had the rare ability to code-switch and sound less like a yacht owner from Maine and more like a textile factory manager from the Midwest.

It took me a while to remember that he'd grown up doing this with his politician father. Reagan Wellbridge had practically been raised in front of the press. Granted, it had been small-scale early on, only local media in and around Honeybridge, but then Trent had moved up to a state senate position. Now, as an influential politician with an eye on the governor's office, he and his whole family, including Reagan, were under a larger national microscope.

It was no wonder Reagan was a master at glad-handing.

As we carefully extracted ourselves from the crowd and headed back to the tour bus at the outer edge of the convention center lot, January called, so I waved Reagan on ahead before answering.

"Good timing," I told her. "Just finishing up here."

January's voice was dry. "It's almost as if I have a way of knowing your schedule. How'd it go?"

"Great. I feel like we did a good job, and we met almost

all of the people on Layla's key contact list. How's the flu situation?"

"Two more people down, but so far, it seems mostly contained to PennCo. I authorized people to work from home, as you suggested. And personally, I'm pushing supplements and fluids, just like I'm sure *you've* been doing. Right?"

"In fact, I have. Took my supplements last night as directed," I said smugly.

"Good. Please keep doing it." She hesitated. "Listen, Layla called. She said she tried calling you a little while ago—"

"She might have. My phone was off during my speech, and I haven't checked messages."

"Figured. Look, this isn't an emergency, in my opinion—"

"What isn't?"

January sighed. "Someone from marketing contacted Layla and said Reagan wanted login credentials for PennCo's social media accounts—"

"Jesus Christ," I muttered. "*I* authorized Reagan to get those credentials. I assumed since Layla was sick, I'd have time to circle back and explain our plan to her later."

"'*Our* plan,'" January repeated. "Yours and Reagan's?"

The way she put our names together made warning bells go off in my brain. I instinctively glanced at Reagan, who was chatting with McGee outside the door to the bus. A grin lit up his handsome face as he explained something to my driver, hands gesturing wildly. Whatever he was saying had McGee nodding seriously.

"Yes. Reagan came up with some great ideas for handling our social media, both to mitigate the Elustre PR crisis and to improve our brand awareness in general. I want

Layla's buy-in before we tackle any Elustre content related to the launch or the PR crisis. But I made the executive decision to have him move forward with some generalized content. Problem?"

"Not from me," January said. "Sounds logical, and you're the boss. But Layla expressed concerns... about Reagan."

"What concerns?" My voice came out sharper than I'd intended.

"Well... Our security team's investigating who sent Nova the shirt, but it's not gonna be easy. Apex Athletics has been sending us samples from the launch for months now. Theoretically, *anyone* at PennCo or Apex—even several former employees—could have gotten their hands on one, printed it with that cheesy slogan, and shipped it off. Unless Nova's people at Rumblefeld Talent come forward with info or we find a note on someone's computer that says, 'To do this week: send shirt to Nova Davidson and unleash PR shitstorm,' there won't be hard evidence. So they're looking at who'd have motive instead." She hesitated. "Obviously, any disgruntled former employee might have done this as revenge. But Layla pointed out that this was also the sort of thing someone would have done if they were trying to convince the company to implement a social media strategy. She's suggested that Reagan could have done it."

McGee jogged up the stairs into the bus, and Reagan turned toward me, catching me full force with his grin.

My god, he was beautiful. A walking wet dream. A thousand pounds of snarky intelligence in one lithe, sun-kissed package. Sharp as a blade, sometimes. Prickly as a hedgehog. Insolent. Provoking. Undisciplined, according to his father—and, *no*, I did not sit around exchanging fatherly frustrations with Trent Wellbridge, but that didn't mean I'd never heard him say it. It would be pure arrogance for me to believe that I knew some deeper, truer version of Reagan after sharing space with him for less than a day—*and a bed for a night*, my brain helpfully reminded me.

But I remembered the way his face had lit up while he was outlining his plan to me earlier. His honest frustration at not having his voice heard. The compassionate, practical things he'd said about Brantleigh.

And I simply couldn't believe he'd have done what Layla seemed to be suggesting.

"That's a terrible accusation to throw around with no proof," I said, allowing anger to bleed into my tone.

Reagan's grin faded at whatever expression he saw on my face, and he frowned. I shook my head, waving him off, but he walked toward me instead.

"That's what I said," January agreed. "In her defense, she backed off immediately, and she's probably half out of her mind between the flu and her meds. Alena told me she was already stressing about the Elustre launch even *before* this Nova thing because she wants to impress you, and she really doesn't want to let her team down. Now she's trying to fix this stuff from her bed while you and Reagan go off to save the day. She's probably feeling left out and proprietary and worried."

I understood this. Layla was the head of PennCo, and Elustre was her baby. It had to be killing her not to be on the front lines. And still...

"I sympathize, but I will *not* condone her or anyone else throwing around accusations. Is that understood?"

Reagan's eyebrows lifted as he wandered close enough to overhear. "What's happening?" he stage-whispered. "Who's accusing someone? What's going on?"

I ignored him.

"I've known Reagan Wellbridge for a long time," I told January. "And I can tell you with confidence that he's a silver-tongued, provoking little shit. But he's not a liar. He's not manipulative. And he's not a person who'd callously put someone else's livelihood at risk for his own gain. He didn't do this."

Reagan froze in shock as I walked past him toward the bus stairs.

"Good enough for me," January said briskly. "I'll make sure Layla knows."

"No. Thanks anyway, January, but *I'll* make sure she knows." I ended the call, then paused with my foot on the bottom tread. I half turned and found Reagan exactly where I'd left him. "Get inside before you freeze your ass off."

Reagan blinked out of his stupor and followed. "I don't... What the hell was that about?"

"Get in here and I'll tell you." I turned to McGee once I was inside. "Did you get me khaki pants?"

"Yep. Khakis, golf shirts, sweaters. Everything on Mr. Fashionista Barbie's list. A full-on discount dork wardrobe is hanging in your closet." McGee thumbed over his shoulder toward my bedroom, then looked at me with a little frown. "You good, boss?"

Was I? A woman I'd trusted for over a decade was throwing around accusations. I was stuck on a bus with a man I absolutely couldn't have and also couldn't stop thinking about. I was already tired of glad-handing, and this was only day one.

But I knew what I needed to say. "I'm good. Just let me get out of this damned suit, and we can go." I looked at Reagan, who was sliding off his coat, and added, "Then you and I need to talk."

Chapter Seven

Reagan

...He's a silver-tongued, provoking little shit. But he's not a liar. He's not manipulative. And he's not a person who'd callously put someone else's livelihood at risk for his own gain...

On the all-time list of compliments I'd received, this should have ranked somewhere near the bottom with the thinly veiled insults. But hearing those words in Thatcher's deep, confident voice, in this particular context, gave them a totally different spin.

He'd defended me.

My chest squeezed at the warm comfort of it. Thatcher Pennington had defended me, and that meant...

Nothing. Come on, Reagan. You're his friend's kid. Of course he'd defend you. It's not personal.

"Reagan? You okay?" Thatcher emerged from the bedroom quickly, wearing casual pants, another of his incredible sweaters, and a concerned expression, possibly because I was standing next to the refrigerator, staring blankly into space.

"Never better. Nothing I love more than randomly

being accused of things." I forced myself to move, to grab a drink from the refrigerator, to keep my cool, though it felt like a losing battle under the circumstances. "I was just standing here wondering what the hell someone thinks I've done now. I haven't fucked up anything that I'm aware of."

"I know."

Thatcher slid onto the front-facing side of the booth, as usual, and I took the seat opposite him. As though McGee had sensed that Thatcher was finally sitting, the bus pulled smoothly out of the parking lot toward Wichita, and I looked at Thatcher expectantly.

But instead of talking, explaining, Thatcher took out his phone and started tapping—maybe another of those incredibly awkward, type-erase-repeat texts he'd sent Brantleigh earlier that had made my stomach cramp with all sorts of gushy, sympathetic feelings—and I found myself filling the silence.

"All I did yesterday was make media packets for the trip. I didn't even write any of it—just formatted it and printed copies and delivered them to McGee," I said.

"Okay." Thatcher didn't glance up.

"I worked all day. I barely took a break. I didn't even take time to go on TikTok and see the Nova footage for myself. I wasn't gossiping or chatting—" I thought of my brief talk with Nataly and hesitated. "—much."

He grunted.

"And the tweaks I made to your speech were solid, based on the talking points that the team already prepared. If you disagreed with any of them, you could've told me—"

"Mmm."

"So what's the issue, then?" I demanded, unable to take him ignoring me any longer. "What am I being accused of? Because if I haven't made it clear, I care about this job,

Thatcher. I care about doing it well. And I'd really like a chance to defend myself—"

Finally, Thatcher set his phone facedown and looked at me. "Calm down."

"Calm down?" I repeated, incredulous. "Are you kidding? Never in the history of humanity has a person calmed down because they were instructed to calm down. And how would *you* feel if you were being accused of something bad enough that it wasn't being reported to your boss, or your boss's boss but to your *boss's* boss's boss? Something that 'could put people's livelihood at stake'? Because I'm pretty sure it wouldn't be with *calm*." I slapped my hand on the tabletop for emphasis.

"Reagan." Thatcher laid his larger hand over mine, holding it firmly in place. His voice was deep and commanding, and I instinctively responded by snapping my mouth shut. "You heard me tell January that you hadn't done anything, right?"

I breathed in through my nose, which was a mistake because all I could smell was Thatcher—woodsmoke and pine, sage and sex—a scent that fried all of my synapses and... alright, *yes*, calmed me down. "What does January think I did?"

"January doesn't think you did anything either." Thatcher's voice had dropped even lower now, and he hadn't let go of my hand. I felt surrounded. Cradled. Like he was holding me together. "You're not in trouble. Layla made some ill-considered comments, probably because she's sick and lashing out—"

"Layla?" Just like that, I was amped up again.

"Take a couple of deep breaths, and I'll explain." His voice was soothing, but when he squeezed my wrist to get my attention, distracting images of the other night flashed through my mind. Of him pinning me down, taking me.

I closed my eyes tight.

Fuck, I wanted the man. I didn't want to, and I shouldn't, but I did, and I was tired of trying to convince myself I didn't.

I tugged my hand back and opened my eyes. "I'm under control. Please explain."

Thatcher nodded once. Palms flat on the table, brown eyes squarely focused on me, he said, "Layla implied you might have been motivated to provide that shirt to Nova specifically to create a situation where PennCo would need a social media campaign. Like a firefighter setting a fire."

"I didn't."

"I know. And deep down, Layla probably knows, too. She backed down immediately when January pushed back. January thinks she was frustrated and reaching for any possible explanation. It's understandable."

Not to me, it wasn't. "That doesn't make it okay—"

"Definitely not." Thatcher's eyes blazed. "Which January *also* told her during their conversation and which I just now reiterated to her by email in no uncertain terms." He tilted his head at the phone he'd just set down.

"Oh." I scrubbed a hand over my face. "Well... thank you. But I still don't get why she'd say that. She knows I don't have access to clothing samples, much less marketing assets like logos. She knows everyone at PennCo is loyal to her, and they'd hate me for going behind her back, even if they agreed with my idea. Why would she think I'd do something that unethical and unprofessional—"

"Hang on," Thatcher interrupted. "Back up. Why don't you have access to the samples or the marketing assets? The logos are on the company intranet. Hell, they're probably available to the public on the internet. Everyone in PR should have access to them."

"I haven't been there long enough, I guess? I don't know." He was missing the point. "For the last month, I've been as hardworking and professional as I know how. I've done every assignment I've been given without complaint, even busywork so mundane that one of those feral beavers in Lake Wellbridge could probably have done it. I've worked on research and presentations on my own time. I've spoken up when I thought I had a good idea and kept quiet—well, mostly—when it didn't work out. I turned over a whole new leaf, Thatcher. I don't know how else to prove myself at PennCo. I still can't get anyone to trust me—"

"I trust you."

The thrill of those simple, direct words made my chest tingle, though I tried to will it away. "Well, sure. Because it's, like, a requirement of your friendship with my dad—"

Thatcher laughed, startlingly loud and deep. "Reagan, I like your father. I do. But not enough to risk my reputation to save yours, let alone risk the stability of my company by continuing to employ you if there was any chance you caused this incident. If I had even the smallest doubt, I would have asked you about it, but I don't have to. Being sneaky isn't your style. And furthermore?" he went on. "From everything you showed me earlier, if you ever *did* decide to go rogue, you'd have engineered something a hell of a lot more effective than this clusterfuck. It wasn't you."

His brown eyes caught mine and held, as though willing me to see that he had faith in me.

God, I wanted to believe it.

"I trust you, Reagan," he repeated calmly, as though he still wasn't sure I was getting the message, and damn if that didn't cause another thrill to race through me.

I let out a breath. "Okay."

"Good." Thatcher sat back and added, almost as an afterthought, "You shouldn't have to prove yourself to anyone."

Was he serious?

"Thatcher, that's... very kind," I said carefully, "but it's easy to say that when you're the head of the company and you've already proven to the whole world that you're a business genius. A little different when you're trying to convince people you're not a... a fuckup or a slacker."

He tilted his head, studying me. "Living up to other people's expectations is a losing game, Reagan. You need to live up to your *own*. And if that's not good enough for the people around you, find new people," he argued before I could interrupt. "Success is hollow unless you're achieving something *you* want. And all those folks you thought you'd impressed will be the first ones to tear you down when things go south. You might not have paid attention to the media headlines after my second marriage ended—"

"I remember," I whispered. "Twice unlucky in love. Billionaire heartbreak."

He snorted. "Right. All bullshit. The more successful you become, the fewer people you let matter to you, because suddenly the whole world expects you to do or be something for them. So, do well for *you*. Succeed for *you*. Other people will be impressed, or they won't. Don't let it touch you either way."

I was caught in the spell of his words, the sincerity nearly glowing in his eyes. And suddenly, I wanted very badly to know... who mattered to Thatcher? Because the life he was describing, the life of a successful billionaire, sounded a little like being a princess trapped in a tower. It sounded lonely.

Fortunately, before I could open my mouth to say something horrifyingly revealing—or, Jesus, *hug* the man—Thatcher cleared his throat and looked away.

"Anyway. This will all blow over, and I'm sure Layla will apologize once she's feeling better. You're an asset to PennCo, Reagan. You've been an asset to *me* on this trip." One side of his mouth quirked up. "I'm pretty damn pleased I let you stay the other day."

I had to be tired or overwrought or something because there was no good reason why those words, that disarming grin, should feel as good as they did. No reason why they should be as much of a turn-on as his bossy voice or his broad shoulders.

Thatcher clapped his hands together once, startling me out of my drooling daze. "Alright. Now, let's post some pictures to social media. Tell me how we do this."

This, at least, was distracting enough to keep my focus where it needed to be. We spent the next couple of hours going through the photos I'd taken at today's event and deciding what kind of posts to make on which platform. It was kind of fun getting to explain it all to him because I finally felt like there was a topic I was well versed on that the great Thatcher Pennington knew very little about.

But I realized while flipping through the photos that we'd made a critical mistake. "We need to put you in Elustre clothing for these photos from now on," I said, specifically imagining him in a particular long-sleeved running half-zip that would accentuate the shoulders I couldn't stop thinking about.

"I can't wear athleisure gear for speaking engagements," he protested. "That's a little *too* casual."

"Hmm." I glanced up at him from the online catalog of samples he'd shown me on the company intranet. "Do you still run? We could get some shots of you exercising before one of the events, especially if it's somewhere iconic that will get good play with people who recognize landmarks in the background."

Thatcher's eyebrows lowered. "You know I run?"

Busted.

"I mean, I sort of vaguely remember you doing that up in Honeybridge." I shrugged like I hadn't made it my business to know how Thatcher spent every waking moment of his day last summer. "I think I saw you on the lake trail once." I cleared my throat. "So, can we have the office overnight us some of this?"

"Of course. I'm not sure what the flu situation in the mailroom is, but certainly someone can get them to us." He moved around to sit next to me in the booth so he could look over my shoulder at the selections, and *holy fuck*, the scent of him wrapped around me again, making me light-headed.

I wanted to lean back into his body heat. I wanted to turn my head and feel the rough scratch of his stubble against my cheek. I wanted—

"That one looks good," he said in a low murmur. I closed my eyes and let the sound move through me before I realized what I was doing.

"Hmm? Oh. Yes. Yup. On it. Copying the item number, pasting the item number on our wish list. Click. Done."

Shut up.

"That one's kind of nice also. It would go with the running tights I brought."

Thatcher in running tights. Check. Check. *Check.*

"Got it." I clicked again to make sure it was added to the list.

He reached a hand out to point to the screen, brushing

against my shoulder with his chest. "What about that pullover? It's going to be cold in Aspen."

"Vail," I corrected absently. "And, uh. Yeah. That's... that one's good."

Thatcher turned to face me. His lips were only inches from my skin, and his eyes were close enough to differentiate his eyelashes. One of them was lighter than the rest and curved slightly in the wrong direction. "What do you want?"

"Me?" I blinked at him. Did he want the whole laundry list of what I wanted? Because I would prefer to start with a kiss, but—

He nodded. I couldn't help but notice his Adam's apple in the center of his stubbled throat. "I think you should get a pullover, but it's up to you, really. You should have something, though. You represent the company, too. We can include you in the photos, too, so they're not all of me." His eyes bobbed to my mouth before he blinked three times and then quickly shifted out of the booth. "Anyway, send that list to January, and she'll see to it."

As soon as he returned to his side of the table, he was all business again.

I followed his lead and got back to work, forcing myself to focus on the emails I wanted to draft to a small list of influencers I'd targeted for this response campaign.

By the time we stopped to pick up McGee's replacement driver and eat a late dinner, things were back to being whatever the relationship equivalent was to business casual again.

Which was fine.

Incredibly, sufficiently, thoroughly *fine.*

I was being professional. I was being polite.

And if Thatcher's voice saying, "I trust you, Reagan,"

was the background to most of my dreams, that was no one's business but mine.

———

"Ready for your interview?" I asked Thatcher the following day as we moved past the exhibits at the Century II in Wichita, headed for the private room we'd reserved specifically for that purpose. "You've got your talking points, right?"

Thatcher made a grunting noise that conveyed both agreement and disapproval and walked faster, forcing me to bob and weave through the noisy crowd so I could stay by his side. I'd never been to Wichita before that I could recall, but apparently, Kansans loved textiles. I hadn't seen a mob like this since Gaga had played Dodger Stadium.

"Look, I know you don't like small talk, but you do it well," I insisted. "You had the whole table hanging on your every word at lunch, and the interview will go well, too. Chris Acton's a good journalist—hardworking and fair."

I didn't mention my own past with Chris, such as it was. Admitting to sleeping with a high-profile business reporter at one of my father's leadership conferences last summer didn't exactly scream "trustworthy professional," and I was still buzzing at the idea that Thatcher trusted me to begin with. Besides, it was hardly relevant to the situation.

Thatcher managed to glare sideways at me without slowing down. "I don't need you to manage me, Reagan," he grumbled, exactly like a person who needed to be managed. "I'm not a child."

I tried, mostly unsuccessfully, to hide my smile, but I could do nothing about the way my chest squeezed. It simply wasn't fair that a man as sexy and compelling as

Thatcher should be low-key adorable, too, and I hated that I knew this about him.

"Of course you're not," I said in a fake-soothing voice that conveyed exactly the opposite. "You're a successful billionaire. A titan of industry. You don't care what the media says about you."

The glare intensified, and he finally slowed. "You're right. I don't allow their speculation about my personal life to bother me. But I also don't trust them, and I definitely don't like relying on them. There's a reason I only gave this reporter fifteen minutes last time we spoke."

"You sound like my mother talking about vulture journalists," I noted, amused... and then further amused when Thatcher scowled at the comparison. "Chris is a decent guy. The only reason Patricia doesn't like him is because his article about my father suggested that the Senator wasn't conversant with aspects of his own political platform as laid out on the Wellbridge campaign website." I shrugged. "That was accurate, unfortunately."

"I read that piece," Thatcher said. "Your father made some errors, and Chris Acton jumped on them. He's ambitious. Wants to make a name for himself."

"Don't we all?" I said easily. "It's not a crime. He was just doing his job. In my experience, Chris is thorough and very focused on transparency. If someone has something to hide, he'll want to ferret out the story, sure. But don't forget, Layla and Alena set up this interview. I expect a bunch of softball questions that you, being your charming self, will hit out of the park."

Thatcher stopped entirely, forcing the crowd to veer around us, and raised an eyebrow. "My charming self."

I shrugged again. "Sure. Last summer in Honeybridge, you charmed every person you met." Including me, without trying at all. "Tap into that. Smile a little when you're making small talk. Don't do the commanding-and-grumpy thing you sometimes do when you're talking to someone you dislike."

His eyes turned flinty as I spoke. "How do you know when I'm talking to someone I dislike?"

I scraped my upper lip with my bottom teeth to hide a grin. "Uh... because you become grumpy and commanding?"

His gaze met mine, the warm brown as deep and impenetrable as mahogany. "Sometimes I'm commanding with people I *do* like."

The memory of his deep voice shot through me like the unexpected and overwhelming zing from a live wire.

Come for me... Now.

I opened my mouth to respond... somehow... but thankfully, the rapid *clip-clip-clip* of footsteps on the industrial tile floor behind us reminded me that we weren't alone.

"Thatcher! Excuse me, Thatcher?"

We turned at the same time and found the thirty-something brunette woman Thatcher had been seated next to at lunch nearly sprinting in her sky-high stilettos to reach us. To reach *him*.

"Thatcher. I'm so glad I finally caught you." She panted like she'd run the entire length of the exhibit hall, but that didn't stop her from smiling with teeth white enough to sear my retinas. "I just happened to see you passing by, and I... had a follow-up question from our conversation at lunch." She tossed her hair lightly. "About industry trend forecasting?"

I was irked by the interruption but stood patiently while he responded to her questions with his usual calm assurance, and I tried not to roll my eyes when she nodded vigorously after every word he spoke, her eyes shining with admiration that wasn't solely professional.

Who could blame her, really? Thatcher Pennington was magnetic. He also didn't seem to notice the effect he was having on her. At least, not the way I did.

"Boost to the ego, hmm?" I said lightly after he managed to extricate himself from the conversation, and we continued on past the next few exhibits.

He side-eyed me. "Being solicited for my opinions on industry trend forecasting? Always thrilling." He smoothed down the pine-green polo McGee had purchased according to the list and color swatches I'd texted him and looked around the space. "Where's this meeting room?"

"Over there." I pointed left, and he headed in that direction so quickly I found myself hurrying like the brunette again in order to catch up. "And you and I both know that's not the only thing she was interested in. She gave you her business card."

"People often do."

"With her personal cell number on it," I countered. "She offered to buy you dinner."

"To discuss—"

I grabbed his arm and pulled him to a stop outside the meeting room. "You're not that naive. If you're not interested in her, fine, but at least acknowledge—"

Thatcher turned toward me, face set. "What are you doing, Reagan?" he asked softly.

I blinked up at him and swallowed. What *was* I doing? I didn't have the faintest clue. It was not professional in the slightest.

"I'm just saying, she gave you *fuck me* eyes under her lashes." I demonstrated the look, and Thatcher's own eyes narrowed. "She held on for a whole minute when you shook hands. And she's pretty—not my type, but you go for women, too, right? So..." I swallowed. "Is she the kind of person you usually go for? Because she was definitely flirting with you. She was playing the game. And I bet if you wanted—"

Thatcher stared at me while my heart pounded its way out of my chest, and my breath came faster. "I told you before," he said in a soft voice that reached right into my brain and snatched away all logic. "I'm not interested in games."

My muscles locked tight as I waited for him to say something more, to close the space between us—

"Holy shit! Reagan Wellbridge! I didn't expect to find you in Wichita, of all places."

I whirled away from Thatcher just as Chris Acton strode out of the meeting room, all bright eyes and delighted smile.

"And you're looking *good*," he added with an appreciative up-down that took in my tailored pants and crisp Oxford. "As usual. I haven't seen you since we—"

"Met at the leadership conference in June," I cut in quickly. "Yes. Hi. Good to see you again." I shook his hand and managed to smile, but I couldn't come up with a single word to continue the conversation because all my attention was focused on the man standing like the world's tallest, most impenetrable fortress at my side.

Be charming, I reminded myself. *Be professional.*

God, I was beginning to loathe that word.

"I'm here on business," I said, trying to recover. "I work in PR at PennCo now. I'm assisting Mr. Pennington today." I tilted my head in Thatcher's direction.

"Oh." Chris darted a startled glance in the direction of my head tilt, almost as if he hadn't noticed Thatcher—the man he was supposed to interview—until that moment. "Of course. I remember hearing that somewhere, but I was expecting to meet Layla James today." Chris dropped my hand so he could offer his to Thatcher. "Chris Acton, Mr. Pennington. Not sure you remember me from our quick meeting last year..."

I waited for Thatcher to turn on the charm, but despite our conversation about this just minutes ago, he simply nodded and shook hands without saying a word. In fact, he looked grumpier and more aloof than I'd ever seen him.

I could practically smell disaster in the air.

Shit. I closed my eyes and bit back a sigh of frustration. This was supposed to be a friendly interview that would hopefully convince Chris to say good things about Thatcher and his company. But there was a reason a PR person accompanied a CEO on a press tour, and this was it. I needed to fix this. *Head in the game, Wellbridge.*

"Actually," I said, throwing Chris an apologetic smile. "Can you give us a moment? There's a message I forgot to relay to Thatcher from his assistant, and I want to make sure it's not urgent." I gave Thatcher a pointed look and directed him to the hallway.

"January did not call you."

"No. I just..." I leaned in close and lowered my voice. "You remember that man is here to help you help PennCo, right? So maybe stop frowning at him."

"I'm not frowning." His eyes flashed a warning. "And stop telling me how to conduct my business. I told you I don't need to be managed."

I threw up my hands. "That's not what I'm trying to do," I hiss-whispered. "I'm just reminding you that you're here to schmooze the press, even if you don't like it. Even if you don't trust them. If you're going to act like you have a stick up your ass, what's the point of this whole tour?"

Thatcher's gaze seared through me. Up close like this, I noticed a faded freckle tucked in a laugh line next to one of his eyes... which were not laughing now. "You're acting like I've never done this before. I know what I'm doing, Reagan."

I opened my mouth to remind him that he'd once been quoted by a Wall Street Journal reporter saying he hated giving interviews. But then I remembered that I'd read the quote during a late-night drunken internet search one hot summer in Honeybridge when Thatcher Pennington lay only a few doors away from my bedroom and shut myself up.

I folded my arms over my chest. "Fine, then." I nodded at the doorway. "Proceed."

Thatcher cocked his head in challenge, as if he knew I wouldn't be able to leave it at that.

Unfortunately, he was right.

"But it wouldn't hurt to smile," I blurted, because I was right, too, damn it. "Just smile, okay? Chris is gay, Thatcher. He's not immune to another sexy man."

One eyebrow lifted, and he gave me a look that was hard to read. "I'm not going to ask how you know that about him."

My face heated, and I straightened my shoulders defensively. "Just... be nice to the reporter, and he'll be nice to you. You said you trust me, so... trust me. Okay?"

Thatcher's nostrils flared as though he wanted to argue, but he gave me a clipped nod and thrust a hand toward the door, ushering me ahead of him into the room.

Chris either didn't feel the tension in the air or chose to ignore it. Neither option said much about his journalistic instincts, but I was grateful for it. I needed time to get myself back under control.

Chris waved Thatcher to the far side of the long conference table where he'd set up his microphones and recording equipment, then took the seat opposite with his back to the door. Instead of taking a seat, I leaned back against the wall behind Chris where I could keep an eye on the proceedings... and yes, fine, watch Thatcher without being noticed, because apparently, I hadn't seen the man enough in the past few days.

"Ready?" Chris asked Thatcher as he got comfortable.

Thatcher gave a clipped nod, as friendly as a block of wood. "Ready."

Chris began with a series of getting-to-know-you questions that I imagined were designed to set people at ease, and they seemed to work. "What were the early days of Pennington Industries like?" he wanted to know. "What's been your greatest achievement to date? Can you talk a little bit about your companies' commitments to sustainability and fair employment practices?"

Little by little, Thatcher relaxed into the rhythm of the questions, and as he did, his charm emerged, like the sun peeking out from behind a cloud. He was self-effacing and funny, intelligent and passionate, caring and genuine. He *did* know what he was doing, just as he'd said.

I'd never wanted to peer into someone's head as badly as I did at that moment. What had been wrong with Thatcher before? Why was he okay now? Had he recognized my jealousy over the brunette woman? God. Was he upset that I'd pushed him to talk about it?

The idea was horrifying. My entire purpose for being at this interview was to make sure things went smoothly. Thatcher was trusting me to do that. *Do your job*, I told myself firmly. *Obsess about Thatcher's potential hookups on your own time.*

I spied several rows of water bottles lined up on a table in the far corner of the room, so I sidled over as unobtrusively as possible and grabbed a couple, the way my father's PR people often did when he was in an interview. Leaning across the table, I set one in front of Thatcher and the other in front of Chris.

"Hey, thanks." Chris shot me an appreciative grin before cracking his bottle open.

Thatcher's eyes met mine as he lifted his chin in acknowledgment.

I resumed my place at the wall, feeling much better about things... which, of course, was when the vibe in the room shifted in a decidedly unhelpful direction.

"So," Chris began casually as he recapped his bottle. "Let's get down to it. Where did Nova Davidson get the Elustre shirt, Mr. Pennington?"

The question wasn't a surprise—the Nova situation was the reason Chris had agreed to do the interview, after all—but the change in his tone was. In an instant, he'd gone from amiable to insistent, and though Thatcher's smile didn't waver, his eyes cooled all the way to subarctic.

"That's a great question, Chris," Thatcher said. "Unfortunately, I don't have the answer. I'm afraid you'd need to ask her."

Chris sat back in his seat almost challengingly. "Her team isn't responding to inquiries beyond the 'no comment' they put out after the arrest and claim she's concentrating on recovering from her injuries. Are they trying to hide something?"

Thatcher's expression turned appropriately serious. "I

don't have the answer to that either, although we at PennCo Fiber certainly wish her speedy healing from her injuries."

"Did PennCo Fiber send Nova the shirt?"

A sliver of unease curled in my gut. I'd sat in on dozens and dozens of interviews like these with my father. Chris should have allowed Thatcher a few chances to say our prepared responses to the Nova situation and then moved on. He wasn't supposed to be pressing the issue like a television attorney interrogating a hostile witness.

"Not to my knowledge," Thatcher said. "As I said, I really think the appropriate person to ask would be the person wearing the shirt."

Chris waited several beats, obviously hoping Thatcher would elaborate and say something useful. He didn't.

"Is it possible someone at your company could have done it without your knowledge?"

What the hell was Chris asking? Of course that was possible. Thousands of people worked for Pennington Industries. Was it *probable*? Definitely not, unless someone was really trying to get fired.

Regardless, did Chris actually think Thatcher was going to confess to a conspiracy theory? Hell, even if he had something to confess, Thatcher wouldn't be fooled into doing it here and now.

"I believed we were here to discuss PennCo Fiber's innovative new product and commitment to sustainability." A muscle ticked in Thatcher's jaw. "Please let me know if you have any more questions related to those topics."

"Was this part of a plan to seek social media attention for your 'innovative new product'? Be honest, Thatcher: were you hoping that having a celebrity wear it would snag you some free media coverage?"

I felt heat creep up my neck as I recalled Thatcher's words about Chris Acton.

He's a vulture.

I'd promised Thatcher Chris was a good guy. Fair. That he'd be lobbing softball questions, not repeatedly hammering Thatcher on the same point as though hoping to catch him in a lie.

Thatcher took a slow, silent breath before responding calmly. "No comment. Shall I interpret this line of questioning to be your request to end our conversation?"

Chris hesitated. Thankfully, he changed the subject.

"What's next on the horizon for PennCo Fiber? Any exciting announcements coming in the new year?" Chris asked. Maybe the easy question was meant as a peace offering, but if so, it was too late. Thatcher was no longer smiling.

He proceeded to explain the "exciting" renewable resource initiatives the company was investing in and implied there would be further announcements coming soon. I could tell by Chris's reaction he was less than thrilled.

Chris cocked his head. "While preparing for today's conversation, I discovered you invested recently in property in a small town in Maine called Honeybridge. The property is being used to expand Honeybridge's unique mead offerings. Is this an indication of a new direction Pennington Industries is moving in?"

Thatcher's face was granite. "Not at all," he said. "That's a personal investment of mine, unrelated to Pennington Industries."

Chris nodded like he already knew this. "That's a great segue to my next question. What's on the horizon for

Thatcher Pennington? Tell us more about what you have going on... *personally*."

The question, or maybe Chris's arch tone, made Thatcher stiffen in his seat. At first, I worried that I'd missed something, but then I remembered how Thatcher had looked on the bus yesterday when he'd talked about how he'd made tabloid headlines after his second divorce. Defiant. *Lonely*.

This was not what Layla had agreed to when she'd set up the interview, I was sure, and I was furious that Chris had taken advantage of the situation. Thatcher didn't owe anyone anything, damn it.

"Pennington Industries and the people who work there are my primary focus, both personally and professionally," Thatcher said, firm and cold. "They always have been."

"Of course," Chris agreed in a voice that said something else entirely.

I shifted on my feet, ready to intervene and tell Chris that our time was up. I wasn't sure if that was what a true PR handler would do, but I didn't want to subject Thatcher to any more of this.

Before I had a chance to speak, though, Chris stood and offered Thatcher a handshake and a polite thank-you. Thatcher barely shook his hand before muttering his own goodbye and striding from the room without glancing at me.

Great.

I pushed off the wall to follow when Chris turned and offered me a handshake as well, all smiles now that the interview was over. "It really is good to see you, Reagan. How have you been?"

I didn't bother to hide my annoyance. "I was doing fine until five minutes ago. What the hell was that?" I thrust a hand at the conference table. "PennCo didn't set up this interview so you could rake my boss over the coals or try to get the gory details of his personal life."

Chris's easy smile didn't fade. "Please. That wasn't raking, and you know it. I asked him a couple of off-the-cuff questions. Getting to the deeper story is my job." He shrugged. "Besides, your boss handled them well enough."

"Because there *is* no deeper story," I insisted.

"There's *always* a deeper story. But enough about that." Chris's grin turned friendlier, more open. "Are you staying at the Sheraton while you're in town? I'd love to buy you a drink later."

Chris was sexy—unquestionably so—and a few months ago, I would have jumped on that kind of opportunity in a heartbeat. *Had* jumped on it, in fact. Even a few weeks back, I might have been tempted to go for a repeat. But at the moment, I couldn't think of anything I wanted less than a quick hookup, especially with someone who'd upset Thatcher.

This was concerning on many levels.

"Can't. Work trip, remember?" I said shortly. "We have a business dinner thing. And since we're traveling by bus, I think we'll be leaving for Colorado tonight anyway."

Chris tilted his head. "Bus? Oh... right. That makes sense. I, ah... I saw Thatcher's driver earlier. Not that I know him. The driver, I mean. I don't know him at all, really. Just saw him the one time I had a quick interview with Thatcher. And then again earlier today at the coffee stand." He cleared his throat. "McGee is his name, I think. Right?"

I didn't pay much attention to what he was saying because I was still hot with embarrassment about the way I'd tried to handle the situation between Chris and Thatcher. "Yeah, so we're heading to a dinner later and then getting back on the road. It's a whole PennCo whistle-stop tour thing."

Chris shifted away from me to slide his messenger bag over his head and onto one shoulder. "You know, when I heard you were working for PennCo, I almost didn't believe it," he said off-handedly, reaching for his coat and frowning at it. "I'd figured you'd end up working for your father's campaign. You seemed eager to get involved last summer, and you're killing it on Instagram. God knows the Senator needs someone on that team who actually understands how to use social media."

My face went hot, but I fell back on my default politeness. "There's no deeper story there either, Chris," I said. "My father's team is very experienced. He trusts them implicitly."

"Sure. But who could he trust more to lead them than his own son?" Chris seemed genuinely puzzled.

Movement near the door caught my attention, and I saw Thatcher pacing a few feet away, possibly within earshot. I really hoped he hadn't been listening. Of course, Thatcher probably knew my father's low opinion of me as well as anyone did, but I really didn't need him to be reminded of it. Coming on the heels of this interview, it would only highlight how wrong Thatcher had been to trust me himself.

"Always nice to see you, Chris," I said, forcing a smile. "But I've gotta go. Can't keep the boss waiting."

"Yeah." Chris glanced at Thatcher before his own smile faded. "You're sure everything's alright, Reagan?" he asked, suddenly serious.

I waved this off. "Of course," I said over my shoulder. "Perfectly fine. As always."

But as I hurried out of the room, I felt the opposite of perfect. I was unsettled and frustrated—feelings that only increased when Thatcher marched beside me, utterly silent and wearing the scowl of the deeply, rightfully pissed—as we made our way through the convention center.

Guilt and shame clogged my throat and made my stomach ache. When we exited the building and headed toward the bus, I almost broke the silence with a blurted apology. Thatcher had been right about Chris, and I'd been wrong, and now he was angry. He had every right to be.

Trust me, I'd said. And look where that had gotten us.

I felt stupid and immature. Naive. I knew plenty about media and interviews, yes, but I'd been so desperate to prove myself that I'd let myself believe I knew better than Thatcher about Chris's intentions.

In hopes of not embarrassing myself further, I kept my mouth closed. We were supposed to attend a formal dinner event with other high-level executives attending the symposium, but I expected any minute to be politely excused from accompanying him.

It didn't happen. When we boarded the bus, Thatcher finally spoke, though he still didn't look at me. "Be dressed and ready at seven. January arranged a car to take us to dinner."

I stared at his back as he disappeared into the back bedroom and closed the door.

"Problem?" McGee asked, appearing out of nowhere and scaring the shit out of me. I jumped and nearly fell back down the stairs and out the door of the bus.

"No, not at all," I lied. "Why do you ask?"

McGee looked at me, at the closed bedroom door, and then at me again. "You're acting weird."

"*You're* acting weird," I said, confirming once and for all I was an immature brat who couldn't professional his way out of a paper bag. "Have you considered wearing sunglasses? They really help with the crow's feet."

"Nope." McGee's lips quirked. "You're not distracting me this time. What's up with the weirdness?" He lifted a pierced eyebrow, which was way hotter than it should have been.

Once again, I wondered how much of this man Thatcher had seen up close. Had touched. Had *tasted*.

This was my punishment from the Universe.

I closed my eyes and took a breath.

"I fucked up," I admitted, opening my eyes and rubbing a hand over my mouth.

This time, both of McGee's eyebrows lifted in surprise. "Really? How?"

"I thought I could trust a reporter," I said, making a flicking gesture with my fingers. "I told *Thatcher* to trust him. Stupid, right?"

He reached over and pushed a button that made the door close with a whooshing sound, blocking the frigid air from filling the bus. "Meh. We all do stupid shit, Reagan. Trusting someone you shouldn't... well, maybe it means you're the kind of guy who wants to see the best in people. That's not a bad thing."

I narrowed my eyes at this frank, fair, *kind* reply, but I couldn't even come up with a snarky retort. I glanced back at the closed bedroom door and let my shoulders droop. "I let him down."

He let out a laugh. "Join the club. But Thatcher's not an asshole. He'll get over it, and you won't make the same mistake again."

"Maybe," I said glumly. But I was starting to think making the same mistakes over and over was my dubious superpower.

I moved further into the bus to shrug out of my coat before searching my luggage for a nicer pair of pants and a button-down shirt for dinner.

While I dressed in the tiny hallway bathroom, I couldn't help but think of McGee's claim that Thatcher would get over my misstep. Logically, I knew he was right. One uncomfortable interview wasn't going to destroy Pennington Industries, especially since Thatcher had managed to stick to the script, even when Chris hadn't. And Thatcher couldn't have been surprised that he was right and I was wrong either. After all, who'd take business advice from Trent Wellbridge's fuckup son?

But none of those truths made me feel better. In fact, they somehow made me feel even worse.

I glanced at myself in the mirror as I buttoned my shirt. Thankfully, I didn't look quite as young as I felt, but at that moment, I was pretty sure I understood what my parents saw when they looked at me. A whole bunch of ego and no life experience. A whole bunch of ideas and no practicality. A pretty, decorative shell.

"From now on, stop talking and start listening, asshole," I muttered to my reflection. I made a vow there and then to stop trying to be Thatcher's peer and remember I was on this trip as a gopher-type underling. The CEO of a multibillion-dollar corporation didn't want or need my opinions on how to run his business, and even if he had, my opinions were clearly wrong.

I swallowed my pride and stood up straight. Reagan Wellbridge wasn't exactly a quiet wallflower. But tonight, I'd be the best damned wallflower Wichita fiber executives had ever seen.

Chapter Eight

Thatcher

If Reagan didn't stop whatever the fuck he was doing, I was going to scream.

We'd been together in enough business social situations over the past couple of days to have fallen into a kind of comfortable routine. He might sometimes be temperamental in private, but in public, Reagan was pure charm, engaging every person we met, from swaggering executives to the most timid assistant's assistant, with a warm, genuine interest. He was intelligent and well researched enough to tee up conversational opportunities for me to capitalize on and to subtly remind me of why each person we spoke to was important. And he seemed to do it all effortlessly.

He'd become my secret weapon at these events.

Tonight, my weapon was missing.

All through the welcome cocktail hour, he'd been a ghost, standing slightly apart from me while wearing an insipid smile that held no warmth whatsoever. He nodded politely when spoken to and replied with as few bland words as possible. The only thing that differentiated him from the silent and efficient Newport Grille waitstaff was the luxury brand name and tailored fit of his clothing. And I was pretty sure it was because of today's clusterfuck with Chris Acton.

The interview itself had been no worse than I'd expected. The guy had tried digging for dirt, but I hadn't been surprised, and I'd managed to stick to the prepared responses Reagan and the rest of the team had provided. But from the moment I'd set eyes on Chris—from the moment *he'd* set his greedy little eyes on Reagan—I'd felt the nearly irresistible urge to commit violence. Every innuendo-laden word out of the asshole's mouth had only fueled the fire, and when he'd taken a lingering look at Reagan's ass as Reagan leaned over the table to hand me a water bottle, I'd come closer to laying hands on someone than I had in decades.

Worst of all, I was pretty sure the reporter had caught a glimpse of my anger before I locked it down.

It was inexcusable.

So what if Reagan and the reporter had history? Reagan was no shrinking virgin, and I wouldn't want him to be. Moreover, I had no claim on Reagan, which meant he was free—absolutely, perfectly, entirely free—to hook up with Chris Acton or any other man with a come-hither smirk and a sexy gleam in his tiny, beady, vulture eyes.

The problem here was *me*. I shouldn't be fantasizing about the tattoo hidden under Reagan's tailored pants, shouldn't see a flash of bright aquamarine even when I closed my eyes, shouldn't want my hands on Reagan so badly that imagining Chris touching him made me stalk out of the interview and all the way back to the damn bus before I could trust myself to speak. I shouldn't want Reagan at all... and I couldn't fucking stop.

I had to assume Reagan was pissed that I hadn't taken his very good advice and made nice with the reporter. Or maybe he was upset because he'd noticed the possessiveness —the *jealousy*—I had absolutely no right to feel. I wasn't sure why any of that would make Reagan go radio silent rather than shedding his polite mask and calling me out for it, but I needed to figure it out. Because of all the versions of Reagan I'd seen so far—provoking, sexy, earnest, thoughtful, and ridiculous—this silent, cowed Reagan was the only one I couldn't handle.

I excused myself from a conversation and turned to him. "Come with me."

He looked surprised but nodded with a robotic politeness that made me want to growl. He followed me out of the private dining room and into a quiet nook off the main foyer.

"Tell me what the hell is going on with you," I demanded without preamble.

Reagan opened his mouth and then shut it. He tilted his head and then frowned. "Pardon?"

"Are you sick? Would you like to go back to the bus? Are you... Did I... If you're pissed off, say so." I folded my arms over my chest. "I've told you to speak freely with me often enough, haven't I?"

"Yes, but..." He opened his mouth, then shut it again. "I'm letting you do the talking. You're the boss, and this is your show. I'm being polite. Respectful."

"Fuck politeness. You're polite with *them*." I jabbed a finger toward the dining room. "Not with me."

Reagan stared at me like I was speaking gibberish... which, okay, was a fair assessment.

"Have I ever asked you to be polite and respectful with me?" I clarified, leaning in to pin his gaze. "Since when have

I given you the impression that I want you to stand back meekly like a good little foot soldier?"

His nostrils flared, and his lips tightened. "You didn't, exactly. I just realized..." His voice trailed off.

I grabbed his upper arms. "What?"

The scent of his soap and aftershave swirled between us, clean and crisp. It brought a wave of sensory memories with it from New Year's Eve. I could almost taste this scent on his skin.

"I fucked up, and I know it, okay?" he said at last. "You were angry with me, or annoyed, or... whatever, and I get it. I told you not to worry about Chris. I told you it'd be all soft-ball questions. I told you to smile and be friendly. And then he came after you. He tried to *gotcha* you. He tried to get you to comment on your personal life." The outrage on Reagan's face burned nearly as hot as my earlier jealousy had... and made me feel far better than it reasonably should have. "I was wrong. And I'm sorry."

"That's what's bothering you? You... think *I'm* angry?"

Reagan lifted his chin. "Obviously. You've barely spoken to me since then. And I get it. You knew better than I did. I fucked up, as usual. I need to learn when to keep my big mouth shut and remember I'm better at smiling for the cameras."

It was said in his voice, but those were his parents' words. I'd heard Patricia and Trent talk about Reagan as an irresponsible kid, a directionless young man who didn't take things seriously enough, all the while plastering his hand-some, youthful face all over Trent's campaign.

For a moment, I wasn't sure what to say, and in that silence, Reagan looked away and shuffled his feet, revealing insecurity miles deeper than I'd ever suspected in a man who usually glowed as brightly as he did.

It was shocking.

It was infuriating.

And then, suddenly, I knew exactly what needed to be said. Exactly what he needed to hear.

I leaned even closer. "You listen to me, Reagan Wellbridge," I said in a voice too low to be overheard. "Whatever the fuck voice you have right now in your head? It's wrong. Do you understand? Dead. Ass. Wrong."

His gaze flew to my face.

"First of all," I continued, "you didn't fuck up. You liked Chris. You believed the best of him. You wanted to give him the benefit of the doubt." *A benefit of the doubt that no one had ever shown Reagan himself*, I thought but didn't say. "That's a *good* thing. That's an incredible thing."

Reagan frowned.

"Second, I was going to be on guard with the reporter no matter what you said. Because I *don't* give reporters the benefit of the doubt." I met his eyes. "My comportment around the media is on me."

"But you trusted me," he whispered, "and I—"

"Did exactly what I trusted you to do, which is to give me your best. Your best work, your best advice, your best... you. I don't trust you to be *perfect*. Jesus, Reagan. Who'd ever hold someone to that kind of standard?"

He swallowed without speaking, but we both knew the answer, and I deeply regretted every second I'd spent hearing Trent and Patricia sigh about Reagan without speaking up.

Never again, I promised myself.

"And third," I said, "what did I tell you yesterday? You don't need to prove yourself to anyone. You're talented. And dedicated. And savvy. And good with people. You're..." Beautiful. Irreplaceable. *Important*. "You're good at a hell of a lot more than smiling for the cameras. So even if you do make a mistake someday—make the worst fuckup in the history of fuckups—you don't for one second let that cause you to dim your damned light."

Those gorgeous aquamarine eyes were so wide it might have been funny... if the moment hadn't felt so significant.

"I don't want to embarrass you," he whispered.

My chest burned like every inhale had to pass through jagged glass. There was something incredibly wrong with this sassy, cocky man second-guessing himself. "Never. You will never embarrass me. You couldn't."

"Oh, I assure you," he said ruefully, "I—"

I set my hands on his shoulders and shook lightly. "Couldn't," I insisted. "I'm responsible for my choices. Fuck anyone who's made you feel differently. That's a sign of their own weakness."

Reagan blinked. The dim lights of the restaurant corridor glinted warmly on his lashes. "So... you weren't angry?"

"Not at you," I assured him. "And even if I was, I still wouldn't ever want you to be anyone but yourself."

He swallowed. His prominent Adam's apple bobbed, drawing my eyes down to a throat I longed to map with my tongue. "So, you're telling me that a 'silver-tongued, provoking little shit' is what Fortune 500 companies should look for in a public relations person?"

I felt myself smiling almost despite myself. It was a rare occurrence these days for someone to call me on my bullshit, and I couldn't deny that was part of what drew me to Reagan.

One *small* part.

"If it's not, perhaps it should be. I'll ask HR to update

the job description," I teased, and he grinned. I shook him again, gently, because he was right there under my hands, finally. Because I *could*. "From now on, talk to me instead of doing the silent wallflower routine. It doesn't suit you. Tell me you understand."

His smile faded. "Yes, sir," he breathed.

Tension jangled between us like wires stretched too tightly and on the verge of snapping. I wanted him saying those words to me naked and begging in the center of a large bed.

My head swam with memories. It had only been one night, but his submission had been enough to imprint on my brain for a lifetime. I caught myself swaying closer to him. The soft light in the corridor left sharp shadows across the planes of his face. His warm, unsteady breath fanned against my cheek. If I closed my eyes, I could almost feel the smooth skin under his eyes against the tip of my nose.

The clatter of plates startled me out of my inappropriate trance. I blinked at Reagan and took a decisive step back.

We were here for work.

Reagan Wellbridge *worked* for me.

I would not put him in the untenable position of thinking his boss was coming on to him.

I cleared my throat and nodded. "Let's get back in there and charm some people, damn it."

On my way back into the private dining room, I heard him release a sigh of relief behind me. The sound made my own shoulders unknot.

We hadn't been back in the dining room for five minutes when Reagan began telling a funny story to a local textile executive about how the PennCo Fiber public relations team had welcomed him to the team by making him write a fictional press release in the style of a stand-up comedian. I knew Layla's management style and Reagan's exaggerated storytelling habits enough to know the story was most likely ninety-five percent bullshit, but it had the executive, along with several other people nearby, laughing their asses off.

Reagan then used the story to slip in several key points about Elustre's natural fiber content and PennCo Fiber's commitment to sustainability, but he did it in a way that didn't seem obvious or sales-y.

And just like that, we were back in our rhythm.

But that night, when I was finally alone in bed and the bus was rambling west again, I stared at the ceiling with one hand propped behind my head and remembered what I'd overheard Chris Acton saying that afternoon as I'd paced outside the interview room. *I'd figured you'd end up working for your father's campaign,* he'd said. *You seemed eager to get involved last summer, and you're killing it on Instagram.* I turned over and grabbed my phone from the side table to check Reagan's social media profiles the way I'd meant to days ago.

I quickly logged in to my own barely used account and found his name on a quick search, then blinked, sure I was reading wrong.

One point four million subscribers? Seriously? How the hell had he gotten so many? Those were celebrity numbers.

As I scrolled through his feed, the answer became clear. The man was snarky and fun, relatable and kind—the very same attributes that made him so damn appealing when he was networking at these industry events—and, yes, I was sure his breath-stealing gorgeousness didn't hurt either.

Who *wouldn't* want to find his perfect face and fit body in their feed every day?

I swiped back past photos of last night's sunset at a truck stop outside Topeka, an earlier one of him in the kitchenette booth on the bus, and him in that damn feather mask and glorious tuxedo at the gala on New Year's Eve. Never had a tuxedo cradled a man's body with so much precision and flattering emphasis.

Scrolling further, I found with some surprise that the man had sponsors for some of his posts. Three different clothing brands had sent him things to wear in December alone, and if I hadn't already known that he wasn't responsible for the Nova situation, seeing these pictures would have confirmed it. Everything about his posts was professional, classy... and incredibly arousing.

My dick stirred between my legs, and I reached down idly to stroke it. One sponsored photo featured Reagan in a couture version of gray sweatpants with a matching hoodie. The outline of his dick was *just* noticeable in the play of light breaking through the wintry clouds and reflecting off the patchy snow in the park behind him.

A snowflake sat on the apple of his cheek as he grinned into the lens. Hashtags about winter in NYC, Central Park in the snow, and freezing his balls off littered the bottom of the caption. He was breathtaking.

Further back, there was a shot of him with friends in a sports bar watching a football game one afternoon and another the same night dressed for clubbing in the West Village. The man seemed to be a chameleon, able to fit into any group of people whether he wore team colors or skin-revealing mesh. He was the same way with his friends that he'd been on this trip—adaptable, inclusive, engaging, and social.

But how many of them actually knew him? How many of those people saw the vulnerable, tender heart beneath his attractive exterior?

Over the next hour, I went down rabbit hole after rabbit hole, smiling the entire time. It turned out Reagan had done a whole series of posts about Honeybridge. One showed the Welcome to Honeybridge sign and the dozens of smaller signs below that proclaimed it the home of the "Honeycutts: Ice Festival Heroes" and, bizarrely, "Wellbridges: Best Leaf Peepers." Another was a collage of highly decorated window boxes, with a caption explaining the "rules" of the Honeybridge Box Day competition. A post about the Tavern and Meadery showed Flynn Honeycutt, strong arms folded over his chest, staring down the camera with fierce eyes, and JT Wellbridge, arm thrown over Flynn's shoulders, grinning proudly down at him.

How do you want to make people feel? Reagan had asked the first time he and I had discussed social media, and I hadn't understood it until now. Seeing the town like this was more effective than a loud, splashy tourism campaign ever could be at making people want to visit Honeybridge and see the place for themselves.

In my scrolling, I also found linked accounts for Reagan's influential friends that I could see at a glance reflected Reagan's organizational style and well-branded aesthetics. Was Reagan managing them, too?

The man didn't just *want* a career in social media; he already had a thriving one. One that showed his talent, vision, and determination. And while I didn't fully understand how much income that translated to, I knew it had to be a significant amount.

So why the hell did he work for me?

And why did Chris Acton assume that Reagan had planned to work for his father?

Trent Wellbridge was a moderately conservative state politician who'd made a name for himself through strategy and networking. We'd met at various parent events when our children were at school together, and I liked him well enough to consider him a friend—he was smart and sociable, an excellent host who shared my enjoyment of good scotch, an above-average golfer, and most of all, he respected my privacy—but I didn't hold out high hopes for his campaign. From what I'd heard, he hadn't gained much traction with voters because while he was passionate about winning, he wasn't specific about anything he might do once he'd won. I couldn't imagine why Reagan would want to help him get elected, unless it was out of a sense of family loyalty.

On a whim, I searched Instagram for Trent's political account and nearly laughed out loud. It was almost as bad as PennCo Fiber's account—or maybe *worse* since PennCo's account simply lacked content while Trent's account had plenty of content and zero appeal. Most of his posts were recaps of mainstream media coverage of Trent's appearances and blasts of official press releases. There was absolutely nothing dynamic that illustrated who Trent Wellbridge was as a person or even as a resident of the state of Maine.

Chris Acton was right. Trent's campaign needed someone like Reagan on his team.

Too bad. He's mine. I took a deep breath and held it before repeating the silent words in my head. *He's mine.*

It felt so damn right.

But he'd taken the job at PennCo for reasons that were important to him, even if I still didn't totally understand them, and... the hell of it was, I didn't want to fuck that up for him. I didn't want to give *him* a chance to fuck it up, if he still wanted me the way I suspected he did.

I liked him. A lot. I genuinely wanted to get to know him better. To enjoy his company as a coworker and friend. To appreciate his imagination and talent for relationship marketing. To pick his brain, as an entrepreneur, and learn from him. To *protect* him. And if that meant locking my lust away, surely I could do that.

I blew out a breath and closed the app before tossing my phone on the bedside shelf and rubbing my face with my hands.

Respect him as a professional.

I fell asleep repeating the words like a Human Resources training video stuck on a loop.

And then I dreamed of a million filthy ways of making his body mine.

———

"SUGAR," Reagan said, handing me two packets over his shoulder as I scooted past him to the table. I took the packets and shook them before tearing them open and pouring them into the mug that was already waiting at my spot.

He fished a spoon out of a drawer and took the seat opposite me before peeling off the top of his yogurt. I silently passed him a napkin from the small stack on the side of the table before taking a sip of my coffee.

After six days together on this bus, we'd fallen into an easy routine... for a certain definition of "easy."

It had been three days since I'd felt his breath on my cheek in the corridor of the Newport Grille in Wichita. Three days without any near-miss kisses or glances that lasted several breath-stealing beats too long, without accidentally-on-purpose brushing against him in the hallway or crowding onto his bench to check out his tablet while tiny electrons of arousal bounced between us.

Instead, we'd spent a lot of time talking. We'd discussed social media in general and which of his (casually sexy) posts got the most interaction in particular. I'd told him about the musicians I loved. We'd even traded intramural softball horror stories, which had necessitated Reagan dragging the collar of his shirt down and trailing his fingers over the clavicle he'd broken years ago in illustration. I'd watched him eat a lot of yogurt, which was his favorite breakfast food and apparently so delicious it needed to be licked off the spoon.

It *had* been easy.

It was also fucking torture.

Fortunately, things with Pennington Industries had been easy, full stop. In the office, flu cases were way down. Our social media accounts were in better shape than they'd ever been and were getting good engagement. And our tour was proceeding smoothly. After Wichita, I'd had meetings in Colorado Springs and Denver, both of which had gone spectacularly well. Today was a rest day, and tomorrow, we'd head to Vail for a meeting with Maya Martinez, the CEO of Zen Activewear, who was hosting a social event at her family's ski lodge. Since the Martinez family owned the Boise Thunderbolts baseball team, the event would feature lots of pro baseball players (which meant plenty of free media coverage), and I was hoping the informal setting would give me a chance to talk to Maya about the use of Elustre in Zen Activewear's yoga line for next fall and winter.

This wasn't how I usually spent my days. If I was being

honest, I rarely thought much about the PennCo subsidiary at all, let alone the nitty-gritty of marketing a particular line of fabric. But somehow, with Reagan around, it had become... fun.

"Will there be skiing?" Reagan asked before shoving a heaping spoonful of yogurt into his mouth. I blinked away from the sight of his Adam's apple bobbing as he swallowed and tried to distract myself by shooting off a quick check-in text to Brantleigh.

"Not sure. Why?" I said without glancing up.

Brant still hadn't replied to any of my texts, and I'd gone from concerned to annoyed and back again. Fortunately, Thalia had gotten a quick text from him—a question about why his Centurion card was no longer working—so I knew he was alive and well enough to be out shopping.

"Because it might be fun to ski with the Thunderbolts. You know, hot guys, formfitting ski onesies, all that bending..." he teased.

I did glance up then and arched one eyebrow, which earned me a smile so sunny and innocent I nearly laughed.

"Kidding, kidding," he said. "But it really would be nice to ski. Don't you feel cooped up from all this time on the bus?"

He sounded wistful, even as he pushed his tablet over the table, turning it so I could skim today's media summary.

As it had every day since Wichita, coverage of the Nova situation was trending down while coverage of our press tour heated up. Even though our Colorado Springs and Denver meetings hadn't been directly related to Elustre or PennCo Fiber, the PR team had arranged interviews with local business reporters at each stop to help keep the positive coverage coming.

I made a satisfied sound and pushed the tablet back. "I

do feel a little cooped up," I admitted. "I can't run at this altitude, but skiing would be nice. Do you have gear?"

Reagan pulled the tablet close and shook his head. "I didn't think to pack anything like that, and it's probably too cold to try skiing in sweats."

We were currently parked in a campground near Silverthorne for a planned overnight stop. Here, we could receive packages, get our clothes washed, resupply the bus with groceries, and allow McGee time to freshen the place up. I'd originally planned to catch up on work, but now I had another idea.

"After breakfast, let's find some ski clothes, then we can Uber to Keystone and hit the slopes."

Reagan stared at me like I'd grown several extra heads. "But... January packed your schedule full today. You have at least two online meetings and a call from the Zurich people. There's no way she'll let you duck out of so many work commitments."

I pulled out my wallet and slid a credit card free. "You forget she works for me, not the other way around. If I tell her to change the schedule, she will. Besides, most of those meetings are scheduled for this morning. If you pick up clothes for me, too, I can knock out the most important things while you're shopping." I handed him the card. "Charge it all to me. Oh, and make sure you get us good socks. Thick wool ones. Cold feet on the slopes are the worst."

He continued to stare. "I'm not charging my stuff to your card," he said.

I waved this away. "Consider it a bonus. Or, hell, hazard pay. You've been a real asset on this trip, Reagan, and I'd like to treat you to a nice afternoon on the slopes. We can even strategize tomorrow's meeting with Maya and plan some more social media posts while we're on the ski lift."

Reagan shoved my card in his wallet. "I'll charge your stuff, but I can afford my own ski clothes." Something in his stilted tone alerted me to the fact I'd struck a nerve, and I frowned.

"I didn't say you couldn't," I agreed slowly.

"I don't need handouts. I'm an adult, and I've been paying my own way for months." His cheeks went pink. "That might not sound like much since I was living off my parents for years, but—"

"It is. Rent in the city isn't cheap." Especially not in a neighborhood like Reagan's, on the PR assistant's salary he'd been collecting for the last few weeks. That said a lot about how much he had to be earning from his social media management... just like his prickliness said a lot about how Trent and Patricia had tried to keep him in line.

I reached out and laid a hand on his forearm. "I didn't offer to pay because I think you can't afford it. I offered because you wouldn't need to buy anything if you weren't on this business trip or had been given more than twenty minutes to pack for it. It's only fair that your employer carry the cost." I lifted an eyebrow, hoping he saw a spark of challenge. If he continued to fight me on this, I was not going to be happy.

"Fine." Tension in his jaw belied his easy response.

Reagan got busy with his tablet while tearing into a granola bar. I took another sip of coffee before pulling my phone out to message January about the change of plans. After a few minutes of texting back and forth with her while Reagan chewed savagely, the bus door opened, and McGee climbed aboard in a blast of frigid air.

"Package from corporate," he said, tossing a large vinyl

mailer bag at Reagan. "Laundry will be ready at four. And I got a menu from a cute little sandwich shop around the corner we could try for lunch or dinner." He set a small flyer on the table between the two of us, which was when he must have sensed the tension in the air. Instead of asking what was up, he rolled his eyes, muttered something under his breath that sounded like *"stupid fuckers,"* and closed himself off in his bunk.

Reagan ripped open the vinyl shipping bag with a pleased little "Oh!" and began stacking Elustre garments on the table. I tried to look away, but it was unexpectedly entertaining to watch as he sorted items into piles, apparently based on how much he liked them.

He took out a shirt and sucked in a breath as he stroked the fabric. "Like butter," he murmured to himself. "Hell yeah. I'm stealing this at the end of the trip." Meanwhile, a pair of compression shorts earned a disgruntled expression and a muttered "Ew. Sexy online, garish in person."

"Anything we could wear on the slopes?" I asked.

His face lit up, earlier frustration forgotten. "Yes. In fact, I know exactly what kind of shot I want to get with this piece," he said, putting his hand on a sharp green-and-blue patterned running shirt. "You're going to wear it as a base layer under your other stuff."

As he excitedly tapped notes into his tablet, I let out a slow breath. It had only taken me a few days of a cross-country press tour to learn that seeing Reagan Wellbridge happy improved my own mood exponentially and that the happier he was, the happier I wanted to make him. Like so many things with Reagan, this was easy and natural... and torture.

Thankfully, Reagan finished his breakfast at the same time McGee emerged from his bunk and collected his supplies to begin cleaning the common areas of the bus. Reagan quickly pulled on his coat, exchanged pleasantries with McGee—a too-sympathetic comment about high altitudes being absolute *murder* on skin that showed early signs of aging and a muttered "don't get lost in the snow, kiddo"— and left to find a ski shop. While McGee got to cleaning, I focused on my task list for the morning.

Item one: check in with Layla.

Though I'd spoken to Layla since we left town, so far, I'd managed to keep our contact brief and direct. She had what Reagan called a "raging case of FOMO" from missing out on the tour, so she'd wanted to postmortem every event in detail—who I'd spoken with, what we'd said, how much she wished she could have been there to make some point Reagan and I had missed—but I'd firmly shut this down. For one thing, I'd written up memos about each event and meeting, so further discussion would be a colossal waste of time. For another... I hadn't been feeling particularly warm toward Layla since she'd made those accusations about Reagan, despite her repeated, abject apologies and assurances that it was all a misunderstanding.

This was a perfect example of why this connection with Reagan was such a problem. Being protective was one thing, but allowing it to skew my objectivity and make me side-eye my loyal vice president and friend was another. My goal for this morning was to rectify that.

Layla answered my call on the first ring.

"Thatcher! I was just about to call you." Her voice through the phone speaker was so warm and excited McGee's shoulders tensed, and he gave me an incredulous look that I ignored. "I have *excellent* news."

"I assume it's today's media summary," I said. "Reagan already showed me, and I'm very pleased."

"Well... yes," Layla agreed after a brief hesitation. "*That*, obviously. You've been doing a wonderful job—not surprising since I've known how brilliant you are for decades now, but I do feel terrible that you were thrust into it all on your own." She laughed lightly. "And *that's* the excellent news—you won't have to go it alone anymore! I'm feeling so much better that I'll be flying out in just a few hours to join you for the Vail meeting tomorrow."

"Oh." I tried to sound pleased, told myself that objectively I *was* pleased, though disappointment was a hard jab to my solar plexus. Not only had I looked forward to spending the day tomorrow with Reagan, but I'd let myself forget that his presence on this tour was only meant to be temporary. *Priorities*, I reminded myself. "That's great."

"I expected a *bit* more enthusiasm," she teased. "I'll be taking over a good bit of the socializing for you, after all."

I chuckled half-heartedly. "Obviously, I'm glad you're feeling better. I was concerned about you. I'm just surprised since I hadn't heard that you'd gotten a negative flu test yet."

"Well, I haven't officially. But I've been fever-free for two days, and I'm barely coughing anymore. Besides, the flu test requirement isn't a corporate policy; it's something January came up with, and January works for you," Layla said with certainty. "She'll make an exception if you ask her to."

"I put January in charge of handling this situation with the facilities people, and I make it a habit not to override January unless absolutely necessary," I found myself saying, glad Reagan wasn't around to comment on my abrupt about-face. "She's holding everyone in the office to the same standard, so please confirm you're well by getting a negative flu test before you fly."

"Alright," she agreed. "I'll stop on my way to the airport.

Oh, and when I get to Colorado, I'll fill you in on my strategy for closing Zen Activewear. I spoke to Ron in Sales yesterday, and I'm prepared to negotiate hard with Martinez—"

"Hang on," I interrupted. "Tomorrow's a social event, not a formal meeting. I think it would be more appropriate to treat this like an initial conversation rather than a negotiation."

"Ron and I think it's better to fast-track it. A win like signing Zen would help shift the focus toward the future of Elustre. We desperately need that right now, Thatcher."

Despite my goal of smoothing things over with Layla, I found myself frowning at the phone. "Take a breath. Negotiating from a position of desperation is a bad deal. Besides, media reports about Nova have all but disappeared—"

"Only because Nova's been quiet all week," she broke in. "She's playing a show next weekend, and as soon as she shows her face, the images from New Year's Eve will resurface. Plus... I've gotten an initial report from Nova's people at Rumblefeld Talent Management. Apparently, the shirt she wore just *showed up* in a package with some other articles of Elustre clothing, and they didn't save the packaging. None of the garments were labeled from any fashion brand, so we're no closer to finding out who did this. I'm not suggesting we panic, but we need to keep our momentum going."

"Let's talk specifics when you get here," I said. "You might feel less anxious when you see how we've been running things. As far as I'm concerned, we're well on track, thanks to your team setting up this tour, and our meeting tomorrow will be the cherry on top."

"We'll make sure it is," she agreed. "Oh, before I go, will

Reagan be taking care of his own travel arrangements back to the city, or should I ask my assistant to make them?"

I stretched my neck from side to side and tried not to catch the eyeballs McGee was giving me. "Those arrangements won't be necessary. Reagan's been a true asset, and I'd like him to stay and support the tour. You'll be impressed with his ability to put people at ease and speak eloquently about PennCo and our products without sounding like a sales pitch. And I'd love for the three of us to discuss some future plans for our social media accounts. I'm seeing some good interaction on the content Reagan's put out there already."

There was silence for a few beats. The only sound was McGee's cleaning spray and paper towels swishing over nearby surfaces.

"That's... an option," she said cautiously. "But Thatcher, we can discuss our social media accounts later, and there's no reason to have three people on this tour. I'm more than capable of doing whatever Reagan's been doing for you."

You're really not, I thought as Reagan's teasing smile flashed through my brain.

"Three heads are better than one," I said firmly. "If you're worried about space, don't. There's plenty of room for both of you. If you need additional privacy, you're welcome to take the bedroom, and I can sleep in a bunk."

Her voice was tight but cordial when she responded. "That won't be necessary. Won't be my first time on the company coach. First time we'll be together for this long, though. It'll be nice, won't it?"

The swish of paper towels stopped. McGee's eyes met mine again as his eyebrow ring lifted. I waved him back to his task.

"Layla, I need to go. My next meeting is about to start. Let me know what happens with the flu test," I said before disconnecting the call.

Well, that didn't go as planned, I thought. Followed quickly by, *Please let her still be testing positive.* Which was a horrible thought.

McGee slid into Reagan's empty booth seat and widened his eyes, not even pretending he hadn't heard the entire conversation. "She's intense, Thatcher. Too intense. It's creepy."

"Not creepy," I argued, though his opinion about her intensity confirmed my own. "She's objectively excellent at her job, and I'm fortunate she's part of my team. She might be a bit opinionated, but only because she's dedicated. Enthusiastic."

I wasn't sure which of us I was trying to convince, but McGee wasn't buying it. "Enthusiastic about *you*, maybe. She'd like to be the next Mrs. Pennington."

"Don't be ridiculous. She knows that's not a position I'm looking to fill, ever." It was none of McGee's business, but in an attempt to silence him, I added, "Look, Layla tried to start something once, years ago. I declined, and we both laughed it off. She's not interested in me that way anymore."

"Mmm, sure. The same way you're not interested in the kid?"

It was too much to hope McGee hadn't noticed. With one eyebrow popped, I stared him down. "If Reagan were here, he'd tell you meddling causes fine lines and wrinkles."

McGee grinned unrepentantly and kicked my foot under the table. "You like him. I knew it from, like, minute one, even when you were trying to pretend you didn't. He pissed you off. Got under your skin. But now you like him fine."

I focused on my laptop again. "I like that he's good for business. Because he's my employee."

He kicked me again, harder this time. "You like *him*. And don't give me excuses about being his boss. There's probably five levels of management between you two."

In fact, there were only two managers between us: Layla, as head of the PennCo Fiber subsidiary, and Stephen Price, PennCo's head of PR. In most other Pennington subsidiaries, there would have been more—four or five—but PennCo was small, and Layla liked to be closely involved with her teams. It worked well, so I'd never had reason to give the hierarchy any thought... until the morning after Reagan and I slept together.

"Besides," McGee added, "that shit only matters if you're taking advantage of a power imbalance. As far as I can see, the fact that his dad is well-connected evens the playing field."

"Right. Obviously. Those two *gigantic* complications cancel each other out." I rolled my eyes. "I had no idea I employed a certified relationship expert, McGee. How fortunate I am."

"Hey, I read articles. *Lots* of articles," McGee said loftily. "Aren't you the one who told me education was the path to success back when I was younger?"

"Yes, and I'm sure this was precisely what I had in mind." I waved him off. "Go away. I have a meeting, and you should be catching up on sleep."

"I didn't know if I liked him at first," McGee continued, ignoring me.

I huffed, exasperated. "Yes, so you said the first day. And then he insulted you, and now you're BFFs who communicate *exclusively* through insults. It's a heart-warming story."

"Nah, I mean, I thought he was funny and all, but I could tell you were into him, and you were acting all squirrelly about New Year's Eve. I wasn't sure if I could vibe with the two of you... you know, getting it on. 'Cause that's a whole different thing."

"We're *not*—" I insisted.

"But then, I saw how *he* looked at *you*, and I changed my mind." McGee paused for a long moment while I looked at him expectantly, and then he braced one tattooed hand on the table and pushed himself up. "*Buuuut*... you've got that meeting, so I'm sure you don't want to hear about it."

I opened my mouth. Shut it again. I would regret this. I already regretted it. "How does he look at me?" I demanded.

McGee sat back in his seat and smiled smugly. "Like he's a hungry man and you're one of those disgusting yogurts he keeps in the fridge. Like he wants to eat you alive."

A vivid image of Reagan curling his tongue around his yogurt spoon flashed through my brain, and I squirmed involuntarily. "Nonsense. He's... he's my son's age." Though I didn't know what that had to do with anything.

"Still older than me," McGee reminded me cheerily. "And age is about the only thing he has in common with Brant. Last summer or the summer before, looking at Reagan from a distance, I might have said different. He was kind of a troublemaker, just like I used to be. But I think he's straightened out now. Somebody gave him a chance to do a job, and he gives a shit about it. I feel that." He patted his own chest, then shrugged. "Besides, you said Reagan practically handed you that medical company deal on a silver platter because you let him talk, right? That's not kid stuff."

This was true. The meeting in Colorado Springs

yesterday had been with the owner of a small medical supply company that I'd been trying to acquire. For two years, our lawyers had negotiated terms, but over and over, the owner had killed the deal at the last minute for no discernible reason. Then, at lunch yesterday, Reagan had spent a solid half hour discussing the man's love of floral arranging, charming him with descriptions of Honeybridge's annual Box Day event, and making him howl with laughter over stories of his mother's incessant need to cheat by bringing in flower-box experts to win the grand prize. The signed contracts had been emailed to me last night, along with a sincere thank-you note for "the most delightful business lunch I've ever had."

Still.

"That's all well and good," I said, shaking off the memory of Reagan's contagious smile as he'd described the elaborate small-town festivities. "But it just means I need Reagan to work for me. Not that he and I should..." I cleared my throat. "I do like him. I want to see him succeed and be happy. And you know my track record with relationships. He and I would never work out longterm."

McGee hooted. "Jesus, who said anything about longterm? I meant road trip nookie. I meant hot and heavy backseat hookups. A scenic detour down the orgasm highway. A quick pit stop for a full-service lube job. I meant don't come a'knockin' if the luxury coach is a'rockin'. I meant *sex*," he clarified when I only stared at him in horrified fascination.

"Yes, I got that. Loud and clear." I shook my head, trying to clear the mental images away. "But it's still an epically bad idea. Impossible if Layla's joining us. Besides, I thought you were anti-hookup these days."

"Oh, *me*." McGee waved a hand. "That's because I'm a

sensitive soul, but no one ever sees it beneath my hot-as-fuck tattoos."

I snorted. "And your overwhelming modesty?"

"That, too." He smiled. "All I'm saying is you've got an opportunity here: a guy you want who wants you back. And sure, there are complications, but it doesn't have to *be* complicated if you just stop overthinking. Why deny yourself a little bit of enjoyment? Why deny *him* that?" McGee leaned toward me. "You know what else you taught me when I was a kid? Opportunity knocks, but it doesn't pick locks. You gotta open the door." He winked and slid out of the booth.

As McGee put away his cleaning supplies and went back to his bunk to rest, I signed on to my next call and tried to put his little pep talk out of my mind—to put *Reagan* out of my mind, to focus on my work and my priorities—but it was impossible. When January texted an hour later to say Layla was still positive for flu and would have to delay her trip by at least a day, I gave up trying. I closed my laptop and decided to make the most of my solo time with Reagan while it lasted, starting with our afternoon on the mountain.

Once we were both dressed in the gear Reagan had bought, we took a ride share to the slopes and got fitted for rental equipment. On our way to get in line for the lift, I realized I had no idea how much ski experience he had.

"Are you a Timberline guy, living it up on the logging trail, or do you favor heavier stuff like Widowmaker?"

Reagan wrinkled his nose in thought. "I can definitely hang on Widowmaker, but it wouldn't be pretty. I'd say my sweet spot is a good blue run like Tote Road. What about you, old man?"

"I skied for Cornell," I said, feeling my chest puff up.

He laughed. "Pfft. Isn't that a club team?"

I nodded. "Yes, but it was established in 1932. Do you dare impugn the honor of the Big Red?"

The teasing sparkle in his eyes was brighter than sunlight on snow. "Oh, I dare."

His gorgeous face and exciting company were almost enough to distract me from the fact that I was going to have to get on a ski lift in a moment. In many areas of my life, I could get around my fear of heights, but I hadn't found a work-around for mountains where the only method for getting to the top was ski lifts. Which meant today, I had to white-knuckle it.

But right before we got on the lift, my phone rang, giving me a temporary reprieve.

At least until I checked the caller ID.

"Thalia, what's up?"

At the sound of her name, Reagan veered away from me a little to give me some privacy. It wasn't necessary, but I appreciated the gesture.

"You sound different. Where are you?" Her voice had its usual clipped tone, like she was on her way somewhere and running late.

"Colorado. About to go skiing. Everything okay with Brant?"

"He's fine. I spoke with him a little while ago. He apologized profusely to his stepfather and says he's ready to make amends." She sighed. "Paul offered to give him back his production assistant job at the studio, but... this is it, Thatcher. Last chance. And we've made it very clear to him that our financial support is at an end, too. He can continue to live in our guest house, but beyond that, he needs to take responsibility for himself. I'm sorry if that leaves you carrying the weight, but—"

I closed my eyes briefly. "Don't apologize. I understand." I only wished I had a magic solution for our wayward son. "Now's not a good time for me to talk, but... I'll handle it."

"You sure? He'll be done with his program in about a week, and then you might want to meet up with him to have a conversation. I wish you could find a way to get through to him. He has so much potential, but no matter how much of a boost we try to give him, he can't seem to appreciate the chances he's being given."

"Yeah," I said gruffly. "I'll handle it," I repeated, softening my tone. "I promise."

She blew out a breath. "Thanks, Thatcher. We'll talk soon, okay?"

I ended the call and followed Reagan on autopilot while my brain churned through thoughts about Brantleigh's future and our collective past.

It wasn't until the chair lifted my boots off the ground that I realized we'd even boarded the ski lift. I took a deep breath and held it. The sky was a cloudless blue, and though it was plenty cold, the sun made it feel less bracing than I usually felt while skiing back East. I forced myself to drop my shoulders and pretend everything was fine. "This is nice. Thanks for suggesting it."

"Pretty sure that was you, boss," he said softly, almost as if he was allowing me to stay distracted in my own thoughts.

I glanced over at him and realized that was the opposite of what I wanted. I leaned over and bumped his arm with mine. The water-repellant fabric of our parkas *shushed* together.

"Is there any way we can pretend I'm not your boss today?" I said without thinking. "I mean... I seem to recall you talking smack about my skiing prowess a minute ago. What if we agreed to some kind of... contest?"

"Oh, now you've done it, Thatcher Pennington." He shook his head sadly. "Don't you know better than to challenge a Wellbridge?"

He turned his head to face me, but instead of teasing aquamarine eyes, I saw the reflection of my own face in his sunglasses. I wanted to lift them off his face and fling them hundreds of feet to the snowy ground below. Instead, I clenched my grip on my ski poles.

"I think I can handle it," I told him and said a silent prayer of gratitude that there were no shades covering up his giant, gorgeous grin.

Chapter Nine

Reagan

I WAS desperate to know what Thatcher's ex-wife had called about.

While everything I'd heard about Thalia said she was a better person than his more recent ex, Heather—who had, incomprehensibly, been hooking up with her tennis coach when she could have been fucking Thatcher—Thalia was still someone I significantly side-eyed. How anyone who'd had a chance to settle down with Thatcher Pennington could have given him up was a mystery I'd never solve.

Since it was none of my business, I forced myself not to ask, even though we'd agreed not to be boss/employee today. If we weren't boss and employee, though, then what were we? Friends? Was he back to being my dad's friend? After spending one night in his bed and nearly a week soaking up his presence, every part of my soul rejected that idea.

The sun bore down on us, taking the edge off the frigid temperature this high up. I took a few moments to enjoy the deep blue sky and crystal-clear mountain air while I thought of something impressive and mature to say to the man sitting next to me.

"Did you ever think about having kids?" Thatcher asked after several beats of awkward silence.

I swiveled my head to stare at him in shocked disbelief, and his body shook with deep, rumbling laughter.

"Sorry, sorry," he said. "God, the look on your face. I didn't mean it the way it sounded. I, ah... Thalia called to talk to me about Brant, and I... never mind."

Thatcher sounded uncharacteristically unsure of himself, which got my attention more sharply than the brisk air on my face. I rubbed my lips together, considering. "I've never given much thought to children one way or the other. The question's never come up." I shrugged. "But then... Brantleigh's not really a kid, is he?"

"No," Thatcher agreed a bit sadly. "He's not."

"If you want to talk," I offered, "I could listen."

But Thatcher was silent for so long I decided he was trying to come up with a way to politely turn me down, and I felt stupid for offering. Thatcher probably saw me as being not much different from Brantleigh, after all.

"Sorry," I muttered, leaning away from him toward the side of the chair to peer over to the pristine snow below. Suddenly, Thatcher's gloved hand shot out and grabbed my arm, nearly scaring me out of my seat. If his ski pole tether hadn't been looped around his wrist, it would have dropped to the ground far below.

"Don't get too close to the edge!"

I turned to stare at him. The sound of sheer terror was something I'd never heard in his voice before.

"Thatcher," I said calmly. "There's a safety bar. I'm not going anywhere."

The blood had drained from his face, and his grip stayed tight on my arm. The ramp to disembark was quickly approaching. I moved my hand over and held his, removing it from my arm. "Hey. *Hey*. It's okay," I said softly. "Take a breath."

He shuddered and cleared his throat, pulling his hand out of mine and nodding his head. I could tell he was trying his hardest to pretend it had never happened. He gripped the safety bar in front of us like it was the only thing keeping us from plummeting to our deaths. Was he scared of heights the same way he was scared of flying? Were the two things related?

When we reached the off-load ramp, we lifted the bar and skied off the lift, stopping when we got to the flat area at the top of several runs.

"What trail do you want to start on?" he asked, not meeting my eyes.

I tossed my poles down on the ground and then took his off his wrists to do the same. I grabbed his shoulders and duck-walked until my skis bracketed his and we were face-to-face. "Talk to me."

"I'm fine."

I bit back an affectionate smile. It was rare to see the tender underbelly of a man as strong as Thatcher Pennington, but god, he was adorable. "You're scared of heights."

"It's a common fear."

The sun slanted across the pristine surface of his high-tech ski parka, making the dark blue look almost purple and the silver accents throw speckles across my vision. "Your reaction is a little more intense than the standard fear of heights. Babe... you're pale as a ghost."

I didn't know if it was his anxiety or the casual endearment that got to him, but he let out a shuddering breath and brought his hands up to grasp my hips.

Then, before I could adequately prepare my racing heart, he pulled me closer until I slid into his body with a thud of parka padding between us. His arms banded around me, and I flailed only a little before my arms locked around him, too.

Holy shit.

Brightly attired skiers streamed past us on their way to the various runs, but I barely noticed. I was entirely focused on the man in my arms. The man who trusted me... enough to let me see this rare moment of vulnerability. I vowed to myself that I would claw out the eyes of anyone who approached us for any reason.

"Talk to me," I murmured. "Please."

"I will. But not now, okay?" His words were low against my ear. The warm breath from his cold lips tickled my skin.

I must have made some kind of noise of agreement because he murmured a thanks before releasing me.

Our eyes met, and... *god.* My lips were desperate for his. The hunger in my gut clawed at me to lean forward and take his mouth in mine, but his skin still held the pallor of real fear.

I yanked off my gloves and dropped them on the ground before taking his face in my hands and forcing Thatcher to meet my eyes. "Today," I insisted. "You'll tell me today."

His eyes stayed hidden behind his sunglasses, but I could see the laugh lines quirk around the edges, like he enjoyed me being bossy and demanding. "Yes. Today. I promise."

I leaned in and pressed a kiss to his cheek, inhaling the familiar woodsmoke and sage scent that clung to his skin. Then I pulled away, pushed back from him, and picked up our gear before yanking on my gloves. "We'll start on Spring Dipper," I said, nodding toward an intermediate trail to our left. "There's a small section of moguls near the end if you insist on a *prowess* contest. Otherwise, smooth sailing to the bottom."

Thatcher's steel gaze followed me as I moved away from him toward the top of the trail. The taste of his skin remained on my lips, and I tucked them together to keep it there as long as possible.

We pointed our skis down the run without saying a word. Unlike the last time I'd skied, back in Vermont, there was no crust of ice on top of the powder, and I relished the soft sounds of my skis cutting through it. The sun warmed my back as the winter air froze my face. My muscles loosened with every turn and filled my lungs to capacity before exhaling and allowing the stress to melt away.

Thatcher skied silently a few yards away, taking long, graceful turns down the wide slope. His muscular thighs looked amazing in the slim-fitting ski pants I'd bought him, and his shoulders looked even broader in the parka. At one point, I was so busy drooling over his form I nearly crashed into another skier to my left. After that, I forced myself to keep my eyes on the slope with only a few glances over to make sure he was still with me.

Thatcher's silence lasted all the way to the bottom. With unspoken agreement, we'd stayed on the smooth trail instead of tackling the moguls. At the end of the run, we moved wordlessly to the ski lift line, and this time when we loaded, we ended up sitting much closer together. Thatcher transferred one of his ski poles to the other hand, removed his glove before shoving it in a pocket, and reached for my hand.

I wasn't sure if this was to ensure my safety or express some kind of affection, but I wasn't complaining either way. His hand was warm in mine, and his thumb stroked my skin softly.

"Brantleigh fell over a cliff when he was four."

I turned to stare at him. His words made no sense. "He... he fell off a cliff? *How?* Where?" What I really meant was, *how the hell did he survive?*

"Hawaii. Our family Christmas vacation. It was one of the rare times Thalia and I had agreed on a place to go. We'd both wanted to have a quiet holiday, just the three of us. At least, I thought so. But when we arrived, it turned out she'd invited a bunch of her friends to stay at the same place. So, I spent my time with Brant. And it was *fun*." He smiled out at the blinding snow like he was seeing some long-ago tropical scene imprinted there. "He was a ball of energy back then. Exploring in the surf, swimming in the pool, running along the beach, finding a ball and kicking it in the grass. And I... well, I secretly enjoyed the excuse to avoid Thalia and her friends. One day, the hotel concierge suggested a hike and said it was easy enough for Brant. It sounded like a great chance to tire out my little boy while getting to see a different part of the island."

His hand had pulled mine into his lap so he could hold it between both of his. Both ski poles tangled by their tethers on his far side.

"On the trail, Brant raced back and forth ahead of me, babbling nonstop. He'd run ahead, then run back and grab my hand so I could come see whatever cool thing he found. And I told him, 'Stay where I can see you, remember? Don't get lost,' but I wasn't worried, really. The trail was easy. No more dangerous than the walking trails at the park." He sucked in a breath. "Until you got to the waterfall."

"What?" I demanded.

"Yeah. I don't know if the concierge assumed that everyone knew Liliha was a famous cliff-diving waterfall or if he mentioned it and I was too busy chasing Brant around the lobby to hear him." He shrugged. "All I remember is hearing a woman's scream a few beats after Brant raced out of my sight around a curve in the trail."

"Oh god," I murmured, holding my breath in fear, even though I knew Brant had survived.

He nodded. "As I raced around the corner to see who was in need of help, I saw a woman standing at the edge of a cliff. It was the top edge of the waterfall. Brant had apparently run ahead and slipped over the edge right in front of her. I remember my body shaking, my head swimming, the blood roaring in my ears as I neared the edge. I leaned out to find him, expecting the broken body of my beautiful baby boy on the rocks below. But instead, he was in the water. There was a giant pool at the bottom full of swimmers, and several people were racing through the blue water to reach his tiny body."

I felt the clammy hand in mine, the slight tremble. I wanted to pull him into my arms and wrap my entire body around his. I couldn't even imagine the terror of a parent in that situation. "What happened next?"

"I flung myself off the edge—shoes, backpack, and all. I did it without thinking, just to get to him as fast as possible. The free fall felt like it lasted a lifetime. Hours of knowing he was probably inhaling water or sinking or at the very least trying to keep his head above water and crying for his daddy." He took a breath. "I found out later the distance of that cliff dive is forty feet, as high as a four-story building. I hit the water hard enough to knock the wind out of me. I still don't know how I managed to make it to the bank with Brantleigh in my arms, and I definitely don't know how he survived hitting that water at such speed. His little body was shivering with cold and shock by the time I got to him. Thankfully, one of the swimmers had been a lifeguard and had training. Brant didn't need resuscitating, but the woman helped make sure he didn't aspirate the water coming up, and she managed to organize people around us to get towels and stuff to warm him up."

His chin wobbled as he spoke, and my heart wanted to break. I'd known he loved Brantleigh, of course, but I hadn't seen the depth of that love until now. Thatcher's vaunted confidence and self-control had blown away in the mountain air like a puff of powdery snow from our ski tips.

"I carried him out. Four miles, one up to the top and three back to the trailhead, where emergency services were waiting. Thalia met us at the hospital. He was hurt—broken leg, broken wrist. I'd *let* him get hurt."

"Thatcher," I whispered. "You didn't *let* him."

"You can say that. I can see, logically, how you might even be right. But that's not how parenthood works. You think you've figured life out, more or less, then they put this tiny baby in your arms, and you realize you don't know *anything*. You love them so much. And you think, I'm going to do this differently. I'm going to make this kid's life so much better than mine. I'm not going to push him to succeed the way I was pushed. I'm going to make sure he knows he's loved whether he wins or loses. I'm going to make his life so damn easy. I'm going to keep him perfectly safe. But then..." He stared down at our joined hands.

"You can't." I shifted carefully on the chair so I could look up into his face. "I mean, not *you*. No one can."

Thatcher nodded, looking as troubled as if Brantleigh had fallen hours ago rather than decades, and looked off in the distance, where colorful parkas floated down white ski slopes. "Doesn't mean you don't try, though. Or that you don't feel guilty when you fail. After Brant's accident... it was a dark time. I realized I had no business raising a kid. Thalia agreed," he added with a ghost of a smile. "Things between us were already bad, but there was no coming back from that. She moved to California with Brant."

"You didn't fight for custody," I murmured, pieces fitting into place.

"Hell no." Thatcher scowled. "I wouldn't have him flying across the country every week or two. He needed stability. And he had Thalia."

And who did you have? I wanted to ask, but I already knew. He'd had Pennington Industries. His company. His work.

"That's bullshit," I proclaimed.

He turned that scowl in my direction.

"Would you have blamed Thalia if he'd fallen on her watch?" I demanded. "Maybe, for a while, but you would have gotten over it. Continuing to blame yourself is ridiculous martyr-level bullshit, Thatcher. Every parent makes mistakes. I mean, obviously, I've never been on the parent side of it, but from the kid side?" I snorted. "I fell off a hotel bed when I was a newborn and bumped my head on the wall. My mother had set me in the middle of the bed while she blow-dried her hair. Should she have lost custody of me?"

"Of course not. But that's hardly the same—"

"Isn't it? Weren't you the one who said I can't hold myself to a standard of perfection... or something like that?" I added, as though I didn't remember every second of that conversation in the hallway of the Newport Grille.

"It's different when it's your child," he insisted.

I lifted one shoulder. Maybe it was. What did I know? I shifted back to the reason he'd begun this story. "You've been afraid of heights since then?" I asked gently. "But...

how does that work? Your office is on the top floor. And don't you live in a penthouse?"

"Yeah. When there's something solid beneath my feet and a wall around me, it doesn't bother me." His voice was gravelly. Broken. "But when I get on a ski lift or, god, an *airplane*, I feel like I'm in free fall with nothing under me. Pretty sure that's one reason Thalia decided to move to California. It cut way down on the number of times I'd simply turn up to visit. I still forced myself to do it four times a year, but it was—*is*—a fucking nightmare. I have to plan ahead. Take meds to knock myself out, which make me sick afterward. A full recovery day after each flight. And nothing helps," he added before I could ask. "I've tried therapy. Many times."

I thought of the years he must have carried this guilt, the impact it had made on Brant's upbringing, and the impact on Thatcher himself. He'd told Chris in that interview that Pennington was and continued to be his top priority. But the company couldn't love him back. And if I'd ever met anyone who deserved to be loved, to be appreciated for all that he was, it was Thatcher.

As the chairlift rumbled through a transfer point, the seat swayed a little. I watched Thatcher closely. He gripped my hands tighter but kept his cool. "You're able to ride this lift," I said. "That's something."

He huffed out an unsteady laugh. "Only because I want to make you happy."

Such a simple sentence, but it slingshot my heart around my chest cavity like a ping-pong ball. "Me?"

Thatcher's hand released mine and reached out to tug my beanie down over my ear before running a thumb along my cheek. "You."

It was the only word he spoke, but the look in his eyes

said much more. I stared at him. Was the pull between us all in my imagination? Was I the only one tumbling helplessly toward the other? He crowded my waking thoughts and made me want things I'd never truly craved before.

Like a partner in crime. Someone to share this rollercoaster life with.

The rumble of another transfer point snapped me out of my delirium. I'd wanted to lean forward and taste the winter air on his lips. Instead, I murmured my thanks and turned to look out at the trees covered in snow, simply enjoying his presence by my side without doing anything to mess things up between us. I enjoyed his companionship, and for now... that was enough.

THE FOLLOWING DAY WAS A WHIRLWIND. I'd met several pro athletes through my parents, which meant I wasn't nervous or intimidated in a room full of hot, fit millionaires.

But I was jealous as hell.

Thatcher wasn't just sexy to me; he was sexy full stop. The man gave off toppy silver-fox vibes in a way that caught many pairs of eyes in any room he entered. Half the ball players' wives eyed him up and down, and even a couple of the men there gave him a second look when they thought no one was watching.

They weren't alone. All day long, I couldn't keep my eyes off him. He spoke with authority on topics ranging from long-term real estate investments to complex global trade agreements. Hell, even children and animals seemed drawn to him. At one point, I caught him laughing at a story the Martinezes' young son was telling him about his winning science fair experiment, while Thatcher sat pinned under the weight of their incredibly pudgy cat, who'd sprawled on his lap. When Thatcher caught me staring, he looked over the boy's shoulder and winked at me.

My stomach tightened, and my inner slut whimpered. Instead of asking if I could sit on his lap, I busied myself in the kitchen, fetching another beer.

It wasn't until later that evening, after several hours with the group on the slopes and then a long dinner full of sports gossip and a dessert course full of whiskey tasting flights, that I realized I was losing my ability to keep my feelings for Thatcher hidden behind any kind of poker face.

"I'm going to head back to the bus," I said to him as I pushed my chair back from the long dining table. The two of us had stayed at the table with Maya and her husband, Dom, long after everyone else had scattered around the living room to watch a late football game on the large-screen TV. Cheers and jeers had erupted periodically as Maya and Dom discussed Elustre and PennCo Fiber with Thatcher, but once the nanny had appeared to let Maya and Dom know one of their kids was asking for a late good-night kiss, they'd gotten up with their apologies and headed out of the room.

As I moved away from the table, Thatcher caught my wrist. I turned to blink at him. My reflexes were sluggish from the alcohol and the seeping warmth from his grip.

"Today was a good day," he said.

"Yeah. A really good day," I murmured.

But then, yesterday had been, too. And the day before. And the day before that.

Every day of this damn trip that I'd thought would be a catastrophe had been incredible, and even the low points had been better with Thatcher there. But the closer we'd gotten, the more we'd talked and shared, the harder it was to remember why I needed to keep my distance. Why I should bother being professional.

Thatcher might still technically be my boss, was still my father's friend, but he was *mine* now, too, and it was getting harder not to show it.

Especially when I was tired and a little bit drunk.

His thumb stroked the skin of my wrist while his eyes stayed on mine. "You sure you don't want to take Maya up on her offer of a bedroom? You'd be more comfortable in a real bed."

The Martinezes' huge house was already full of guests. They'd only had one extra bedroom to offer us, but they'd been able to offer McGee a nice parking spot with electricity hookup next to one of the detached garages on the property.

"No," I said, shaking my head unnecessarily. "I don't mind the bus." Honestly, I preferred the bus at this point because it was just for us. On the bus, I was able to stay closer to Thatcher, almost like sharing a suite in a hotel instead of being in separate rooms.

"Want me to come with you?"

I knew he'd promised Dom and a few of the other guys he'd watch some of the game with them after dinner. He'd been having a good time with everyone, and I didn't want to be the cause of his cutting the night short.

I shook my head again and gave him a reassuring smile. "Nah. Stay and have fun. I'm going to crash. All this fresh air at altitude has worn me out. And the whiskey flight didn't help."

It wasn't a lie, but Thatcher kept his eyes on me a few extra beats as if testing the truth of it.

"If you're sure."

He released me, and I made my way to the living room,

waving a quick but hazy goodbye to several of the people I'd talked to during the day. I knew I'd have the opportunity to thank Maya and Dom in the morning before leaving, so I didn't bother waiting for them to return from wherever they'd gone to check on their kid.

The cold air outside woke me up a bit but didn't sober me up much. When I wove my way down the driveway and knocked on the bus door, McGee was laughing. "Need help?"

"Never try to keep up with pro ballers when they're tasting fancy whiskey," I muttered, kicking bits of snow off my shoes before stepping up into the bus.

He closed the door behind me and followed me back to the kitchen area, fussing at me about storing my coat and shoes before dripping all over his floors. When I was finally in my socks and had grabbed a bottle of water from the fridge, I threw myself down in one of the recliner seats.

"Hey, kid." McGee took the seat next to mine and turned to face me. "How'd it go with the Martinezes?"

"Good. Maya loved the samples and is going to put Thatcher in touch with... whatever the name was of the... whoever... needs to..." I wasn't all that in touch with my memory at the moment.

McGee laughed softly. "Good to know. Where's the boss?"

I thumbed over my shoulder in the wrong direction. "Still there. Mr. Popular with the ball boys."

"Okayyy," he said with a chuckle.

"Baseballers. Pro ballers. The guys on the team. The Boise Thunderclap."

"Thunderbolts," McGee corrected.

I waved my hand dismissively. "Whatever. They all want him. Or their wives do. Or I do. All of them."

McGee looked at me funny, but I didn't realize what I'd said to give him such a strange reaction. "Did you have a nice time?"

"Mmhm. Good skiing. Good food. Good company. Good prospect with the Zen yoga line. Thatcher was great with them. Got them to agree to an official proposal."

"He said you've been a big help on this trip with the business side. He likes having you here."

I picked at the label on the water bottle. "I like being here. Being with him. I mean... *working* with him. Learning from him has been... an honor."

"Uh-huh." McGee slouched into his seat. "So why'd you come back early? I figured you'd stay and drink with all those guys."

"Pfft. They were drinking me under the table hours ago. If I'd stayed any longer, I would have..." I snapped my teeth closed and made a grunting sound of annoyance at myself for almost saying too much to Thatcher's... whatever it was McGee was to the man.

McGee studied me. "You know, you're not who I thought you were."

"Gorgeous, witty, and charming? Of course I am," I said loftily. "And my skincare recommendations have done wonders for you."

He grinned. "I thought you were a spoiled smart-ass."

"Oh, well." I waved a hand in agreement. "That too. For sure, that too."

McGee laughed. "Maybe. But you're also good at what you do. You're respectful and kind. You learn from your mistakes. You don't treat me like shit, even though I'm the bus driver."

"Please." I rolled my eyes. "You're not *just* the bus driver. You're like... Thatcher's second son. If Thatcher were younger—and larger, and tatted, and pierced... you know, looked like you—you'd be exactly alike." I paused and stared at him blearily. "That made more sense in my head."

"Holy shit." His smile grew comically large. "If I didn't like you before, I would now. You need to drink at altitude more often, son."

I snorted.

"You know how me and Thatcher met?" he asked.

I shook my head and tried not to look too curious, even though I was desperate to hear it.

He pulled up a foot on the edge of his chair and tucked it under his other leg, settling in. His tattoos shifted in and out of the shadows coming from the dim kitchenette lights nearby.

"When I was a teenager, my mom used to work nights cleaning offices, including Thatcher's. His big-ass office at Pennington Industries HQ. You ever been there?"

I shook my head.

"Well, lemme tell you, it's huge. Way fancier than the apartment my mom and I had at the time. Used to make me angry that she had to clean for a bunch of rich pricks. But then, everything made me angry back then." He rolled his eyes. "I didn't like where I was. Had no plan for the future. I was two hundred pounds of attitude in a hundred-forty-pound sack. So I used to get in fights." His pierced eyebrow quirked. "A lot."

"You shock me. You're literally shocking me right now, McGee."

"Shush." He kicked my leg with one booted foot. "I'm talking now. Where was I? Oh, right. So one time, I got suspended from school for fighting in the cafeteria. My poor mom." He shook his head with genuine regret. "She felt guilty because she was a single mom, like *my* shit was *her* fault. She thought maybe a dad in the picture would have made a difference—"

I scoffed at the idea that a dad was calming magic on a boy's upbringing.

McGee snorted his agreement. "Right? Anyway, Thatcher found her crying in the hall outside his office one night, and he... he offered to help. Brought me to his big, fancy office. And I was shitting myself, I promise you, but all cocky, too, you know?"

"Yeahhhhh. Been there," I admitted.

"So I told him, right off, he had no idea what it was like to be me. I *had* to fight. And I wasn't gonna stop because some rich asshole told me to."

"Ooooooh," I said, faking a shiver. "So badass."

McGee laughed again and pointed one tattooed finger at me. "Like you've never pretended to be bigger and badder than you are?"

"Perhaps once or twice." Or every damn day. "Go on."

"Well, it turned out Thatcher didn't want me to stop fighting." McGee chuckled at my skeptical look. "Seriously. He offered me martial arts classes instead. Which, like, looking back, is the lamest, cheesiest thing. Probably got the idea from Dealing With Asshole Children for Dummies or something. But... I did it. And I hated it at first, but I was just guilty enough about my mom that I agreed to do it for a couple weeks, and honestly, part of me just wanted to screw him out of his money." He let out a soft laugh. "Rich asshole wants to come in and save me? Pfft. Fine. Let him waste his coin. I didn't realize at the time it was pocket change to him. And I didn't realize it wouldn't be a waste." He rubbed a hand over his mouth. "Turned out I was good at it. So good I started competing. Won competitions. Moved up. Tried different styles. Even became a teacher, part-time, for a little while, before I started working for Thatcher full-time." He met my eyes. "Thatcher Pennington saved my life. Not even being dramatic."

I nodded, enthralled.

"If he hadn't intervened, I'd have been on a fast track to nowhere. I'd already done some petty shit I never got caught for, but the kid I was then, the crew I hung with who were even angrier and more directionless than I was? Shit, I would have gone all in with that stuff. I know it as sure as I'm sitting here." He rapped the table with his big hand. "Might even have started with the hard drugs, ended up in a cell or on a slab like a couple of those guys did." McGee's jaw tightened. "Instead, I had Thatcher giving me jobs so I could earn money, then standing with my mom at my high school graduation. He's the best guy I know."

"Wow." My chest tightened. Thatcher *did* have people in his life who loved him, who saw him, and it helped to know that. "Did you ever tell him this?"

"Sure. Sorta. Got real emotional right after my graduation and tried to thank him for helping me. You know what he told me?"

Thoughts of Thatcher's guilt and regrets over his own son tumbled through my whiskey-soaked brain. I shook my head.

"He said sometimes the thing people think is your weakness can be your greatest strength. That maybe I needed to fight and I was just picking the *wrong* fights."

There was a good point in there somewhere, but I was too tired and drunk to sort it out. "God, he's such a good man. And you're lucky to have him, but he's lucky to have you, too, you know? He deserves to have people who care about him and are loyal to him. Who *love* him—" I swallowed hard.

"Hooo, boy." McGee shook his head. "I knew you were drunk, but you are *drunk*." He smiled, maybe a bit too sympathetically. "Or else you've got some powerful emotions going on. Anything you'd like to share?"

"God, no."

"You sure? You wouldn't be the first young man in the throes of capital-F Feelings I've counseled," he said solemnly, though his eyes twinkled. "Not even the first this week. I've never suffered from that particular affliction myself, but I'm an understanding listener."

I rolled my eyes. "Right. So I'm sure you'll *understand* when I say that I hope a case of capital-F Feelings smacks you in the face someday."

McGee laughed out loud, but my face heated with embarrassment. I stood up to escape to my bunk. "I think you're right. I'm even drunker than I thought," I muttered. "Sincerely, thanks for the talk, but, um... good night."

McGee stretched out his legs before standing and looked at me for a long, long moment. Finally, he said, "Why don't you use the bedroom in the back? I'll have Thatcher take a bunk when he comes in, or he can take a room in the Martinezes' house. He said they'd offered you guys one."

I snorted. "Take my boss's bed? Has that moisturizing serum I gave you gone to your brain?" I demanded. "Hell no."

"Hell yes. You're wobbly as fuck, and that bunk is narrow. If you fall out of it, it'll be a whole liability thing. Take the bed," he repeated. "Thatcher will sleep in the house."

"What about you? You could take it."

He shook his head. "I'm heading out in a little while. An

old friend's picking me up, and we're gonna hang out at his place in Eagle. It's all yours."

There was a flaw in this plan somewhere, but I couldn't quite reason it out. There really wasn't any point in wasting the large bed if Thatcher was going to sleep in the house. And by the time I made my way to Thatcher's room, stripped down to my undershirt and boxer briefs, and really stretched out in a bed for the first time in a week, I decided I was too tired to worry about it. I grinned dopily at the neatly stacked books and the reading glasses on the side table as I turned out the light, and then I rolled up in the blanket, shoved Thatcher's pillow over my head, and fell asleep wrapped in woodsmoke and sage.

Chapter Ten

Thatcher

After Reagan left the house, I couldn't focus.

The game was in full swing on the enormous television, and the remaining few guests were talking and laughing, but I didn't care. Whatever I was drinking tasted flat on my tongue, and the entire room seemed less bright than before.

When there was a break in the action on screen, I pushed myself off the sofa. "I'm going to head out," I told Don and Maya, who were curled up in an easy chair. "Thanks again for a great day."

Maya grinned without getting up. "Thanks for coming. I was intrigued by the idea of working with PennCo before, but I'm even more eager now. You and Reagan made quite an impression."

"I'm glad to hear that."

"Still have that extra bedroom upstairs," Don reminded me. "You're welcome to it."

I shook my head. "Thanks anyway, but we have to get on the road early. I've got a vendor in Omaha I'm meeting up with next. If I'm asleep on the bus, McGee can simply start driving."

After thanking our hosts again profusely, I slipped out the front door and made my way across the snow-dusted driveway to the welcoming warmth of the bus. McGee was just shrugging on a coat.

"Gotta go, boss. My friend's waiting for me down the driveway. I'll be back around six, and we'll get on the road," he said softly.

I'd forgotten his plans to watch a pay-per-view fight with a friend nearby, but I was glad he was getting out to have some fun. After watching him jog off the bus, I closed the door behind him and made my way to the back, pointedly ignoring Reagan's bunk on my way past it.

The man had been tempting me for days, and I'd managed to stand firm. But after our time on the mountain yesterday pretending I *wasn't* his boss, after I'd told him things I'd never spoken aloud to anyone else and he'd given me kindness and compassion in return, I'd felt the barriers I'd tried to erect between us crumbling, one after another. Tonight, buzzed and tired and riding the high of an excellent day, I had no defenses left at all.

My room was still and quiet. Only the low hum of the bus's electrical system filled the small space around me. The scent of Reagan's aftershave was faint, but it reached me, even in here. Or maybe it was simply imprinted in my nose after so much time spent together. Like I carried him with me everywhere now.

I walked to the opposite side of the room and slid between the sheets with a grateful groan, then turned on my side to stretch one arm out under the opposite pillow... and encountered warm, firm muscle.

I opened my eyes and squinted through the darkness. From this close, the scent of his faded aftershave was clearer, and I could just make out the outline of his messy, sun-kissed hair and prominent chin.

The breath punched out of me. *Reagan.*

I stared at him, begging my eyes to do a better job of seeing in the darkness.

"Th-thatcher?" His voice was a sleep-rough whisper, but he managed to lever up on one elbow. "Hey. You want your bed back?"

I sucked in a breath and felt the last barrier crumble. "No," I breathed, moving closer and reaching out to cup his cheek, feeling the prickle of stubble along my palm. "That's not what I want."

He turned his face toward me as I inched closer. I'd had just enough alcohol and sleep deprivation to pretend this one night—like our last *one* night—wouldn't count. That I could have him here like this, naked and willing, sleepy and submissive, and we could go back to our easy routine in the morning.

Reagan made a small noise in his throat. A noise of need, of desire, of confusion... I wasn't sure. I only knew that it carried with it barbed hooks that dug deep into my solar plexus and reeled me inevitably closer to him.

"Let me have you," I murmured, afraid speaking at full volume might awaken him enough to push me away.

"Yes." The sound was deep and hoarse. It carried through my chest and down to my balls. I closed the remaining distance between us and finally, *finally*, took his mouth in mine.

The taste of him brought exquisite relief and immense excitement. The combination made me feel an even stronger buzz than the one I'd entered the bus with. Reagan was sleepy-soft and pliant under my hands. I shoved the covers down and found the hem of his T-shirt before rucking it up to run my hand along his abs and chest.

His skin was warm, and the hair on his chest brushed softly against my fingertips. The skin around his nipples puckered when the air hit it, or maybe it was my touch that set them off. He let out a sound of pleasure, and I swallowed it down, hungry for more of his lips and tongue.

His hands forked into my hair, pulling me closer until I was practically on top of him. As soon as I felt the hard ridge of his erection against my hip, I couldn't pretend politeness anymore. I was too desperate for him, too frantic with the need to bury myself in his body.

"Clothes off," I said, pulling away enough to strip my own underwear off and toss them over the side of the bed. Reagan must have done the same because when I leaned back over him, he was blessedly bare, displaying all that tanned skin and the wickedly sexy tattoo I'd been dying to see again. "C'mere."

I kissed him again, reaching down with a hand to stroke his cock. He was hot and hard against my palm. His hands clasped my shoulders before moving down my back in firm strokes until he grabbed my ass and squeezed. "Fuck me."

It was a plea. One I was happy to grant. I pulled off his mouth only to clarify his consent. "You sure?"

"Fucking fuck, Thatcher."

I leaned over to fumble in the bedside drawer for the lube I kept there for solo use. "Do I need a condom, sweetheart?"

He didn't respond. When I turned back with the lube, I could see his eyes wide and bright in the moonlight cutting through a gap in the shades. "No," he said softly. "On PrEP. You?"

"Negative. Haven't been with anyone like that in a long while."

"Really?" he asked, seemingly incredulous.

"Well," I drawled, leaning back in to nose his jaw over so I could suck a spot on his neck. "There was this one guy at New Year's..."

"Was he hot?" he asked while sucking in a breath.

"So fucking hot. He talked back. Sassy little thing. Not polite at all." I sucked another spot, then another. "But good in bed. You know the type?"

The low vibration of his laugh made me grin against his skin. "Sounds like a brat."

"Yes. Definitely a brat," I agreed. "But it seems to work for me."

This made him laugh more, and I wondered if I would ever hear that sound and not feel a tiny firecracker go off in my gut.

I grabbed his wrists and moved them above his head while I shifted my weight to kneel on either side of him. My mouth moved down to his collarbone. As I settled above him, our cocks pressed together. His laugh turned into a groan, so I pressed even harder.

"Want that cock inside me," he said before yanking a hand out of my grip and moving it between us to grasp my shaft.

"Fuck," I hissed, arching up into his fist. "You make me fucking crazy. Don't stop."

It wasn't easy fumbling the lube open while his hand was on me, but I managed to slick up my fingers and reach between his legs, shoving one of his thighs wide so I could reach his hole. "Let go, or I'm going to come."

Reagan released his hold on me before grabbing his

knee and pulling it back, opening himself up to me. "Wanted this for so long."

The words were so low I wasn't sure he'd meant for me to hear them, but they wound around my chest and pulled tight. Did he mean he'd wanted me since New Year's? Or, like me, had he felt this long before then?

"Those fucking eyes of yours," I muttered, remembering the way they'd tracked over me last summer, bright Caribbean blue in the sunshine. "They kill me." It was too dark now to see them properly, but the vivid color was seared into my brain.

I leaned in to bite his lip and swallow his gasp. "Tell me what you want," I growled to distract myself from the tight stretch of his channel around my fingers. Even imagining myself inside him made my heart thunder and blood roar in my ears.

His glassy eyes met mine. "To be close to you."

My stomach lurched. I lunged forward again and slammed my lips on his, taking complete possession of his mouth while I continued to fuck him with my fingers. The noises he made fueled the need in my gut, and within seconds, I was slicking up my cock to press against his hole.

"Legs back," I grunted. He grabbed his knees and held them wide. "Good. Stay still. Just like that. Breathe."

As I entered Reagan's body, I wondered if I'd ever felt this combination of fear, excitement, anticipation, and homecoming. This young man was brave and brazen, snarky and opinionated beneath his manners and charm, transparent as cut glass to me. I saw his vulnerabilities and wanted to give him the safe haven and purpose he seemed to need so badly.

"*Nghh.*" Reagan's eyes slid closed, and his mouth opened as his body stretched around me. He was hot and tight. My head spun with the effort not to slam into him and take what I wanted as fast and hard as I could. I knew he was bisexual, but I didn't know how much experience he had with men. The last thing I wanted to do was hurt him. "More," he urged in a lazy slur. "God, please."

I pulled back and pressed forward again, repeating the process until I was as deep inside him as possible. I leaned down to kiss him. "Okay?"

"*Mmm.*"

"You feel so fucking good. I've wanted you like this. Imagined being inside you, fucking you, touching you. Kissing you."

"*Thatcher.*"

I continued to thrust in and out of him. "Do you have any idea how hard it is to sit across from you each day and pretend I don't want to tear your fucking clothes off and make you mine all over this damned bus? Do you?"

His eyes opened wide, the whites visible in the darkness. "Yeah?"

I wasn't quite sure if it was agreement or a question, but I nodded and nipped his jaw and throat. "You're so fucking sexy. I want you every minute of every fucking day. Can't fucking keep my hands off you one minute more."

His lips turned up, and his hands reached for the back of my head, drawing my face back up to kiss him on the mouth again. "Tell me," he begged against my lips.

I hesitated. Reagan's fingers tightened in my hair. "I..."

"Don't you dare say you shouldn't," he said fiercely. "Don't you dare tell me you'll regret this tomorrow."

"No. Never."

He let out a cry as I pounded into him harder. His head went back, and I took the opportunity to suck on his Adam's apple while reaching down to stroke his cock. I was close, so close, and I needed him to come before I lost control.

Reagan's words came out between gasping breaths. "Tell me this won't be the last time. I can't... I don't..."

"Not the last. I can't stay away from you anymore." Even if I knew better, even if it was the wrong thing to do, I knew there was no way this could possibly be the last time I'd feel this way with Reagan Wellbridge.

He exhaled before sucking in another breath. "Fuck. Gonna come."

The words choked out in his broken breath were all it took to trigger my own release. Hot fluid hit my hand as white stars exploded in my head. I released deep inside of him while the sounds of his own cries filled the space around us.

After a few moments, I reluctantly pulled out of him and moved my weight over to lie beside him, keeping a hand on his heaving chest to feel the rapid thump of his heart. Reagan covered my hand with his to hold it there.

"I'm staying here tonight," he said softly but defiantly.

"Yes."

"And I'm staying here tomorrow night, too."

"Yes," I answered before remembering a slight problem with that plan. "But Layla—"

Reagan turned and slapped a hand over my mouth. "Ew. We are not talking about Layla. Not in this room. Don't ruin my glow."

I huffed out a laugh against his warm hand before kissing his palm. "Okay."

"Good," he said, relaxing back onto the pillow. "We'll figure something out."

"Okay," I repeated. It was a word I imagined saying to him over and over again if given the chance.

"Thank you," he murmured. "Now, be a good boy and fetch me a washcloth or something. I have spunk all over me, and it's mostly your fault."

I snorted. I enjoyed his prickles, his teasing nearly as much as I liked it when he showed me glimpses of the vulnerability beneath. Knowing him well enough to see his various defense mechanisms felt like a gift. One I wanted to enjoy for as long as I could.

I got up and went to the tiny bathroom to do as he asked. When I came back and began to clean him up myself, he seemed surprised. The light from the bathroom illuminated his expression.

"Gimme the cloth. I can do that."

"Obviously." I happily continued my task. "You're very capable."

He grumbled but allowed me to care for him. When I was finished. I returned the cloth to the bathroom and turned off the light before sliding into bed next to him and pulling the covers over us. Reagan snuggled up against me unapologetically. I wrapped an arm around him and pulled him even closer.

After a few minutes of silence, his voice sounded sleepy but firm. "Don't change your mind."

I hesitated before responding. "Reagan..."

His voice was less sleepy this time. More firm. "Not kidding, Thatcher. You, me... this is good, right? And I'm tired of fighting how much I want you. So don't fucking change your mind."

"It *is* good. And I want you, too." Part of me wanted to leave it at that, to enjoy our time together and let things happen naturally, but I owed him the truth. "But I'm also a realist. All the reasons we've been fighting it are still there —" I didn't need to spell them out.

"Just for this trip, then," he said quickly. "We can be together until we're back in New York."

"Yeah." I let out a breath. "Just for this trip."

As I fell asleep, my brain continued to tackle the issue, desperately seeking a solution. The trip would be another eight... no, I realized with a pang, seven days. It didn't feel like enough. But how could it last longer? Openly dating a junior employee wouldn't be good for either of our reputations. I couldn't imagine telling Trent that I was dating his son. And my track record with relationships was... well, any tabloid reader could explain in detail why I shouldn't bother trying for a long-term relationship.

But somehow, despite these swirling thoughts, I managed to sleep better with Reagan pressed up against me than I had on any of the nights I'd managed to stay away. I was still deep asleep when my brain figured out the buzzing in my dream was actually the buzzing of my phone in real life.

I grabbed it off the nightstand and answered with a mumbled "'Lo?"

I expected it to be January or possibly Thalia and had just enough consciousness for a spark of worry about Brantleigh before I recognized Trent Wellbridge's voice on the other end of the line.

"Thatcher, sorry to bother you first thing in the morning."

Reagan must have recognized his father's voice because he lifted his head off my chest, and his body jerked against me. Our eyes met in shock as memories of the night before flooded my mind.

"Trent," I said as casually as I could. "This is a surprise. Are you calling for Reagan?"

Reagan shook his head, his eyes huge.

"Reagan...? Oh. No, no. I was calling to chat with you. Although I heard from Jonathan that you'd taken Reagan along on a business trip of some sort. Going well, I assume?"

"Yes. Even better than I'd imagined." The absurdity of the situation hit me, and I ran a hand over Reagan's shoulder.

Trent had *never* called me to "chat," that I could recall, and I was profoundly annoyed that he'd decided to start now. But when I glanced down at his son, who still looked thoroughly debauched from taking my cock last night, I managed to find an extra supply of patience.

"What can I do for you?" I asked.

Reagan moved slightly, an innocent gesture that made his naked leg rub against mine, and I found myself growing incredibly, inappropriately hard. I braced my feet against the bed and shifted myself up against the pillows.

"Kind of you to ask," Trent said. "There's an award ceremony coming up here in Honeybridge. A way to honor the folks who've made important contributions to our community, both large and small, while also celebrating the winners of the various contests that make up our winter festival. I'm sure you've heard Patricia mention the Honeybridge Festival of Ice?"

"I..." A warm tickle on my stomach had me sucking in a breath as my tongue lost connection with my brain. Looking down, I realized that my new position had left Reagan with his face pushed against my abs, and he was taking advantage of the situation by tracing them with his tongue. "No," I told Reagan, low and stern.

"Oh," Trent said, unperturbed. "Well, it's one of our larger town events every January. We've got ice skating, of course, and ice dancing. Ice racing, ice wrestling, ice sleighing—"

Reagan's face—those glorious fucking eyes—turned mischievous, and my heart rate kicked up instantly. I knew that look. I shook my head resolutely.

I only caught the barest hint of Reagan's grin before his disheveled hair disappeared beneath the edge of the blanket.

Oh fuck.

"—ice fishing," Trent went on happily, "ice plunging, ice golf, ice bowling, ice painting, if you're into that sort of thing—"

His voice was lost beneath the pounding of blood in my ears as Reagan leaned forward to run his tongue up my shaft.

I sucked in a loud, sharp breath.

"Ahhh, you're a fan of ice painting, then?" Trent said with a chuckle as his son sucked me off and I tried not to make a sound. "Patricia, too. We also have ice sculpting and ice music. Oh, and this year, we'll have ice *yoga*, thanks to those Honeycutts—"

Holy *fuck*. This was so fucking wrong. And I had never felt anything so good in my life.

I grabbed Reagan's hair and yanked, half intending to pull him off, but when he made a deep sigh of pleasure from the pain, I nearly came in his mouth right then.

A deep, hoarse, needy noise escaped me.

"Thatcher?" Trent asked. "Everything alright?"

Reagan took me deep in his throat and gagged on my cock.

"Yes. Hell yes. Oh my god."

He chuckled. "Glad you're excited about it. I'm going to be winning one of the awards myself for, well, my tireless commitment to getting state funding to improve local infrastructure," he said modestly. "And the town would also like to honor *you*, Thatcher, for investing in one of our beloved small businesses—"

Reagan swallowed around me, sending my thoughts scattering like paper-thin leaves picked up by the winter wind, and I gripped my phone so hard the plastic case creaked.

"So we can count on you being there to receive the award, then? It would mean quite a bit to everyone, I'm sure—"

"Yes. *Yes.*" I thrust my hips up, unable to keep them still. "I..." Reagan dug his fingernails into my inner thighs, tiny pricks of pain that lanced straight to my balls. "I have to call you back."

I didn't wait for Trent's reply before mashing the red button on the screen and tossing my phone over the side of the bed. Then I grabbed Reagan's hair and yanked him up to kiss me, pushing the blanket aside. We attacked each other's mouths until I manhandled him around to finish what he started. As soon as my face was poised above that sexy tattoo, I grabbed his dick and sucked on the tip, savoring the salty taste while running a thick finger up and down his crease, across the hole I'd abused only a few hours earlier.

It was quick and gloriously dirty. We sucked each other off, hot and wet, filling the room with the scent of men's bodies and eventually hot spunk as I pulled off him and jacked him while I came down his throat.

"*Fuuuuck,*" he croaked after swallowing. "Fucking Christ, Thatcher."

"Yeah." The single syllable was the best I could manage. I lay back and gulped oxygen like a drowning man, concerned for a moment that I might pass out when the sunlight in the room began to flicker. It took me far longer than it should have to realize the bus had begun moving.

If I had ever had sex this good before in my life, I couldn't remember it... and I *definitely* would have remembered it.

"So." Reagan turned to face me a moment later, and I was pleased to see he looked every bit as wrecked as I felt. "Did you have a nice conversation with my dad?"

I laughed. "You are..." I grabbed his hand and brought it to my mouth. "Filthy." I nipped one finger.

Reagan whimpered, then sighed and cuddled against me.

"I think he's giving me an award," I said. "Or maybe I'm giving him one? Or both." I shook my head. "I literally can't remember a word he said. I'll have January get details."

My phone rang again, buzzing against the floor, but I pulled Reagan closer and ignored it.

"Ooh, that could be my dad calling you back," Reagan teased. "Would you like to ask him for those details now?"

I slid a hand down to pinch his ass, and he yelped. "Shush."

"He could be asking about *me*," Reagan continued. "You could tell him how very *talented* I am."

"Jesus," I muttered, simultaneously amused and horrified. I climbed out of bed, dragging him with me. "Come on. I'm gonna shower that filth off you."

"Isn't the shower kinda small for both of us?" Reagan wondered, allowing himself to be dragged.

"Definitely. But I'm going to enjoy watching you like a lecher."

His laughter dispelled any remaining tension from the mention of his dad's call.

In the end, we both tried to fit in the shower together

anyway, making a soppy mess of the small space as the bus trundled east again and reality remained thousands of miles away.

It wasn't until we were dressed and ready to face the day that I retrieved my phone and saw who the missed call had been from.

Layla.

Her flu test was finally negative.

Chapter Eleven

Reagan

We had exactly fifteen hours to enjoy each other's company—and naked bodies—before picking up Layla in Omaha, so of course, Thatcher's first priority was... checking his email. After our shower and performing the synchronized kitchen dance we'd choreographed that allowed two people to prepare breakfast simultaneously in the tiny space, Thatcher had immediately pulled out his laptop to deal with some urgent business matters happening in Zurich.

I didn't mind at all. For one thing, consuming enough calories to replace the ones I'd burned last night and this morning was a high priority—sex with Thatcher was like a high-intensity workout, and I'd be damned if I couldn't keep up with the man's stamina. For another, I enjoyed the routine we'd developed. I enjoyed that we *had* a routine. And I especially enjoyed that today, for the first time ever, I didn't have to hide the way I watched Thatcher as I shoveled yogurt into my mouth. If I wanted to drool over his long, strong fingers as they tapped his keyboard, I could. If I wanted to stare greedily at the sexy V of exposed skin just below his neck where his shirt was unbuttoned, nobody would stop me. If I wanted to imagine rubbing my lips all over his heavy stubble and licking my way into his mouth, today, I could *finally* do so without a single repercussion—

"If you don't stop doing that with your spoon," Thatcher said conversationally, his eyes still on the screen, "I'm going to take you back to the bedroom, spank your ass, and fuck you so hard you won't be able to walk for the rest of the day."

I shivered so hard I choked on my yogurt. Holy fuck, why was that so hot?

"When did you shave your beard?" I demanded after getting my coughing under control with a sip of coffee— Thatcher's coffee since mine was already gone.

At this, he looked up, a crease between his brows. "Pardon?"

"Your beard. Last time I saw you, a few months ago, I guess, you still had it. But then at the gala, you didn't. And now... Are you growing it back?"

Thatcher scratched at his stubble and shrugged. "I am. I like the beard. I'm not sure what prompted me to shave it New Year's Eve. I wanted a change, I guess. A wild impulse." He smiled wryly. "But I quickly remembered I'm not an impulsive sort of person."

"Oh, I don't know." I smiled slowly. "Propositioning a *man* at a gala?" I whistled through my teeth. "Seems pretty impulsive, Thatcher, especially for someone who usually... plays it straight."

His cheeks went red above his beard. Had I known Thatcher could blush? "I wouldn't say *usually*. I've been actively bisexual for a long time. A great many people are aware of my sexuality."

"Meaning, the men you've hooked up with," I said with a smirk.

He spread his hands in a gesture of agreement. "I think it's great for people to come out publicly if it feels right or important to them, but that'll never be me. The last thing I want is to give the media more reason to speculate about my personal life." He cocked his head, studying me. "I imagine it's the same for you? Patricia's never mentioned any nice *gentlemen* you've dated."

I shrugged. "I've never officially come out to them, no. My parents are supportive of my brother, and I'm sure they'd support me, too. My mother would have no problem throwing eligible bachelors my way. But if people don't have to come out as straight, why should I have to come out as pan? Someday, if there's a good reason, I'll have that conversation, but for now, I seem to be doing an okay job of finding my own eligible bachelors." I wiggled my eyebrows suggestively. "Hell, sometimes they find me."

Thatcher snorted. "I had *meant* to find a man I arranged to meet on an app," he admitted. "I was supposed to recognize him by his distinctive feathered mask..."

"No," I breathed, leaning toward him in delight. "So you're telling me that some poor schmoe was waiting and waiting for a hot, dominant Roman warrior to make his New Year's Eve..."

"And instead, I ended up in bed with my friend's son? Yes. If you hadn't been wearing that same mask, if it hadn't been too dark in that ballroom to see your hair and your eyes..."

"And if you hadn't shaved your beard and my mother hadn't specifically told me you were supposed to be out of town..."

We stared at each other across the table, thinking of how

impossibly small the chances of this—*us*—happening had been. In a million alternate realities, one of us would have made a different choice and we'd have missed each other entirely. I found myself once again wishing I could read Thatcher's mind. If he could go back to that night and change things, would he?

Would *I*?

"I like your beard," I said. The words came out husky and low, and the slight tension in the air morphed into something hotter.

Thatcher leaned back in his seat and smirked a little. "Is that right? Maybe you should come over here and show me how much."

But before I had a chance to move from my seat, the bus slowed, and a quick glance out the window showed that we were pulling into a truck stop, probably for one of McGee's scheduled breaks. The man pulled back the curtain that blocked off the driver's area and joined us a moment later.

"Morning," he said, darting a shit-eating grin at both of us before turning to fix himself some coffee. "Did everyone have a... restful evening?"

Thatcher and I exchanged a look.

"Very," Thatcher said blandly. "You?"

"Yup. Got to sack out on a real bed at my buddy's place and stretch out—*oh*." He snapped his fingers in an exaggerated gesture. "That reminds me. Thatcher, I meant to mention last night that Reagan was taking your bed, and you were supposed to sleep at the Martinezes' house. But I guess you two figured it out, huh?" He leaned back against the countertop and lifted the mug to his lips, all innocence.

I covered my snicker with a cough. So *that* was how Thatcher had ended up in my—well, *his*—bed? I suddenly felt bad for every wrinkly comment I'd made. I owed McGee a solid.

"Did you get my message a little while ago?" Thatcher asked.

McGee's sunny smile faded, and he nodded. "Picking up your new passenger at the airport in Omaha tomorrow? Yeah, I got it. Also got a weather alert about dangerously cold weather and the possibility of an ice storm in the region." He shook his head. "Who the hell voluntarily flies to Nebraska in the dead of winter?"

"Someone dedicated," Thatcher said, though he didn't quite manage to sound enthusiastic about it.

"Or obsessed," McGee muttered under his breath. He sipped more coffee. "Gonna be crowded."

"Not really. One more person won't matter much either way," Thatcher replied.

"If you say so," McGee said darkly.

Interesting. McGee might be the only person I knew, besides me, who didn't seem to like Layla these days. But my issues with her were personal since she'd dismissed my ideas, accused me of causing a PR disaster, and... okay, possibly there was a little lingering resentment over the way she'd touched Thatcher in the leadership meeting since the only one allowed to be inappropriately proprietary about Thatcher was me. I wondered what McGee disliked about her.

"Anyway," McGee went on before I could think about it too deeply, "if there's ice, we're pulling over. She'll just have to get a room at an airport hotel. Assuming she makes it here at all, that is. My mom says there's bad weather back in New York, too." He sounded way too cheerful about this fact. "I sure wouldn't wanna be hanging out on a dinky aircraft at twenty thousand feet while it's snow—"

"McGee," I said sharply, noticing the way Thatcher's jaw flexed.

"Ah, shit." McGee winced and ran one large hand over his jaw. "Sorry, boss. I didn't think."

"It's fine," Thatcher said. "Really."

But I wasn't feeling quite so forgiving. I lifted my chin and glared at McGee. "Those sagging jowls of yours aren't the only signs of your advanced age, are they?"

McGee sighed. "Yeah, yeah. I deserved that one." He gulped down the last of his coffee. "Anyone need to step outside while we're here? You sure? Okay, then." He rinsed his mug, set it in the dish drainer, and stretched his muscular arms to the ceiling. "Gimme five, and then we're back on the road."

McGee headed for the hall bathroom, and an awkward silence descended over the table. Thatcher's eyes lifted from his screen to meet mine, and a small smile tilted the edges of his lips. "You don't need to defend me, Reagan—"

My face went hot. "I wasn't *defending* you, per se—"

"—but I appreciate it nonetheless," he finished.

Oh. The warmth in his voice had little flocks of rebellious butterflies flinging themselves between my stomach and chest, and I couldn't think how to answer. Everything with Thatcher felt... different. None of my usual responses ever seemed to apply.

I grabbed my tablet and pulled it in front of me, hoping there were a few critical emails that required my attention as well... or that I could manage to pretend there were long enough for Thatcher to stop looking at me.

Unfortunately, the only important message was so unexpected my stomach dropped, taking all the happy butterflies with it.

I blew out a breath. "Wow. So, change of plans, I guess.

Layla's assistant booked me a flight to New York tomorrow afternoon."

McGee came out of the bathroom just in time to overhear. "I told you!" He pointed at Thatcher. "Didn't I call it, boss? The creepy Mrs. Pennington wannabe doesn't wanna share you."

Thatcher flashed McGee a glare. "And I told you, it's nothing like that. Layla's a trusted employee, and when she's on this bus, you'll treat her with respect. Understand?" But when he turned his gaze to me, it was clear McGee wasn't the only one he was annoyed with. "Layla's been in charge of PennCo for a long time, and I allow her to handle most matters at her discretion. I told her yesterday that you were staying on the tour, and apparently, she assumed it was a suggestion. It was *not*. Please email Layla's assistant and explain the situation to her. Tell her to cancel your reservation. That's a direct order from me."

"Yes, sir," I said while McGee climbed back into the driver's seat.

God, it was hot when Thatcher was commanding, even when it wasn't me he was bossing around. My fingers flew over the tablet screen as I responded to Alena's email, and while I tried not to sound too smug as I relayed Thatcher's command, I probably failed.

Once it was sent, Thatcher seemed preoccupied with his ever-present emails, so I went back to my inbox to handle a few less-urgent emails of my own. I got a revised list of talking points from the PR team, sent the marketing folks notes on some posts they'd drafted, and chatted with the event organizers in Madison, who were very eager to see us later in the trip.

What I did *not* do was pull Thatcher away from his work and drag him back to the bedroom to lick every inch of his body. I was still determined to show that I could be professional... though admittedly, I'd allowed that to fall much further down my priority list in the last twelve hours than I should have.

Thatcher had made it clear that this thing between us was temporary, so part of me wanted nothing more than to enjoy it while it lasted. After all, I'd have all the time and energy in the world to prioritize work once the tour was over because Thatcher would probably—god, the idea turned my stomach—go back to ignoring my existence. And for right now, I realized, I was happier than I'd been in a really long time.

My phone clattered across the table, and both Thatcher and I glanced over to see my mother's name and picture appear.

I sighed. "Hello, Mother." I stood and stretched, moving back toward the bedroom so I wouldn't disturb Thatcher.

"Reagan, darling, I'm so pleased!"

I pulled the phone away from my ear and glanced at the screen. The voice *sounded* like my mother, and the call was coming from her number, but...

"Is this one of those things where you want to let me know you've been kidnapped but can't say so directly?" I demanded. "Cough if you need me to call the police."

She gave a long-suffering sigh. "Reagan, honestly."

There we go. "Sorry, Mother. How have I pleased you?"

"Oh, not you, dear. I'm pleased because your father's just informed me that Thatcher agreed to attend the awards ceremony after the Festival of Ice. Such a coup having him here in person! I've let all the organizers know. Of course, I'll expect you back in town well before then. By... oh, Wednesday at the latest."

"What are you... Wait, Wednesday? *This* Wednesday? Three days from now Wednesday?"

"Naturally. We have more events than ever this year, and it's so important that the Wellbridges present a unified front at as many of them as possible. Oh, speaking of which! You'll need to bring your dark Ralph Lauren suit to coordinate with my dress for the Friends of the Honeybridge Art Council luncheon. None of that flashy stuff you get from your internet friends."

I ignored her swipe at my sponsors and gritted my teeth. "Mother. I'm working. I'm on a *work* trip. I know I've told you this—"

"Yes, and I told *you*, Thatcher will understand. I'll call and check with him myself if I have to. Your father and I are very proud of you for doing your... work things, I'm sure, Reagan, but reporters will simply be *flocking* to town to cover the festival and the awards ceremony, and we cannot miss this opportunity. You know how small-town family values ignite your father's voter base."

I opened my mouth to ask how Maine voters would feel about a mother contacting her adult son's boss to arrange time off so her son could pose for pictures, but then I caught myself. "Wait... reporters?"

"Yes! Dozens of them. From Maine, mostly, but Channel 5 in Boston might be sending up a crew for one of their features on scenic New England towns, and I believe your father's convinced the *Wall Street Journal* to give him —I mean, the *town*—some coverage, too. He reminded them the Honeybridge Investment Summit is happening the same week. It's a veritable whirlwind of newsworthy events here in Honeybridge!"

Right. I was sure the *Wall Street Journal* would be sending a team of journalists to cover a meeting of ten commercial real estate investors in a tiny, rural Maine town. For as savvy as my mother could be about certain things, she was utterly delusional about the importance of Honeybridge on a global scale.

But if there really *were* going to be a bunch of reporters and an investment summit in town...

"You know, Mother," I said thoughtfully, "you might be onto something. Let me speak to Thatcher."

"I felt sure you'd be reasonable about this... eventually. Oh, and don't forget to get a haircut, dear. Something tidy this time, hmm? Your internet friends don't have the same high standards as our family."

I'd learned long ago that trying to get the last word with Patricia Wellbridge was an exercise in futility, so I didn't bother. Instead, I said goodbye and made my way back to the kitchenette.

"What's wrong?" Thatcher demanded.

"Not wrong exactly." I slid into the booth and drummed my fingers on the tabletop, still pondering. "The Honeybridge Festival of Ice starts this week, and my mother insists I come to Honeybridge to fill my usual spot as a member of the Senator's faithful family in press photos, especially since there might be some national reporters on the scene. I told her no, but then I got to thinking. You already committed to attend the awards ceremony at the end of the festival—"

"Did I?" he demanded.

"Yup. You told my father so this morning, and my mother is over the moon. It's a good thing the Senator didn't ask you to sign over your company or donate him a spare kidney, eh?" I grinned.

Thatcher rolled his eyes.

"Anyway, what if we made Honeybridge part of our

PennCo tour? There's an investment summit happening in town at the same time—which I'm sure is small potatoes compared to what you're used to—but it might make for some good publicity. All the same hokey, small-town festival things that make great photo ops for my dad—baby kissing, helping old ladies cross the street, building snowmen with little kids—would be good for you, too. So I'm thinking... what if we schedule some press meetings and have photos taken of you and Flynn at the Tavern? We'd get a much more personal and home-baked image of you and PennCo Fiber than the industry stuff we've gotten on this trip. Imagine the TikToks of Nova's drunken arrest stitched with a video of you wearing a puffer jacket and khaki pants, drinking some local mead, and checking out the festival's winning ice sculpture—which, last year, was my cousin Alma's eight-foot-tall depiction of Peregrine Wellbridge, one of the town founders, looking like he might bust out of his breeches and join the cast of *Magic Mike*. There was a *lot* to check out."

Thatcher frowned in thought, and I couldn't tell whether he was envisioning a sexy, frozen pioneer or considering my proposition. "Would Flynn feel like I was taking advantage if I used him for a photo op?" he finally asked. "I promised him I'd be a silent partner."

"We can ask, but he and my brother are savvy businessmen. They recognize the power of press coverage, and I can't imagine them balking at potentially having Honeybridge Meadery featured in the business section of a national news site... and we could get that kind of coverage if we told them you were going to be there and were willing to take some meetings."

"True. Okay, I'll give him a call. If he agrees, I want you to set up the meetings. Don't be afraid to pitch high-level publications." He met my eyes. I could see the confidence he had in me, and I wasn't sure it was warranted.

"Are you sure you want me—"

"Yes," he said in a low growl. Our eye contact became exponentially more intense.

I swallowed. "I, ah... I mean... wouldn't someone else in PR do a better job of convincing—"

"No. Besides, this is good practice. If you can't get them to agree, we can have Layla make some calls tomorrow. Meanwhile, you'll get experience. When do we need to arrive in Honeybridge? If I know Patricia, she's expecting you yesterday."

I let out a nervous laugh. "Yeah. But obviously, we don't need to cancel anything already scheduled. We'll get there when we get there."

He shook his head. "McGee made a good point about the weather. Spending too much time on the northern roads this time of year isn't smart."

Thatcher pulled out his phone and made a call. "Layla. Change of plans. Instead of flying to Omaha tomorrow, I'm going to need you to fly to Portland later this week. Yes, Portland. No, the one in Maine. I'm making some changes to the tour schedule." With every clipped sentence out of Thatcher's mouth, I could hear Layla's voice rise in pitch, but it didn't seem to bother Thatcher. As he spoke, I felt his leg slide between mine under the table and press my knees open. I glanced up at him in surprise to see a dirty, teasing look on his face.

"Reagan and I will still attend the event in Omaha," he continued. "But everything after that will need to be canceled. We're going to push on to Maine directly. January will arrange replacement drivers so we can make good time.

Should arrive by..." He lifted an eyebrow at me, and I did some quick googling.

"Tuesday night," I murmured. Today was Sunday. The Omaha event would finish by lunchtime tomorrow, and the drive to Honeybridge would take at least twenty-four hours. I shot my mother a quick text letting her know to expect not only me but Thatcher and his crew as well.

"Tuesday night," he said into the phone. "January will send you the details of where to meet us. I'll be staying with friends, but I'm sure we can find you a room in a nice ho—"

I shook my head at him. *Sold out*, I mouthed. All the hotels in the Honeybridge area sold out around the festival.

"H-home of some friends as well, perhaps," he finished awkwardly. "I'll have January figure it out and let you know."

Once he finished the call, he phoned his assistant to discuss the necessary arrangements. Within a half hour, January had reported back that she'd made arrangements with my mother to house Thatcher's "people" in our guest wing while Thatcher, who was "practically family," according to my mother, would stay in the family wing with us. The very idea of Thatcher staying in JT's old room right near mine made me squirm.

When he got off the phone, Thatcher must have noticed a look on my face. "You're upset."

"No! Not *upset*." Not exactly.

He narrowed his eyes. "You don't want me staying at your parents' house?"

I sighed and lowered my voice so McGee couldn't hear me over the sound of the road. "Of course I want you to stay with us. I just..."

His lips turned up. "You're worried I'm going to make you scream my name under your mother's roof."

I loved the fact he knew it would be my *mother* rather than my father who would mortify me. But that wasn't it either. The truth was, I was worried I wouldn't be able to keep my giant crush on my boss a secret from my family. "You're not going to make me scream because you're not going to touch my dick in Honeybridge."

"Oh, yeah?" Thatcher's eyes flared as if accepting a challenge. He sat back and crossed his arms in front of his broad chest. "Is your dick on board with that decision, Reagan?"

My dick was actively urging my big mouth to shut it. "M-maybe not, but, um… also…" I tried to block out the mental images dancing their way across my vision. "Also, my goal is to convince my parents that I'm serious about a career in social media. Like, serious enough that my dad will give me a job working for his campaign. And that's not going to happen if they catch wind of us…" I gestured between us with a flapping hand. "Doing whatever."

Smooth.

"Interesting," Thatcher said slowly. "Later, I want to know all about why you're planning to leave PennCo and why you'd want to work for your father's campaign in the first place. But first…" He reached down and adjusted himself, showing that he was already half-hard after just a casual mention of my dick. He grinned. "Would you care to 'do whatever' right now?"

"Fuck yes," I said on an exhale.

"Bedroom. Quickly."

I shot out of the booth like a rocket, knocking my hip against the corner of the table and nearly tripping over my own feet on my way down the narrow aisle. Thankfully, I heard the faint but recognizable sound of McGee's music pumping through the unused earbud hanging around his neck while its twin was plugged solidly into the ear closest to the center aisle of the bus.

As soon as I cleared the doorframe into the bedroom, Thatcher moved behind me and closed the door. His hands quickly rucked up my shirt before spreading out across my stomach and chest. "Your cheeks turn pink when you get flustered," he murmured against the skin at the top of my spine as his chin scraped the collar of my shirt down. "Makes me hard. Want to see that blush streaked down your neck and chest."

His words did nothing to cool the heat in my face or in my groin. "You fluster me."

Thatcher let out a soft chuckle. "Don't know why. I find you enticing and sexy as fuck, but I also enjoy your company." He continued to kiss and suck the skin on the back of my neck. "You're smart and funny. Irreverent and engaging. Why would that make you uncomfortable?"

His words were too kind. I didn't want to start believing them because it would take me about half a second to knit the threads of those offhand statements into a giant happily-ever-after sweater... and Thatcher had made it clear he wasn't interested in that. He'd had at least two serious relationships that ended poorly, which was only slightly better (or worse, depending on your perspective) than my history of *zero*. Still, there was something about the man—the same something that had kept me obsessing about him this whole week, even when it felt hopeless—that now made me want to imagine an impossible, permanent future with him. One where I'd close off my DMs, delete my hookup apps, and lay down roots that wrapped around his legs and ankles to keep him tied to me.

Something about the man that made me want. Need. *Beg* for more.

My breath came faster, but I didn't respond.

"Reagan. Answer me."

"Dunno."

He turned me around and pressed me bodily against the door, grinding his dick into my hip while shoving his knee between my legs. Every time he dominated me physically, my thoughts scattered like multicolored confetti tossed into an industrial fan.

"W-what?" I breathed, unable to look away from his full lips.

The edges of those lips turned up. "Why do I fluster you?" His voice was deep and sultry, and it turned the fan speed to wind-tunnel levels.

"You make me... w-want..." I closed my eyes and swallowed. "More."

His lips ghosted the corner of my mouth, the knife edge of my cheek, the top of my eyelid. "*Reagan.*"

I leaned into him, inhaling woodsmoke and sage. "You... I want... you." Air moved in and out with my hesitation. "You. *You.*"

He moved me around until I was on my back on the large bed. His fingers unfastened buttons and zippers until I was laid out on the bed like a sacrificial offering on an altar.

Without taking his eyes off me, he moved his hands to his own clothes and stripped slowly. When he was finally naked, he dropped his tongue to my ankle and began tasting me, moving up my body slowly with nips, and licks, and open-mouthed kisses until my dick leaked sticky trails into the hair below my navel.

Surely this wasn't how he was with those hookups he'd mentioned. Surely this had to mean something to him the way it did to me. With his dark eyes focused on me so fiercely, I felt like... the only fucking person in his world.

My eyes slammed closed as his mouth reached my thighs. His tongue traced the outline of my phoenix tattoo with reverent thoroughness. Then he moved to the inside of my thighs, and his nose brushed against my balls.

I sucked in a breath and reached down, tangling my fingers in his hair, guiding him further up until his tongue was right where I needed it. As soon as I felt wet suction, I opened my eyes to stare at his mouth. His eyes met mine with their usual intensity, flipping everything around in my stomach and my brain until my entire body felt like it was filled with useless, mismatched parts.

His words from the night before slid through my memory.

I want you every minute of every fucking day.

Was that just one of those overly dramatic things people said while they were thinking with their dicks? The kind you cried out while fucking and maybe even thought you meant in the moment that made you cringe when the hormones had burned themselves out?

Or was it possible that he actually meant it?

God, for the first time in my life, I really wanted someone to mean it. But why, oh why, did it have to be *him*?

I reached down and grabbed his hand, yanking him up until he was pressed on top of me, crushing my mouth with his. My hands clutched the back of his head like I was afraid someone would pull him off me, ending this dream and bringing us both back into the stark impossibility of our reality.

"Easy," he murmured against my mouth. "Shh. Easy, easy..."

Oxygen sawed in and out of my lungs. I couldn't get enough. Things were already so impossibly complicated, and once we got to Honeybridge, the complications would quadruple. Layla would arrive. My parents would be waiting with their truckloads of expectations. And then, once the festival was over, I'd be back in New York...

Without Thatcher. Forever.

I was overthinking. Panicking. Ruining the short time we had by worrying about what would come after. But it felt like this thing I'd wanted for so long was slipping through my fingers, and I didn't know how to convince Thatcher that we could be good for more than a week any more than I knew how to convince my parents I was good for more than camera fodder, and—

"Shh, *shhh*." Thatcher's words barely registered. I squeezed my eyes closed, cutting off any possibility of embarrassing myself with a leaked tear of desperation and panic.

My hands tightened in his hair.

"Reagan. Sweetheart. Look at me. Look. At. *Me*."

I opened my eyes to see him staring down at me with a furrowed brow. His hand brushed the messy hair off my forehead as his eyes flicked between my own. I tried offering him a reassuring smile. I was fine. Truly, I was.

Whatever he saw deepened the furrow between his brows. "Talk to me."

I flashed the smile again. "Don't want to talk. I want you to fuck me."

Thatcher's nostrils flared. "Don't lie to me—"

"I'm not. I *really* want you to fuck me." I ground out the words. If he would simply flip me over and use my body as roughly as possible, I could lose myself and these uncomfortable feelings in the mind-blowing pleasure I knew the sex would bring.

He opened his mouth to speak but stopped. Something

in his expression changed as he studied me. "You want to fuck? Okay. But this time, you're topping."

A shudder ripped through me that was partly from nerves—ridiculous since I'd never been nervous at topping a partner of any gender—and partly from excitement.

I'd wanted to give myself over to him. To have him drive away all my hopelessness and relentless *thinking* with the power of his body. Topping him meant staying in the moment. Staying in control.

But god, the idea of Thatcher wanting that from me and trusting me to give it to him... the idea of me holding him down and thrusting into his body... made my brain short-circuit. Multicolored confetti blew everywhere.

"Okay," I whispered. "Then get on your back."

Chapter Twelve

Thatcher

I WOULD DO anything to snap Reagan out of whatever had come over him.

The panic on his face was clear, and I figured I knew why. We'd finally given in after fighting our attraction to one another for what felt like much longer than a week, and that had put us on shaky ground even before the calls from his parents and our change of plans.

But seeing the man who'd engaged crowds across the country lose his confidence made me even more irrationally upset now than it had back at the Newport Grille in Wichita.

I treasured the vulnerable parts of him, but I'd fight like hell against his fear. And I'd be damned if I lost the witty, warm, engaging man to the dull, polite shell or even his prickly defensiveness again.

What he needed was to be in control, to remember his power and take charge of it fully. I'd never bottomed for anyone, but I was so incredibly hot for Reagan I'd take him any way he wanted or needed. And right now... right now, he needed to take charge.

I rolled onto my back and grabbed his hand, tugging it until he blinked at me and scrambled over to climb on top of me. "Fuck," he grunted under his breath. "Gonna make me come just thinking about it."

The weight of his muscular body pressed me into the mattress. His leg hair scratched against mine as our limbs tangled together, and the hard press of his dick against mine proved he was just as into the idea as I was.

"Lube," he muttered, reaching across the bed to find the bottle. While he was distracted, I took the opportunity to run my hands up and down his broad back to his narrow waist and rounded ass. His body was perfection despite the hours I knew he spent in the office, and I wanted to trace the lines of that fucking tattoo until I knew them by heart.

His hands shook as he knelt over me and flipped the cap open. When his fingers reached down to find my hole, his eyes finally met mine again. "You sure this is okay?"

I smiled at him, which made his entire face light up. "Very okay."

As soon as Reagan's slick fingers began pressing against my sensitive rim, I shivered. If I hadn't been so obsessed with watching his facial expressions, I would have thrown my head back and squeezed my eyes closed in over-whelming pleasure. Instead, I took in every detail. How his exploring fingers felt stretching me open, how his inky eyelashes brushed together when I reached down to tweak his nipple, how his breathing hitched as I let out a deep groan of satisfaction, and how his eyes—those gorgeous sea-glass eyes—watched me carefully for any sign that I wasn't on board.

"Have you... do you..." He sucked in a breath before meeting my eyes. "Do this with... other men? Bottoming, I mean."

"Never." The word came out like a bite, fangs bared and snapping, but he needed to know the truth. "Just you."

Something about those words flipped a switch in Reagan. Gone was the uncertainty and worry, the young man who couldn't seem to believe he was in a position of power with me.

His eyes darkened. "Good. Fucking keep it that way."

The tone of his voice, deep and commanding—almost angry—made me finally throw my head back and close my eyes in surrender. His questing fingers stretched me more aggressively, and his knee shoved one of my legs wider. "Fuck. *More*," I moaned.

After working me over for what seemed like forever, he withdrew his fingers and slicked himself up before shoving me over onto my stomach. "Ass up. Like that. Knees apart. Good."

Reagan manhandled me into position while I tried not to feel the vulnerability that came with the removal of his thick fingers. I felt strangely empty and unsatisfied while I waited to feel his cock inside me.

Instead of his cock, I felt the hard press of his hand between my shoulder blades. As soon as my forehead hit the soft sheet, I shuddered again. With anyone else, I would have told him to back off, but for some reason, with Reagan... it only made me hotter.

When his hands spread my ass apart and the blunt head of his cock slid against my hole, I reached back and grabbed his knee.

"Shh," Reagan said. "Easy. *Easy*." There was humor in his murmur. The repetition of my earlier words to him didn't go unnoticed. I grinned stupidly against the sheet as I gripped his knee more tightly.

"Fucker," I gritted out as my ass began to stretch impossibly wide around him.

The rumble of his laughter made my stomach flip over. "Mm-hm. I feel the *anger* coming off you in waves."

Now it was my turn to laugh, only... the feel of him invading my body was too overwhelming, and my laughter ended in a groan. "Fuck," I breathed.

He leaned over me, letting me feel the heat of him along my back. "You're killing me." Reagan's voice carried the slightest hint of a tremble, enough to let me know I wasn't the only one thrown incredibly off-kilter by this encounter.

As he grabbed my hand, tangled our fingers together, and pressed our entwined hands to the mattress above my head, his lips brushed my ear. "Breathe out. That's it. You feel so fucking good, Thatcher. So *fucking* good."

It felt like Reagan's thick cock was deep enough inside of me to be up in my throat. I felt him everywhere until my skin prickled with it. How he was able to move this slowly was beyond me, but I was grateful for it. My body adjusted, but it was still a lot to take.

He continued checking in with me through murmured encouragement and gentle touches until I finally felt ready for him to speed up. Feeling Reagan on top of me, pressing me face-first into the bed while he shoved his fat cock into me, was not an experience I'd ever thought I'd want... and not one I could ever imagine sharing with another person. He held me down and fucked me with a unique combination of commanding determination and exquisite care, his words of praise washing over me while I struggled to take it all in. It was both too much and not enough.

Reagan's thrusts sped up until he was pegging just the right spot to make me beg. I managed to free one hand from his hold and get it under me so I could jerk myself in desperation. His muttered curses joined the steamy heat in the space between us just as my orgasm reached the tipping point.

I screamed into the sheets, still clutching tightly to him with my other hand. The feel of his warm, jagged breath on my skin, of his sweat-damp chest hair against my back, and the heavy press of his hips against my ass joined the chaotic mess inside my head.

When Reagan pulled out, the empty, messy feeling left in his place echoed the chaos in my thoughts. Thinking about what awaited us in Honeybridge put a dark cloud over my plans to continue enjoying Reagan's company.

"Turn over," he said softly. "Let me clean you up."

I managed to push myself onto my back with all the finesse of a turtle and blinked at him. He sat back on his heels, his sun-kissed hair sticking up at odd angles, forehead damp with sweat. Bright aquamarine eyes peered intensely at me, making me feel more exposed and defenseless than I had when he was fucking me.

Slowly, as though I might stop him, he climbed over me, hovering on his hands and knees. He bent to brush his lips to mine in a kiss that was achingly tender.

"Thank you," he said softly.

"For what, bottoming?" I gave him a teasing grin, trying to lighten the mood. "If it wasn't obvious, I enjoyed the hell out of it."

But Reagan didn't take the bait.

"For that," he agreed. "For trusting me. For knowing what I need and giving it to me. For not immediately regretting this." His soft smile was a little bit wry. "Unlike our first time."

I lifted a hand to his messy, damp hair. "I didn't regret

that night," I found myself saying. "I regretted the circumstances around it. I regretted that I'm your boss, that I'm friends with your parents. I regretted that it was so good I wanted more... even though I shouldn't have. And I worried you'd have regrets, too."

Reagan shook his head but gave me a small smile. "That night, my only regret was that I hadn't jumped you last summer. I mean, think of all the days we wasted cruising around on my father's sailboat when we could have been doing this."

"And now?" I prompted, trying to pretend that I wasn't holding my breath, waiting for his answer.

"And now..." His smile brightened, though it didn't quite reach his eyes. "I think I'm going to make sure I don't have any more regrets by enjoying you as much as possible before you—I mean, *we*—get back to the city." Reagan winked, then pushed himself off the bed.

I watched as he moved through the motions, retrieving a wet cloth from the tiny bathroom and returning to attend to my body. I hissed as he gently moved one of my legs out of the way, and he pressed a reassuring kiss to my knee.

My breath stuttered in my chest.

I couldn't remember the last time anyone had taken care of me. Couldn't remember the last time I'd *let* anyone. But like so many things, with Reagan, it simply felt... right. Necessary. Just as right and necessary as it felt for me to care for and protect him.

There was no logic to the feeling. It wasn't anything I could explain or excuse to the rest of the world. And it didn't suddenly eliminate all the multitude of ways that the two of us having anything more than a temporary arrangement would be *wrong*.

But as he finished his task and bent to kiss me again, his

eyes met mine, and an emotion-drunk voice slithered silently through my mind.

This can't be an ending.

I won't let it be.

Chapter Thirteen

Reagan

I WAS in love with Thatcher Pennington.

That had become clear the moment he'd called me *sweetheart* instead of running in horrified disgust when I'd gotten emotional during sex—a thing I'd never done, *ever*, in my entire try-sexual history, with any partner or variety of partners, no matter how hot they were or how inebriated I was, no matter how wildly inappropriate the setting or the participants.

I had always said you could enjoy sex better when you kept the emotional significance out of it. It was easier to concentrate on getting off when you weren't worried that whichever side of the bed you flopped on postorgasm was going to be *your side*, forever and ever amen.

And yes, okay, maybe after JT and Flynn found each other again, I'd started to think it might be nice to fall in love someday. To have someone look at me with the fiery devotion Flynn gave my brother in every passing glance. But I'd thought about summiting Mount Kilimanjaro, too, when I'd seen someone doing it on Instagram, and that didn't mean I was going to throw on my flip-flops and start climbing willy-nilly.

It figured that with Thatcher, nothing about love had gone the way I'd expected, not from the moment I'd agreed to a proposition from a bossy mystery man and found myself kissing my actual boss. Thatcher was so much more than the hot, unattainable teenage fantasy I'd thought he was. He was dominant, yes, but also open-minded and fair, and my heart squeezed thinking of how very responsible he felt for the people in his life—his employees, his lover, the son who hadn't bothered answering *one* of Thatcher's dozens of check-in texts this week. When I was alone with Thatcher, even before we'd come together last night, his proximity had made my heart pound in a way that it simply hadn't for anyone else, with a strong, fast rhythm that showed the stakes were higher.

It also figured that I found myself in this predicament—up this damn mountain—with no plan for how to get down gracefully. Confessing my feelings might make me feel better for half a second, but what good would it do? Thatcher liked me, I knew he did, and trusted me, too, but was he going to push aside all his priorities, all those things he felt responsible for, to date his most *junior* junior employee, who was almost twenty years younger than him, his politician friend's son, *and* no longer on speaking terms with Brantleigh? In the immortal words of Trent Wellbridge when I'd asked him to let me manage his campaign social media, "Hahaha! Reagan, son, what would a man want to do that for?"

So, I fell back on doing what I always did when I had things to say that couldn't be spoken—I smiled and charmed and said nothing of substance while trying very hard not to get snippy with the beautiful man who'd done nothing to deserve it. The rest of the drive to Omaha was filled with a mix of shallow banter, shop talk, and an unusually high number of odd looks from Thatcher.

I understood his confusion. I was giving him the kind of hot-and-cold treatment one might have expected in a medieval torture spa. But I was confused and conflicted, too. And if he felt me attempting to pull away from him like I had in Kansas, at least this time, he didn't question me about it. On some level, he had to understand that the more we talked, the more we shared, the more... entwined we got, the harder it would be to unpluck ourselves from one another in Honeybridge.

The good news was I managed to get a lot of work done. I contacted several news outlets, explaining our change of schedule, and even though it was a Sunday, a surprising number got back to me immediately and agreed to cover Thatcher's Honeybridge appearances. I created some reports on our increased social media engagement and copied them to everyone in PR. And I managed to draft a couple of new posts for the PennCo Instagram using photos Thatcher and I had taken in Colorado.

One of the shots I found in our shared picture library was a solo picture of me that Thatcher had taken during our ski trip when I wasn't looking. I was standing alone in my brand-new gear, hands on my hips, staring out at the snowy mountain and the brightly colored skiers just outside the frame. I was pretty sure I'd been thinking sappy thoughts of Thatcher at that moment—about the irony of having the lift *up* the ski run being the terrifying part of the experience, rather than the moguls and the death-defying speed on the way down, and wishing I could always be there to hold his hand when he needed me—but if any of that had been visible on my face, you couldn't tell from the angle of the shot. Instead, I looked strong. Resilient. *Capable.* So I stole the picture and uploaded it to my personal Instagram, needing the little dopamine rush I always got when I posted.

It took me a lot longer than it usually did to come up with a caption, though. I typed and deleted more than Thatcher did when he was sending a text to Brantleigh. In the end, I decided on *To fresh powder and new adventures! #wanderer #eyesonthepinnacle #keepmovingforward* and hit Post. And if the cheerful words felt a little forced this time, more like a lie than a reframing of the truth, well, that was just a sign that I really needed the reminder they provided. I needed to control the things I could control, like building my career, attaining my goals... and not making it any harder or more humiliating to end this fling with Thatcher than it already would be.

When it came time to sleep for the night, I didn't even need to fake the excruciating headache that my stress and confusion had caused. Thatcher had insisted I head back to his room to lie down shortly after our dinner stop, and I'd fallen dead asleep before he'd even finished talking to McGee about the arrangements January had made for replacement drivers.

Upon our arrival in Omaha the following morning, we rushed to a sustainability event hosted by Union Pacific. Layla had arranged a private brunch with several key executives from the railway company, and we knew there would be a couple of reporters included to cover the high-level meet-up to give both companies good coverage for their efforts at sustainability.

When we walked into the elegant dining room, Thatcher was immediately hailed by the event organizers. Meanwhile, I was met by another familiar, smiling face.

"Reagan," Chris Acton said warmly. "Nice to see you again so soon. I'd heard a rumor your schedule was changing. Wasn't sure you were going to stop here after all."

I shook his outstretched hand. "Thatcher didn't want to miss it. But your rumor was correct. We're headed to Maine after this. To Honeybridge—"

"Oh, I know," Chris interrupted with a smile. "I'll be there, too. Layla called me to make sure I followed along." He began to add something else but stopped himself, and I wondered if he was hoping to try to ferret out more information about Nova Davidson like he had in last week's interview.

If so, good luck to Chris because I had no new information to give him even if I wanted to. We'd been getting updates on the security team's investigation, but they didn't seem any closer to finding the culprit... and probably never would. There were simply too many people who had access to the samples and too few people who had the desire to defy Layla. Last I'd heard, they were looking into former employees to see if anyone was holding a grudge.

If Chris wanted a scoop, he'd be better off talking to Nova—or cultivating a source close to her since Nova was keeping quiet on the advice of her legal team—but that seemed like a lot of effort for a story that didn't seem to be generating much public interest anymore. PennCo had weathered the storm, thanks to our quick action—thanks to *Thatcher*—and we'd be ending the tour in better shape than we'd been even before the Nova debacle.

"So..." Chris went on. "You, me, Honeybridge?"

Thinking of Thatcher had me scanning the room for him, watching as our host introduced him to several other executives. "Mmm? Oh, yes, Honeybridge is lovely," I said with an absent nod. "You'll like it."

Chris folded his arms over his chest. He was shorter and slighter than me, and the pose made him look a bit like my mother's dog when she was irked about something. "I *already* like it. I especially liked sucking you off in your parents' boat house last June... remember?"

"Huh?" I swiveled my head to look at him fully, then darted a look around us to make sure no one had overheard. "Shit, Chris," I whisper-hissed, face flaming. "Don't talk about that here. It's a professional gathering, and I'm *working*."

"Is that what you call it?" His smile was back but wry this time. "You haven't taken your eyes off your boss since you walked in."

If my face got any hotter, I would have to leave the room and throw myself into the snowy parking lot.

"Because I'm his PR assistant for this trip," I said haughtily. "He might need a rescue."

"Right." Chris cocked his head. "So what's it like working for *the* Thatcher Pennington? Some people claim he's an asshole. Others say he's fair but incredibly demanding."

Apropos of nothing—and inappropriate as fuck—a memory of Thatcher's voice saying, "Come for me. Now," flitted across my brain as it seemed to do on a regular basis.

I cleared my throat. "Er... not really? He has high standards for himself, but he's very gracious and..." I swallowed. "It's good. I'm learning a lot. It's especially nice being out of the office, getting to meet people across the country." All of that was true. I mentally nodded in self-approval.

Chris narrowed his eyes. "That was a bullshit PR response if I ever heard one. Straight from the Trent Wellbridge playbook."

I let out a surprised huff of laughter. From twenty feet

away, Thatcher turned his head and met my eyes as though he'd heard me. I quickly looked back at Chris before the reporter could see me mooning in Thatcher's direction.

"The truth is, it's been strange working with him," I told Chris honestly. "I've known Thatcher for years as a, uh... family friend, but it's different interacting with him as a boss. He's a brilliant entrepreneur—which, you're right, makes him a bit intimidating—and this opportunity to travel with him feels a little bit like a second job interview." I smiled winningly. "I want to learn from him, to impress the hell out of him. I also don't want to let him down or put my foot in my mouth."

I shrugged, suddenly feeling put on the spot. While it didn't seem like Chris was pressing me for insider information, it still felt awkward to discuss Thatcher in this way with another person, especially someone I'd slept with before, so I quickly added, "You might have heard from Layla that I was only put on this tour because there was a serious flu outbreak at the office. Normally, Thatcher's very hands-off at PennCo, and since I'm new to the company, I haven't worked closely with him until now. It was an unexpected opportunity."

Chris nodded thoughtfully. "I've researched the man quite a bit. His second wife was very vocal, post-divorce, about how career-driven Thatcher is, probably because his parents always pushed him to succeed. I remember her saying, 'Thatcher cheated on me with Pennington Industries long before I was ever unfaithful.' She claims he's a very cold man."

"Cold? Thatcher?" I demanded, incredulous. "No way."

"Interesting," Chris said. "So you're saying she lied?"

It was on the tip of my tongue to say *fuck yes* and to add

my opinion of the beautiful woman who'd been fucking her tennis coach while wearing Thatcher's ring, but I caught myself at the last moment, shocked at how close I'd come to giving Chris a hell of a sound bite. *Jesus, Reagan.*

"Not at all," I said smoothly. "Thatcher and I have never discussed his marriages, so I have no idea what he was like in a relationship." And I never would. "But I can tell you that the Thatcher Pennington I know is generous, hard-working, and caring. He's dedicated to his company, yes, but he's just as dedicated to the people who work there as he is to making a profit. He recognizes the power he has to impact things on a global scale. Sustainability, for example."

Chris's lips twitched. "Nicely done. But... off the record," he said, leaning closer. "What's it like working and traveling with someone so damn gorgeous? I would be *all* over that if he wasn't so damn straight."

I barked out a laugh. "No comment."

He groaned and waved a hand. "I swear you used to be more fun than this, Reagan. Then you spend ten days on a bus with the CEO, and suddenly, you're a corporate drone spouting off PR talking points. What have they done to you?" Before I could answer, Chris leaned closer—too close—and added in a teasing murmur, "But I could forgive you for that... if you make time for me in Honeybridge. C'mon. Let's grab a drink and catch up."

I assumed "catch up" was code for more boat house action, which definitely wasn't going to happen. Thankfully, before I could give him a stammered, hedging response, Thatcher appeared at my side.

"Reagan." He picked an invisible piece of lint off his shirt. "Sorry to interrupt, but I need your assistance. *Now.*" He glanced at Chris and firmed his jaw. "You'll find Reagan is extremely busy with work. I doubt he'll have free time in

Honeybridge, especially since he'll be spending part of his time with his family."

Chris's smile slid away, and his lips tightened. "That's disappointing, but we all have our jobs to do," he agreed. "Speaking of my job, I was hoping to schedule another sit-down with you in Honeybridge—*not* about the Nova situation," he added before Thatcher could speak.

Thatcher stepped closer. The familiar, warm scent of him reached my nostrils, and I gritted my teeth to keep from letting my eyes close. "I'm sure we can sit down again. Contact Layla, and she'll find you some time on my schedule. And speaking of Layla..." He turned to me. "She just called. It seems she chose not to change her flight, and she's waiting for us to pick her up at the airport. Here in Omaha," he added when I continued to stare at him blankly.

"Oh," I managed. Determined as I'd been not to get any closer to Thatcher over the next twenty-four hours, this should not have felt like such a blow. But deep down, I'd still craved that time where it was just the two of us. One last hurrah when we could speak and look at one another freely.

Thatcher dipped his chin, and the look in his eyes—banked rage—spoke volumes. "I'm afraid we need to cut our time here short and go pick her up. Then... we'll head to Honeybridge." He reached out a hand to Chris. "See you there."

I mumbled a goodbye to Chris, our host, and two of the other executives I'd met, but I couldn't remember any of it. By the time we boarded the bus in the freezing cold parking lot, I was shivering with nerves more than cold.

McGee greeted us at the door to the bus, his usual smirk missing. "The fuck is this nonsense?" he demanded before glancing over our shoulders as if looking for someone else.

His eyebrows dipped together for a split second before he focused back on the boss.

"I take it you got my message," Thatcher said.

McGee nodded, but he was frowning at me. "Take Reagan to the back, boss, and warm him up. You want coffee or tea?"

I shook my head, but before I could speak, Thatcher did.

"Reagan's not cold. He's probably wondering, like I am, what the *fuck* Layla James was thinking." Thatcher's voice shook with anger, but still he helped me out of my coat as I unzipped it almost without realizing he was doing it. "I told her to change her flight. Told her directly—"

"You don't want to hear this," McGee said grimly, "but I'm not surprised. I also wouldn't be surprised if she didn't cancel Reagan's flight back to New York. She wants to be alone with you, boss. She wants to start something. And I know you said that you've already told her you're not into that, but that doesn't mean she heard you. Maybe she thinks things are different since you divorced Heather, and she's given you an appropriate time to recover. But Layla seems like the sort of person who capitalizes on opportunities, and this tour is an opportunity. One she doesn't want to give up."

Thatcher shook his head, and I couldn't tell whether it was because he didn't believe McGee or because he couldn't believe Layla's behavior, but I kept my mouth shut because it wasn't any of my business.

Thatcher narrowed his eyes at me. "Right," he said, then nudged me down the narrow aisle toward the bedroom.

"What are you—?"

But he ignored me. "McGee," Thatcher called over his

shoulder, "find us a place to park for a bit. I don't care if Layla's waiting for a while. I'm going to get Reagan sorted."

"Good call," McGee called back.

"What do you mean 'sort Reagan'?" I asked, trying to shrug Thatcher off me. "I don't need sorting."

He pushed me the rest of the way into the bedroom before closing the door. "Sit down." He nodded at the bed.

I shrugged and didn't argue, but I couldn't help remembering how he'd all but thrown me onto the bed this time yesterday. It was funny how quickly you could get used to a thing you had no business getting used to—

Thatcher dropped to his knees in front of me and caught my hand. "Stop it," he said. "Stop it right now."

Shit. Had he read my mind? My stomach dropped. "Sorry?"

"No," he snapped, shaking his head. "No apologies. Stop acting like you're the junior gopher to the mid-level assistant. You're Reagan Fucking Wellbridge. You're a valued member of this team. You're... you're a valued member of *this* team," he added, releasing one of my hands to point to his chest.

The gesture, the words, and the way he knew me well enough to see what I was feeling and call me on it made my chest ache with want and gratitude. But it was a bittersweet feeling, too, because having this and losing it was going to hurt like fuck, even if I never let it show.

Was this what love felt like? Jesus, why would anyone actually *want* to feel this vulnerable on purpose?

I cupped Thatcher's cheek and smiled a smile that made heat kindle in his eyes. "That's sweet and all," I said archly, "but how about you stop treating me like I'm an injured bird who needs rescuing and do something useful?" I leaned back, resting my weight on my hands, and spread my legs slightly. "I'd like my cock sucked before we get to the airport since apparently the rest of the drive is an endless expanse of blue balls."

Thatcher's eyes darkened, and his nostrils flared. "Demanding."

I flashed back to Chris's description of Thatcher as the same and couldn't help but grin. "Like recognizes like."

"Baby boy, you can demand whatever you want of me, but we both know who's in charge here."

His words lit me up and drove all the blood to my dick. "Yeah. *Me.*"

The deep rumble of his laugh accompanied a sincere smile that went straight to my gut. "Thinks he's Mr. Important," he murmured. "I see."

Hearing that nickname on his lips was another sweet ache, though I knew him using it was pure coincidence—he hadn't been around Pop enough to hear it, and he sure as heck wouldn't have heard about it from my parents, who thought Pop's nicknames were silly and borderline slanderous.

"The clock is ticking, Mr. Pennington. We don't have much time until we pick up my *boss* from the airport. Do you want to spend it—"

His lips crashed into mine as he pushed me all the way to my back, hands gripping and knees shoving my legs wider to make room for him. I allowed my rational brain to take a much-needed break so all I could do was feel.

And try to forget that within the hour, I'd be back to being very *unimportant* once again.

Chapter Fourteen

Thatcher

DESPITE TELLING myself for an hour that I wouldn't allow Layla's sudden appearance to disrupt the trip, things began to go wrong the moment she arrived.

She swanned onto the bus in a cloud of perfume that nearly drowned out the remnants of Reagan's scent lingering in my nose and on my tongue, apologized over and over for her "misunderstanding" of my instructions, tossed her leather computer bag onto the dinette, and declared the bus "incredibly cozy." She inspected the bunk situation and assured Reagan with a smile that she wouldn't "pull rank" and claim the bunk he'd been sleeping in, even though it was her "favorite." Then, while I was trying to catch his eye and tell him without words that he'd only switch bunks over my dead body, Layla took advantage of my distraction to run her hands down my biceps appreciatively and tell me how amazing I looked in my Elustre shirt.

Sixty seconds into our journey, she'd sucked all the air out of the space like an oncoming tornado and left Reagan vibrating with tension.

But while every protective instinct told me I needed to

fix this and make it okay for him, there was nothing she'd done that I could actually take issue with. Could I tell her to stop being... aggressively cheerful? To stop... smiling? To stop casually touching someone she'd known for years, when the only reason I even registered her touch was because I was so aware of *Reagan* that I noticed his eyes locked on her hands and mentally replayed our mutual jealousy at the expo back in Wichita?

Fortunately, McGee whipped us back onto the road immediately. I could tell by the set of his jaw he wouldn't mind making Layla feel every miserable minute of the long drive ahead of us, but I also knew he cared enough about me to get it over with as quickly and efficiently as possible.

Layla continued talking as she made herself comfortable, taking the seat at the table that I usually claimed, and patted the bench beside her. "Come sit, Thatcher. We can make the most of the long trip by putting our heads together and discussing some tweaks to the Elustre summer launch strategy. I've received updates from Apex Athletics and Sierra Outfitters, and I think we should loop the folks at Zen Athletics in, too, since you had such a great meeting with them..."

Instead of taking the spot next to her, I slid into the booth next to Reagan. When he scooted over to make more room for me, I reached under the table to squeeze his leg in reassurance, and he gasped at the unexpected touch.

Layla frowned. "Problem, Reagan?"

"Er, no." Reagan's face went beet red, and he studiously avoided even glancing in my direction. "Not at all. Zen is an excellent fit for the brand. I'm excited to see them added to the list."

"Good." She turned back to me. "Now, Ron and Tanya had several ideas—oh, Reagan, make some notes while we're talking, please." She motioned toward his tablet. "Thatcher, I think you'll be most excited about—"

I tried to concentrate on Layla's words—to give her the respect and attention she deserved—but it was difficult for several reasons. First, textiles weren't my day-to-day business, which was why I left the bulk of the decisions for the PennCo subsidiary in Layla's hands while I focused my energy on Pennington's more critical holdings. And second… it was hard to care about anything she was saying when Reagan was sitting beside me, taking notes like Layla's personal scribe and growing more tense with every passing second.

The realization of how much Reagan meant to me had been sneaking through my subconscious for days now, but this situation made it impossible to ignore. I cared more about him and his comfort than I did about closing the Zen deal and for damn sure more than hearing Layla's marketing talk. In fact, I suspected I cared more about him than anything to do with Pennington Industries at the moment.

I had no idea how I'd let that happen. I also had no idea how the hell to get my priorities back in alignment… even if I wanted to.

That was a knot to be untangled later, though. When Reagan and I were back in New York, we could make an appointment to discuss our wants and needs and challenges, rationally and without distraction.

For now, I had more immediate problems to focus on.

A quick sideways glance showed Reagan's jaw flexed while his thumbnail flicked at the cuticle on his fourth finger. I casually shifted in my seat and, while pretending to nod along with whatever Layla was saying, moved my leg over until it lay alongside his. Air silently *whooshed* out of his nose, but this time, he didn't startle. In fact, little by little, his body settled, as if I was calming him by osmosis, which settled me, too. After a few moments, his flicking fingers moved down to rest on my leg, and I pretended to scratch my leg so I could give his hand a quick, reassuring squeeze.

Encouraged by what probably seemed like rapt attention from both of us, Layla pulled out her laptop to get my opinion on some marketing images.

"I like the red one. It's bold." I shrugged. "But I'm not a public relations expert. Reagan, thoughts?"

Reagan and Layla both seemed startled that I'd asked, which was so ridiculous as to be borderline annoying. Hadn't he single-handedly resuscitated PennCo's dying social media accounts with his twice-daily posts from our tour? How could he doubt that his opinion would be wanted and valued? And why did Layla not see what I did when I looked at Reagan—a person capable of so much more than note-taking?

"Well..." Reagan said slowly. "The red's nice, but the green ties in nicely to the sustainability vibe I've been using in the social media posts I've drafted for the launch. Not sure if you've had a chance to take a look at those yet, Layla? If we go with that, I think it'll set us apart for a lot of consumers—"

"We're not *talking* about social media right now. This is for print. Magazine ads, primarily." Layla gathered her laptop toward her again. "I'll tell Ron we like the red."

"But why aren't we talking about social media?" I asked. "Our accounts are getting more interaction after just a week of Reagan posting. Doesn't that prove there's an audience for this?" I nudged Reagan, who never failed to come to life when the words *social media* were mentioned. "Pull up the data—"

Layla sighed. "Thatcher, I don't need to be convinced. I..." She closed her laptop and spread her hands on top. "Look, the truth is, I've been working behind the scenes to put together my own social media campaigns around the Elustre launch. I didn't want to share with you until things were perfect, and in our business, perfection requires coordination with our marketing partners... rather than going off willy-nilly and posting all sorts of random things for the world to see." She darted Reagan a look. "We won't have a clean slate to launch from now since some *eager beavers* were determined to have their way. But when it's finished, Thatcher, I think you'll be quite impressed at what a professional social media campaign looks like and the impact it will have."

I stared at her—at the tidy auburn hair and bright smile of a woman I'd known and worked with for decades—and impressed was not at all what I felt.

"Let me be sure I understand," I said slowly. "When you were specifically asked about social media in your meeting with Reagan weeks ago *and* in the leadership meeting last week *and* in our subsequent conversations about this, you said it was irrelevant in the textile industry. A waste of time. Now you're saying that you've secretly been working on it all along and keeping us in the dark?"

"Not *in the dark*." Layla blinked, genuinely confused by my outrage. "This is the way we've always worked. You let me handle PennCo my way—coordinate with my people, make my own timeline based on the needs of the organization—and I come to you with a finished product for your approval. Right? I admit I haven't been entirely forthcoming, but I felt... well, cornered. Pushed to discuss the topic before I was ready to make an announcement." Another look at Reagan. "But I assure you, that's only because I have the company's best interests in mind, and I wanted to make sure all my ducks were in a row before I brought my ideas to you." She reached across the table and clasped my hand earnestly. "PennCo is my first and last priority," she vowed. "Just like Pennington is for you. Nothing has changed."

But things *had* changed for me, though I didn't know how to quantify the change just yet.

I couldn't blame Layla for sticking to the status quo and caring about PennCo, exactly as I'd encouraged and expected her to do all these years. And still, thinking of the effort Reagan had put into the campaigns he'd drafted, the pride and passion he'd displayed while doing work that Layla now seemed to imply was wasted effort—was enraging.

And this is why conflicted priorities don't work, I reminded myself. Because what was good for PennCo and what was good for Reagan in this instance might not be the same thing.

"You created a campaign all on your own?" Reagan asked softly. His face was inscrutable.

Layla tilted her chin up. "Yes. I have been working with some of the graphic artists in Marketing to flesh things out, but I came to them with the concepts, as I'm sure they'll verify."

"No one doubts that, Layla," I assured her.

"Of course not," Reagan agreed. "But I'd love to see what you have so far. What a *professional* campaign looks like."

The edge in his tone was clear to me but apparently not to Layla. She smiled slightly. "I told you, it's not ready yet."

Reagan held up his hands, the picture of innocence. "Of course, of course. I know it's a rough draft. I wouldn't expect perfection."

Layla darted a glance at me, as if hoping I'd intervene and put Reagan in his place, but I had to admit my own curiosity was piqued. She pursed her lips. "Well... alright, then."

She clicked a few keys on her laptop and brought up some images that even to my untrained eye were good. Actually, better than good. Like the content Reagan had been creating, these images hinted at a larger story. They made me *feel* and shifted my perception of the brand.

"The pictures are stock images of people hiking and kayaking, as you can see," she explained. "I'll need to arrange a photo shoot once Apex and Sierra Outfitters finalize their product lines, but I already have a short list of models and locations. I'd hoped maybe we could get some celebrity endorsements—" She winced. "But after what happened last week, I've changed my mind."

Reagan's eyes didn't move from the laptop as she scrolled, but I could sense his stunned disbelief. "You definitely need the right photos, but the branding here is... it's cohesive," he murmured. "Totally on-target for Elustre, completely in line with the PennCo brand." He flicked a glance at me, looking faintly troubled. "This *is* professional quality."

Layla smiled tightly and reclaimed her laptop again. "Of course it is."

Reagan nodded, and I could practically see his face icing over in slow motion as his polite mask settled into place.

I was very glad when McGee chose that minute to pull off the highway into a truck stop to change drivers. I needed to get Reagan alone to talk, to reassure him, or to kiss him senseless. Anything that would melt that mask off again.

"Oh, thank goodness," Layla groaned as McGee parked

the bus and jumped out to find his replacement driver. "I was up before five, and I'm *dying* for coffee. Reagan, two creams, no sugar, please."

Reagan opened his mouth and shut it again. "Sure," he agreed... *politely.* "No problem."

"Actually, Layla—" I began, prepared to explain that Reagan would be far too busy assisting me and she should fetch her own coffee, but I broke off when my phone rang.

I scowled down at the display, but what I saw there made my heart flip.

Brantleigh. Fucking finally.

"I need to take this," I murmured to Reagan, tilting the screen so he could see. Reagan gave me a slight smile and nodded.

"Brant?" I answered as I hurried out of the booth and down the steps. Outside, the Nebraska landscape was frost-covered, the air so cold it shocked my lungs and stole my breath. "Hey! So good to hear from you."

"Hey, Dad."

I couldn't remember the last time he'd called me "Dad" without resentment in his voice, and hearing him say it warmly now made me hopeful.

"How are you?" I demanded. "Your mother said you're at a yoga retreat or something...?"

He laughed a little. "Yeah. She packed me off to the Quick Lake Artists' Retreat and Chakra Centering Center. It's actually been... well, not entirely awful. Not much different than California, except for the shit weather."

I blinked. "The Centering Center. Why does that sound...?"

"Familiar? Because it's in Honeybridge," he said with a laugh. "Remember that dinky little town where you made us have forced family fun time last summer?"

I was so happy I was finally having a civilized conversation with my offspring that I ignored the jibe about the town —it *was* small, after all—and didn't argue the idea that I'd "forced" him to spend time with me, which I supposed was a matter of interpretation. "I remember. I can't believe your mom sent you to Honeybridge. I'm headed there now."

"Wait, you're coming here? To see me?"

"No." I winced. "I mean, I *would* have come to see you, but I didn't know where you were until just now. I'm actually on a press tour for PennCo Fiber..." I gave him a condensed version of my past week—one that assumed he hadn't read a single one of my text messages or seen much social media. I also omitted any reference to Reagan that didn't have to do with work, reminding myself that I'd never discussed my sex life with Brant before, so there was no need to start now. Instead, I focused on the Nova incident, the stops we'd made, and the upcoming festival and investment summit that drew us to Honeybridge.

"Holy *shit*." Brant chuckled. "I saw the Nova thing on TikTok, but I didn't even realize that was about your company." He yawned. "What a clusterfuck. And you said Rea Wellbridge is working for you? Damn. That hard to find qualified employees these days?"

"Not at all," I said firmly. "Reagan's got a ton of experience with social media, and he excels at public relations. He's been an asset to the team. He works hard."

Brantleigh was silent for a long moment. "I could be good in public relations," he said thoughtfully. "I mean, I've created enough work for PR people over the years; I should know how to handle them."

It was my turn to fall silent, staring at the cracks in the pavement of the parking area while the wind whipped at my hair. "You want to work at Pennington?" I demanded.

"Because in the past, you've said you had no interest in my company. You said you preferred the West Coast, and working with your stepdad at the studio—"

"I do," he agreed. "And I want to get back to that eventually. But, like, the studio won't be starting a new project for weeks. So Mom's all, *Stay in Honeybridge, Brant. Keep working on yourself. You'll only get into trouble if you come back here and sit around until March.* Which, first off, is just bullshit. I don't get into trouble; I live my life and shit happens, which isn't my fault. But second... Dad, it's boring as fuck up here," he said plaintively. "You don't even understand. The new moon is next week, and the lady who runs the center wants me to do some crystal-cleansing ritual in the freezing cold. So I'm thinking... what if I came to work for *you* for a little while? Maybe earn a paycheck while I soak up some of that famous Thatcher Pennington brilliance?"

He sounded close to begging, and I hated that I hesitated for a long moment, wondering what was really going on. But in the end, I thought of Reagan. I still didn't know why he wanted to work for his father's campaign or why Trent hadn't immediately recognized his talent and snapped him up for the job, but he'd spilled enough over the past week that I could guess how things had gone, and imagining it had the same shriveling effect on my respect for my friend as the Nebraska cold was having on my balls.

Brant wasn't Reagan, no... but I sure as hell wasn't Trent Wellbridge. Brant deserved a chance, just like Reagan did.

"I think that's a great idea," I said with a confidence I didn't totally feel. "I'll be arriving in Honeybridge tomorrow, probably late, so we can discuss details the day after.

Reagan's going to be busy doing family stuff, so I think you'll be a big help handling press at some of the events."

"Fuck yeah. And... the paycheck?" he prompted.

I frowned. "There'll be a salary commensurate with what the other junior PR associates make. If you want details, I'll put you in touch with Margot in HR."

"Cool. And..." He hesitated. "You'll tell Mom?"

"I can, but don't you want to tell her yourself? You're twenty-eight, kiddo. I'm sure she'll be proud—"

I could practically hear Brant's eye roll. "Nah. She freaks out about nothing. It'll be better coming from you."

"Alright. I... I love you, Brant. I'm glad that the retreat worked for you."

"Yeah." He laughed lightly. "See you soon, Dad."

Three *Dads* in one conversation? This was good, I told myself. This was really good. My other priorities might be skewed after this week with Reagan, but Brantleigh was right at the top where he'd always been.

Since it was too cold outside for a conversation with Thalia, I got back on the bus. As usual these days, Reagan drew my attention like a lightning rod, but for the moment, he seemed to be engrossed in something on his tablet while Layla was busy with her laptop. I nodded to McGee, who was resting on his bunk, and hurried to the bedroom in the back. As I engaged the call, the replacement driver started the engine to keep us moving east.

"Hi," Thalia answered in her usual clipped tone.

It only took a minute for me to explain Brantleigh's new plan, but I wasted at least ten more attempting to calm her fears about the situation while reminding her that our son was an adult. I wasn't sure why dealing with my ex-wife always left me feeling like a frustrated failure while calming Reagan made me feel ten feet tall, but that was another thing I'd have to puzzle over later, once I was back in the privacy and quiet of my penthouse in the city. For now, I promised to check in with Thalia again from Honeybridge and ended the call with a sigh.

I gave the bed a longing look. This day had felt a week too long, and I wanted nothing more than to curl up, preferably with Reagan in my arms. I'd missed him last night when he'd been sleeping off his headache, not just because I'd wanted to touch him but because I'd wanted to talk to him, too. I appreciated his fresh perspective on the world, which was often so different from mine.

For now, though, I had work to do, and I didn't like the idea of leaving Reagan alone to cater to Layla's every whim.

The more I thought about her treatment of him, the more I wondered about it. Layla was a good manager—at least according to her staff—and even Reagan agreed that her team was loyal and devoted. But was this another situation where I hadn't gotten involved and Layla had been keeping something from me? Or was it a personal issue with Reagan—irrational resentment that he'd taken her spot on the first half of the trip, perhaps, or that I'd heard *his* ideas for social media campaigns before she'd had a chance to impress me with hers? Stroking her ego and reminding her that I respected her skills and authority as vice president might go a long way to fixing the situation... if I could get over my instinctive urge to jump in front of Reagan every time she said anything, like I was protecting him from one of those feral beavers back in Honeybridge.

"There you are," Layla said when I walked back out. She offered me a smile and nodded to the spot next to her in the booth. "Come join us. I was just tasking Reagan with researching local media contacts in and around Honeybridge so we can invite them to a meet and greet."

Just that quickly, I forgot all my good intentions.

I glanced at Reagan, who was sitting in his usual seat. He made a point not to raise his eyes to meet mine. "Actually, Reagan's *from* Honeybridge," I said. "Between that and his dad's position, he probably already knows the key contacts there."

"Oh." She blinked. "I didn't realize." And she probably hadn't given him a chance to volunteer the information either. "That works out well, though. Reagan can be on hand at the meet and greet to hand out press kits and make sure everyone's comfortable. He's arranging for the catering now, so he'll be able to coordinate with the servers to ensure the reporters have what they need. Happy media, happy coverage," she added with a wink before focusing on her laptop again.

I moved to the small refrigerator to grab a bottle of water, automatically grabbing one for Reagan, too. Layla seemed to still be working on her coffee from our pit stop, so I assumed she didn't need anything. When I set the water down in front of Reagan, I used it as an excuse to slide into the booth next to him again.

"Thanks," he murmured without taking his eyes off the screen.

I glanced at what he was working on and saw an online order form for the bakery in Honeybridge. "Layla, wouldn't your admin be a better person to handle this?" I waved a hand at Reagan's tablet. "Reagan's a PR associate—"

"A *junior* associate," Layla reminded me. "Arranging catering is definitely within his job description."

It was on the tip of my tongue to tell her that we should change the job description—not just for Reagan, but for every other junior associate who should be spending their time learning skills related to their field—but Reagan pressed his boot against mine as though imploring me not to speak.

I knew he was right, so I kept my mouth shut for now. This was the man I'd trusted to charm textile executives across the Midwest, I reminded myself. He'd handled himself in his job without my interference; he'd handled his parents for years. Obviously, he could handle this, too.

I cleared my throat. "Layla, I'm not sure if Reagan's discussed this with you yet, but he has some family obligations while we're in Maine. Since he's been working around the clock on this press tour, it seems only natural to allow him time for that. Meanwhile... my son, Brantleigh, will be joining our team. You can have him help out with whatever tasks you would have assigned Reagan this week. Please ask January to forward Brant our event schedule."

Reagan and Layla's twin expressions of surprise almost made me chuckle. Reagan was the first to speak. "My parents are aware that my job comes first. I'll work my family commitments around PennCo's events—"

And he'd run himself ragged rather than ask for time off. I held up a hand. "There's no need. Brant seems excited to get involved, and he and I haven't spent time together in a long while. I'm looking forward to seeing him."

A muscle ticked in Reagan's jaw, but he managed a polite—too polite—smile. "Sure."

Once again, my hands ached to grab hold of him and force him to tell me what he was actually feeling. I clutched them into fists on my thighs instead.

Layla's lips pursed for a moment while she considered this. "I mean, of course Reagan can take the time he needs for his family... obligations. And obviously, I'll be very pleased to welcome young Brantleigh to the team. But I want to make sure this event is a success. I wonder if we need to bring in Nataly or someone else from PR if Reagan isn't going to be able to fulfill his duties."

Reagan remained conspicuously silent, and I hated it.

"Honeybridge is a small town," I explained to Layla, trying to ignore the vat of stress sitting next to me. "Even busy events there are easy to manage. I'm sure between the two of us, we'll be just fine."

"You're right." She smiled. "The two of us can handle anything, can't we? Hopefully we'll even have time for you to show me around town. I remember you spent a fair amount of time there last summer."

Once again, Reagan's reluctance to add to the conversation got under my skin.

"It's a beautiful town," I agreed. "In fact, Reagan is from one of the original founding families. His father is the state senator for that part of Maine."

Reagan shifted in his seat before finally closing his tablet and indicating his desire to stand up. I moved out of the booth to let him pass and bit my tongue against the need to ask if he was okay. Clearly, he wasn't. Even more clearly, he wouldn't say so in front of Layla.

Layla watched Reagan with undisguised interest as he grabbed a yogurt from the fridge. "Is that right, Reagan? A local politician might be good for a photo op. I bet the local press would eat that up. Do you think you can arrange for something with your father and Thatcher?"

I took a sip out of my water bottle to keep from laughing.

Reagan's eyes shifted to mine, and he pretended to consider. "Hmmm. Would my parents make time for *the* Thatcher Pennington? Hard to say, really. They're not the sort of people who are impressed by money and status—"

Water shot out of my nose, and I began to cough.

"Ignore him, Layla. Trent Wellbridge and I are friends. In fact, he was the one I was visiting in Honeybridge last summer." I shot Reagan a glare as I mopped up the mess on my face with a napkin. "Sarcasm is the lowest form of wit, Mr. Wellbridge."

His lips curved up in a reluctant smile, and those gorgeous eyes twinkled at me as he peeled the lid off his yogurt. "Don't quote Oscar Wilde at me, *Mr. Pennington.* 'Most people's thoughts are someone else's opinions, their lives a mimicry, their passions a quotation.'" He gave me a pointed look. "You'd do well to remember that."

I stared at him. He'd responded to my Wilde quote with one of his own? Reagan Wellbridge never ceased to surprise me. There was so much more depth to him than he let most people see.

"Rea-*gan.*" Layla sucked in a shocked breath and pressed a hand to her chest. "Mind your tone when you're talking to your CEO, if you please."

I opened my mouth to speak, but Reagan cleared his throat to cut me off. He stuffed a spoonful of yogurt in his mouth, licked the spoon thoroughly, and swallowed. "Sorry," he said, dropping his gaze demurely.

Layla nodded in smug approval.

What she didn't notice was that his gaze only dropped to the approximate vicinity of my cock, which had begun thickening behind my fly at the reminder of what his talented tongue could do and only got harder under his attention. I quickly slid back onto the bench before accidentally giving Layla an eyeful, but the situation didn't improve when Reagan slid in beside me...

Or for the rest of the awkward, frustrating afternoon.

I couldn't recall how I'd kept my hands and eyes off Reagan our first week on the bus, but doing so now was nearly impossible. Every moment, I was so viscerally aware of the inches between us it required a concerted effort not to let it show. And I craved his intelligent comments, his wry humor, and his sincerity nearly as much as I craved his touch. McGee had been so right when he'd said that three people would make things far more crowded than two... at least when the third person was Layla. I couldn't *wait* to get Reagan alone.

We stopped to eat dinner and stretch our legs, and I could see from the strain on Reagan's face that I wasn't the only one having difficulty. When we got back to the bus, I gently suggested that Reagan head to my bedroom to call his family in relative privacy, and he took me up on the offer with an enthusiasm that had more to do with escaping the awkwardness than excitement to chat with Patricia and Trent.

I half expected Layla to ask if the offer to use my room extended to her, but she didn't. And the reason why became clear when Reagan had shut the door to my room behind him.

She let out a breath and smiled broadly. "Finally, some time to catch up just the two of us."

I studied her face, scanning for any sign of the sexual interest McGee kept talking about, but of course, there was none. She seemed relaxed. Friendly.

I spread my hands. "I think we've already covered everything."

Layla laughed. "About work, yes." She leaned her elbows on the table. "But how are you, Thatcher? How has the tour been, *really*? I'm sure it's been challenging."

I shrugged, thinking that the most challenging part had been today, mostly due to her arrival.

Layla and I were friends, but not close ones. Certainly

not close enough to trade stories about our weeks or talk about our deep feelings. "It's been great, just as I said. Reagan's been a trooper, and he's carried me through more than once."

Her smile turned cagey. "Your fondness for him makes more sense now that I know you're friends with his father. I missed that information somehow. I assumed he was a friend of your son's—"

"My feelings about Reagan have nothing to do with his father," I said flatly. "I assure you, I hardly remembered that this week." Even when I'd tried to remind myself. "Let me be clear, Layla: the success of this tour rests largely on Reagan's shoulders. I'm not discounting the terrific job you and your team did in planning and providing support, but day to day, it was all him. He engaged the people we met, he knows a ton about our products, he thinks on his feet, and he's genuinely likable. He's the sort of person who should be mentored for a much higher position." I lowered my voice. "And if you disagree, I'd be interested to know why."

Layla blinked. "I... I do like Reagan. Of course I do. He's sweet. It's just..." She sighed. "Look, I know it's difficult for you to think ill of someone you've known for a while. You're a very constant sort of person, and it's one of the things I like best about you—once you've established a routine or opinion, you rarely change it."

Is that true? I frowned.

"But I don't trust Reagan. I know, I know," she said quickly, holding up a hand at whatever expression she saw on my face. "I admit that it was wrong of me to make accusations about his involvement—*potential* involvement—in the Nova situation. But watching him today, I can't help thinking that he's hiding something from me, and he's quite self-satisfied about it. I don't tolerate that sort of attitude on my team. In fact..." She hesitated, then admitted, "if you hadn't vouched for him, Thatcher, I'd probably suggest that he'd be happier at another company. That's one of the ways I ensure harmony in my team."

"Is that right?" I asked softly.

"It is. And I know you'll say he's young and eager." Layla's mouth tilted up. "But you must admit you're a little bit biased—"

"Reagan's not that young, and being eager is something I value in an employee," I interrupted. I lowered my voice, very aware that Reagan could come out of the bedroom at any moment. "But understand this, Layla: I trust Reagan. Full stop. Not because he's Trent Wellbridge's son, not because I've known him for years, but for the simple fact that he is *trustworthy*. He's not only creative and good at his job, as his one million Instagram followers would agree, he's also hardworking, honest, and dedicated to PennCo—a quality the two of you share. So perhaps consider that you're the one who's a bit biased. And that perhaps you should reevaluate the way you run your team."

I smiled a bit to soften the rebuke but also made a mental note to have January schedule a meeting with Layla after the tour so we could discuss her management philosophy and possibly restructure her division. All of the missing steps in the hierarchy at PennCo now seemed problematic for reasons that had nothing to do with me and Reagan sleeping together.

When I heard Reagan come out of the bedroom and head directly for the hall bathroom, I stood. "Bedtime," I told Layla. "Take the bedroom tonight. I insist. I'd like you to be comfortable."

Her features softened. "You're so good to me, Thatcher. And I'll think about everything you said, I promise."

If she'd known I would have gladly signed over my pent-house for the chance to spend the rest of the night alone with Reagan, I doubted she'd have thought quite as much of my generosity, but I merely nodded, grabbed the few things I needed from my bedroom, and perched on the edge of a bunk, waiting for Reagan to emerge from the bathroom.

But when he did, I took one look at his troubled face and realized that my plans for the night were about to go to shit.

Chapter Fifteen

Reagan

Is THERE anything worse than sitting next to the sexy billionaire boss you're hopelessly in love with, trying to pretend you're focusing on work stuff when you're really just picturing him naked while you do dirty, dirty things to him with your tongue?

Yes. Yes, there is.

It's infinitely worse when you catch his eye and know he's imagining the very same things, but you can't do a damn thing about it because your fling has to stay a secret, your feelings are one-sided, and, *oh yeah*, because there's a sniping, treacherous, handsy *harpy* watching you both a little too closely.

When Thatcher had offered me his bedroom for a little while, I hadn't hesitated, even though I hated leaving him with Layla. I'd needed a break from the tension, and I'd needed to make a few crucial business contacts... which had been extremely enlightening, although the guy I'd been messaging probably wasn't anyone Thatcher had thought I'd be contacting. Then, I'd sat for a long time, staring out the darkened window, wondering what to do with the information I'd learned.

Eventually, I'd left the room, but when I'd heard Thatcher and Layla getting ready to go to bed, I'd quickly ducked into the bathroom. I was the king of polite masks, but facing Layla after DMing with Terrance Fisher, Layla's former marketing director, and hearing about his experience at PennCo Fiber might have been too much even for me.

"Fuck," I breathed, peering at my scraggly appearance in the mirror. The fun part of this road trip was definitely behind us, and now it was simply a matter of surviving the remaining hours, even if it meant spending most of that time hiding out.

I took my time washing my face and brushing my teeth. By the time I came out of the bathroom, I'd decided to keep my newfound knowledge and suspicions to myself, at least until the trip was over. For now, I'd go to sleep in my narrow bunk and avoid everyone until we arrived in Honeybridge.

Thatcher had other ideas.

Arms folded over his chest to strain the seams of his shirt, knees spread, he slouched against what I'd thought would be Layla's bunk, waiting for me. "Sit."

The bossy voice got to me. I was afraid it always would. But I forced myself to continue standing. "Did you switch spots with Layla?"

He nodded.

"That was nice of you. I'd love to chat, but I was going to go to bed. I'm tired." I kept my voice modulated so as not to sound like a whiny child.

Thatcher looked at me for a long moment, then nodded slowly. "Okay, then. Go to bed."

I hated that I was a little bit disappointed when he gave in so quickly. I forced myself to look away and move toward the bunk. I'd already changed into pajama pants and a T-shirt, so I pulled down the comforter and slid into the bed. When I reached over to yank the bunk curtain closed, my hand hit Thatcher's warm body as he leaned forward to shove in next to me.

"Move over," he said in a voice that was sexy enough to light my clothes on fire.

"Are you insane?" I hissed, glancing over his shoulder and noticing he'd already closed the curtain on the other bunk.

"Nope. You said you wanted to go to bed, so we're going to bed. Move over."

I gaped at him. "I'm not sleeping with you when my boss is on the other side of a pencil-thin door."

"Your *boss* is getting in this bed with you. *Move. Over.*"

I moved over because I was nothing if not a slut for his touch, but I wasn't happy about it. As soon as he'd climbed in next to me, I leaned over and yanked the curtain closed. "What is this about?"

He placed his hand on my upper chest and pushed me back down on my back before looming over me. "Checking in with you. You're so tense you're vibrating worse than the engine on this coach. You've been this way all day."

"And you haven't? Of course I'm stressed. It's a stressful situation. But I'm dealing with it. Or I *was*, until someone climbed into my bunk."

He moved his hand up to caress my cheek. My eyes slid closed against my will. "Reagan... I'm sorry for putting you in this situation."

I opened my eyes to take advantage of being this close to memorize his face—the exact warm color of his eyes, that freckle in his laugh line I'd grown disgustingly fond of, and the scar that looked like a teeny little starburst right under the edge of his chin that made him moan when I licked it. I swallowed hard. "You didn't put me in it. I jumped in with both feet. And it's almost over, right? Honeybridge tomorrow, and then we'll go our separate ways."

His eyes widened. "You do remember we're staying in the same house, right?"

"Sure. You, me, *and my parents*. And then during the day, you'll be chilling with Brant and Layla while I'm doing the Wellbridge happy-family fuckery. I don't think there'll be much time for... us." I forced a little smile. "It was nice while it lasted, huh?"

Thatcher leaned in and pressed a kiss to the side of my mouth. "We'll reconnect back in the city."

His words surprised me because they sounded genuine and heartfelt, like maybe in this moment, he actually meant it... though we both knew it would never happen.

"Absolutely," I said automatically, completing the bullshit exchange. I wouldn't hold my breath waiting for his call.

He grinned. "Maybe I'll show you the view from my penthouse."

I snorted so loudly I froze for a second, worried I'd given us away. "*I'll show you my view?* Is that what you say to lure men up to your place?" I teased. When Thatcher said nothing, I turned to face him. "That was a joke."

"I know." He cast his eyes to the ceiling of the bunk, his usual way of indicating that I was being ridiculous, but for just a second, I caught a flash of hurt there that made my stomach flip inside out. "Anyway, I wanted to tell you I was sorry about earlier, with Layla—"

I frowned and poked him gently in the ribs. "Wait. Go back. Tell me about the view."

"It's pretty," he said, like this explained everything.

When I continued to stare at him, waiting, he admitted, "It's vibrant. Full of life and color. At night, a thousand little lights turn on across the city, and every one of them represents a... a person, with a whole life I know nothing about. Makes me feel like I'm part of something larger." He cleared his throat. "The apartment's nice, too. Great investment, obviously. But the view is what sold me on it."

"Holy shit." I cocked my head, a smile breaking over my face. "You make it sound amazing. I definitely want to see it."

And I meant it. I'd seen penthouse views before—dozens of them—but the way Thatcher described his, the cautious excitement on his face as he studied my reaction, made my chest ache with the need to know more about this vulnerable, fascinating facet of an already fascinating man.

"Yeah?" he whispered, sounding unusually raw.

I could practically *feel* my face softening as a wave of gushy emotion nearly swamped me. "Yeah," I whispered back.

Even if today was the end of him and me being like this, the fact that he'd trusted me with this part of himself—a part I could tell he didn't share with many people—filled me with warmth, dispelling the chill that had come over me the moment Layla landed in Omaha and our little bus-bubble popped.

I'd been trying to get some distance from Thatcher to protect myself, but for that moment at least, I didn't want distance. I wanted to share with him like he'd shared with me. To trust him.

I gripped his hand. "Thatcher, I know this might sound crazy, but I want to tell you... I think Layla stole the branding ideas for the Elustre launch," I whisper-blurted.

Thatcher blinked. "You... what?" Which, honestly, was a fair response to my abrupt change of topic and mood.

I pushed myself up so I was braced on one elbow while he was flat on his back—which was incredibly distracting, because god, he was gorgeous all splayed out like that—and spoke as quietly as my excitement would allow. "I wasn't going to say anything until I had a chance to figure it all out on my own. I didn't want to point fingers at Layla because it was awful when she did it to me, and I wasn't sure anyone would believe me anyway unless I had proof. But then you told me about the view from your apartment, and I..." *Remembered that you trust me. Remembered that even though you can't love me back, I can still trust you.* "I wanted to tell you."

"Okay," he agreed cautiously.

"When Layla showed us that presentation earlier," I whispered, "I had concerns right away. It *was* professional. Too professional. And I'm not saying putting together a presentation is rocket science, it's not, but it does take some experience and knowledge of the topic I'm not sure she has."

"Reagan—"

"So I remembered Nataly telling me that Terrance Fisher, the guy who worked for PennCo until a few weeks ago, had storyboarded an entire social media campaign for the launch and presented it to Layla, but she gave him her whole song and dance about not doing social media. So when I was in your room earlier, I found Terrance's Instagram, and I DM'd him. He was really nice and *really* talkative. He described his concept to me, and it sounds exactly like what Layla showed us," I said. "More than that, he told me some other stuff that happened while she was his manager, and—"

"Reagan." He rolled into me, pushing me back into the bed. "Stop. I don't want to talk about Layla. Not like this. Not now."

I frowned. "You don't understand. Thatcher, she flat-out took credit for his ideas. And if the other stuff he said is true—"

"*Quiet*," he said low and firm and sexy. His tone, combined with the press of his half-hard cock against my thigh, made it tough to remember why I'd wanted to talk in the first place...

But not impossible.

"You're not listening to me," I breathed. "Thatcher—"

"I'm listening." His words were a hot wash against my neck as his lips nudged the sensitive skin there. "You think Layla's taking credit for Terrance's work. Maybe she is —*maybe*," he repeated when my body tensed at the doubt in his voice. "But the truth is, any presentation Terrance did while he worked at PennCo is PennCo's property, and for all you know, baby, Layla may have influenced his design or changed it up after the fact."

I shook my head, trying to clear the lust haze that formed when he called me *baby*. "N-no. She didn't—"

Thatcher dragged his hand up my side under my sleep shirt, and I shivered. "I can't blame you for thinking the worst of her right now—she was awful to you earlier, and I'll be addressing that with her once we're back in New York, I promise—but she's still your supervisor. This, *us*, doesn't change that." He nipped lightly at my jaw. "So tonight, let me take your mind off it."

I let out a shaky breath. "I'm not complaining about the way she talks to me. I'm trying to tell you, it's way bigger—"

He cut me off with a kiss to my lower lip. His hard length moved against my leg in tiny, frustrated circles.

"Shhh. I told you, I'll take care of it. I'd have said something to her already if I didn't know you'd be too busy over the next few days to be fetching her coffee—"

"Stop." I rolled, pushing him onto his back. "Look, I appreciate you being protective or whatever. It's sweet," I whispered. "But I'm not sharing gossip or hoping you'll take my side against my boss. I can handle myself, and I can handle Layla, too—"

"Bullshit," he said, low and fierce. His eyes were a dark storm of lust, affection, and frustration.

"Pardon?"

"I said that's bullshit. You *didn't* handle it, Reagan. You were cold and polite to her." He said the word like a curse.

"Of course, because she's my boss," I pointed out, keeping my voice down though it wanted to rise.

"So am I, but you don't try that shit with me," he hissed back.

"Because I don't want to sleep with Layla," I said in the same tone. "And I'd rather not be *fired*. I'm trying to succeed at my job here—"

"So that you can get a job with your father."

His words, like the rest of our conversation, were hardly more than a whisper, but they landed on the bed between us with an almost audible *plop*, like a rock thrown into the center of Lake Wellbridge, sending out ripples that pushed us to opposite sides of the bunk.

I sat up, ramrod straight, and stared down at him. "That... is none of your business."

"Isn't it?" he shot back. "You're *mine*—I mean... my employee," he corrected quickly. "And you've already admitted that your goal is to convince your father that you're serious about a career in social media so he'll give you a job on his campaign. Of course, you still haven't said why the hell you'd want that. Your father campaigns for big business and family values. He's never, to my knowledge, spoken up for any LGBTQ issues. Doesn't it bother you that he won't take a stand?"

"Yes, of course it does," I whispered fiercely. Then I frowned.

How the hell had we gotten to this? How the hell had Thatcher missed the point so damn badly? We'd both been on edge all day, but this tense, whispered conversation—while my whole body ached to feel Thatcher inside me and one small woman on the far side of one thin-as-fuck door held us back—had me clinging to the "edge" with my fingertips.

I took a deep breath and tried to speak calmly.

"My dad's attitude hurts JT," I admitted. "And I *hate* that. For a long while, I told myself that since I'd never come out to my parents, it didn't hurt me personally, but that's not true. It does hurt that he doesn't go to bat for people like me. But... my father's not evil. He does decent things, too. He's got a moderate voting record compared to other people in his party, and he supports charities and programs that provide training for underprivileged people. But he can't do anything unless he can get elected, and to get elected, he needs my support." I sounded like one of his campaign ads, and judging by Thatcher's lifted eyebrow, he knew it. "I'm just saying, refusing to be seen in public with him or making a giant, public stink about his platform isn't the way to get him to make a stand on the issues that are important to me. Once he's elected and I'm on the inside, I'll have the ability to push him on those issues."

Thatcher's mouth twisted up in an expression of fond skepticism that I recognized well because I'd been seeing it on my parents for years. It was like setting a match to dry paper.

"Look, I love my family," I whispered. "They don't have to be the very best people for me to love them. Heck, they don't have to understand me or even support me for me to love them. Apparently, I go around loving people with zero regard for my personal needs." And wasn't I staring down at a prime example of that? "I'm not going to change my mind because you don't like it."

Thatcher's annoyance crumbled into concern, and a line appeared between his eyebrows. "Reagan, I wasn't criticizing you." He blew out a breath and sat up also. "Talking about this was the furthest thing from my mind when I was waiting for you tonight, and I apologize for leading us down this road. I was only trying to convey that I don't want you to ever accept less than you deserve or to... to feel like you need to be anyone you're not. I want you to feel empowered to stand up to Layla when she's asking you to do things that aren't in your job description. I want you to realize there are bigger, more fulfilling jobs out there than working for your father if you decide to leave PennCo. I want you to know that your voice, your perspective on the world, are valuable and deserve to be heard—"

"Right." I huffed out a laugh that expressed more pain than humor. The things he was saying, the sincerity in his eyes, was exactly what I'd wanted from him a week ago. Now, what I wanted from him was so much more... and absolutely never gonna happen. "You want me to stand up for myself and what I deserve, but you definitely don't want anyone to know you're in my bunk right now. You want to protect me from Layla, but you don't want to hear what I learned from Terrance, which means you won't help me protect *myself* and anyone else at PennCo. And you're side-eyeing *me* for giving in to my family when *you've* spent so long taking ownership of Brantleigh's life he might never learn to take responsibility for his own happiness or his own fuckups."

Too much. I'd said too much. As soon as the words were out of my mouth, I wanted to suck them back. Instead, I firmed my jaw and refused to utter another word.

Thatcher pulled away, literally and figuratively. Storm clouds crashed across his expression. "I can see we've gotten into the inadvisable act of exchanging unsolicited advice. My bad. I'll find my own bunk and leave you to your sleep."

As usual, I couldn't let him have the last word, even though I betrayed myself with my final jab. "Might as well sleep in the bedroom. Layla's probably in there fantasizing about you anyway. McGee totally called that whole situation... not that you listened to him either."

The only indication Thatcher heard me was the slight widening of his nostrils. "Good night, Reagan."

As he escaped through the bunk curtain, I felt that strange kind of emptiness that comes from pulling out of a lover. It was enough to make me low-key nauseated and edgy at the same time.

I opened my mouth to call him back, but the words didn't come. Maybe it was better this way. It would be easier to keep our distance from each other if we couldn't stand the sight of each other.

As I counted out the next two hours with the steady *thrum thrum thrum* of the bus tires, I did an awful lot of fantasizing about someone I couldn't stand the sight of.

———

When we finally reached Honeybridge late the following day, I shot off the bus like I'd been fired from a cannon. Layla had treated me like a brainless bridge troll the entire day, and Thatcher acted like he didn't have a single concern outside of work. It was a stark reminder of the truth. Thatcher Pennington was married to his job and always would be.

"Reagan, darling!" My mother's voice cut through the thin winter air as she strode down the shallow front steps to greet us. Her crisp navy wool trousers and cream turtleneck sweater were a calm contrast to the bright silver metallic snow boots JT and Flynn had given her for Christmas. Thankfully, they'd refrained from telling her they'd only selected those particular boots because they were called "Cougars." I was saving that tidbit for just the perfect moment.

"What took you so long?" she demanded, throwing air-kisses in my general direction before reaching out to grasp Thatcher's hands. "Oh, and Thatch-*errr*." She beamed a bright-white smile. "It's always *so* lovely to see you. Come in, come in. It's forecast to be utterly *frigid* the entire week of the festival. I'm so put *out*." Her forehead might have creased with a scowl, if such a thing were possible.

One would think frigid conditions would be optimal for an Ice Fest, but I knew better than to say this out loud.

We all trundled to the foyer, and I inhaled the warm, welcome scent of home. My mother's custom-blended botanical room spray was a cross between fresh pine and the glossy pages of a home-decor magazine. The usual bowls of wooden balls and vases of monochromatic feathers had replaced the holiday decorations since my previous visit over Christmas, but there was a roaring fire in the stone fireplace, giving the main living room a cozy feel.

As much as I enjoyed the bustle of Honeybridge in the summer tourist season, I liked the winter here just as well. And although I'd been dreading this interruption to our trip, I was surprised to find there were things I'd missed about this place.

My father stood in the living room, his cell at his ear, staring out over the rooftops of the town at the glittering waters of Lake Wellbridge in the distance. He was using his Senator Voice, so I knew better than to interrupt him with a greeting.

My mother continued her welcoming speech as our housekeeper, Rosalia, took Layla's and Thatcher's coats. Patricia was in her element, inviting everyone to sit and enjoy a "preprandial cocktail" before the other guests—*you remember Bunty and Magdalena Lamb, don't you, Thatcher? And the Parks and the Jains?*—gathered for dinner. Her overly enthusiastic discourse contrasted with the rude continuation of my father's phone call, reminding me what I *didn't* love about coming home.

And then, as only Patricia Wellbridge could, my mother made it ten times worse.

"Reagan, dear, take Mr. Pennington's bags upstairs and show him to his room while I help get Layla settled in the guest house."

Thatcher's eyes met mine as the heat of embarrassment crawled up my neck. "Yes, ma'am," I said, keeping the sarcasm volume as soft as possible while still allowing it an escape.

I moved back toward the door to fetch the bags McGee had deposited in the entryway. The expression on McGee's face was understanding and kind, which only made my humiliation more complete.

Once I had his bags in hand, I turned toward my boss. "Right this way, *sir*," I bit out.

Chapter Sixteen

Thatcher

REAGAN REFUSED to look at me as we made our way upstairs.

Perhaps that shouldn't have been as surprising as it was, given all that we'd said to each other the night before and the way we'd avoided each other most of the day. Maybe he'd intended for us to simply disappear from each other's lives as suddenly as we'd crashed together. But seeing the way his parents had treated him when we'd arrived—his mother commanding, his father flat-out ignoring him—had raised my protective hackles, and I wanted to somehow reassure him that I cared about his feelings and was on his side...

Which was difficult when he was pretending I didn't exist.

It was immature, I decided, which was probably why everyone said it was a bad idea to date someone so much younger. And it was pretty fucking ironic that Reagan was behaving this way after making remarks about *my* parenting skills. Reagan had no idea what it was like to raise a child. He also knew exactly why I blamed myself for Brant's behavior. So how dare he cast judgment on me for feeling responsible? Furthermore, Reagan's parting shot last night—accusing Layla of thinking inappropriate thoughts about me—was the pot calling the kettle black, not to mention completely off base and, once again, *immature*.

And I was going to tell him so. As soon as he deigned to look at me.

"You going to give me the silent treatment for a matter of minutes, hours, or days? I'd like to know so I can plan accordingly," I said drily as soon as we were alone.

Reagan's chin lifted a fraction, but otherwise, he pretended not to hear.

"You'll be in JT's room here on the right, Mr. Pennington." His voice was crisp and scrupulously polite. Patricia would be so proud. "There's an en suite bathroom that should have plenty of supplies, but if you need anything, Rosalia is usually in the kitchen and will be happy to help. I'm sure you've met her before. She's the one who keeps this place running."

He sounded like an automaton as he led me into the room and set my bags down on the crisply made bed. "I assume dinner will be served at seven. I suggest freshening up quickly unless you want to hear Patricia's passive-aggressive statements about busy schedules leading to the downfall of the American family."

I nudged the door closed behind me and moved closer to him, but he sidestepped around me and reopened the door. "See you at dinner," he said stiffly before escaping across the hall to his own room.

I stared after him, torn between feeling bad for his obvious discomfort and feeling annoyed at his petulance.

Before I could follow him and insist upon talking it through, my phone buzzed.

"Yeah," I snapped.

Brantleigh's familiar voice immediately reminded me to take a calming breath. "Dad. Hey. Are you picking me up or are you going to text me a location so I can get there myself?"

"A location?" I repeated. "I don't understand. Are we meeting somewhere tonight? Didn't we say we'd talk first thing tomorrow? You got the schedule of events January forwarded you, yes?"

"I did. But I thought... I mean, I'm working for you now, right? I figured you'd get me a room wherever you're staying. God knows there's no Four Seasons anywhere near this backwater, but I'm not picky. I could make do with a Marriott."

I literally shook my head like I was trying to clear away buzzing mosquitos. "I'm not at a hotel, and from what I gather, all the hotels in the area are at capacity because of the festival. I'm staying with the Wellbridges. So are Layla and, obviously, Reagan."

"Oh." Brant paused a beat. "Then I'll meet you at Patricia's?"

I rubbed a hand over my forehead. "I thought you already had a place to stay."

"I'm booked at the retreat for another week, yeah, but... Dad, they turn the electricity off every night at eleven so the molecules won't disrupt your sleep. My phone hasn't been fully charged in a week. And the internet is too weak to stream *anything*." He sounded pained. "If I'm working for you, don't I get treated like any other employee?"

"You do," I informed him. "Which in this case means finding whatever accommodations you can. Remember, I've been sleeping in the bus for a week, and now I'm staying in

JT's old room since all the Wellbridges' guest rooms are full. That's simply how things are right now."

"But if you asked—"

"I won't," I interrupted. "Not when you have a perfectly fine place to stay... and not after what happened last time you stayed with Patricia and Trent."

"Oh, fuck me," Brant groaned. "You think they're still pissy about last summer? I told everyone it was all a joke! People took it way too seriously and turned it into a whole *thing*, but you made me apologize. Like, get over it already."

"Apologizing doesn't mean a guarantee of forgiveness or that there won't be consequences," I said sharply. "One of the consequences in this case is that you'll have to stay where you are. Understand?"

After a moment, Brant sighed. "Yeah. Whatever."

He sounded a bit unhappy, but frankly, I'd expected a lot more pushback and to offer a lot more bribes to make Brantleigh accept the situation—which was not because I'd *taken ownership of his life*, as certain people had incorrectly suggested, thank you very much, but because I'd given in too often and spoiled him too much.

"So what time did you want to meet tomorrow?" he asked again. "And when do I fill out the paperwork to get paid and stuff?"

"I'll have HR call you tomorrow morning." I sat on the edge of the bed and smiled a bit for the first time since Reagan had walked out. "You're eager to get to work, huh? Like father, like son," I teased.

"Huh? Oh. Yeah. Definitely. I have some ideas about my job title and whatnot. But first, I'm gonna need to get some decent clothes. Not sure there's anything designer in a hundred-mile radius, but there have to be some boutiques in Portland—"

"Whatever you have is fine, and I have a bunch of Elustre samples I can give you, too. Send January your sizes, and I'll have her send you more. That way, we can post your picture to the company Instagram, if you're okay with that—"

"Hell yeah. That would be sick," he agreed. "You can tag me, too."

I chuckled. "Great. You know, I'm really pleased that you're so enthusiastic about this job. Just promise you won't go too far overboard and become a workaholic like your old man," I joked. "Balance is the key."

He snorted. "Like you know any damn thing about balance."

"Hey! I know plenty, even if I don't always put it into practice. Focusing too much on work and making it your *only* purpose is almost as bad as not having any purpose at all. It can prevent you from having relationships with the people in your life who matter." I cleared my throat. "I never wanted that for you."

I wasn't sure when I'd started wanting it for myself.

An image of Reagan surfaced in my mind, as it did so often these days, and I wondered what balance would look like with him in my life. Though I'd never been the type to sit on a couch and watch the snow fall, or stroll Central Park in spring sunshine, or cut out of work early for a long summer weekend, it was shockingly easy to picture myself doing all of those things as long as a pair of aquamarine eyes were at my side, warm and teasing and steady.

But that was just a fantasy. In reality, critical eyes would follow us anytime we strolled together, noting the difference in our ages. People at work would whisper when Reagan took time off to vacation with the boss. The media would have a field day as the *Billionaire Dates Politician Friend's*

Son headlines wrote themselves. And what were the chances Reagan wanted to curl up on a sofa when he could be out with younger, non-workaholic friends, doing Instagrammable things?

"So, tomorrow," Brant said, bringing my attention back to the call. "Meet at twelve or twelve thirty? Maybe at that Tavern place with the cute bartender?"

I frowned. "Brant, our first event at the Investment Summit starts at twelve thirty. You did see the schedule of events, right?"

"Yeah. Sort of. I mean, I didn't *memorize* it—"

"Never mind. Layla might need your help with preparation, so let's meet at ten."

"In the *morning*? Dad, I'm still mostly on West Coast time..."

"Fine," I conceded. "Noon, then, at the Tavern. McGee's picking up a rental car, and I can have him grab you at eleven forty-five—"

"McGee." Brantleigh said my driver's name sourly. "Not necessary. I have a rental."

"Alright." My lips twitched. I'd never liked the animosity between McGee and Brant, but if it spurred Brant to take more personal responsibility, that could only be a good thing.

I changed into a suit, and pausing for only half a second outside Reagan's closed door, I made my way back downstairs for dinner with the Wellbridges.

Faint murmurs of conversation floated out of the living room, overlayed with Patricia's much-louder voice as she held court on something *those Honeycutts* had done, but before I took a step toward the door, Trent spotted me and silently beckoned me down the hall to his wood-paneled study.

"Thatcher," he said, clapping my shoulder warmly once we were inside. "Great to see you. Drink?" Without waiting for a reply, he moved toward the built-in bar on one wall of the room and poured me a scotch. "You must be glad to be off the road. Those trips can be exhausting, especially at our age."

I refrained from pointing out that Trent was at *least* a decade older than I was. "It's even less fun in winter," I said, accepting the crystal low-ball he offered. The smoky scent hit my nose before I took the first sip. "Seemed like you were busy when we arrived." Too busy to greet your own son. "Problem with the campaign?"

Trent shrugged dismissively and gestured me to a leather club chair before taking his own. "Not a problem, exactly. Just something we need to keep an eye on." He leaned back in his chair and sipped his drink thoughtfully, watching me with blue eyes ten shades duller than his son's. "Speaking of which... *Reagan*," he sighed, in much the same way I imagined he'd say "...*taxes*," or "...*woke politics*," or some other harbinger of societal collapse.

I remembered him saying Reagan's name just like that many times. But I remembered, too, standing with Reagan outside the Newport Grille in Wichita and vowing that I'd never again hear that sigh without speaking up to let Trent know he was wrong. Annoyed as I was at Reagan, I wouldn't stay silent.

"God, yes, let's talk about Reagan," I said. "Trent, I think you've been holding out on me. The man's incredibly talented—you should see the uptick in engagement since he took over our social media accounts—and he's a hell of a hard worker, too." I took another slow sip of scotch.

Trent's eyes narrowed for a moment like he was trying to puzzle out some hidden meaning in my words, and then his face brightened. "Ah, I see. You're trying to make me feel better. I know my son, Thatcher. You don't need to bullshit about him just because of our friendship. That's above and beyond."

I clenched my back teeth together to keep from sputtering the expensive drink. "It would be, yes," I said flatly. "But I'm not bullshitting. I don't keep nonperforming employees on the payroll, even for the sake of friendship."

He smiled wryly. "Patricia and I appreciated you putting him on the payroll in the first place... not to mention all the help you must've given him since. To be honest, we expected Reagan home before Christmas. He's always been a bit... high-spirited, as Patricia calls it. Follow-through's not his specialty." He stared down into his drink glumly. "You know, Thatcher, children are like the stock market."

I blinked.

"You can do as much preparation as possible," Trent went on, "invest in their education and extracurricular opportunities, monitor them diligently—I mean, you couldn't ask for a more loving and involved mother than Patricia—"

I coughed into my scotch.

"—but still, sometimes they underperform." Trent took a considering sip of his drink. "Ah, well."

Meanwhile, I clutched my glass in shaking hands and tried very hard not to throw it. *Underperform?* Were we talking about the same Reagan?

"On the plus side, though," Trent continued more brightly, "Patricia and I make good-looking children, and the boy's great for optics. Housewives love him, and the young voters can't seem to get enough. He's... what's the word? Relatable." He let out a little laugh. "My campaign manager says the click rate's astronomical when Reagan's in a campaign photo, whatever that means. They tell me it's a positive thing."

The liquor burned in my chest and gut. "Your son is more than a pretty face. He's incredible with people—seriously masterful in a crowd—not to mention creative and knowledgeable and funny—" I broke off, afraid I was speaking too passionately, giving too much away. "He's wasted on photo ops. And he's ambitious enough to want more—"

"Ambitious?" For a moment, Trent looked confused. "You sure you're not confusing him with JT? Now, *there's* a go-getter. Would've made vice president in the city if he hadn't fallen in with *that Honeycutt*—"

"You mean Flynn." My eyelid began to twitch. "Remember, I like Flynn. I believed in his meadery enough to invest in it."

Trent nodded. "Of course, of course! It's great for Honeybridge, and it's good for Maine. We need more young entrepreneurs like Flynn."

He sounded like one of his own campaign ads. Like a parody of himself, talking out both sides of his head. Had I really never noticed this side of him before? Or had I simply not cared until now?

"Did you know *Reagan* is an entrepreneur?" Though I tried to stay calm, I couldn't keep a thread of anger from my voice. "He has a lucrative social media business with over a million followers across multiple platforms. Lifestyle brands throw sponsorship opportunities at him left and right—"

"Of course I know about his social media thing." Trent looked more confused than ever, like he could hear my anger but couldn't understand the reason for it. "I just don't think receiving free sweatpants with a giant logo on the ass qualifies him as an 'entrepreneur.' Mainstream media would love for you to believe a social media guru can make grown-up money, but I've seen the truth firsthand. Reagan receives packages of free stuff all day long, but it's not cold hard cash. I know they're throwing him a few bucks here and there—he made quite a scene about paying his own way when his mother expressed concerns about him moving to New York—but in a few months, he'll be bored of 'adulting,' as the kids say, and tired of commuting to work by bicycle from whatever Hoboken hovel he's rented. Then he'll come home to Honeybridge and lay in bed staring at the ceiling until Patricia offers to send him off to the Amalfi Coast. Trust me, Thatcher, I've seen this before." He stared down his nose at me and repeated his words from earlier. "I know my son."

But he didn't. He didn't at all.

"Trent." I leaned forward. "Your son probably makes half a million dollars a year posting on social media."

As soon as the words were out of my mouth, I realized it wasn't my place to say them. For all I knew, Reagan was purposely keeping his parents in the dark. But Christ, it felt like Trent was determined to hang on to the false narrative where his son was an incapable, dependent slacker, and I needed him to see how wrong he was.

He barked out a laugh. "If that were true, Thatcher, why would he bother working for you?"

Because he wants his parents to take him seriously, you idiot. Because part of him believes he can't take himself seriously unless he has a traditional job.

But I didn't say that out loud. We were expected at the dinner table in less than ten minutes. It wouldn't do to start a fight with my host, especially when he might start to wonder why I was so passionate about defending his child.

A moment later, Trent set his glass down and gave me a

campaign smile—wry, friendly, and insincere. "Have to say, I really hope you're right and that he's started thinking about things more seriously. Once we're in the governor's mansion, the boy's not going to be any use to me at all, and you'd better believe I'll be a whole lot less likely to keep paying his way. Time he stood on his own two feet." He nodded to himself. Then, he added with no trace of irony, "But Patricia and I appreciate you giving him time off to help the family out."

I stepped closer and reached out to slam my crystal glass on the table between us when I was interrupted by a soft knock and the creak of a door opening behind me.

"Dad? Mother would like you to come immediately and lead us in to dinner. I think—oh." Reagan paused when he saw me, then flushed from his carefully styled hairline to the collar of his shirt. He straightened. "Sorry to interrupt. Bunty Lamb has been telling Layla how beneficial climate change will be for Bunty's tan lines, and while Flynn has been holding back admirably from correcting her, he's turning an unhealthy purplish sort of color. JT flat-out refused to '*control your boyfriend if you absolutely must have him here, Jonathan*' and threatened to leave if Mother said a single critical word. I think she hopes that getting everyone in their assigned seats will prevent Firecracker from... well, exploding."

Trent stood and moved around the desk toward the door. "She's right, no doubt. I don't know why people get so upset over trivialities when we're having a nice dinner."

"Yes, it's in extremely poor taste to worry about the fate of the planet when Rosalia's made pavlova for dessert," Reagan agreed blandly.

Trent nodded. "Well, let's go, then. Oh." He paused and clapped Reagan on the shoulder. "Mr. Pennington was just telling me he has no complaints about your job performance thus far. Keep up the good work."

Reagan's ears turned red, and his jaw tightened. "Yes, sir. I'd hate for *Mr. Pennington* to be dissatisfied."

I sucked in a slow, silent breath. I needed to say something, to correct Trent's statement, but I couldn't. Emotions bubbled just beneath my skin—anger from my conversation with Trent, annoyance from Reagan avoiding me, hurt from our pointless argument last night, helpless frustration from every fucking minute of the last two days when I hadn't been able to take care of Reagan with my hands and mouth and cock—and if I said a single word, all of it might erupt like a volcano. Instead, I silently *willed* Reagan to look up, to let me reassure him without words.

He turned on his heel and walked out after his father, never lifting his eyes from the ground.

The scotch in my stomach turned sour as I followed.

The meal was two hours of eye-opening performances, not only by the politicians in the room but also by Reagan himself. There was no hint of hurt or anger in his polite demeanor. He was all cheer and charm, easy flirtation and eager attention. He said nothing of interest but nodded intently when spoken to. His smile never faltered.

I hated every minute of it.

This was the Reagan I'd known for years. The Reagan I'd *thought* I'd known. Handsome but shallow. Courteous but aimless. Adorably sexy but hopelessly immature.

If I hadn't spent the last week cataloging his expressions, listening to his thoughts on a variety of subjects, and obsessively replaying them in my head every damn night, I might still believe his act was genuine. But the Reagan I'd come to know was opinionated, and snarky, and endlessly interesting. His charm and flirtatiousness were warm and friendly—a way to make connections rather than a defense mechanism. My Reagan's smile lived in his beautiful eyes.

Worse than seeing him retreat behind his polite facade was that I could see now how much it cost him to maintain it. His cardboard smile was limited to the lower half of his face while those aquamarine eyes that lived hook-deep in my soul remained shuttered.

I wanted to scream. I wanted to ball the pristinely pressed tablecloth into tight fists and yank with all my might, sending crystal and china crashing to the floor. I wanted to wrap Reagan up in my arms and carry him from the room like some movie hero while the music swelled and the credits rolled.

And then what? What the hell could I offer Reagan that was better than what he had now? A romance built on secrecy and half-truths with a man who'd managed to drive away his own son, his two ex-wives, and most of his friends?

So I stayed calm and silent... and watchful.

"Patricia tells me you're a friend of the family," the white-haired woman on my right said, leaning close enough to waft expensive perfume my way. "Are you here for the festival?"

"In part. There's also a small investment summit in town where I'm making an appearance since I invested in a local business last summer." I shrugged. "Reagan suggested it, and there's a reason why he's handling the entire social media arm of my company. He's absolutely brilliant."

"Reagan works for you?" Her face lit up. "How lovely. I know he's been doing campaign appearances for Trent, and I must admit..." She leaned closer and lowered her voice. "I had some concerns."

I paused with my wineglass halfway to my lips, then set it down. "Really."

"Mmm. It's not healthy to keep your adult children dependent the way they have with Reagan. An article in the *Times* a few years ago suggested that seeing your children as problematic and flawed could be a destructive, self-fulfilling prophesy because you end up catering to that narrative rather than trusting them to find their own solutions to problems. That's precisely what Trent and Patricia have done. I'm not sure they realize it."

I glanced over at Reagan and caught him staring at me. As soon as he saw me glance in his direction, he turned away and nodded at whatever his mother was saying, fake smile firmly in place. My chest tightened. "Yes," I murmured. "I... I see your point."

After finishing dinner, I managed to make my excuses and retire to my room sooner than was polite. Falling asleep before Reagan came upstairs was the only way to keep myself from sneaking into his room and begging him to share his bed—and his body—with me.

As soon as I woke the next morning, I busied myself with a run on the trail around Lake Wellbridge—also known as Kiss Me Quick Lake, if you fell in the Honeycutt camp— and out of habit, I took several partial selfies of myself in Elustre wear to post on social media. Thankfully, I stopped myself before sending them to Reagan to post. Considering we pretty much weren't currently speaking to each other, I assumed he wouldn't welcome texted selfies.

When I returned to the house, I showered, dressed, and threw myself into work in the privacy of JT's borrowed bedroom until it was time to meet Brant.

January wasn't surprised by my call and jumped right into work mode with me. The only hint she knew something was off with me was when we were wrapping up the call and she hesitated before asking me one final question.

"So... how's it going with Reagan?"

"What do you mean?" I snapped, responding without using my brain first. As soon as my own clipped tone hit my ears, I closed my eyes in resignation. "He's fine. It's going fine."

"*Huh.* Interesting."

"What's interesting? January, I don't have time to sit around gossiping—"

"I just got an alert from your Apple Watch that you were having a cardiac event, right around the time I mentioned Reagan. Oooh, look, it's happening again. So *odd.*"

I glanced down at the offending item on my wrist. "Stop spying on me through my health app."

"Dr. Anderson only let you out of your frequent blood-pressure checkups if you promised to provide him regular cardiac data, remember? And you tasked me with it, and I quote, '*to keep that nosy asshole off my back.*' So don't complain to me when I want to know what's causing you stress right now."

I took a silent breath and forced myself to calm down. "I'm not stressed. I'm busy. The Apple Watch can't tell the difference. Also, I've been exercising like he told me, and I've taken all the damned supplements you pushed on me. Just ask McGee."

"McGee," January said thoughtfully. "You know, he had some interesting things to say about Reagan Wellbridge—"

I stood up from the desk and searched for my wallet. "I don't have time to discuss this right now. At this rate, I'm going to be late meeting Brant before heading to the Investment Summit."

"Good luck! And say hi to Reagan if you happen to see —oh, wow! Would you look at that heart rate spike?"

"Goodbye, January," I said drily.

After finishing the call, I grabbed my coat and made my way through the house, not bothering to look for Reagan since the housekeeper had said he and Trent were at a campaign breakfast meeting.

So when McGee dropped Layla and me off outside the Tavern, I was surprised to see Reagan there.

And even more surprised to see him hauling my son out of the front door and shoving him bodily against the side of the building and snarling in his face.

Chapter Seventeen

Reagan

I SLEPT LIKE SHIT, tossing and turning while actively keeping myself from throwing myself across the hall into Thatcher's bed. Maybe if he hadn't been sleeping in JT's old room, I would have tried it, but the thought of sleeping with my dad's friend while in my brother's bed was simply a bridge too far.

That, and the fact I was angry at him. Mostly, I was angry at him for being mature and correct, faults that I considered unforgivable at the moment.

He'd pushed one of my buttons by calling me out on my participation in my father's campaign. The problem was, I hadn't realized it was a button until he'd smashed it.

But sitting here in the country club's private dining room listening to a bunch of old white men congratulate themselves on keeping change to a minimum in state government made my insides begin to boil.

Dad's campaign manager was a woman named Violet. While most of the time she seemed to hold her own in conversations like this one, today, she seemed to be losing every battle she attempted to fight.

"I'd like to get back to the issue of activating the college student population," she said, leaning forward in her seat and peering at my father over her reading glasses. A notebook full of scribbled pages lay in front of her now that the breakfast dishes had been removed. "As I told the Senator yesterday, our campaign is floundering amongst younger voters, and the polling is... concerning. Research shows that firing up this demographic can have an exponential impact on disseminating critical talking points—"

Arnold Duffer's jowls jiggled as he frowned. "I don't see how that's possible. Those young folk don't seem to give a good goddamn about *real* issues."

As the ancient CEO of one of the largest sawmill companies in New England, Arnold didn't seem like the best person to chime in on issues related to young folk, but no one had asked me. As usual.

Violet nodded sympathetically. "I certainly understand your confusion, Arnold. But they are reactive. Get them excited about an issue, and they'll spread it through word of mouth to everyone they know."

"Social media," I added softly to mark the importance of the moment in my overall strategy for boosting his efforts in that arena.

My father shot a look at me before nodding. "Reagan can help us with that. He's been doing social media things for Thatcher Pennington over at PennCo Fiber. It's one of the reasons I brought him here today."

It was?

I'd assumed my father had voluntold me to attend this meeting because he'd wanted a show of familial support, and I'd been too tired and frustrated by all things Thatcher to balk. But if he was finally ready to give this the attention and credit it deserved, if my plan to become his social media strategist rather than his camera fodder was finally working, I was *all in*.

I straightened in my chair and tried to blink away my fatigue. "I... yes. Absolutely, Dad. Let me know what issues you'd like to focus on, and I can create some videos for them while I'm here."

"I'm sure Violet can get you the approved graphics from our marketing group," he said, gesturing with his coffee cup. "Just add the pound signs, or whatever you call 'em, and get the attention of the college boys. Then we'll be good to go."

"Hashtags," Arnold scoffed. "If only the kids put half the effort into their classes as they do their hashtags, the world would be a better place."

A man named Brian Raffey tapped a thick finger on the table next to his coffee cup. "Can you blame them if their classes are all about how to gallivant around in the wilderness? My son tried to convince me to let him take four credit hours on something called Independent Study in Outdoor Recreation. What I want to know is how the youth in this state plan to pay their bills if that's what they're studying in school?"

"Outdoor recreation makes up five percent of Maine's economy," I said, trying to maintain a neutral tone. "That's more than double the national average. It's one of the reasons our state universities offer programs in those areas."

Violet looked thoughtful, but the rest of the table looked either confused or annoyed by my addition to the conversation. My father fell on the annoyed side.

"Be that as it may," Dad said, ever the diplomat, "I agree that galvanizing the youth is important but challenging. I expect Reagan will reach this audience."

I let out a slow breath of relief and began to get excited. This was the opportunity I'd been waiting for. Social media strategy for a political campaign was everything, and targeting the college-age demographic made it more fun. I could try some off-the-wall stuff I'd been thinking about and really boost engagement. My parents wouldn't understand what I was doing, but they'd be impressed when they saw the numbers—

My impromptu brainstorming session almost caused me to miss Violet's next comment.

"We'll have to clarify your stance on tuition assistance before we get too involved in the student groups, Senator. After your comment at the food bank press event, we've been receiving increasing pressure to speak to that in more detail."

Arnold sighed, and Brian shook his head. My father's eyes flicked between the two men before glancing up at the ceiling. "These kids," he murmured. "They just don't understand reality."

Brian tapped his finger on the table again. "Ask them how they're going to pay for it. That's what I want to know."

I opened my mouth to comment, but my father shot me a look that very clearly commanded me to stand down. I clenched my teeth against the urge to defy him. As a politician's son, I knew better than to make a scene in front of influential campaign donors, regardless of how strongly I felt about the topic.

They bandied language around before coming up with a more detailed way of saying... very little of substance, which seemed to be exactly what my father wanted.

When he finally finished his coffee and said his farewells to the others, he turned to me with a smile. "That went well. I'm glad to have Brian on board. His campaign contribution alone is funding our entire ad budget for this quarter."

I swallowed a groan. "And in exchange, all you have to do is ignore Maine's youth when it comes to affordable college tuition."

"You've been begging to work on my campaign's social media, and I'm allowing it. I didn't ask for your opinion on my platform, son."

"You're letting me add hashtags. There's so much more I could do."

"I'm giving you a chance here, Reagan—a limited-time, one-shot chance—in part because Violet had some grave concerns yesterday just before you arrived and in part because Thatcher said some positive things about your performance—"

"He did?" I felt my face go hot at the surprise in my own voice. "I mean... I appreciate him volunteering that information." Especially since Thatcher and I hadn't been on speaking terms all day yesterday.

My father grunted. "I disregarded what he said at the time, but upon reflection, I decided you might be useful. Consider it an unpaid internship for the time you're here, which might be extended if all goes well." He smiled benignly at the server who'd come to collect our dishes and waited until she was gone before continuing. "But continuing to argue with your boss is a surefire way to get yourself fired before you even start. Understood?"

I inhaled sharply. This was the job I'd wanted badly enough to endure months of frustrating busy work at PennCo, badly enough to embark on a cross-country bus tour in the dead of winter with the boss I'd probably already been falling for, even if I hadn't known it yet. And while part of me wanted to flip a table, tell my father exactly where he could shove his disrespect, and flounce out... I also knew that was precisely what my father expected me to do.

To quit.

So I nodded once, accepting his terms.

"Good." He grinned at me for real, then slapped the table and pushed himself to his feet. "Now, I'd like to head to the festival and meet up with your mother. Violet's sending over a photographer to capture us shaking hands while the volunteers set up the booths."

When we arrived in the center of Honeybridge, people were buzzing around bundled in their parkas, all bright eyes and friendly smiles. Thankfully, the sun shone brightly, and despite my mother's dire predictions, the temperature wasn't as bad as it could have been in mid-January. I'd never understood why our town insisted on holding any outdoor event this time of year, but once something was declared a tradition in Honeybridge, it became sacrosanct.

My mother stood in the middle of the crowd, holding a clipboard and directing the action. A chilly breeze stirred the hem of her long, red cashmere coat, but her blonde bob did not sway one inch. At her side stood a balding man with a camera—no doubt the photographer Violet had hired—and the poor guy already looked harried and exhausted. I felt for him.

"Ah, Trent!" She waved at my father from two feet away like he was a solider coming home from war, and the photographer dutifully stepped back to capture their joyful reunion. "And Reagan, darling." She cupped my cheek with one hand and beamed at me lovingly. "You didn't even *try* to make time for a haircut, did you?" she said, voice low and reproving. "*Tsk.* What's done is done, I suppose."

When the camera shutter stopped clicking, she stepped back. "Doesn't everything look particularly lovely this year? I do think we've exceeded everyone's expectations. Now, where will we begin? We want to get some shots of the Senator inter-acting with the townsfolk," she instructed the photographer. "But we'll want to be careful about where we go first. The Senator's endorsement is bound to draw attention."

"Oh! There's Willow Honeycutt," I said, waving at Flynn's mother, who was decked out in a colorful, hand-knit hat, scarf, and mittens. "Why not start there? They're prac-tically family now."

"Darling, while I have accepted that your brother's inamorata may become a Wellbridge at some point in the future, let's not be too hasty in using the f-word when describing Willow's brood, hmm?"

I fought not to roll my eyes. "Right. Of course not."

"Besides, she's on that Clean Waterways committee that's looking to clean up Lake Wellbridge," my father pointed out.

"Hmph. As though the water needs protecting now that the beavers are gone," Mother scoffed. She touched a hand to her perfect hair. "Oh, look, Trent. There's Justine with a group of young mothers. That would be a perfectly whole-some photo op."

My cousin Justine waved from where she sat in a folding chair, attempting to nurse her newest baby while preventing her other two kids from knocking down a folding table and using it as a snowball shield. I grinned and waved back.

"Indeed." My father smoothed his coat and checked that his lapel pin was straight before heading us in that direction. "Nothing says family values like mothers and their precious babies."

The photographer and I stood back and shared a look that clearly said, *I'm not telling him, YOU tell him.* Apparently, sharing the Senator's DNA meant I'd drawn the short straw.

"Uh, Dad? I do think this could make for an awesome photo, but since the women are here representing the La Leche League, we're going to have to stage the photos a certain way—"

"The what?" My father stopped dead. "What's that?"

My mother seemed to be equally mystified, though I wasn't sure how that was possible.

"It's a group that advocates for breastfeeding mothers—" I began.

"Oh, my word." My mother grabbed my father's arm and wrenched him away. "Under no circumstances will the Senator be photographed while those women..."

"*Feed* their precious babies?" I finished, deadpan. "It's simple biology, Mother."

"Exactly," she exclaimed, scandalized. "Reagan, avert your eyes. It's inappropriate."

I rubbed the spot between my eyes where a headache was beginning to form. "What *would* be appropriate, then?" I demanded, unable to hide my impatience.

The four of us—if I included the hapless photographer—turned in a slow circle, surveying the various clusters of Honeybridgers, but my parents found a reason to quickly and quietly veto each, from the local organic farmers' guild ("It's not that I *don't* support organic farmers; it's just that I don't know if I *do* support them."), to a troop of lollipop-selling Wild Explorer Girls ("Do we really want to encourage wildness in our youth?"), to a bake sale to benefit the Senior Center ("Trent, you cannot be photographed with Ernest Chandler and his fig bars after what he said about my hibiscus lemonade at the Arbor Day Foliage Fiesta.")

Finally, at the end of the row of stalls, my father found a group he approved of.

"The Box Day Committee?" I asked, trying not so successfully to hide my disgust. "Are you serious? That's Mother's committee."

"So it is," my mother approved. "And look, Tommy Strickland is manning the table. He's on the town council," she reminded my father unnecessarily. "And his brother-in-law—"

"Represents the teacher's union," they recited in perfect harmony, smiling at one another.

This time, I was the one scandalized. "No," I said firmly. "Dad, you cannot take pictures with a man who tried to get his wife to organize a boycott of Alden's salon simply because the man displayed a Safe Space sticker on the door—"

"That was *not* why," my mother sniffed. "It was because he hired Oona Frank to sweep floors when she was underage—"

"Two weeks underage, and only because she needed the money to help her mom pay the electric bill," I pointed out. "And since the boycott didn't come up until months later, I highly doubt the two were related, no matter what Tommy claimed after the boycott failed."

"Well. We'll never really know, will we?" But my mother bit her lip in an uncharacteristic show of indecision.

I laid a hand on her arm. "Mother, you go to Alden's salon religiously. You said he was one of the most gifted hairstylists you've ever come across. Surely you don't need to be photographed with the person who tried to destroy his business for no other reason than because Alden wants to support gay youth. For heaven's sake, your own beloved eldest son is—"

"Reagan, modulate your voice, please," she interrupted. She adopted a pleasant smile and raised a hand in greeting to a woman passing by. "I believe I told you how many reporters there are here, dear. Some from national news organizations—"

"So what?" I demanded. "Is it a secret that JT is gay? Because if so, he probably shouldn't be standing over by Willow with his hands in Flynn's back pockets." I tilted my head toward where my brother stood, gazing at his boyfriend with his heart in his eyes.

"Of course it's not a secret! We love Jonathan... *and* Flynn," she added, grudgingly but sincerely. "Your father and I are truly happy for them. But Reagan, there's a difference between knowing a thing and... and screaming it out loud. They're a part of our family, certainly, but they're not what the Senator's platform represents. Surely you understand the difference."

I closed my eyes, which were suddenly scratchy and throbbing in rhythmic counterpoint to the pounding in my head.

The sad thing was, I did understand... sort of. Hadn't I said something similar for years? That being pansexual was only one part of me and arguably the least interesting? That there was no need for me to "come out" to my parents or the public because I already *was* out to my friends and brother and sexual partners, and no one else needed to know?

It was true, damn it, and I stood by that—no one *should* feel like they had to come out, *ever*, if they didn't want to. In fact, I'd always thought the whole notion of "coming out of the closet" implied that everyone on the LGBTQ spectrum was born into the world's shittiest, darkest escape room and had to fight to free ourselves, using someone else's rules, on someone else's timeframe, if we ever wanted to be taken seriously. I rejected the whole fucking concept.

But...

In that moment, I also recalled two snippets of conversation I'd had that week. The first from that night in Colorado when McGee had recounted Thatcher's words of wisdom to him. *Maybe I needed to fight, and I was just picking the wrong fights.* The second, words Thatcher himself had spoken. *Living up to other people's expectations is a losing game. You need to live up to your own.*

The two thoughts fused together in my brain, and suddenly, the world came into a different sort of focus, much like pulling on tinted ski goggles after being snow-blind for hours.

What the hell was I doing?

Had I really just agreed to work for my father—*unpaid*—so I could prove myself to him? Was I agreeing to give up the life I'd been building in New York, my job at PennCo, the possibility of ever being with Thatcher in any capacity? And what about my *own* social media and the brand I'd been building? Would I give that up, too, if my father asked it of me?

What kind of endgame was that? Why had this ever been my goal?

If I'd hoped to affect political change from the inside, I'd been deluding myself. Deep down, I knew I didn't have a hope in hell of changing my father's views on political issues because the man tried as hard as he could not to *have* views on political issues. He chose his platform based on exit polls and donors. He wasn't an evil man—he really wasn't—and he'd even been a pretty decent dad for most of my life, but as a candidate... he sucked.

And if I'd been doing this to gain my parents' approval,

that was even more fantastical. Working for my father, my life would become a daily drip of condescending head pats and warnings that I'd better not screw up as he projected his own fears of losing the election onto me. This morning's confrontation and set-down would only be the tip of the iceberg. Even if I hadn't spent the last week working for a man who'd told me "I trust you" point-blank after two days of being on my worst behavior and didn't have that example to compare it to, I knew having my dad as a boss would break me. I'd lose myself entirely and become a Reagan-shaped robot, permanently set to Overly Polite Mode.

Worst of all, Trent and Patricia wouldn't even know the change was happening because my parents didn't have a clue who I really was... and that was on me—at least in part—because I'd never told them.

I wanted their respect so badly, but how could they possibly respect me when I didn't respect *myself* enough to stand up and say, "This is who I am, this is how I'm choosing to spend my life, this is the line in the sand I will not allow you to cross, and no, I will not be taking comments or questions at this time"? Proving myself *was* a losing game, exactly as Thatcher had tried to tell me, because my parents wanted me to prove that I was just like them... and I *wasn't*.

I didn't want to be.

So instead of fighting for my parents' respect no matter the cost, it was time to pick a different fight. The one where I fought to be a person *I* could respect instead. A man who chose his own path, achieved his own goals, and had a future that included loving and being loved by whoever I wanted, whether that was Thatcher—*please, baby Jesus, let it be Thatcher*—or not.

I'd spent a long time hiding behind a mask, and was that really any better than a closet?

"Mother. Dad." I smiled, bright and honest. "I should probably tell you that I'm pansexual." I caught my mother's confused frown and felt laughter bubbling inside me. It felt a lot like *relief*. "FYI, pansexuality has nothing to do with actual pans," I said gently, knowing my father would have no idea what I meant. "It means that I am attracted to people regardless of their sex or gender. My most recent... relationship—" I stumbled a bit over the word before deciding it fit. "—involved a man."

"I see." My mother blinked rapidly. "Well. That's..." She looked around, as if hoping that the assembly of happy, pink-cheeked Honeybridgers would help her find the right word... and maybe they did. "...good," she said at last.

My father said nothing but pursed his lips and studied me thoughtfully.

"It is good," I agreed. "But I think you'll understand that when I hear you say JT and Flynn don't represent Dad's campaign platform, I can't help but think that platform doesn't represent *me*. And I can't continue working with you. Not on your social media strategy and not in front of the cameras either."

"You're quitting," my father said. He nodded once, as though this confirmed something for him.

I couldn't deny twenty-eight years of habit made me quail a bit at the disapproval in his voice, but I straightened my shoulders. "You might see it that way. I prefer to think of it as *not* quitting... on myself, what I stand for, and my own happiness."

"But Reagan..." My mother sounded truly shocked and unhappy, which hit me even harder than my dad's reaction. "Don't you want to help your father win?"

I studied them both for a minute—my mother's perfect hairstyle and perfectly unlined face, my father's perfectly straight lapel pin—and said, "To be honest, I'm not sure he can win. Not on the platform he has now. Dad, your donors like to talk a lot about what's wrong with *young people today*, like we've all been corrupted by hashtags, but all social media's done is teach us that anyone can look great with a filter on. They want a repre-sentative who cares more about what and who he stands for than how he looks while he's doing it, and if you don't get on board with that..." I shrugged. "Anyway. I love you both. I'll plan to see you back at the house later, if that's alright?"

"Yes. Yes, of course," my mother agreed, still looking shell-shocked. She wrapped her hand around the Senator's elbow. "Your father and I will see you then."

I kissed her cheek gently, nodded at my father, and walked away. As I did, my hands trembled.

Holy shit.

I knew I'd done the right thing—the only true and honest thing I could do. And it felt *good*. Heady. Empow-ering as fuck.

But I'd been raised not to make waves, especially when my father was in campaign mode. To be seen and not heard around donors. To smile, smile, smile whenever we were in public as a family, no matter what I was actually feeling. Today, I'd broken a cardinal rule—in public, no less, even if no one else had heard—so I was also low-key, irrationally afraid that I'd earned myself seven years of bad luck.

I found myself in front of the Tavern in hopes of finding my brother. No one else would understand exactly what I'd done—how simultaneously amazing and embarrassingly terrifying it felt to stand up to Patricia and Trent, even as an adult man—like JT would. But it wasn't until I'd pulled open the door and found Castor Honeycutt pulling pints behind the bar that I remembered JT and Flynn were back outside.

I took off my coat and slid onto a stool anyway.

"Hey, Reagan. Haven't seen you in a bit." Castor's smile was sweet and warm, as usual. There was a reason his grandfather had nicknamed him *Sunshine*. "Can I get you something?"

"Maybe... Actually, yeah." It was almost noon, right? And I could really use a drink. I scanned the menu hanging over the bar that listed all the mead varietals Flynn brewed right on-site and grinned. Flynn used to serve only five varietals, each named for one of his siblings. Now, there was a sixth option.

Honeybridge Kiss Me Quick - Tasty enough to turn a Frog into your own Prince Charming! An invigorating blend of wildflower honey, crisp apples, and zesty citrus.

"Flynn made a mead for JT?" I asked with a sigh. "How cool is that?"

Castor glanced at the board, too, and his gentle smile softened even further. "Oh yeah. He started working on it last summer, but we only started serving it maybe a month ago. Flynn tried claiming it was inspired by Kiss Me Quick *Lake* and the old legend, and JT said he knew *exactly* what inspired it, and then the two of them just looked at each other—you know how they do?—until Alden threw a bar cloth at Flynn and said they were both insufferable." He lifted one thin shoulder. "Personally, I think it's kind of amazing. Love conquers all, even family curses and a bunch of old hurts."

I blew out a shaky breath. God, I really hoped that was the case. I'd give a lot for Thatcher Pennington to appear at my side at that moment. Today was a day for telling truths, right? And suddenly, I found that I *wanted* to tell Thatcher all sorts of things I'd been holding back. Like how sorry I was for what I'd said the other day and how hard I'd fallen for him. Like how very badly I wanted to curl up in his arms, feel the soft scratch of his growing beard as he kissed my hair, and let him know I was ready to fight for *us*, even after the bus tour ended and we were back in—

"Fuck off! I've been living on grass juice for a week, and *I'll* say when I've had enough. My father practically owns this place, remember?"

The drunken shout made me swivel on my stool just as Brantleigh Pennington lurched to his feet at one of the tables in the far corner of the mostly empty Tavern and began gesturing wildly, nearly clocking PJ Honeycutt with a half-empty glass of mead.

Castor gripped the edge of the bar so tightly his fingers squeaked on the polished surface. "Damn it," he whispered.

"What the hell is *he* doing here?" I muttered.

"He came in maybe twenty minutes ago and ordered a pint, and I think... I think maybe he'd already been drinking? But Brantleigh said he was here to meet someone, and he sat down by that guy over there, so PJ and I decided to play it cool and serve him *one* pint. I'm guessing he just tried to order another and PJ said no... and Brantleigh decided not to play it cool," Cas finished in a small voice.

"My father is basically your *boss*, asswipe." Brant took a stumbling step toward PJ, who retreated a pace. "When the bastard croaks, who do you think is gonna take over the reins? Me! I'm the heir. And I will shut this place *down*."

Yes, it was clear Brantleigh had decided *not* to play it cool. But worse than that, when the *that guy* Cas had pointed out turned around, I saw that it was none other than Chris fucking Acton.

Damn, that man got around.

Shit shit shit. Damage control tactics from my time in PR raced through my head, but none of them applied to the situation. How did you beg a reporter—even one you'd hooked up with—not to write a sensational story unfolding right before his eyes?

Chris spotted me at the bar and immediately stood up. He squeezed his slight frame between Brantleigh and PJ, who were staring each other down like dogs getting ready for a fight, and hustled over to the bar.

"Reagan, you've got to get him out of here," he said without preamble. "Like, now. At the hotel this morning, a bunch of reporters made plans to grab lunch here, and they'll be here in twenty minutes, tops."

I pushed a hand through my hair. "Yeah, okay, I'll—"

"But wait, you need to know..." He grabbed my hand as I slid off my stool and towed me toward a small, relatively private alcove near the glass window that showed the inner workings of the meadery. "Brantleigh's *do you know who my father is* schtick isn't even the worst of it. He was already drunk when he walked in here and was only too happy to tell me about his cash flow problems—how his 'shitty mom' cut him off financially, and he found out this morning from Pennington HR that his 'heartless, cheap-ass father' isn't going to be paying him the big bucks Brantleigh thinks he deserves." Chris rolled his eyes, disgusted. "He also volunteered some information about his former stepmother's affairs. Stuff that made *me* clutch my fucking pearls, and I thought I'd heard everything."

As Chris spoke, I felt my temperature spike until I was fever hot. After everything that had already happened that morning, there was no mask on earth that could contain my rage. And when he mentioned Heather, I lost my mind.

"Thatcher Pennington is a good man. No one deserves a single *shred* of his private information unless and until he's ready to share it." I seethed. "So help me, Chris, if you write this story—"

"Oh, shut up, Wellbridge." Chris bristled, making his slight frame puff up. "You think I told you all this because I intend to make a story out of a spoiled child showing his ass in public? No fucking way... But if someone else covers it first, upper management will force me to cover it, so you and Thatcher need to get on this. Got it?"

I let out a breath. "Yeah, I got it. Sorry I jumped the gun. Thatcher owes you one."

"He does. And I'll take him up on that." An easy grin replaced Chris's look of frustration. "You're a good man, too, Reagan Wellbridge. And you and Thatcher make a good team." His smile went a little lopsided. "Though, if you're trying to hide that the two of you are involved, you're gonna have to try a little harder."

My heart thundered in my chest. "There's nothing—" I began.

But Chris cut me off again. "Save it. He looks at you like he wants the two of you to occupy the same molecules or some shit, and when you look at him..."

I swallowed. "Yeah?"

"You look happy, Reagan." For a moment, he looked a little wistful, but then he recalled himself and slapped my arm. "Now, go get that jackass out of here and figure out a way to shut him up."

I nodded and quickly spun away. Across the room, Brant had resumed his threats at top volume, though fortunately, the bar remained fairly empty, so there was no one to hear. Without wasting a minute, I grabbed Brant by the upper arm and yanked him out the door.

"R-Reagan? Where'd you come from? Hey, did you hear? I'm taking your job. And when I'm in charge, you—"

I shoved him up against the side of the building. "You will never be in charge, you sniveling sack of entitlement," I said fiercely.

Brant seemed to have trouble focusing on me, but that didn't stop him from spluttering and trying to get away.

I shoved him harder, locking my forearm over his chest to keep him in place. "How fucking dare you? Do you have any idea how much your father cares about you? How much he's sacrificed for you? How hard he's worked to make your life easy? The man texted you daily this week, Brantleigh. Daily! Just hoping you'd reply. He didn't ask you for anything. He didn't expect you to give up anything for him. He didn't want you to perform for him. He just wanted to love you. To let you know he was there for you. He would give you the shirt off his back, the breath out of his lungs, every piece of wisdom he's got, and a billion fucking chances to make something of yourself... but all you want from him is *money*. For him to bankroll your life while you slander him in public like a drunken fool." I tightened my arm—not enough to cut off his air, though that was more luck than care on my part—so Brantleigh was balancing on his tiptoes. "You don't deserve that man as your father."

"You know *nothing*," Brant ground out, still trying to squirm away. He was about my height and weight, but he had a minibar's worth of alcohol running through his veins while white-hot fury ran through mine, so he was no match for me. "You have no idea what it's like to have a father everyone thinks is so great at everything. Everything Thatcher Pennington touches turns to gold... except me. Maybe because he spent more time with his company than he did being a father."

"Oh, please," I sneered. "Did it ever occur to you that he was trying to give you stability and security? Huh? Did it? Jesus. Stop blaming your father's mistakes twenty years ago for the choices you're making today. He *loves* you, Brantleigh, and if you're loved by Thatcher Pennington, that makes you the luckiest person in the goddamn universe. So stop throwing it away—"

"Hey!" Strong hands grabbed me from behind and pulled me off Brant. "Hey, hey. That's enough." Thatcher's deep voice cut through the red haze of my anger. "Take a breath. What the hell's going on here?"

"He's drunk off his ass," I accused, shaking Thatcher's grip off me. "He tried to start a fight in the Tavern *after* spouting off a bunch of bullshit about you—and bullshit about *Heather*—to a reporter." I thrust a hand toward the bar. "Chris Acton is in there."

Brant snorted. "I didn't tell him anything but the truth. And don't think I missed the way you and that little reporter were getting cozy. Does your dad know you're fucking—"

Now, it was Thatcher who got in Brant's face. "Finish that sentence," he growled, low and dangerous, "and it'll be my arm across your throat."

Thatcher's words, the emotion behind them, and the intensity in his eyes shocked the hell out of me. I'd thought I'd seen Thatcher angry before, but this was different.

My hand snuck out to touch his back, to ground him somehow, but fortunately, I caught myself before I made contact because Layla scurried up at that moment with McGee jogging toward us, half a block behind her.

"Everyone *calm down*," she instructed, hands out like a crossing guard. "Thatcher, I recognized a man from the *Wall Street Journal* heading this way. I think we need to—"

McGee arrived on the scene at the moment the Tavern door opened. The corner of the door caught him in the nose and forehead, and at the speed he was going, he practically bounced off, landing hard on his ass.

Layla gasped and glanced around in concern. Brant barked out a laugh that quickly turned into an annoying giggle. And poor Chris Acton dropped to his knees in an effort to help McGee after knocking him over with the door.

"I'm so sorry. Oh shit, oh fuck. I didn't think. I wasn't thinking. I wouldn't have—"

McGee tested his face with one large hand and reached the other out to grab Chris's flailing arm before it could do more damage. "Peace. It's okay." His words came out muffled, which made sense when his nose began to pour blood. Thatcher met my eyes over their heads and tilted his chin toward the Tavern. I shook off my stupor and raced inside to get some napkins and ask Castor for help putting together a bag of ice.

When I returned with supplies, Chris was halfway onto McGee's lap, holding a bandana to the bleeding nose while murmuring soft apologies, McGee's eyes were riveted on Chris's pink cheeks and bright eyes, Brant was still laughing and pointing at McGee, and Layla was quietly urging Thatcher to get the hell out of there before anyone else from the media showed up.

But Thatcher... Thatcher stood calmly in the center of the chaos, seeming not to hear Brant's drunken laughter or Layla's increasingly frantic pleas. In fact, he looked devoid of all emotion, as if his anger had hit the boiling point in a pressure cooker and simply... sealed the pot closed.

After handing off the napkins and ice, I took a step closer to Thatcher, but when he raised his eyes to mine, I saw all the emotion Thatcher had been hiding, a veritable cauldron of guilt and anger roiling just beneath his controlled exterior.

I sucked in a breath. How much of that anger was directed at me? I couldn't even remember what I'd been saying before he'd pulled me off Brant—pulled me off his one and only *son*, who I'd been pinning up against the building like I was ready to knock him out.

A million apologies rose to my lips, but I choked them back. I wanted to explain, somehow, that I'd lost my temper and gotten careless because I couldn't stand to hear the things Brant had been saying, but I didn't. I wanted to tell Thatcher that I loved him and to thank him because his faith in me had helped me stand up to my parents the way I should have years ago, but I couldn't do that either.

Because we had an audience. And saying anything to him would only make the situation worse.

Later, I told myself.

Layla settled a hand on my shoulder and leaned in close. "Reagan, I need you to get Brantleigh off the side-walk. *Now*."

Right. Okay. That was something I could do. I snapped into work mode and nudged my way between Thatcher and his son, grabbing Brant by the arm, more gently this time. "Come back inside, Brant. It's cold out here, and you don't have a coat."

Thatcher made a noise and stepped forward to inter-vene, but Layla blocked him bodily. "Thatcher, we're supposed to be at the Investment Summit in five minutes. There's nothing to be done here. Reagan will take Brantleigh inside and make sure he gets some coffee, and we'll resolve everything when we get back."

I didn't hear Thatcher's reply if he made one, but he allowed Layla to turn him and point him down the street.

"We'll meet you at your parents' house after the Summit," Layla said. "I'll take care of Thatcher."

My stomach flipped and landed with a sick *thud*. "Right," I said, though she'd already hurried away. Then I turned and shuffled Thatcher's dick of a son back into the Tavern.

The warmth of the restaurant caused my throat to tickle, which made me glance fondly at the soothing mead I couldn't allow myself to sample. I was on the clock. And my job right now was to protect Thatcher Pennington... even if it meant spending the next few hours with an insufferable, ungrateful asshole.

My brother and Flynn returned in time for the lunch rush, and while Cas and PJ caught them up on everything that had happened, I spent the next hour trying to sober Brant up in Flynn's tiny office while trying *not* to think about how I'd finally shed my polite mask for good... only to jeopardize my relationship with the man I loved because I'd let my emotions get the best of me.

Brantleigh didn't seem to notice my distraction, probably because he didn't shut up. He quickly moved from ranting about his rich, stupid father to describing in uncomfortable detail the hot women Thatcher was able to attract simply because of his wealth.

"I mean, what girl wants to put up with someone who's cold as ice? But they do," Brantleigh assured me. "They all do. You shoulda seen this one chick he bagged on the Cape last summer. Fucking Christ, the body on that woman. And her *lips*. If he was into sharing, I would have done it with that one for her mouth alone."

Hot bile inched up my throat at the thought of Thatcher fucking someone other than me. Of a woman's mouth on his dick and his head thrown back in ecstasy.

"TMI," I warned tiredly, knowing it wouldn't stop him. "Besides, I thought you were gay."

He waved his empty coffee mug through the air, nearly knocking it into Flynn's laptop, which perched precariously on his cluttered desk. "That doesn't mean I can't ap-appp-appreciate a hot woman. You know what's funny?"

I stared at him frostily.

"One time, I convinced Heather to show me her tits out by the pool. All natural, if you can believe it. And she shaved. *Everywhere.* I know 'cause I caught them in the outdoor shower once. Oops." He dissolved into a fit of giggles, bending at the waist and laughing into his knees while his mug rolled to the floor.

I stared at the ceiling and tried not to vomit or murder him. Was this what Chris had been alluding to? If so, Brantleigh Pennington was a horrible human being, and he didn't seem to want to change. What kind of person fucked around with his *stepmother* behind his father's back? It made me hate Heather even more than I already did, which I hadn't thought possible.

"Stop talking," I growled. "You disgust me."

Once he'd kept down a cup of coffee for half an hour and the Tavern was nearly empty again, I decided it was safe to take Brantleigh back to my parents' house. Fortunately, his giggles and verbal bullshit had subsided to the point where he seemed ready to curl up and sleep, so it was easy enough to grab the keys to his rental car and drive him up the hill to my parents' place. I considered giving him some Tylenol before I put him to bed in Thatcher's room but decided I wasn't that merciful. Brantleigh deserved the hangover he was about to have. He deserved a hell of a lot more than that.

I went back downstairs to wait for Thatcher's return,

and as I paced the living room, my headache from earlier came back with a vengeance, almost like I'd caught Brant's hangover. The only saving grace was that my parents still weren't home, so I didn't have to hear whether there was any town gossip about my display or hear any smug recriminations about my total lack of control.

If I could get Thatcher alone for just five minutes and talk to him, I might be able to resolve things. Thatcher had stood up for me when Brant was about to make a comment about Chris Acton, and that had to mean something, right? He trusted me. He believed in me. Surely he'd understand that extenuating circumstances had led me to... throw his son against the side of a building, pin him there against his will, and scream in his ear.

In public.

Fuck, even in my own head, I couldn't make it sound forgivable, so how could I convince Thatcher to forgive me?

At four in the afternoon, just as the sky was turning pink from early sunset, Layla arrived back at the house. Alone.

"Where's Thatcher?" I asked immediately... and maybe a bit rudely since Layla was running her hands through her hair like she'd had a rough day, too.

"I couldn't say." She dropped heavily into a chair. "He took off after the event and had McGee bring me back."

Had Thatcher not come back because he didn't want to face his son? Or me?

I squeezed my eyes shut. "Shit."

"Yes, well." Layla gave me a sympathetic smile. "I can't speak to what Thatcher is thinking, of course. He didn't seem happy when he left, but I'm sure that's not *entirely* a result of your incident with Brantleigh today. There's also a clusterfuck in Madison that's very stressful. The organizer of one of the original press tour stops we tried to cancel is throwing a fit because PennCo won't be there, and I'm sure Thatcher is as worried as I am that it'll generate bad press just when we're emerging from the Nova catastrophe. It's critically important for the business that we send someone, *tonight*, but of course, most of my team back in New York is still recovering from the flu or scrambling to keep things going while we're short-staffed. You're the only one who's free... but then, you've got your family obligations."

She said nothing more but watched me expectantly.

"Are you... asking me to go?" I wondered.

"If you could, I'd really appreciate it." Layla gave me a hopeful look. "I do think it would go a long way toward... let's say, smoothing things over after whatever that was between you and Thatcher's son earlier today."

I bit my tongue until it hurt at this reminder. After standing up for myself in such a huge way earlier, the realization that I was still the tiniest cog in the PennCo wheel, the guy who could be kicked off the tour and sent to Madison on a moment's notice, was hard enough to swallow. The fact that *Layla* was the one doing the sending, when I hadn't forgotten Terrance's list of grievances or forgiven the way she'd treated me on the bus, was like swallowing jagged, broken shards of glass.

But I hadn't decided what my next career goal was going to be, now that I wouldn't be working for my father's campaign, and I was unsure of my future at PennCo, so I definitely didn't want to burn bridges. More than that... she was right. I'd fucked up today, and maybe this was the way to smooth things over with Thatcher and give him the space to deal with Brant however he needed.

"Okay," I said in a low voice. "Tell me what to do, and I'll do it."

"Excellent! I already got you a room at the hotel for tonight, and Alena sent a bunch of marketing materials and event credentials that will be there when you arrive. The plane is on standby, and I'll let the team know." She walked out of the room with her phone to her ear, leaving me gaping after her.

If there was already a waiting plane, a hotel room, and event credentials in my name, why had Layla made it seem like I had a choice in the first place?

I would never understand her, I decided as I rubbed my tired eyes and trudged upstairs to pack, but I'd said I was going, so I would.

McGee drove me to the small private airport outside town, where the company jet waited to whisk me to Wisconsin. He spent the whole ride darting glances at me in the rearview with a furrowed brow. "You don't look so hot, princess," he said after the fifth time I caught him.

"Pfft. Says the man with the busted nose. The good news is those black eyes really hide the crow's feet."

The jab had no force behind it, but I must really have looked tired because McGee didn't comment. Instead, he asked, "Does Thatcher know about this little trip?"

I shrugged. "I figured Layla told him... or she would, once he got back. I haven't seen him since... you know. Earlier."

"Fucking Brantleigh," McGee sighed.

Yeah, and fucking *me. Reagan Wellbridge, you stupid fucker*, I thought for the first time in nearly a week. If only I'd known then just how much worse things could get.

I was horrified to find my eyes stinging. "Thatcher has enough to worry about right now, so if he asks, please tell him I agreed to go and I'm fine with it," I said, though my voice was so rough with the lie on my tongue that I coughed. "I'll see him back in the city. If he wants to, I mean. Maybe things won't be so crazy then."

Though I could feel his disagreement, McGee kept quiet after that, and I was glad because contemplating a future where Thatcher *didn't* want to see me—one where he decided he couldn't forgive me and went back to ignoring me—made me feel awful. I wanted nothing more than to fall asleep, kick the headache that was beating my brain against the sides of my skull like ice in a blender, and forget my troubles for a while. I succumbed to sleep...

And barely noticed when the shivers started.

Chapter Eighteen

Thatcher

I let Layla pull me away from my son at the Tavern because I knew if I'd stayed there, I would have done something unforgivable.

Reagan Wellbridge was many things—gorgeous, courageous, and annoyingly astute, to name a few—but he was not quick to anger. For him to have physically restrained Brant and barked in his face, my son had to have done something egregious, and I would have lost no time in addressing it, right in the middle of the sidewalk.

If I'd stayed, I might not have resisted the temptation to pluck Chris Acton off McGee's lap and remind him once and for all that Reagan was not *his* to be "getting cozy" with.

And had I stayed there, I definitely wouldn't have been able to keep my hands off Reagan either. It had taken every ounce of my control not to grab him by the arms, pull him against me, and cement him to my side, especially after I'd heard him defending me. It hadn't mattered in the slightest that Reagan had been red-faced and screaming the words *if you're loved by Thatcher Pennington, that makes you the luckiest person in the goddamn universe,* because the sentiment behind it had punched into my chest, making my heart thump and flip over for him like a besotted spaniel.

When was the last time anyone had stood up for me like that? *Had* anyone? I didn't think so. Not either of the women whose fingers had worn my ring, not any of the people I'd spent time with over the years. And the fact that Reagan, the man who so often neglected to stand up for himself, was the one who'd defended me didn't feel as strange as it might have. Instead, it felt right that we should stand stronger with and for each other. We were simply *better* together... even though we had every reason not to be.

So what the hell was I going to do about it?

I had no more idea what to do about that than I did about Brantleigh.

I'd managed to go through the motions at the Investment Summit, glad that Layla had been there to take the lead. But when it was over, I couldn't wait to get away. I'd told Layla I needed to run errands, and when she'd offered to come along, I'd made it clear I needed time alone.

By the time I'd walked through the town, the sun had sunk low in the sky, and most of the Honeybridgers had packed up their festival booths for the night. The Tavern was open, and a few clusters of hearty souls chatted outside the door, bundled up in their parkas, but I didn't want to socialize. Instead, I headed for the warm, golden lights of the Honeybridge General Store, where I could grab a drink and possibly a quick sugar fix.

The bell over the door rang when I opened it, and Pop Honeycutt nodded a greeting at me over the messy blond pigtails of a little girl buying two lollipops with a handful of coins. I took a minute to wonder when I'd last seen anyone buying something with cash. Honeybridge was a special place, and Pop's General Store was the heart of it.

I passed down the aisle toward the drink coolers in the back as my phone buzzed.

Thalia. It figured. I wondered what Brant had told her.

"Yes?" I murmured, trying to keep my voice low so as not to disturb anyone else browsing the store.

"Thatcher, Brant sent me a string of unintelligible texts." She sighed. "I was calling to see what's going on."

I let out a long breath before sucking in a new one that tasted faintly of sour apple candy. Instead of answering, I asked, "Was I a terrible father, Thalia? Wait, don't answer that. I know I was. But shouldn't a twenty-something-year-old man begin taking responsibility for his own life regardless of whether his parents were shitty or not?" I trailed the toe of my shoe over the shiny floor. "Never mind. Don't answer that either."

"Thatcher, stop. What did he do?"

I gave her a quick recap, from my not-so-brilliant plan to have him work for me through my arrival at the Tavern. "He got drunk and spouted shit about me to a reporter. Things about Heather—"

"No!"

"Yes. And that's not all. The head of HR sent me an email this afternoon stating that Brant was belligerent to the woman who called to complete his new hire paperwork. He was very upset to learn that he wouldn't be earning six figures at his entry-level position, which may be what led him to get drunk off his ass before twelve o'clock. Thalia, be honest... does Brant have a substance abuse problem?"

"Not to my knowledge," she said firmly. "What our son has is a lack of give-a-shit problem, and he's been handed every opportunity to fix it—therapy, meditation retreats, admission to great schools, paid internships with incredible career potential—and he hasn't taken advantage of any of them to build a life for himself."

"I gave him too much stuff and not enough of my time," I said softly.

"No. Look, I understand why you're feeling guilt. I feel it, too. But you made every effort to spend time with him when he was growing up. You visited on his birthday, you took him on vacations, you made it to his graduations and sports events. Were you there every minute? No. Was I? Also no. We weren't perfect parents because we're not perfect people, and we're still, to this day, sorting through the shit that *our* parents did to *us*."

I huffed out a laugh. "I guess."

"Brant wasn't abused or neglected, physically or emotionally," she went on. "And lots of people with bad parents turn out okay. Surely you know one or two."

"Yeah." I pulled a bottle of orange juice out of the drinks cooler and closed the door before moving slowly toward the front of the store. "In fact, Reagan Wellbridge— you remember he and Brant were in the same class at Grandview for a year or two?"

She hummed agreement.

"He grew up with wealthy parents. Trent and Patricia weren't *bad*, but they also weren't great. His father is a state senator and as obsessed with winning elections as I am with Pennington Industries. His mother's involved in everything outside the house—committees, boards, directing Trent's career..."

"And Reagan grew up okay?"

"Way better than okay. He's amazing, Thalia. Smart, dedicated, kind, and hardworking. And despite his parents' machinations and political aspirations, he's managed to stay grounded. He's been working at

PennCo, and we've been traveling together on business. It's been mind-blowing to see the way he interacts with people. And he has this amazing perspective on the world—"

"Whoa."

"What?" I demanded, pausing beside a circular rack of postcards.

"It's just... are you talking about a kid Brant went to school with or someone you're involved with? Because you never so much as strung two adjectives together about Heather, and you for sure never went all dreamy-voiced when you talked about me."

"I..." I licked my lips. I couldn't bring myself to deny it, which was all the confirmation Thalia needed.

"Oh. Shit. You're falling for a guy?" she breathed. "Well, damn. I owe Paul five hundred bucks."

"You what? Hang on, you bet with your husband about..."

"Sort of? Not really. It was just a theory he had about why you dated women you didn't seem to like very much. Something about you not allowing yourself to go after what you really want. But that's not the point. Do your parents know about this? Shit, do *his* parents know?"

"No." I all but shouted the word, then immediately lowered my voice. "No one knows. Hell, Thalia, *I* don't even know how I feel about him." I lifted a hand and sent the carousel of postcards spinning. "That's a lie," I admitted. "I... care about him. A lot. I want to be with him. I might even... feel more than that."

"Meaning you're in love with him?" Thalia's normally clipped tone was gentle. "You can say the words, Thatcher. It's okay. In fact, it's *more* than okay—"

I snorted. "It's really not. Jesus, not only is he beautiful and bright and *young*—Christ, so young—he's my employee."

"Circumstances," she said flatly. "Excuses. Keep him around and he'll get older. That's how life works."

"But *how* do I keep him around?" I demanded, because that was the crux of the damn problem. "I've been married twice. My first wife moved across the country to escape me—"

"Don't flatter yourself."

"—and my second wife cheated on me for most of our marriage. My only child will happily sell me out to reporters rather than talk to me when he's unhappy. And I didn't make it to my mother's second birthday party this year because I couldn't stomach the idea of flying out there—"

"I went," she said in a bored voice. "You didn't miss much. And I'm not understanding at all what this has to do with you and Reagan."

"The only lasting relationship in my life is with Pennington Industries," I admitted. "Eventually, I drive everyone else away. Why the hell would I do that to someone I lo—care about?"

"Well," she said practically. "At a guess, I'd say you *wouldn't*. The answer's in the question. I never got the sense that you loved Heather. She was pretty, and she never asked for more than you wanted to give, so it was easy enough to be with her and then just as easy to let her go. With me... we were teenagers when we got together, more interested in the *idea* of being in love than actually doing the work it would have taken to stay married."

"Yeah." I'd accepted that truth a long time ago.

"So, you picked the wrong people. Twice. Big deal. Are you telling me you've never made a wrong turn in business?

Never... I don't know... funded the wrong project? Never put too much faith in the wrong people?"

"Obviously, I have." I thought uncomfortably of Layla and all the things I'd stopped Reagan from telling me the other night. "Possibly recently."

"Right. But you're not breaking up with Pennington, are you? And you haven't run it into the ground, unless I've missed some really big headlines. You care too much to let it fail, so you make the company a priority—figuring out what it needs, how to make it thrive, all that good stuff. And when you make a mistake, you take the time and trouble to correct it, even when it's complicated and it'd be easier to say 'fuck it.'" I could almost hear her shrug. "Hate to break it to you, but relationships with humans are pretty similar. The difference is, unlike a billion-dollar corporation, a human partner will simultaneously be prioritizing *you* and *your* needs... while also fucking you on the regular, which is a nice bonus if you're into that sort of thing."

She made it sound so simple, and maybe it was. But it definitely wasn't easy. I had no idea where to begin. And the not-knowing was uncomfortable.

"Back to the original subject," I said roughly. "We need to figure out what to do about Brantleigh. Or," I said, remembering my conversation at dinner the night before, "what *not* to do. Have you heard about some article in the *Times* that says parents who view their kids as problematic create a self-fulfilling prophesy?"

"Actually, yes," she agreed. "Because we jump in to *provide* them solutions rather than letting them learn they're capable of figuring out solutions themselves. That's why I told you that Paul and I aren't giving Brant money anymore. If he wants to come here, he can live with me. I don't want to see him on the street. But if he needs more out of life than a bed and three hot meals—and I really hope he does—he can figure out a way to get it without my interference. Or rescue," she added. "It's the failures in life that teach you what you really want and the kind of person you want to be."

I blew out a breath and moved toward a display of candy and selected a toffee and chocolate bar for McGee, a Snickers for me, and a pack of watermelon bubble gum for Reagan. After so many days together stopping at rest stop gas stations, I knew everyone's preferences without having to think. "Someone recently told me it's funny how parents want to give their kids what they need but never seem to get that what they need is independence and respect."

"Mmm. Your Reagan sounds like someone I want to know," Thalia said.

"How do you know Reagan said it?" I asked, amused and more than a little excited about the idea of someone else calling him *my* Reagan.

"Dreamy voice," she said succinctly. "Listen, talk to Brant. Explain that we're giving up running his life for him but not giving up on *him*. And then I'll get him back here, and we'll figure out where to go from there."

"Agreed. Thanks a lot, Thalia."

When I put my phone away, I approached the counter and mumbled an apology to Pop.

He smiled and shook his head. "Nah. Family comes first. You're Thatcher Pennington, right? The boy who helped our Flynn expand his business? We're all grateful."

It had been a while since I'd been called a boy, and I found myself smiling. "I'm the grateful one, sir. Your grandson is a keen businessman. You must be proud."

"Of course." Pop took my candy and rang it up on his giant, old-fashioned cash register. "Firecracker was always going to be a success. You couldn't stop him even if you wanted to. Just like Mr. Important." He leaned across the counter like he was imparting a secret. "I heard you talking about Reagan on your call. I should probably apologize for eavesdropping, but I love hearing someone say nice things about one of my favorite Honeybridgers."

I was too distracted by this information to be embarrassed that he'd overheard. "You call Reagan... Mr. Important?" I grinned. I'd heard about the nickname tradition before—it was one of those quaint and quirky things I enjoyed about Honeybridge—but I'd somehow never known Reagan's or even thought to ask until now.

"Yep. Figuring out a person's true nature is... well, I suppose you might say it's a hobby," he said modestly. "That's why Flynn is Firecracker, and Jonathan Wellbridge is Frog, and my boy PJ is Daydreamer—or at least he *was*, and I have faith he will be again." Pop's eyes twinkled. "Not surprised you've never heard Reagan's nickname, though. Patricia's sure as heck never called him that."

"No," I agreed slowly, registering the double meaning behind his words. "I don't think she ever has."

"You, on the other hand." He set the final candy down and placed both hands on the counter before meeting my eyes. "I think you might understand why he earned that name."

I shrugged. "Because he *is* important, obviously. He's smarter than anyone gives him credit for and can succeed at anything he puts his mind to."

"That," Pop agreed easily. "Smarts is part of it, sure. Lord, he was a bright young thing. Biggest eyes you ever saw, and they didn't miss a trick. But that's not the whole reason." He reached over and pulled out a stool so he could sit down, handed me my bottle of orange juice, and nodded at me to enjoy it if I wanted to. I cracked it open and took a sip, appreciating the cool, sweet slide of it on my parched throat.

"Reagan Wellbridge was born smiling." Pop settled himself comfortably, like he was telling a bedtime story. "He was curious about everything, and I mean every dang thing. 'Pop, what's air? Pop, why's it *positively indecent* for me to swim in the lake with no pants on? Pop, why's my nanny watch that show about the doctors if it's only gonna make her cry? Pop, what's 'children should be seen and not heard'?"

He chuckled, and I did, too.

"He still hasn't learned that one, has he?" Pop asked fondly.

I gave him a half-smile. "Oh, I don't know. Sometimes I think he's learned that one too well."

Pop looked at me frankly and nodded. "Maybe so. Maybe so." His eyes went unfocused as he recalled himself to his tale. "All his life, wherever he went, Reagan made other folks smile, too. Turned out that curiosity of his was really a natural talent for setting people at ease and making 'em feel like they're the only one in the room when he gives them his attention. When tensions are high, he'll deliberately cause a ruckus just to get folks laughing, and when they're sad, he'll talk 'em 'round. He always seems to know just what people need... except himself." He smiled ruefully.

"I think you're right," I managed, my chest tight.

"He'll figure it out in time, though. Got a heart as big as the whole world hiding inside him, and those eyes still don't miss a trick. Honeybridge wouldn't be the same if he wasn't around, and for sure the Wellbridges wouldn't—their noses would've been too high in the air to get oxygen if Reagan wasn't around to bring them back to earth. He's the glue that holds 'em together and the grease that keeps 'em humming along. Nothing more important than that, far as I can tell."

"Have you told him this?" I demanded hoarsely. "Have you ever explained why you gave him that name?"

Pop glanced at me in surprise. "You know, I don't believe I ever did. But then... telling a man he's important is all well and good, but *showing* 'em they're important, the way Reagan does... well, that's a different and better thing altogether, isn't it?"

It was. Assuming you were the sort of person who knew how to do that.

Pop slapped his hands to his knees and pushed to his feet with effort. He threw my empty juice bottle in a recycling container and put my candy in a bag.

"I don't think I want to know what you'd nickname me," I said as I pulled a twenty out of my wallet.

He hit a button on the big register that made the cash drawer open with a satisfying *ding*. "That remains to be seen," he told me seriously, handing me my change. "But I sure hope you're around long enough for me to figure it out."

After I said goodbye and took my candy haul, I stepped out into the cold and texted McGee to come and get me. Despite it being just after five o'clock, the sky overhead was already a dusky gray-blue, and what little sunlight remained had gathered into a single white-gold band above the treetops on the west side of town. My breath fogged the air, and I huddled deeper into my coat. I hadn't anticipated how much colder it would be when the sun was gone.

Missing Reagan was like a visceral ache, even knowing that he was only across town, and sleeping across the hall from him tonight was just too damn far. I still couldn't puzzle out how he and I would work once the tour ended, but... hadn't I been telling everyone who'd listen how damn brilliant and creative Reagan was? How he had a different perspective on the world than I did? So, I'd talk to him. I'd tell him what I wanted and what I feared. I'd listen when he talked—with no limitations, this time, on what was appropriate for me to hear, as his boss, since I wanted to be a hell of a lot more to him than merely his boss. I'd apologize for what happened with Brant earlier and thank him for taking care of the situation when I couldn't. And then I'd ask what Reagan wanted for us... or whether he still wanted there to be an *us* at all.

It was scary as fuck, no two ways about it. I had more money than I could spend in a lifetime, and with that came a certain amount of power to make things go my way. But one thing I could not control—or even predict half the time —was the sexy, silver-tongued little shit who'd managed to steal my heart.

When McGee finally pulled up in the rental car, I slid into the passenger seat and handed him the toffee bar. Sunglasses covered his eyes despite the gathering darkness. "Ooof. How's the face?"

"Fine. Been a minute since I've had my bell rung like that, but it looks worse than it feels. And Reagan says the black eyes hide the crow's feet." He grinned. "So there's that."

My quick bark of laughter caught me by surprise, and some of the stress of my day fell away. "How is Reagan?" I asked McGee. "Did anything else happen with Brant?"

He snorted. "Brantleigh's sleeping it off in your bed, last I heard. And Reagan... he looks rough. Dealing with his parents, then Brant, then Layla... it's a lot." McGee darted a glance at me. "Not the best condition for flying out."

"Uh-huh." My chest was so busy twisting in sympathy it took a minute for my brain to catch up. "Wait, flying out? *Reagan?* When? To where?"

"I freaking *knew* you didn't know," McGee muttered in disgust. "Layla sent him to the hinterlands of Wisconsin. He took off like half an hour ago. I was on my way back from delivering him to the private airport when you texted."

My heart rate kicked up, but every third or fourth beat hit wrong. My lungs expanded and contracted, but they didn't seem to be doing a decent job of getting enough oxygen in. "Why?" I asked stupidly.

"You want the real reason or the bullshit reason? Because Layla *claimed* that he was the only person who could possibly go to whatever event you guys canceled in Madison, but I don't believe that for a hot second." His voice was hard and uncompromising.

I rolled down the window until the bitter wind stung the skin on my face. "So what's the real reason?" I was pretty sure I knew what he was going to say, and I didn't want to hear it, but I thought maybe I needed to.

"She's jealous. And *no*, I don't think she knows you and Reagan are getting it on," he added quickly. "She doesn't know you well enough to even suspect that. But she knows you like him. She knows you listen to him and respect his opinions. And she feels threatened by that."

I thought about it for a long moment, really considered it, but still shook my head. "I'm not brushing you off this time, I promise, but I just don't see it."

"You probably *can't* see it because you've known her a long time, and you've mentally put her in the platonic column. You don't see her as a potential romantic partner...

and she knows it." He slowed down as we approached the Wellbridges' house. "So, like, how do you get a person to un-friend-zone you? Well, first, you make them notice you. If they've got a dog, you become the dog's best friend. If they're into rock climbing, you watch a few YouTube videos, strap on a chalk bag, and then show them pictures of you free climbing in Acadia." He affected a bored tone. "Oh, you didn't know I was a *climber*, Reggie? Ha ha ha! Goodness, yes. Been climbing for *years*. We should climb together sometime!"

"Jesus," I muttered.

"And if the person you want is your *boss*," McGee went on in his normal voice, "a mother-freaking billionaire who's been quoted a dozen times saying that his company is his priority..." He pulled his sunglasses off and looked at me expectantly.

I groaned, running a hand over my face. "You show me how competent you are at your job. How I couldn't possibly get along without you."

"Ding, ding, ding. You might decide that an in-person bus trip—so cozy, just the two of you, with plenty of opportunity to show your dedication and brilliance—would be the perfect way to handle a PR crisis. You might be righteously pissed when little Reagan Wellbridge, the most peon of peons, steals your thunder."

"He didn't *steal*—" I began hotly.

"Obvs. But from Layla's point of view? She was sidelined in the playoff game. And she *thought* the dude you were taking was, like, the team mascot, except it turned out the guy could throw a perfect spiral. Suddenly, you're giving him the nuclear launch codes for the social media shit and ruining the big reveal of *her* strategy. And then, when Layla finally joined you, you were like, 'Nah, I'm keeping Reagan with me 'cause he's just so talented. Screw your seduction game.'"

As the truth of what he was saying hit me, I concentrated on breathing in and out. I'd recognized parts of this before—January had told me plainly that Layla was feeling replaced, and I'd realized on my own that Layla resented having her social media ideas upstaged by Reagan's, but hearing it laid out like this was eye-opening. How had I not seen it before?

"Fuck," I said succinctly.

"Yep. That about sums it up," McGee agreed. "So what are you gonna do now?"

I laughed weakly and closed the window to spare McGee the frigid temperature. "About Layla? I was already planning to speak to her about her management style. I'll be looping HR in on that meeting. About Reagan...?" I shook my head. "This is yet another thing I'll be apologizing for next time I see him. He tried to tell me some things about Layla the other day, but I was too concerned about the propriety of him tattling on his boss to hear him out. *Fuck*," I said again. "How long is he gone? When will he be back?"

"I don't think he's coming back to Honeybridge. He'll probably fly back to New York when the event is over. He said something before he left, like, 'Thatcher has enough to worry about. Tell him I agreed to go, and I'll see him back in the city... if he wants to.'" McGee pulled into the Wellbridges' long driveway. "So do you want to?"

"Yeah," I said without hesitation. "Yeah, I want to. I need to make sure he's okay, and I..." I cleared my throat. "Thalia thinks I'm in love with him."

"Oh, does *Thalia*? Well then." McGee sounded way too amused. "I've known you were in love with him since

Colorado—hell, since *day one back in New York*—but nobody listens to McGee."

I shot him a glare. "Smart-ass. Let's get on the road tomorrow. We can be back in New York before he arrives." I no longer cared about anything other than clearing the air between us, and I couldn't do that if I was stuck here or still caught on a highway somewhere between here and there. I wanted to pick him up at the airport and take him back to my apartment. I wanted to show him the way the city looked when its glittering lights spread out beneath my penthouse window.

McGee grinned as he shifted the car into park. "Fuck yeah. We ride at dawn."

I managed a slight laugh as the decision settled my heart a bit, though I still wished I was a person capable of hopping on a plane and simply flying to Madison to tell him how much I... cared.

I still found myself tripping over the other word, even in my own mind. I wasn't normally this hesitant. I usually knew the way forward and took it. But right now, what I knew and what I *needed* were at odds. Once Reagan and I had talked, once he was in my arms again, once we'd figured out what the future would look like and I was confident I wouldn't make the same mistakes I'd made, then I'd be able to say the word that was pulsing in the back of my brain. I'd be able to say it... and *mean* it.

———

When we entered the house, I found Patricia and Layla sitting in the living room, chatting happily over a bottle of wine, as though they hadn't noticed how the whole damn world had gone colder the minute Reagan left town.

"Thatcher!" Layla twisted in her wingback chair and greeted me with a smile that, since my eyes were now open, I saw was probably too wide and friendly. "I was going to ask Patricia to send out a search party in a little while."

Patricia patted the sofa beside her. "Come sit. We missed you at the festivities today, though I know you were busy with your Investment Summit and spending time with Brantleigh. Er... Reagan mentioned Brant was a bit under the weather? He's been napping upstairs for hours." The knowing look in her eye suggested she'd heard about the altercation outside the Tavern but was trying to be discreet.

"I appreciate you hosting him unexpectedly, Patricia." I gave Layla a significant look. "I was also sorry to hear that we had to cut Reagan's family time short so he could fly to Madison."

Layla's cheeks flushed, but Patricia waved my words away. "Don't give it a thought. We'll miss him, of course, but it hardly matters if he's here for the Festival of Ice now that he's quit the Senator's campaign."

"Quit?" I shifted on the couch to stare at her more fully. "I don't understand."

"Neither did *we*." Addressing herself to Layla, Patricia explained, "For months, Reagan's been dying to work as Trent's social media manager. We had doubts about the idea, of course, but after Thatcher raved about Reagan's performance at PennCo and we realized Reagan could help us reach younger voters, we decided to give him the job on a trial basis. Then, not an hour later, he quit! Children." She sighed as if to say *What can you do?* and gave a commiserating pat to my knee.

Layla nodded sympathetically. "That happens with young people, doesn't it?"

"Not always," I said tersely. "He's not a child. Reagan is

twenty-eight. And not at all fickle. There must have been a logical reason why he chose not to work for Trent."

"Weeeell, there *may* have been a bit of a kerfuffle at the festival this morning," Patricia allowed. She played with the collar of her cashmere sweater. "A... a misunderstanding. Imagine Reagan implying that his father isn't supportive of his children simply because Trent wanted to take a few campaign photos with a constituent who doesn't, ah, wholly endorse rainbow flag stickers. Ridiculous, really! Everyone knows we are *extremely* supportive parents. I mean, our eldest is practically living with a Honeycutt, and I've hardly said a word about it."

There were a lot of things I wanted to say, like "Is Trent really so desperate for votes that he'd willingly pose with an asshole like that?" or "Surely Reagan wasn't upset about the sticker but what it represented..." but my brain had snagged on something else she'd let slip.

Children, Patricia had said. Reagan implied Trent didn't support his *children*. Plural. Did that mean...? Had Reagan come out to Patricia and Trent and then taken a stand and quit the campaign, all in the same morning?

If so, I was both proud as fuck of him and his bravery... and devastated that he'd had to handle that on his own. I knew he was capable—beyond capable—but the idea of Reagan going through something so difficult without someone—*me*—at his back made it difficult to catch my breath.

What the hell was happening to me?

"In any case," Patricia went on airily, "Reagan can be very dramatic at times—I have *no* idea where the boy gets it —but Trent and I are willing to hear his apology and smooth things over when he's ready. We do love him very much, and he has *so* much potential, if he'd just stop wasting his time connecting with online people and find his true call-ing. We're hopeful that his job at PennCo is a step in the right direction—he seems very dedicated, don't you think? You know," she confided, leaning toward Layla's chair with a satisfied smile, "Reagan's very like me in that way. *Dedicated.*"

Dear god. Connecting with people *was* Reagan's call-ing. How could someone who claimed to know him not understand that? And was she really taking credit for Reagan's dedication to his job? The idea was not only absurd but disgusting. Reagan was his own person. An adult. He'd been raised by Patricia and Trent, yes, and he'd learned things from them, but what he'd forged himself into after a whole lot of trial and error was nothing that they could take credit for, any more than they could take the blame for... oh.

Oh.

I was not a person given to epiphanies or over-the-top realizations, but sitting there on Patricia's sofa, I had a light-bulb parenting moment. More accurately, it was as though I'd been trying to solve a jigsaw puzzle in the dark, and hearing the way Patricia talked about her youngest son was like turning on a klieg light. Under its glare, the things the woman at dinner had told me, what Thalia and I discussed, every parenting book I'd ever read, and what I'd known deep down all along, all slotted into their proper place easily, and I was able to see the full picture at last.

Brantleigh was my son. But the things I'd given him as a parent—all my love, my wealth and privilege, the pieces of my own fears and phobias, my poor priorities, my need to keep his life safe and happy and easy—were raw material. Building blocks. What he chose to keep and discard, what he chose to make with them, was entirely up to him. It had to be. Until that moment, I'd never truly accepted that the most painful and terrifying part of parenting wasn't rushing around trying to fix things for my child before they got derailed but stepping back and accepting that it wasn't my place to control any of it.

I pulled in a deep breath and let it out.

"Thatcher?" Layla asked in concern. "Are you alright?"

"I am," I said honestly. "I will be." I pushed to my feet. "If you'll excuse me, I'm going upstairs to find Brant."

But I'd barely gotten to the base of the stairs when I heard footsteps behind me.

"Thatcher?" Layla said too softly. "If I can help, I—"

I paused without turning. "I don't need your help, thank you."

She rushed toward me. "I can see that you're unhappy I sent Reagan to Wisconsin, but I really had no choice. Cath Woodall with ImagineTex has been frantically texting me all afternoon, demanding that we make an appearance at the Textile Tech Trends event. I didn't think it prudent to risk negative publicity right now, and Reagan was the only available person—"

I hadn't planned to have this out until we got back to the city, but I couldn't help turning and saying, "Not true. You could have gone yourself."

"Me? But..." Layla's smile faded, and she smoothed back her auburn hair into its tidy bun. "I couldn't go. I'm the head of PennCo. And you need me here."

"*I'm* the head of Pennington Industries and all of its subsidiaries, but when you told me that we needed to do an in-person publicity tour, you knew I'd agree and find a way to balance it by relying more heavily on my other team members temporarily, right? Because that's what leaders do. Reagan and I have handled the tour just fine with the PR team's support." I cocked my head. "Did I not make it clear that I wanted Reagan to remain on the tour, even *before* I explicitly said that Reagan was to have time with his family this week?"

"I... I didn't think that applied to... He was happy to go, Thatcher. Reagan understands his place in the pecking order," she said firmly.

"Actually, I don't think either of you understand it," I said frankly. "Reagan is incredibly talented, and I told you that I expect him to be mentored for a much higher position. Otherwise, we'll lose him to a competitor, especially now that he won't be working on his father's campaign. If your responsibilities as vice president make it difficult for you to see where we could be promoting employees from within, then I think we need to discuss adding some levels of hierarchy to PennCo."

Layla gaped. "But things run perfectly fine as they are. Haven't you been pleased with our profitability? In the past, you've said—"

"I know what I said," I interrupted. "I've wanted you to run your division your own way without micromanagement as long as you got good results. But good results mean more than turning a profit, Layla. It also means maximizing our employees' talents and making sure they're satisfied." I shrugged. "Just think about it. We'll discuss it later." I turned back toward the stairs.

"I... I did hire someone, actually!" she called.

I turned again. "Oh?"

Layla licked her lips. "Yes. Just today, I hired a social media manager. After talking with you and Reagan and seeing your excitement about my plan, I realized I needed to speed up my timeline for launch. A friend recommended Greta, so I contacted her this morning and had a wonderful interview. She's starting Monday. I asked HR to send her a contract just this afternoon."

I stared at her for a long moment. "You hired a social media manager from outside the company when you already have someone on staff with social media management experience who knows about our products and is eager to step into a larger role? Why wouldn't you promote Reagan to that position?"

Her eyes widened at my tone, which I hadn't bothered to modulate. "I made this decision based on the needs of the company. Greta has years of additional experience, but she's also very grounded. PennCo wouldn't merely be a stepping stone on the way to a better job, and you heard what Patricia said—that's exactly what Reagan thought it was. Plus, Greta will fit perfectly in our corporate culture—"

"Meaning Reagan doesn't? I highly doubt that. And have you asked Reagan whether he views PennCo as a stepping stone? Perhaps if he'd seen an opportunity for such a role at PennCo, he wouldn't have tried to get the position with his father's campaign."

Layla opened her mouth and shut it again. "Thatcher, I know you're fond of Reagan, but..." She broke off with a little head shake and stepped closer to lay a hand on my arm. "Never mind. I shouldn't have brought this up when you're already so agitated. Just take care of yourself and your loved ones right now, and we'll talk about personnel concerns when we're back in the city." She smiled at me from under her lashes. "In the meantime, trust me to take care of PennCo for you, okay? Your priorities are my priorities." Her hand rubbed my arm through my sleeve, and for the first time, I saw her meaningless touches as something more.

I jerked away. Layla and I would definitely be

discussing many things, and soon, because I wasn't sure I *did* trust her—not the way I once had and never in the instinctive way I'd always trusted Reagan—and PennCo was so far from being my priority, I would have happily traded it off in exchange for a rocket-powered car that could get me to Madison by morning.

"Thanks," I said shortly. Then I jogged up the stairs.

I found Brantleigh sitting on the side of the bed in my room, red-rimmed eyes fixed on the floor. I could tell at a glance that he was trying to convince himself he was capable of standing and that it wasn't going well. When I looked at him, I remembered the little boy he'd once been: the way he laughed with his whole body, the way he'd trusted me completely. But that boy and his smiles were gone, and in their place was a grown man.

I closed the door with a *click*, and his eyes shot up before he remembered why he shouldn't make any sudden movements. He winced but tried to hide it.

"Come to yell at me and list my failings?" he said in a bored voice. "Don't bother. Mom said she got the story from you, and she already lectured me via text." He shot the phone by his leg a glare. "She expressed her profound disappointment from three thousand miles away. Isn't technology wonderful?"

"I didn't come to lecture," I said, surprised to find I meant it. I wasn't angry at Brant anymore. "And you're not a failure."

He snorted.

"You're not. You just haven't had a chance to succeed." I pulled out the antique desk chair and straddled it, resting my forearms on the upper rail, my eyes never leaving my son's pale face.

Brant sighed. "Is this some kind of psychobabble? Did

you read a new book? Find a new expert to fix me? Because you'd be better off fixing your fucking HR people. Do you have any idea what they thought a decent starting salary for my position would be?"

"I didn't come here to talk about that either—though I think we both know that after what you pulled today, you're no longer employed at Pennington," I said easily.

He narrowed his bleary eyes. "Figures."

"To be honest, I wasn't sure exactly what I wanted to say to you when I came up here," I went on. "You nearly started a fight with Reagan today—"

"That's a lie. He started a fight with me. Pushed me up against a fucking wall—"

"Why?"

Brantleigh pressed his lips together and looked away.

"Right. Because you were acting like a drunken idiot and mouthing off about me to a reporter. Were you trying to get back at me? Or hoping he'd pay you for the story? Or trying to make me angry?" I shrugged. "Either way, I'm sorry."

He looked at me suspiciously. "*You're* sorry?"

"Yep. I've let you down. I've gone around cleaning up your messes and resenting you for it when it was never my job to do those things. If I'd let you take responsibility for yourself when you were younger, maybe you'd have figured stuff out when the stakes were still low. But this is where we are, so this is where it stops."

"What the fuck does that mean?" he demanded.

"It means I agree with the plan your mom laid out. But I'm still going to text you all the time to let you know I'm thinking of you, and I'll visit you more than you'd probably prefer. I'll give you advice when you ask for it, and I will always answer when you call. I won't be paying your debts or making excuses for you." I took a breath. "It means no one will be happier when you figure things out than I will."

"Yeah, sure. I'll be poor and alone in Mom's guest house. Pure fucking bliss. Thanks for *nothing*," he spat. But I could see the fear in his eyes and the sinking knowledge that this time, Thalia and I were on the same page and would stand firm.

"If you decide to talk to a reporter again," I warned, pushing to my feet, "consider the consequences first. It won't change my mind, and I *will* get my lawyers involved."

"Fine. Great. Are we done now? I'm going back to the retreat for the night." He ran a hand over his face. "As soon as this headache eases up a little."

"I'll have McGee—"

"No." Brant raised his chin stubbornly. "I have a car."

I nodded, "Okay. I'll call you in a couple days. And Brant?" I paused with my hand on the doorknob. "I love you."

"Yeah," he muttered without meeting my eyes. "I know."

Deciding that was the best possible outcome I could expect under the circumstances, I closed the door behind me and headed down to dinner.

Though Patricia's guests were just as lively and the food was as plentiful as the night before, Reagan's absence ached like a sore tooth, and I kept darting glances at the place where he should have been.

I took out my phone and texted under the table.

Me: *You make it to Madison okay? I'm sorry I didn't know that was happening.*

By the time dinner was over, I still hadn't received a reply, so I tried again.

Me: *Please respond and let me know you landed safely.*
Reagan: *I landed safely. Thank you.*

I stared at the screen. I could almost hear the words in Reagan's polite, distant voice, damn it all.

I thanked Patricia and Trent for the meal and rushed upstairs as quickly as I could after dinner so I could call him, but he didn't answer.

Me: *I wanted to talk to you about what happened today. Please call me back.*
Reagan: *Can't. I'm exhausted and half-asleep. I need to be up at six for the event.*
Me: *Get some rest. I'll check in with you tomorrow.*

My finger hovered over a never-used heart emoji, but before I allowed myself to go there, I quickly sent the message without it.

Sleep eluded me that night, and I was still awake at midnight when Thalia texted that Brant was safely back at the retreat and would be flying home to California in the morning. As soon as the sun came up, I rose and packed my bags so I could depart, too. Despite Reagan's prickliness, or maybe because of it, I was still determined to get back to the city as quickly as possible so I'd be there when he returned from Madison. All I needed to do was thank my hosts before hitting the road, and fortunately, I knew Trent and Patricia were early risers.

But when I got to the kitchen, I was shocked to find JT was already there.

"I'm telling you, he sounded awful." JT waved his phone at his mother. "He's coughing so hard he's gasping, and he's not making any sense. I'd fly to Madison myself, but I've got three client meetings scheduled back-to-back today. Flynn said my family was more important, but—"

"Wait, are you talking about Reagan?" I demanded. "He's sick?"

JT turned to me in surprise, either because I was up so early or because I'd butted in on what was clearly a family conversation, but he didn't hesitate to explain. "Yes. Very. He texted me before dawn, asking me to look up an urgent care near his hotel. He says he can't make Google work." JT pushed a hand through his hair and gave Patricia a hard look. "When Reagan can't work his phone, it's serious."

I fumbled for my own phone and called Reagan, but it went to voicemail after several rings. When that didn't work, I texted him.

Me: *I'll find a doctor for you, okay? Baby, please tell me you're alright.*

Surely there had to be a nurse or doctor who would do a house call if I paid them enough. After a few moments, there was no response. *Damn it*. What if he was passed out? What if he was alone in a hotel room with no one to notice whether he was conscious or not? What if he needed me and I wasn't there because I'd made the wrong choices and prioritized the wrong things again?

It felt like for the second time in my life, I was watching someone I cared about fall off a cliff. Only this time, I wasn't there to jump in after him—

Except I could be.

I *could* be.

Fuck.

I glanced up at JT. "Is he answering your texts? Tell him to call me."

He glanced down at his phone, then back up at me. He shook his head, face grim.

Without a word, I raced out of the room to look for McGee. Behind me, I heard Patricia murmur, "Thatcher must be worried Reagan won't make his meeting in Madison. *Tsk.* The poor man. He was too preoccupied with Brantleigh last night to even enjoy our after-dinner conversation, and now he's got to deal with this, too."

"Mother, focus. We're concerned about Reagan right now," JT said.

"I *am* concerned, Jonathan! I told you I was concerned after his announcement yesterday morning, too. I can be concerned about more than one thing at a time," Patricia insisted.

I left JT to handle Patricia because I was already dialing January, who was awake and immediately alert.

"Boss? You never call at this hour."

"I need a plane from Honeybridge to Madison, Wisconsin, January. As soon as possible."

"Uh. Alright." She typed furiously. "The company jet is currently refueling to come back to Honeybridge. It'll be there in three hours."

"Too long." I paced across the living room. "I need something faster."

"Why? What's going on?" she demanded. "Is there a problem?"

"Reagan's in Madison, and he has the flu. I don't know how severe it is, but he's not answering texts. I need to get there as soon as possible."

"You?" January repeated. "You're going?"

"*You're* going?" JT asked from behind me. "Yourself?"

"Yes," I answered both of them.

JT looked instantly relieved. January, meanwhile, sounded anything but.

"Thatcher, the only way to get there faster is flying commercial out of Portland," she said, "and you don't fly—"

"Today I do." I ignored the way my stomach churned and my breathing spiked at just the *thought* of leaving the ground, but I couldn't chance medication if I wanted to be alert enough to see Reagan when I landed. "I'll get through it. I can't let him be alone."

"Alright, I'm booking you now," January said, typing once again. "And I'll send the information to McGee." She hesitated for a moment. "Good luck."

"Thanks." I disconnected and immediately headed for the front door, but JT blocked my path.

"Reagan mentioned you hate flying. That's why you were on a bus tour," he said.

"Yeah." My voice sounded rough. "Look, if you don't mind, I really need to—"

"You don't even know how sick he is," JT interrupted, moving to block me again when I tried to step around him. "There's a possibility he's feeling better and simply fell back to sleep."

"Yes, and there's a chance he's very ill."

"You could ask the hotel to do a wellness check." JT moved in front of me once more. "They can call an ambulance if he needs one."

I blew out a breath and stared him down. "Yes, but he'd still be *alone*. Sick and confused."

He kept his eyes locked on mine, almost like a challenge. "Reagan is used to being alone."

"But he shouldn't be. And he won't be anymore," I said boldly.

JT looked me up and down, then nodded once. "Good." Satisfied, he stepped aside. "Do you need me to handle anything? Contact anyone for you?"

Damn. I'd nearly forgotten. "Yeah," I called as I struggled into my jacket. "Please make my excuses to your parents and Layla. Tell them I'll be in touch when I can, and Layla should handle things here while I'm gone."

"Done. I'll tell them it was a family emergency."

I glanced at him in surprise, and he shrugged. "Details are nobody's damn business until you decide to make it their business." He glanced in the direction of the kitchen and sighed wearily. "*If* you decide to make it their business."

"I'll be back as soon as I can," I promised him.

And, I added to myself, *I'll be coming back with Reagan healthy and whole and in my arms.*

Chapter Nineteen

Reagan

By the time I'd landed in Madison the night before, I'd felt like death.

As the cab had crawled toward the hotel through the darkness, I'd cursed the stupid, naive Reagan I'd been that afternoon. Why had I agreed to come to Wisconsin when I could have been curled up in my bed back in Honeybridge, awaiting the Grim Reaper with dignity? And why had my mind kept latching onto thoughts of Thatcher as I soared through the sky when every blurry thought made me feel weaker?

When the woman at the hotel reception counter handed me an overnight package full of conference credentials and marketing materials along with my key, I'd remembered. *Because this is my job, and I'm not a quitter, that's why.*

I rigged the box atop my suitcase and dragged them down an endless hallway to my room. After a quick shower, I fell into bed naked and was asleep before the covers even settled over me.

It wasn't until I opened my eyes sometime before dawn

that I realized I wasn't merely sleep-deprived—I was sick. Sicker than I could remember being. My head swam, and my skin felt too sensitive. I was both hot and cold, and I couldn't focus my thoughts enough to even google my symptoms... though I was pretty sure I knew what it was.

The flu had finally found me and tackled me face-first into a strange bed in a strange city.

It took me half an hour to retrieve some Tylenol from my suitcase and get a cup of water from the bathroom, and by the time I made it back to bed, I started to feel just a little bit afraid. Black spots danced at the edge of my vision, and I was so cold the entire bed moved with the force of my shivers.

I texted JT and asked him to find me an urgent care place once he woke up, which resulted in a phone call a minute later—it was hardly my fault the letters had moved around so much I hadn't spelled any of the words correctly —and a promise to text me back quickly.

So I crawled under the covers and waited.

And waited.

And waited.

A minute or a few hours later—time was such a tricky bitch, and who knew how time zones worked in Wisconsin, anyway?—my phone buzzed, and I grabbed it, expecting to see a list of clinics. What I found was... not that at all.

I frowned down at the email on my screen. The subject line said PROOF ATTACHED, and the sender was a T. Fisher. I sucked in a breath and promptly started coughing. T. Fisher, as in Terrance?

I clicked the attachment and, sure enough, found it was a slide deck showing images of a storyboard—the exact same one Layla had shown Thatcher and me and had claimed as her own.

Even in my feeble state, I could tell this was the original. Not only had the file been created nearly eight months ago, but there were barely decipherable speaker notes attached, too, showing the deck had been created for use as part of a larger presentation.

Explain increased ROI for managing SM in-house, one read.

Quantifiable data here!!!! said another.

A third note was a list called *Suggested strategies prior to Elustre SM launch: Send samples (jackets?) with catchy slogan (TBD?) to celebrity influencers for indirect social media exposure? Select targets who love athleisure gear, post workout selfies, get paparazzi attention. Popular social media talent managers: Karen Finegold @ Waterworth, Jon Cordero @ Rumblefeld. Customize in-house or @ Apparel Designs on W 31st.*

I stared at the note, and my brainpower was so low I had to read it several times before I realized why it all seemed so familiar. This was the Nova incident, all laid out in black and white, right down to the suggestion of Rumblefeld Talent Management—Nova Davidson's PR agency—as a contact. Layla had been right—someone at PennCo *had* planned the whole fucking thing.

I pushed the laptop away like it was suddenly too hot to hold and tried to remember my conversation with Nataly, which felt like it had happened a million years ago. Hadn't she said Terrance was pissed off about Layla shutting down his ideas? Could he have instigated the Nova thing as some kind of revenge against PennCo, stealing the shirt before he left, printing it with that "Sponsor of Your New Year's Resolutions" slogan—and sending it off as a final *fuck you*?

I climbed back under the covers so I could shiver and think.

As vengeance schemes went, it was pretty flawed. After all, if Nova had been caught by the paparazzi on a New Year's Day run around the park, the stunt with the shirt might have resulted in *good* press for PennCo. Of course, anyone who followed her on social media knew how unlikely that was. Nova was too busy stirring up internet feuds with other influencers to go for a jog. Still, who could have predicted something as attention-grabbing as a car accident?

And why would Terrance have agreed to help me if he'd been the one behind it?

So... what if it hadn't been a vengeance scheme at all? What if it had been an attempt to score good publicity for PennCo... executed by someone who didn't know shit about social media influencers and had no idea what they might be unleashing? What if Layla had done it?

A lot of it still didn't make sense, of course, and I didn't think that was my flu talking. Why would Layla launch a full-out manhunt for the culprit if she'd done it herself? Was it simply to throw suspicion onto others—like, say, me? Or—*ugh*, I shot up in bed as the idea hit me—was it to give herself the opportunity to make it all right with the whistle-stop bus tour, which would also give her a chance to throw herself into Thatcher's bed?

Heat suffused my body, and I couldn't say whether it came from my actual fever or possessive rage at the thought of her using Thatcher like that. And there was no doubt in my mind that she would have. Thatcher might be a good man who chose to give her the benefit of the doubt, but I saw Layla for the evil mastermind she was.

One thing I knew for sure, though, was that Layla "fetch me a coffee, would you, Reagan?" James might have masterminded the plot, but there was no way she'd done the legwork.

After waiting a minute for the dizziness to pass, I called Alena, Layla's assistant.

"Reagan! Hey, early bird. Nataly and I were just talking about you yesterday 'cause we're hitting up your favorite Thai place for lunch today, and—oh, wait! You're probably calling about the event today, aren't you? Did you get the marketing stuff I sent? Should be at the hotel reception counter."

"I got it, thanks. You're the best," I croaked. "Sorry for calling so early."

"Oh, *nooo*. You're sick! You poor thing. How can I help?"

Layla didn't deserve Alena.

"Nothing to do with work," I lied. "I actually need your help with a personal thing. See, my mom wants to have some ball caps and apparel printed for this fundraiser thing my dad's doing, and she put me in charge, but I have no idea where to get that done in the city—" I broke off with a cough.

"Oh, honey, you really shouldn't go to the event today if you're not feeling well."

"Uh, yeah. Um... I definitely don't feel good. But I told my mom I'd—"

"I know just where to get that done," she said. "Send me what you need, and I'll take care of it for you."

Layla *definitely* didn't deserve Alena.

"Oh, I couldn't ask you to do that. If you could just send me the info," I croaked. "I'll have my mom ask someone from the campaign."

"Sure thing. I'll shoot you an email right now. Are you

going to be okay? It sucks you're sick in a hotel all by yourself..."

"I'm going to find an urgent care place," I told her. "If I can get some meds, maybe I can make it to tomorrow's events."

"Well, take care of yourself, and don't push it. I'll let Layla know you can't make it today, and I'm sure she'll be fine with it. She told me this event wasn't that important anyway."

Seriously? My head swam sickly, but it might have been the anger thing again. "Good to know. Thanks again for your help with the apparel place."

After waiting a minute for her email, I forwarded it to JT, asking for more help, and then I collapsed back in the bed. JT texted a minute later to inform me that he'd ordered me a room service delivery of Gatorade, toast, and bottled water, and he'd look into the apparel place.

JT: *When the order gets there, drink as much as you can and get in bed.*

It wasn't until I was falling asleep again that I wondered why he hadn't given me the directions to the nearest urgent care I'd asked him for.

A couple of hours later, his call woke me up. "Huh?" I said.

"Hey. I got the information on the print shop for you."

"Already?" I sounded like my tonsils had been dancing the tango with a sheet of sandpaper.

"Yup. My assistant, Alice, is in the city this week, so she volunteered to investigate." JT snorted. "She went down to the apparel place and pretended she was PennCo's newest, least capable employee. Said her boss wanted her to order some more Elustre gear, but she completely forgot who authorized the last batch, and could they *please* help her? They looked up the purchase order, and sure enough, Alena Jimenez was the contact. Any guesses who it was billed to?"

"Layla James," I said hoarsely.

"Layla James," JT confirmed. "And Alice got the name of the person who helped her at the printer, too. I'll email you her name and cell number. Rea, what does this mean?"

"It means I work for a *snake*," I said so forcefully it set off another round of coughing.

"Oh, man, that does not sound good," JT said in a gentler tone.

"No kidding. I feel like dog shit." I laid my arm over my forehead since my brain felt in danger of exploding. "I was going to go to an urgent care place, but my brother forgot to text me a location."

"I didn't forget," he chided. "I did something better. I sent you help."

"You sent someone? Here?" The sheets felt uncomfortable on my prickly skin, and I couldn't decide if I was cold or sweaty. "If you love me at all, please tell me Mother's not coming."

He chuckled. "Patricia? Voluntarily playing nurse? No. She has people for that, Reagan."

"Rosalia," I said, blowing out a relieved breath. "I could do with some Rosalia mothering, to be honest. But I'd hate for her to get sick."

JT's familiar laugh was comforting. "Not Rosalia either. Don't worry. Just get some rest."

He ended the call before I could ask him anything else, and the ensuing coughing fit was the worst yet, leaving me gasping and sweating despite my chills.

But I couldn't just sit here and do nothing with all this

information I'd acquired. Thatcher needed to know what Layla had done. I grabbed my phone, then hesitated.

Thatcher was probably in no mood to talk to me when I still hadn't had a chance to explain or apologize for the Brantleigh thing. And last time I'd tried to tell him about Layla, he'd refused to listen, like I'd been trying to jump the chain of command.

So, fine, then. I'd follow the chain of command. As soon as I caught my breath, I began an email to my boss.

I know who sent the shirt to Nova Davidson. I have proof. Tell Thatcher or I will.

Then, without considering the consequences, I hit Send...

And passed out.

Chapter Twenty

Thatcher

I WOULDN'T SAY that having McGee along made flying *easy*, but it certainly made it better than it would have been. He sat in the seat beside me, big body blocking out the window so I could almost forget there were clouds on the other side of the shade, and made no comment when I clutched the chair arms so hard my fingers went numb. He turned his black-and purple bruised glare at any passengers foolish enough to attempt small talk. He ordered us each a mini bottle of alcohol and got me to take both. Then he secured us a rental car after landing while I tried unsuccessfully to get Reagan on the phone.

He also kept me from murdering the hotel manager, who refused to let me into Reagan's room and calmly reminded her that the hotel would be liable for anything that happened to Reagan if they refused to enter the room and perform a wellness check immediately.

The second the door was unlocked, I ran inside first and found Reagan on the bed, swaddled under a mountain of bedding, clinging to a half-drunk bottle of Gatorade like it was a security blanket.

"Oh, baby, *fuck*." I peeled the sweat-soaked covers down and saw a pale, shivering Reagan underneath. "I'm so sorry. I'm here now. You're going to be okay. You hear me?"

"Thatcher?" His forehead crinkled as his eyes cracked open, and even though the aquamarine was cloudy with sleep and sickness, just seeing them made me calmer than I'd felt in days.

"Yeah, it's me. I've got you. We're going to get you to the hospital. But first..." My eyes met McGee's. "Get me a cold cloth, please. And you—" I glared at the manager, who'd covered her nose and mouth with her sleeve and was trying to back out into the hallway. "Where's the nearest emergency room?"

"UW Hospital," she said promptly. "Should I call an ambulance?"

"No. I'll take him myself." I grabbed the cloth from McGee and bathed Reagan's face with it.

"Don... ned... a'merency rum." He could barely talk through the chattering of his teeth.

"Baby, you do. You're burning up." I spied a bottle of fever reducer on the nightstand. "When was the last time you took this?" I asked, holding the bottle where he could see it.

He began to speak but ended up coughing. He hacked out something like, "When JT told me to?"

I'd been texting JT throughout the flight, and I knew they'd spoken a couple of hours before. The medicine should have still been working.

"You need something stronger," I told Reagan. "Come on. Let's get you up. McGee, get him clothes from his suitcase."

"'M fine. No trouble," Reagan insisted, squirming away.

McGee threw a hoodie and sweatpants on the bed, then

patted Reagan's ankle gently through the blanket. "I hate to tell you, princess, but you look rough. You'd better listen to the boss man, okay?"

Reagan barely opened his gorgeous eyes. "M'Gee? Sorry I... made fun. You don' have wrinkles."

At that, McGee looked more nervous than he had all day. "Are you fucking kidding? Of course I do. Billions of them. And you'll tell me all about them when you're better, you hear?"

"Out," I barked at McGee and the manager. "I'm getting Reagan dressed."

As soon as they were gone, I pulled the covers back and attempted to wrestle the shirt over Reagan's head and the pants onto his legs. His muscles were too listless to put up much fight, but he seemed not to understand what was happening. Every time he closed his eyes and opened them again, he seemed freshly shocked to find me there.

"Reagan, baby, let me take care of you," I finally said, as gently as I could. "I'm here. And I'm not going anywhere. Trust me."

"H-how?" He sounded like he might cry.

I wasn't sure exactly what he was asking, but I pulled far enough back to meet his glassy eyes and gave him the only answer I had.

"Because I love you," I said firmly. "I love you, so I flew to you—on a fucking airplane, through the goddamn sky—in case you needed me. Because I will *always* come when you need me. And I don't ever want you to be alone."

He stared at me in shock for a long moment before his face fell and tears filled his eyes. "Oh, shit," he sobbed. "I'm ha-*hallucinating*."

I leaned forward and pressed a kiss to his burning forehead. "You're not. I'm here. And I'm not leaving you. Not ever. Understand?"

"Yes," he whispered sadly. "I understand everything now. *Layla did it.*"

I bundled the hotel comforter around him for the journey. "I know, sweetheart. You probably caught Layla's flu, and then she sent you away. She and I are going to have words about that," I said ominously. "About *all* of that."

"No, no," he insisted. "The shirt. It's Layla's..." He let out a breath and closed his eyes. "I told her to tell you."

"Reagan?" I jostled him gently and then more firmly when he didn't respond. "*Reagan?*" He still didn't answer, and his chest visibly shook with each shallow inhale.

Fuck.

"McGee," I shouted. "Time to go. Find his coat. I have his shoes."

The next hour and a half was a nightmare. I spent most of my life in a protective bubble of power and wealth, but ninety helpless minutes watching Reagan float in and out of awareness while struggling to breathe was enough to remind me just how fragile and useless that bubble was when it came to protecting what truly mattered. Holding his body against me in the car and the ER waiting room was the only thing keeping me remotely sane.

"How the hell can they be so calm?" I fumed to McGee as Reagan weakly fiddled with the mask the doctors had given him and looked a bit like he was drowning. "They know he has the flu, for god's sake, and his lips are nearly blue. '*As long as he's conscious, we're not overly concerned*'? That's bullshit. Contact January. Have her find out who I need to call and how big a donation I need to make in order to get Reagan some fucking help."

McGee simply patted my shoulder and forced me to

take the antiviral medication my doctor had called in to the pharmacy across the street once Reagan's flu test came back positive.

Reagan was no longer coherent by the time the nurses had gotten him in a hospital gown and assigned us a bed—technically, the bed was *Reagan's*, but when I'd attempted to set him down and back away, he'd let out a plaintive whimper, so damned if I didn't crawl in beside him. I refused to budge when the nurse who hooked up Reagan's IV side-eyed me.

"Sir, you should probably give the patient a little space. I know it's scary—the flu is particularly bad this year—but we've seen many severe cases like this, and the outcomes are usually good for a young, fit man like your, uh..." He hesitated, waiting for me to explain what Reagan was to me.

Despite everything, a smile tugged at the corners of my lips beneath my own surgical mask as I thought about how to answer that. *Employee? Friend's son? Son's childhood friend?* He was all of those things to me, and for a long while, I'd thought that meant he couldn't—*shouldn't*—be more...

But he was. He was everything.

I was in love with him.

It might have taken a serious illness and a terrifying emergency plane ride for me to acknowledge it, but I wouldn't deny it ever again. Reagan was mine.

Did I have a right to feel such complete and overwhelming ownership of Reagan Wellbridge? Absolutely not. Was it too fast, too complicated, too spontaneous, too risky? God yes, all of that. Would that stop me? No.

I no longer cared how our relationship would be perceived by the nurse, or our families, or anyone else in the damn world. Reagan could decide what label he wanted to put on us—if he wanted to label it at all—but it wouldn't change the underlying truth: we belonged together. I just needed him to get well so I could convince him of that, too.

"...Reagan," I supplied when the nurse still seemed to expect a response.

"Your... *Reagan?*" Eyebrow raised skeptically, he glanced from me to the man whose body was nestled in my arms. Then he shrugged. "Okay, then," he agreed.

"Thatcher?" Reagan's voice was breathy and weak. The nurse frowned at the monitor and reached for a nasal cannula to get some oxygen going under Reagan's surgical mask.

I tightened my arm around his shoulders. "Yeah, babe. Right here."

"Did Layla tell you? Is that why you're here? I have proof, I swear. Get my laptop."

My gut clenched. *This again?* The man was more out of it than I'd thought. "I came because you're sick, Reagan. You're in the hospital now, and you're going to be fine, but please don't even think about work—"

"Layla... *shirt,*" he said, making no more sense now than when he'd said something similar back at the hotel. He winced, coughed raggedly, and closed his eyes for a brief moment before meeting mine again. "Sorry."

The nurse shushed him. "Try not to talk, Reagan. We need to get your blood oxygen levels up. Focus on taking deep breaths in and out."

I cupped the side of his face. His beard stubble was scratchy-soft on my palm. "That's right. Don't think about anything else right now. Just breathe innnnn... and ouuuut."

He shook his head and tried to grab me with the hand that had the IV in it. The nurse and I both reached out to stop him and settle him back down.

He turned pleading eyes on me. "You have to believe me. About Layla. JT knows." He closed his eyes as if gathering strength to say more, so I leaned over and pressed a kiss to his cheek through my mask.

"Okay. Shhh. I'll call JT in a few minutes and ask him about it, okay? Will you just breathe now if I promise to talk to JT?"

"Read the email," he murmured.

"I will. I will, baby. First thing, I promise," I said, trying to sound reassuring, even though I didn't know what he was talking about.

A machine began beeping, and I looked over and saw the pulse ox number drop at the same time the nurse pushed a button and called for help. Reagan's eyes fluttered, and he looked even more pale than when I'd brought him in.

"Reagan?" I shook him a little, panicked and helpless. "*Reagan.*"

The nurse glanced at me, no amusement in his eyes this time. "I need you to step out, sir."

I stood but remained by the side of the bed, clinging to Reagan's limp hand. "I can't leave him," I insisted.

The nurse moved between me and Reagan, instructing Reagan to breathe as deeply as he could, and where everything had seemed to be dragging along far too slowly before, suddenly, they were happening in an urgent blur. The pulse ox alarm continued to blare, and my heart rate tried to keep pace with its frantic beeping. I begged Reagan to breathe, but two more people came into the bay and forced me out of the area so they could assist.

My fingers clenched into fists as I paced a squeaky path back and forth across the linoleum that separated me from him. I understood the need to stay out of their way and let the experts handle it, but the very idea of Reagan unable to get enough oxygen had cold fear squeezing my own lungs like a vise.

McGee appeared beside me suddenly in the restricted area and pulled me into a hug. "Boss, you're not gonna do him any good if *you* pass out. Come on, now. Slow and steady. That's it."

I sucked in a huge breath. "Fuck. I hate this."

"I know. I get it. But I called January on the way back, and she verified that this is the best hospital in the area to treat him. Top-notch emergency room and a... what do you call it? A specialized team of breathing doctors, too."

A young woman came out from Reagan's treatment area, and I stepped into her path.

"Please. Just tell me. Is he okay?" I asked.

Her face softened in sympathy. "His oxygen is low. We're concerned that he's developed pneumonia as a result of the flu, and we'll be bringing in X-ray equipment to confirm. If it's pneumonia—or, frankly, even if it isn't—once he's stabilized, we'll be sending him upstairs so we can monitor his breathing and get him started on some IV meds. Why don't you go to the cafeteria and get some dinner? He'll be resting and won't even notice—"

I snorted. "Oh, he'd notice. And so would I. I'm not leaving."

She studied me as if to see how serious I was. I crossed my arms over my chest and stared her down the way I stared down rival CEOs during intense boardroom negotiations.

She sighed. "Fine, but you need to move back and sit over there." She pointed to a makeshift waiting area—three hard, gray chairs set along a wall between a laundry bin and a vitals cart. "You'll be able to see when things quiet down, and they'll let you back here again."

I opened my mouth to argue, but fortunately, McGee yanked me away and sat me down before I could.

"You can't control this, boss," he reminded me. "And throwing a fit won't help."

I remembered Reagan telling me almost the same thing the first night we spent together—was it really just two weeks ago? *Sorry to break it to you, but there are some things in life you don't control, and you don't get to have a tantrum about them.* Ironically, I'd never felt as out of control in my life as I had in the days since he'd said that.

"He couldn't breathe," I told McGee. My voice cracked. "And here I am, sitting in the most uncomfortable torture chair anyone's ever invented, wearing a paper mask, like a useless lump of shit. Why have millions of fucking dollars if I can't make sure something like this doesn't happen? What if—? What if he—? I haven't even told him…"

McGee's bruised eyes held an expression of mingled affection and pity. "Look around, Thatcher. He's not coding. Nobody's panicking. From what I saw, Reagan has one of those nose things for oxygen, but he's not on a ventilator or whatever. They just needed to get your giant ass out of the way so they could treat him." He bumped his shoulder into mine. "So instead of thinking up worst-case what-ifs, think about *what if* he gets the treatment he needs? *What if* he's wide-awake tomorrow, giving me shit and turning your whole life upside down? What if you get a chance to tell him all your big, schmoopy love-motions. 'Cause that's way more likely." He leaned his huge frame back in the creaky plastic seat and crossed his ankle over his knee. "And I personally can't wait for it. Thatcher Pennington is all up in his feels. Fucking finally."

I glared at him, but activity behind Reagan's curtain saved McGee from getting a fat lip to match his nose and eyes. A short while later, a young doctor came over. "No one's officially read the X-ray yet, but I'm pretty confident it's pneumonia. His ox levels are stabilized, so we're starting him on medicine now and will begin breathing treatment upstairs once he's admitted."

"To a regular room?" McGee demanded. "Not ICU or whatever?"

The doctor seemed shocked we even had to ask. "Definitely not. Standard medical floor. It might take a few days, but your, uh... loved one... is going to be okay."

That look of surprise convinced me she meant it, and the relief that flooded my bloodstream was sweet... though it left me nearly as shaky as my earlier panic.

When the doctor walked away, McGee chuckled and bumped my shoulder again. "You know that doc thought Reagan was your son, right?" he said in a low voice.

"Jesus," I muttered. "Thank you, McGee. That's just what I needed to hear right now."

"Think maybe I should go back there and tell her some of the things I've heard the two of you get up to?"

"Shut your mouth," I warned, but the smile in my voice probably ruined the effect.

"Just sayin'. Not very parental, if you ask me. Oooh, or maybe she thought *I* was your son," he suggested, wiggling his pierced eyebrow. Despite the mask he wore, I could tell his trademark shit-eating grin was in full effect. "That would make Reagan your son-in-law."

I elbowed him. "You wish."

McGee laughed and dropped his teasing. "Hell no. Too mouthy. I like 'em cuter and sweeter, like—" He broke off, looking vaguely guilty, and cleared his throat. "Ah. Like no one in particular."

I stared at him. "Wait. Have you been holding out on me? Did you break your no-hookups rule?"

"No! I mean, not exactly? I'm into someone," he admitted. "Really into him. But I'm not saying anything else until I know *he's* into *me*." His cheeks flushed, and his biceps rippled as he shifted uncomfortably in the chair. "It's fucking weird, man. I've faced big-ass motherfuckers in the cage, and I'm all, 'Let's fucking *go*.' Zero nerves, all adrenaline. But wanting someone this much?" He shook his head, mystified. "Makes my knees weak, it's so terrifying."

"McGee," I said wryly, wrapping a companionable arm over his shoulders, "I know exactly what you mean."

———

THE HOSPITAL ROOM WAS DIM, and the steady, low beep of the cardiac monitor assured me Reagan was still comfortably asleep. The doctor had come in a few hours ago to give an official diagnosis—pneumonia, as a complication of a severe flu infection, just as they'd thought. With the help of IV meds and a breathing treatment, Reagan's fever had subsided, and his oxygen levels were stable, but given the extent of his illness, his body was worn-out. "He's asleep, and it's the best thing for him, so don't be surprised if he doesn't wake up for hours," the doctor had warned in a tone that added an unspoken "...so stop harassing us about it."

I was trying my best, but where Reagan's struggle had left *him* exhausted, it had left me restless and on-edge. I wanted a task. A goal. A target. Something to do or fight or protect or solve.

When McGee took a break to grab some food, I refused to go. Instead, as I stared at Reagan in the semi-darkness, listening to the beeping, I remembered I'd promised him I'd call JT... which, I realized with some chagrin, I probably should have done earlier since no one in Honeybridge knew anything about Reagan's condition.

When I pulled out my phone, I had thirteen missed calls and twenty-two messages from JT alone, plus several more from January and Layla. I ignored those.

When JT answered, he sounded distraught. "Thatcher? Oh, thank fuck. Reagan hasn't replied to me all afternoon. If I need to come out there, I will—"

"Reagan's okay," I said quickly. "He's in the hospital being treated for flu with a side of pneumonia—"

"Holy shit. Pneumonia?"

"He's in good hands, JT," I said, repeating what McGee had been telling me for hours. "He's breathing okay now and sleeping peacefully. And I'm right here with him."

There was a beat of silence on the other end before a very firm and relieved "*Good.*"

"He was, ah... not making a whole lot of sense for a little while there, thanks to the fever and the oxygen thing, but he kept insisting that I talk to you. Something about an email and Layla's shirt? If that doesn't make any sense to you either, he might have been dreaming—"

"Oh, no," JT assured me. "That was very real."

He proceeded to tell me a story about Terrance—the former PennCo employee Reagan had found through Instagram—and some notes he'd made on a presentation slide deck. He also explained how Reagan, sick as he'd been this morning, had managed to trace those clues directly to the source of the Nova Davidson incident...

Layla, herself.

Two weeks ago, I wouldn't have believed Layla capable of it. Even a few days ago, I might have tried to find another explanation. But after everything that had happened, it now seemed so obvious I couldn't believe how blind I'd been.

"Reagan tried to warn me," I murmured, my gaze tenderly tracing the clumps of messy sun-streaked hair that stuck straight up around his pale face in a strange sort of halo. "He's smart, and he's damn good at reading people. One of these days, I'll listen."

JT snorted. "You're not the only one who's underestimated him. I think it's already started to dawn on my parents just how important Reagan was to Dad's campaign—according to Patricia, *everyone who's anyone* was asking why Rea wasn't with them today, since everyone's heard he was back in town, and Dad's campaign manager had some pretty sharp words about him 'letting Reagan slip through his fingers.' Mother's playing it off as Reagan being sent on a crucial mission for *the* Thatcher Pennington since I let everyone believe you were heading to Los Angeles with Brantleigh."

"Perfect. Thank you for that. Eventually, I'd like to tell your parents where I've been, but—" It wasn't entirely my call anymore, what I chose to share or hold back. I needed to see how Reagan wanted to play this.

"None of my business as long as Reagan's okay with it," JT said. "But you should know you might have some company in Madison soon, according to my mother."

"Company? Your mother is coming?"

"Oh, no. *Noooo*. Mother doesn't fully understand how serious Reagan's condition is, and at this point, it's probably better to wait and tell her after the fact. But Mother did mention that Layla packed her bags this afternoon and ordered the corporate jet to take her to Madison. She assumes Layla's going to take Reagan's place at whatever event he was supposed to attend because Reagan's sick and

Layla's *such a lovely woman,*" he said, in a creditable impression of Patricia's voice. "Mother, *not* known for her ability to read people."

"Yeah, well. Layla fooled me, too," I reminded him. "And now I'm wondering..."

It was entirely possible that Layla was coming to Madison because she'd heard Reagan was sick and wanted to take over his role at the event. She certainly wasn't coming to see *me* since she thought I was headed to LA. But something about the timing just didn't add up. What were the chances she was flying out here mere hours after Reagan started investigating her involvement in the Nova incident?

"I've got to go," I told JT. "I'll be in touch, though. And I promise..." I grabbed the hand of the man I'd fallen stupidly and wholeheartedly in love with and said the words like a vow. "I'll take care of your brother."

"I believe you," JT said. "And thanks."

As soon as we ended the call, I dialed January.

"How's Reagan?" she answered.

"He's better. Resting. But we do have a situation, and I'm going to need you to call Legal..."

By the time I finished strategizing with her, McGee had returned with takeout containers of food from the cafeteria, so while he ate, I sat on the side of the bed and filled him in.

McGee scowled around a mouthful of cafeteria french fries. "I don't get it," he said. "Why'd the kid ask his brother for help? Why not come directly to you?"

I toyed with Reagan's long, slender fingers, careful not to disturb his IV. "Because he tried to tell me before, and I wouldn't listen," I admitted. "Our last night on the bus, he said he'd contacted Terrance and heard some concerning stuff about Layla. But I'd already been angry at Layla for the way she'd treated Reagan that day, and it had been really fucking hard to remember that I needed to address her behavior as her boss—through proper channels, in a formal meeting with HR—rather than lashing out like an overprotective boyfriend and telling her to back off. I told myself that listening to Reagan's gossip was inappropriate and that I needed to draw clear lines about what was acceptable if I wanted to keep seeing him while he worked for PennCo." I lifted his hand and pressed a masked kiss to his knuckles. "I was an idiot."

"You really were," McGee agreed way too cheerfully. "I mean, where does flying across the country and carrying Reagan bodily out of his hotel room fit in those lines?"

"It doesn't," I said firmly. I met McGee's eyes from across the room. "I forgot that I'm the head of the damn company. *I draw the lines.*"

McGee grinned fiercely around his sandwich. "Hell yeah, you do. But man, I still can't believe the brass ovaries on her. I mean, I knew she was conniving as fuck—always running around trying to impress you, always so touchy-feely and 'I live to please you, Thatcher,' and whatever—but *this?* Trying to act like she's a fucking hero, saving the day with this bus tour, when *she* was the one who caused the problem in the first place? Trying to throw Reagan under the bus so no one would suspect her? That's some evil villain energy right there. She was your friend, your trusted veep, the fucking Queen of PennCo, and she risked it all for *what?* A chance to stroke her ego and show you she was a superstar?"

"I don't know why." I squeezed Reagan's hand tighter. "But I'm going to find out."

McGee bit into his sandwich like he was tearing someone's head off and shook his head as he chewed. "If she thinks Reagan might suspect her, she's gonna try to blame him again. You know she will."

"Oh yeah."

"She doesn't know how sick he is, so she'll try to meet up with him here and find out what he knows, then she'll twist that information. She'll say he got a copy of Terrance's presentation somehow or that he came up with a similar idea all by himself and he knew exactly which social media influencers to send the shirt to since he's an influencer, too."

"She will," I agreed. "She's been laying the groundwork for that since the beginning, questioning how trustworthy he is."

"She might even claim *Reagan* is trying to frame *her*."

I nodded. "I thought of that."

McGee finished the last of his sandwich and tugged his mask back into place. "So I'm guessing your legal people are gonna tell you to keep your cool and let them handle it?"

I raised an eyebrow. "Probably."

"And you're going to ignore them," he concluded.

I pressed the back of Reagan's hand to my cheek, simultaneously hoping he'd sleep and heal and wishing he'd wake up so I knew he was okay. There was nothing I wouldn't do to keep him safe and happy.

"I'm going to ignore them," I confirmed. That restless energy, that need to *do* something, was thrumming through my veins again. "And I'm going to bury her."

If Layla tried to get in touch with Reagan, I'd be ready.

Chapter Twenty-One

Reagan

I woke to the sounds of beeping and raised voices nearby.

"Don't take another step toward this room, Layla." The man speaking sounded a lot like Thatcher, though I'd never heard Thatcher's voice that cold and flat. It would have made me shiver if I hadn't been surrounded by warm blankets.

"Thatcher? Goodness, you startled me. I didn't expect... I mean, I thought you were heading for California."

"Disappointed?" he asked.

"What? No! No, of course not. I'm always happy to see you. I just thought..." She cleared her throat. "When I heard from Alena that Reagan was ill, I immediately flew out here to take over at the event. Naturally, I stopped at Reagan's hotel to check on him, and I was shocked when the manager directed me here. I imagined the poor kid sick and alone..."

"I'm sure you did," Thatcher said in that same flat voice. "But Reagan's not alone."

"No, I see. It's good that you're here, as a friend of his father's. But... actually, Thatcher, I did need to talk to you about something concerning Reagan—"

"Let me guess: you've found proof that Reagan was behind the Nova Davidson incident."

My eyes flew open. *Wait, what?*

"Well, yes," Layla admitted sadly. "I didn't want to believe him capable of it, and this is hardly the time to discuss it when he's so ill, but—"

"Save it. I already know the truth." Now, Thatcher's voice was a growl of pure venom—the sound of a man betrayed—and everything in me wanted to see him, to comfort him.

My eyes darted around the dimly lit hospital room, and I tried to sit up. Snatches of memories filtered through my foggy brain, and my head swam with the rush of information flooding back in. Thatcher carrying me through the freezing wind and into the busy emergency room. A friendly nurse helping me change into a hospital gown while Thatcher shot him a menacing glare. Murmured conversations between Thatcher and McGee, punctuated by the regular beep and hiss of medical equipment.

The flu. I'd finally caught the damned flu that had caused Layla to miss the road trip out West.

I heard the increased beep of the heart rate monitor before I felt the rush in my chest. *Layla.* Terrance's notes. The Nova scandal. The lies.

And the realization she was even now trying to claim it was all *my* fault.

"Hey," murmured a third voice, much closer to my bed. "Welcome back, princess. You scared us for a minute there, but it looks like you'll be okay now. And I'm, like, ninety-eight percent sure Thatcher's okay, too... but just in case, I'm keeping an eye on him to make sure he doesn't do anything illegal."

I turned my head and found McGee, half-hidden

behind the fabric curtain that screened my bed as he spied on the conversation taking place in the hallway.

"Illegal?" I croaked. I ripped my surgical mask off. "What? I need to go—" I reached ineffectively for the covers.

McGee turned and gave me a wink. "Nah. You sit tight. Thatcher's got this. Trust him. Just listen."

"I'm so glad you and I are finally on the same page about this," Layla was saying. "I know how reluctant you were to see the truth about Reagan—it's a huge betrayal of your trust, of course—but he's young. Overeager. And he was trying to impress you. You shouldn't blame yourself—"

"Oh, I don't," Thatcher said smoothly. "When I said I knew the truth, Layla, I meant I knew it was *you* who sent Nova the shirt."

I gripped the bed rails tightly with both hands. *Oh, god.* "McGee," I whispered. "Get out there. Stop him. He can't do this in a hospital hallway."

"Thatcher, come on," Layla demanded. "After all these years, after all we've been to each other, surely you trust me. You can't possibly think—?"

"The better question," Thatcher interrupted, trying to keep his voice low but failing, "is how, after all these years, you could do something like this. Because I did trust you, Layla. I trusted you to lead PennCo. I trusted you to be honest with me. Instead, it seems your idea of leadership means sidelining employees who might upstage you, stealing their ideas, and trying to blame others for your mistakes."

"How could you possibly accuse me of something like that?" she shrieked.

"Let me be clear," Thatcher continued, unmoved. "I'm not angry that you made the mistake of sending the shirt to the wrong influencer. I'm angry that this mistake happened because you didn't want to share the glory and therefore didn't consult anyone who might have known what they were doing. And I'm *disgusted* that when it went wrong, you tried to ruin a good man's reputation in order to save your own. Go home, Layla," he said witheringly. "Your presence is not needed or welcome here."

"You're letting your personal relationship with Reagan cloud your judgment, Thatcher," Layla insisted, panicky now. "Anyone who looked at these facts impartially would see Reagan had the most to gain. He forged my signature, he corrupted my assistant. He's manipulated you—"

"Dear god, stop. Reagan doesn't have to manipulate me to gain my trust because he already *has* my trust, full stop. He doesn't have to lie to gain my attention because he *has* my attention and always will. And he doesn't need to scheme in order to make himself look important because he's already important—"

My heart leapt at the things he was saying, but... *fuck.* This was getting way too personal. Thatcher was trying to defend me, as usual, but in the process, he was giving far too much away. When he stopped being angry, he might regret having this out in a hallway instead of following the proper protocol. He'd definitely regret saying such sweet things when he realized they might cause speculation about our relationship. And I couldn't stand to see Thatcher look at me with regret ever again.

I finally managed to clasp the blanket in one weak hand and pull it aside. I tried to swing my legs off the bed and nearly fell out.

"Ah, shit," McGee muttered, coming around to stop me from face-planting on the linoleum. "Boss?" he called. "Need a little help in here."

In the space of a single heartbeat, Thatcher was at my side, barking an order for McGee to shut the door and keep everyone out. With gentle fingers, he cupped my cheek. "Baby? Oh, thank fuck you're okay."

"Is this some kind of flu-dream?" I whispered, closing my eyes so I could relish the soft caress of his thumb against my temple. "Karmic payback for how awful and weak I feel? Because if so, I'm kinda here for it."

He chuckled. "It's not a dream. I'm here, and I'm not leaving."

His voice brought a wave of comfort over me. I tried to focus my thoughts, but they seemed to be tangled up. "I heard you and Layla. She must've gotten my email. Is that why you came?"

I opened my eyes to find him staring down at me, shaking his head in fond amusement. "No, sweetheart. I came for *you*. When JT told me you were sick, I came as fast as I could."

A memory of him telling me this earlier tugged at my consciousness. "Wait, I remember. You... you flew? On a *fucking airplane, through the goddamn sky?*"

He nodded. "You needed me."

"Yeah I did," I breathed, gazing up at him like a total sap. "But... wait, Layla... Did you—?"

"I figured out what she did, with some help from JT," Thatcher confirmed. "When you're feeling better, I want to hear your take on it, and obviously, I want you to go to HR and tell them everything, on the record. I don't want a single shred of doubt attached to your name. But in the meantime, HR and our legal team are investigating Layla in an official capacity, including following up with some former members of her team, and— Wait." His brow creased. "Did you say you sent her an email?"

"Yeah." I rubbed at my forehead. "I, uh, told her I knew what she'd done and that she should confess," I admitted. "Dramatic, but in my defense, I felt like death, and I may have gone a little... feral."

Thatcher snorted, but his eyes were still soft and warm on mine, that finger still stroking my face like he couldn't believe I was real. "Like the beavers in Lake Wellbridge?"

He startled a laugh out of me, and miraculously, I managed not to cough my head off at the same time. I wondered dazedly if Thatcher Pennington might be the cure for influenza since he made me feel better than whatever they were pumping through my IV. "Kind of," I agreed.

"I wish you'd come to me," he said softly, sobering me quickly. "I wish you hadn't done any of this alone—"

Just that fast, I remembered why I hadn't. "Oh, god. Thatcher, I'm so sorry about Brantleigh. He was being awful, but I shouldn't have lost my temper. I don't blame you for being angry at me—"

"Angry? At *you*? God, no." He tapped my hip so I'd push over, then sat down beside me. "The way you defended me, the things you said... You were amazing, and the incident led me to finally work things out with Brant, sort of." He rolled his eyes. "I'll tell you all about that later, too. I, ah... figured you felt like you couldn't tell me your suspicions regarding Layla because I shut you down when you first tried to tell me."

"Yeah," I admitted, picking at a loose thread of the blanket with my free hand. "That, too."

He tilted my chin up so I could see the changeable storm in his eyes. "I fucked up. I was trying to keep our professional relationship separate from our personal one, and—"

"I know. I understand," I assured him. Thatcher was an

intensely private man. Naturally, he didn't want to do anything that might invite speculation about just how close we might be. And I couldn't say it didn't hurt—it did—but if that was a boundary Thatcher felt he had to draw so that we could *have* a personal relationship... I would try to respect it. After all, there were a *lot* of compensations. "You flew to rescue me, Thatcher." I shook my head, still not quite able to believe that he was here in front of me. "You're forgiven."

"I do fly sometimes, you know. When I have to. When it's *important*." He leaned closer—so close his lips nearly brushed mine. "Do you remember me telling you *why* I flew here?"

My breath caught, and I knew my eyes were huge because I was staring at him so hard I couldn't make myself blink. "I... I think so?" My heart rate shot up so quickly that the monitors beeped a warning.

Thatcher grinned and moved back a couple of inches, his eyes crinkling at the corners. "Because I love you."

"Oh." The flu must've stolen my dignity along with all my strength because I felt hot tears gather at the corner of my eyes before Thatcher reached out to thumb them away. "Well, that's..." Another tear followed the first. Thatcher brushed it back to the edge of my hairline. "Are you *sure*?" I demanded. "Because I know you said it before, but if it was an adrenaline thing because you thought I was dying or whatever, I would understand." That was a lie. Never in my life had I wanted to believe anything so badly.

"Positive. *I love you*, Reagan Wellbridge. You, with your silver tongue and your gorgeous eyes, with your crazy antics and your big heart, and that sexy tattoo that I've become really, shockingly possessive of." He grinned. "Now, stop crying, love. We need all this liquid to stay inside. The doc said you're dehydrated on top of the flu. You can't afford tears right now."

I snorted and started coughing again.

Thatcher helped me sit up so I could catch my breath and wrapped a supportive arm around my shoulders... but his proximity only made the beeping of the cardiac monitor speed up again. The machine made a shrill warning noise. From the way my heart was hammering in my chest and heat was licking every inch of exposed skin on my body, I thought maybe it *was* an emergency.

"This is mortifying," I muttered, turning my face into Thatcher's shirt. "You told me you love me, and I'm ruining our moment."

He rested his chin against my temple. "You're safe in my arms, Reagan. Nothing could ruin this. In fact," he teased, "I'm kind of wondering if I can keep you hooked up to one of these machines permanently. I like knowing what you're thinking about." His voice was a low rumble that reached deep into my gut, lighting me up in places that had no business being lit, given that I felt about as sexy as a newborn kitten.

The monitor began bleating like a Vegas slot machine hitting the jackpot.

Thatcher burst into laughter. He caught my jaw in one strong hand and kissed my forehead. "God, I love you," he murmured. "It's my privilege to come here and be the one to take care of you, Reagan Wellbridge. Do you understand? I never want you to have to handle anything alone again. I'm a bad bet, but I'm selfish enough to let you make it." He trailed his lips down my forehead to my cheek, then my ear, still wet from my tears.

I swallowed hard. "I...I love you, too," I said seriously.

"Yeah?" He closed his eyes and blew out a relieved

breath. "Thank fuck. I told myself not to expect you to say it back. I know it's only been a couple of weeks—"

Predictably, seeing Thatcher vulnerable made me melt. "Weeks? Ha. I've been into you since... a possibly illegal number of years ago," I admitted.

"Reeeeally." He blinked. "Really?"

"Yes! How could you not know?"

"Baby, before you, it never would have occurred to me to look. I spent a long time keeping my focus on the things I thought I could control. Then, on New Year's Eve, I took a risk. I shaved my beard and hooked up with a masked man—"

"The *wrong* man," I pointed out, smiling despite the tears still leaking from my eyes.

"The absolute right man," he corrected firmly. "Since then, I haven't felt like I'm in control of a damn thing. It terrifies me, but I've never felt more whole. When I'm with you, I see all the things I never could before."

"Blind spots," I murmured, and although I really, *really* didn't want to, just saying the words made me think of Layla and the upheaval that was going to cause for PennCo and for Thatcher himself. What would the investigation entail? "So what happens now?" I blurted.

"Well..." Thatcher settled back against the pillows and pulled me deeper into his arms. "I know I don't want to live without you. I'd like to take you home with me and keep you there permanently—"

"*What?*" I pulled back to stare at him. Was he talking about moving in together? How could we possibly do that while still keeping our relationship under wraps? It wasn't like paparazzi stalked either of us constantly, but people would talk—

"Shhh. Calm down, baby, or that heart monitor is going

to catch fire. I won't rush you into anything," he promised, pulling me back down against him. "But you did ask."

"I... I meant what was going to happen to Layla," I muttered. Despite my illness and the layers of hospital antiseptic on both of us, I caught the tang of his cologne and burrowed more deeply into his side.

"Oh. That." Thatcher's fingertips stroked up and down my arm. "Well, hopefully she went home like I told her to. If she's still here, I'm pretty sure McGee will call security. But if you mean in general..."

I nodded against his rib cage.

"I'm going to follow HR's lead from this point on, but I made it clear that I want Layla out as soon as possible," he said unequivocally. "There's no room for someone with her attitude at Pennington. In the meantime, January's making sure her security badge and login credentials are frozen, pending the results of the investigation, and she's suspended with pay effective immediately."

"Whoa," I breathed. "Just like that?" I lifted my head to gaze into his dark eyes. "How much did I miss while I was out? Did you see the slide deck Terrance sent me? And did you talk to Alena yourself? Because Layla was right— someone else investigating this might look at the facts and think it was me. Alena's the only person who can really tie Layla to it, and she's loyal to her boss, so maybe—"

"Hush, baby. I knew from the first day that you weren't involved, remember? Even before I *knew* you, I knew that much. I trust you, and I'm not going to let anyone else doubt you either."

I wasn't sure how he was going to accomplish that without tipping people off that I was more than an employee and a family friend, but it was still really nice to hear. "You trust me that much?"

Thatcher's gaze snapped up to mine. "With my life. Never doubt it. You're the best thing that's happened to me in a long, long time." He leaned in close, his lips ghosted against mine—

And the fucking monitor began blaring an alarm twice as loud as it had before, complete with a flashing red light like a police siren. Thatcher sprang off the bed.

"Is the machine trying to *induce* a cardiac event?" I grumble-coughed.

"I think this monitor might be malfunc—oh!" A cheerful older nurse pulled back the privacy curtain. "Look who's awake!" She glanced from me to Thatcher, then frowned. "Mr. Pennington, I thought the doctor told you that you need to wear a mask in the patient's room. Antivirals taken prophylactically are only eighty percent effective, you know."

"I took it off out in the hall," Thatcher said apologetically. He grabbed one from a container hanging on the wall. "I'll keep this one on."

"See that you do." The nurse took my vitals while delivering a good-natured lecture on infection control protocols.

If that wasn't enough to thoroughly kill any hope of Thatcher kissing me again, she also took me on a field trip to use the bathroom. One quick look at myself in the mirror had me hoping like hell Thatcher was under the influence of new-love blinders. By the time she helped me back to bed, my legs felt like overcooked noodles, and my head wasn't much better.

"Cockblocked by my cardiac monitor," I muttered when the kind lady left to get me some crackers and water. "That might be the title of my autobiography."

Thatcher, sitting in a chair a respectable distance from my bed, was busy typing something on his phone. "Please don't say *cock*. There will be no cock on the menu for a couple of months," he decreed. I made a squawking noise, and when he glanced up at me, his eyes softened and heated. "Okay, *one* month. But that's as much as I'm willing to concede."

"What? Why?" I sounded petulant, but I was blaming the flu.

"Because I'm going to make sure you get well. Starting by having McGee bring you some soup from the restaurant down the street." Thatcher slid his phone away, leaned forward, and picked up my hand with both of his. "You scared me," he said baldly. "I never want to see you that sick again."

I ran my other hand through his hair gently. "I'm sorry."

Thatcher shot me a glare. "Don't apologize for something you had no control over."

"Seriously, though," I said, "Dealing with me right after dealing with Brant *and* handling the Layla thing... I *am* sorry I worried you."

Thatcher leaned even closer and pressed his hand over my masked mouth to shut me up. "Apologize again and find out what happens," he growled. "If you don't want to worry me, you'll focus on getting better, baby, and understand why we will not be having sex for—" I parted my lips and traced my tongue along Thatcher's palm through my mask. His eyes dilated. "Two weeks," he said in a choked voice. "And that's final."

I grinned. When you were madly in love with a billionaire business tycoon, it paid to master the art of negotiation... especially when it came to sex. I was pretty sure that by the time I was actually well enough to actually consider doing the deed, I'd manage to shave off another week or more. A little bubble of joy welled up inside of me at the idea that Thatcher and I would be together long enough for that to be an option.

I removed his hand from my face and cradled it in both of mine. "You're *not* a bad bet," I said softly.

"Oh no?" His eyes studied me intently over his mask. "I'm eighteen years older than you—"

"Eighteen years more experienced," I countered. "In all the best ways."

Thatcher's eyes flared. "I'm controlling. I don't know if I can change that—"

"I like you bossy," I blurted.

His intense stare softened. "Yeah?"

"*Oh*, yeah," I breathed.

"Hold that thought for another... ten days, minimum," Thatcher instructed. He cleared his throat. "I'm also way too committed to my job—at least, I have been. That's something I'm going to change, but I might slip up from time to time—"

I squeezed his hand tightly. "The work Pennington Industries does is valuable, Thatcher. The technology you develop makes people's lives better in a billion little ways. And you have hundreds—*thousands*—of employees and contractors and investors whose livelihoods depend on the company staying profitable. That's important. I would never want to interfere—"

He shook his head. "It is important, but it's *not* more important to me than you. I've learned that lesson the hard way over the last couple of days." He reached up with his free hand to brush my hair off my forehead. "You know, I was already planning to leave Honeybridge this morning, before I heard you were sick."

"Really?" I frowned. "But the Investment Summit—"

"I don't give a shit about that Summit, Reagan. I'd been

so damn stubborn, and by the time I realized how much I needed you—how little everything else mattered when you weren't by my side—you were gone, and the only thing I cared about was getting you back. I was planning to beat you back to the city so I could pick you up at the airport, maybe take you back to my place, and—"

"And keep me there permanently?" I teased, amused. "So you said. It's a solid plan. I could get on board with being held prisoner in your penthouse with the beautiful view."

Thatcher's face held naked vulnerability. "If I thought I could get away with it. I don't want to pressure you, Reagan. I know there are probably a lot of things we'd need to settle before moving forward together. Whether you'd want to live with me eventually, where we'd live, what you want to do with your career—I mean, I'd really like to offer you a social media strategist position at PennCo since I think you'd be perfect for the job—"

"You do?"

"Obviously." He frowned. "Have I not made it clear that I think you're brilliant? And that's true whether you and I are together or not, Reagan. You would kick ass at that job." He shrugged. "Frankly, there are a *lot* of things you'd do well at, but if that's what you want to do—"

Had anyone ever said the words "there are a lot of things you'd do well at" to me? Hard no. Stupid flu-tears prickled at my eyes ominously again. "That's definitely what I want to do," I croaked out.

Thatcher nodded. "I can't deny that some people would get the wrong idea if they knew you were promoted and that you and I were together—"

I nodded. "I know exactly what they'd say. I've been accused of benefitting from nepotism my whole life. It's not fun, but it was way harder knowing that even my parents didn't think me capable of the job I wanted." Still, I could definitely understand why Thatcher wouldn't want to open himself up to that kind of criticism. That might be the one advantage to keeping our relationship private. "I'd rather not be seen as the boss's arm candy," I assured him.

His eyes darkened ominously. "If anyone ever said that to you, I would sign the company over to you so that *I* could be the boss's arm candy."

I barked out a laugh that set off another bout of coughing. "Honestly, you say shit like that, and then you worry that I feel pressured? I don't feel pressured. I'm in, Thatcher. I'm *all* in. I'm so in, I'm drowning here."

And that was neither a lie nor an exaggeration. Was it a sucker move to give the man a blanket yes when I knew he'd never claim me publicly and our relationship would live in the dark? Probably. That kind of thing had never bothered me one way or the other before, but I already sensed it would be different with Thatcher.

Still, just like that first night at the gala, I could not imagine saying no to this man. I loved him way too much to walk away.

"We'll figure out the details as we go," I told him.

There was a knock on the door. "I got your soup," McGee announced from the other side of the privacy curtain. "I'm coming back there. Fair warning. Walking forward now." He drew the curtain aside and immediately shielded his eyes with one tattooed hand. "Is it safe to look?"

Thatcher and I exchanged a glance. "What exactly are you afraid you might see," Thatcher demanded dryly, "when Reagan's in a hospital bed recovering from the flu?"

"Life-affirming sex, obviously." McGee peeked over his hand cautiously. Once he was sure we were both fully dressed, he set a small takeout bag on my bed tray and plunked himself down in a chair at the end of my bed. "It's a real thing, boss. And remember, I've been with the two of you on a bus for the past couple weeks. Not like you need an excuse, really."

"Jesus." Thatcher dropped his chin to his chest and shook his head while I collapsed into another round of laugh-coughing.

"Don't say *sex*, McGee," I told him when I'd recovered. "Thatcher says we're not doing that for, like, eight days."

Thatcher raised a dark eyebrow. "Eight?"

"Or was it seven?" I asked innocently. "The medication makes it so hard to remember. Also, McGee, I have to compliment you on the eye thing. Not a lot of guys could pull off the reddish-purplish-yellow look, but it really adds some visual interest to your face. Nobody would even *think* of looking at your frown lines."

Bizarrely, this remark made McGee grin hugely. "Aaaand, he's back. So..." He looked back and forth between us, his eyes like ping-pong balls. "Everything good? Did we sort everything out?"

Thatcher kept his eyes on me. "The important parts. Right, Reagan?"

My heart monitor betrayed me again, beeping so loud that my soft "yeah" was almost redundant.

Thatcher's phone chimed, and he dug it out. "Helen from Legal asked me to call her about Layla." He looked at McGee. "She left, I assume?"

McGee nodded. "Threw a hissy fit and tried to come in here, but I stopped her. When the nurse threatened to call security, she took off."

"Good." Thatcher pushed to his feet and bent down to press his masked lips to my forehead. "Eat your soup," he instructed. "I'll be back after I talk to Helen and let January know you're okay. She's been texting me all afternoon."

"Oh, shit." I glanced around the room for my phone. "I should probably call JT and let him know I'm okay, too—"

"Already done, and he said he'd tell your parents," Thatcher interrupted, but he extracted my phone from a bag in the corner and laid it on the bed beside me anyway. "I'm sure they'd all like to hear from you, when you're feeling up to it. FYI, I didn't tell them you're in the hospital —they actually don't even know I'm here. JT thought it would be better to tell them how sick you were after you're feeling better."

"Oh." I nodded. "Right. Sure. Yeah. Makes sense." Telling my mother he was here was *not* a way to keep our relationship under the radar. "I, uh, won't post anything on Instagram either, just in case they happen to see it."

"Smart." He brushed his thumb over my cheek. "I love you," he said firmly, then grinned when my heart rate audibly sped up. "Definitely investing in one of those," he murmured. "I'll be back."

McGee chuckled softly once he was gone. "Pretty sure he means it, kid."

I swallowed and toyed with the edge of my phone. "About getting a cardiac monitor?"

"I meant about loving you... and you knew exactly what I meant." He frowned and leaned forward. "What's going on?"

"Nothing. Just tired, I think, and... *ugh*." I blew out a breath and told the truth. "I love him, McGee."

He snorted. "Not new news, kid. You're pretty shit at hiding it."

"That's exactly the problem!" I lifted my hands and let them fall into my lap. "I worry that I *won't* be able to hide it.

What if we're walking down the street or at the office and I give him a dopey, heart-eyed smile? I mean, I've never done that in my life... but I've also never been in love before, so how the hell do I know how I'll act now that I am? Also, I told my parents I'm pansexual yesterday—"

"Hey! Congratulations."

"Yeah, thanks." I waved this away. "I've never bothered hiding that either, but now that I've made it mom-and-dad-official, I just know my mother has called a dozen friends and told them in *strictest confidence*, which means soon everyone will know. And Thatcher's talking about us moving in together? People will talk, McGee... and Jesus, now I sound like my mother," I groaned, digging my head back into the pillow.

"Whoa, whoa, whoa. Hold up. You think Thatcher's gonna hide you?"

"Not *hide* me. But..." I shrugged. "Well, yeah. I can't see him advertising our relationship, can you? He doesn't share his personal life because he doesn't want to become a news story or have the tabloids crawling all over him the way they were during his last divorce. Telling people that he's not only bi, but he's also dating the much younger son of a friend, who happens to be his employee? That's like sending the tabloids an engraved invitation."

Instead of responding, McGee seemed to stop and think through what I was saying. "Maybe you should talk to him about this," he said carefully.

I blew out a breath. "Yeah." I nodded. "You're right. That's probably a good idea."

And I would. I *would*. Once Thatcher didn't have so much work-related shit on his plate. Once I'd heard the whole Brantleigh story and knew Thatcher was really okay with it. Once I knew he wasn't worried about my health.

Then, I told myself, I'd bring up my concerns in a way that made it clear I wasn't trying to put pressure on Thatcher to do something I knew he'd hate, like take our relationship public.

Which was why I was caught completely off guard four days later when Chris Acton showed up at our hotel in downtown Madison, Wisconsin...

With a film crew.

Chapter Twenty-Two

Thatcher

It wasn't the first time McGee had saved me from a colossal mistake—not even the first time this week—but it was definitely the most critical one.

He doesn't think you want to claim him publicly.

The words McGee had spoken before heading out to find a hotel room that first night had echoed in my mind for two days while Reagan dozed in his hospital bed, joked with McGee, and listened encouragingly while I told him about Brant. They were there when Reagan cajoled me into sitting far closer to him than the nurse strictly encouraged while he ate chicken soup and told me about the morning he'd come out to his parents. And they were there when he looked at me with heat in his aquamarine eyes that made me think eight days was almost definitely too many.

If the words hadn't been there, I might not have noticed the way Reagan sidestepped when I talked about spending time with his parents in Honeybridge this summer or how he only nodded vaguely when I mentioned getting us tickets to a musical he wanted to see. He wasn't wearing a polite mask with me anymore, thank fuck, and there wasn't a doubt in my mind that he loved me and wanted that future we'd talked about as desperately as I did, but my man was holding back in an attempt to protect me.

Which meant I needed to show him unequivocally that I didn't plan to hold back when it came to showing the world how much Reagan meant to me, and he didn't need to hold back either.

When Reagan was finally discharged—after charming the entire nursing staff, of course—McGee drove us to a luxury hotel suite a few blocks away where Reagan could spend a few more days recovering before boarding the jet home. That night, I unapologetically curled my body around Reagan's in the large hotel bed and finally got a decent night's sleep. The following morning, I started making plans.

Two mornings post-discharge, Reagan and I were relaxing on the couch in the sunlit living room of our suite, me with my feet on the coffee table and Reagan with feet propped on the armrest and his head on my shoulder.

I was having a text chat with Thalia about Brant. Apparently, he'd settled into her guest house, started seeing a therapist, would be working for Paul again in a few weeks, and had taken the news that Reagan and I were together better than I expected—meaning he'd rolled his eyes and muttered, "Who *didn't* see that coming after the way they looked at each other last summer?" which was probably a fair comment.

Meanwhile, Reagan was DMing Terrance Fisher, who was in talks with HR and my new VP to return to his old marketing job at PennCo, now that Layla had finally agreed to sign a separation agreement in exchange for a more-than-fair severance package. If everything worked out as planned, PennCo's hierarchy would be restructured, and several new mid-level positions added, which would lead to greater accountability and hopefully prevent another situation like the one Layla had engineered.

Now all that was left on my to-do list was the public claiming of the man I loved. And now that he was feeling better, I was prepared to do just that.

"Come *on*, Thatcher. Six days of abstaining is a long fucking time," Reagan grumbled. He looked up at me with those eyes that still reminded me of warm Caribbean waters and made me want to dive right in. "Especially when I'm perfectly and totally well. Want me to prove it? Come with me to the bedroom, and I'll do jumping jacks." He lowered his voice to a purr. "Naked jumping jacks."

"Pretty sure I said seven days last time we talked about this," I reminded him, although we both knew there was no way we could wait that long. I leaned down and nipped at his plush bottom lip and kissed him deeply but briefly. "But nice try."

"The doctor didn't mention waiting at all, though," Reagan pointed out. "The doctor said *listen to your body* before doing strenuous physical activity, so that's exactly what I'm doing." He pushed himself up to whisper in my ear, "And my body says it really, really needs your co—"

Reagan broke off with a frown when McGee entered the suite, followed by a couple of other people.

"Oh my god." Reagan glanced at me in a panic, jumping off the sofa to put some distance between us. "Thatcher, Chris Acton is here. *And he brought camera people.*"

"Oh, good." I stood, too. "Chris, hey, good to see you again." I shook the man's hand and nodded at his companions. "Thanks for coming on such short notice. I know Wisconsin in January isn't the ideal place to be for an interview."

He smiled and gripped my hand. "I'd have flown to northern Alaska if you'd asked. It's not every day I get an exclusive like this."

Reagan shot me a worried look before he reached out to shake Chris's hand, too. I bit back my jealousy by remembering the taste of Reagan's skin was still on the tip of my tongue.

"Come on in and let me know what your crew needs to get started," I said, gesturing to the seating options of the sofa and chairs or nearby dining area. "I'll be back in a minute."

I strode into the bedroom Reagan and I had claimed, retrieved a charcoal sweater from my suitcase, pulled it on over my shirt, and managed to count to five in my head before Reagan followed me. "Why is Chris here?" he demanded in a low voice.

"Because I agreed to another sit-down. Didn't I mention it?" I leaned over and pressed a kiss to his temple. "You want to watch, or you want to rest in the bedroom?"

"I believe you know the answer to that question," Reagan said. He carefully smoothed the front of my sweater. "When have I ever left you alone with Chris Acton or any other media outlet for that matter?"

"You're right," I agreed. "We're both stronger when we're together, aren't we?"

He frowned. "Well, yes. Obviously. But be careful—"

I wrapped a hand around the back of his neck and kissed him thoroughly, cutting off his protest and leaving him dazed. *Excellent.* "Let's go."

Once Chris's crew had me miked up and seated, Reagan grabbed a bottle of water from the minifridge and moved away to sit near McGee off camera.

Chris took the chair next to where I sat on the sofa. "Just a reminder, the video will be edited with your approval and be available on our website and YouTube channel. According to our agreement, it will be distributed widely on social media. If there's interest from other news outlets, we will, of course..."

I listened with half an ear while I glanced over at Reagan again. He looked concerned, and I could tell he was asking McGee if he knew what this interview was about. McGee grinned and leaned in to bump Reagan's shoulder. I could read his lips when he said, "Trust the boss."

When Reagan looked back over at me, I shot him a wink that only seemed to make him more nervous.

Chris began with an easy question. "Why are you here in Madison, Wisconsin, this week?"

"My partner came here on business and ended up in the hospital with pneumonia. I came to be with him."

Reagan choked on the water he'd been drinking and spent a long moment coughing before getting himself under control.

I smiled at him. "He's still recovering," I confided to Chris.

Chris grinned. After McGee had put the two of us in touch—and I had my suspicions about precisely how McGee had gotten the man's number in the first place—he'd agreed to my specific requests. In exchange, I'd agreed to tell Chris about Nova Davidson.

"No problem," he said easily. "Now, Thatcher, you once said you could never see yourself marrying again.

Would you say this current partner of yours has caused you to change your mind?"

I glanced back at Reagan and made sure his eyes were on me when I responded. "Without a doubt. Yes."

The blue eyes I loved widened... and widened... and widened. *What are you doing?* he mouthed, looking a bit panicked.

"Would you care to elaborate on that?" Chris asked. "Perhaps tell us who the lucky man is?"

"Not really, no. I don't want to put him in the media spotlight by naming him in an interview. But I do want him to know that he's more *important* than anything related to my job or company. He is, and always will be, my priority. I want a future with him by my side. And when he needs me, I will always be there for him."

Reagan's eyes shimmered, and he clapped a hand over his mouth.

Chris nodded. "You sound very protective." He paused meaningfully. "In fact, you sound like a man in love."

"No doubt about that," I said, still laser-focused on the man across the room, the man who had thrown my lonely, controlled world into chaos and then put it back together again with light and color. His face was a delightful deep pink, and I imagined how warm his skin would feel against my lips. "I love him very much."

As agreed, Chris moved on to asking questions about the company. He started with questions about the new social media activity PennCo had shared recently.

"According to this morning's press release, PennCo Fiber has a new social media director." Chris's eyes shot to Reagan.

"Yes. Reagan Wellbridge has accepted the position after proving himself on our public relations team," I said, feeling a familiar pride at being able to speak well of Reagan to others. "As you know, he was an invaluable member of our team on a recent press tour, and he used the opportunity to begin improving our social media presence. The response has been tremendous."

"Several of the posts from your trip have gone viral," Chris said. "In fact, I've seen a few celebrities posting comments about potential partnerships. Do you have anything to announce there?"

"Not today, Chris. Reagan and the rest of the PR team will make any announcements when the time is right," I stated firmly.

Chris shifted in his seat. "There's a rumor that PennCo has had some other leadership changes this week. Would you care to elaborate on that?"

I nodded and smiled. "One of the things I love most about managing a business is the opportunity to recognize and foster leadership talent. The new vice president of PennCo Fiber is a man named Jensen Roberts, who has been with Pennington Industries for over ten years. We are excited to see what he does with the direction of PennCo and the launch of our new apparel fabric this summer."

"Is this new leadership a result of the Nova Davidson situation?" Chris asked.

I nodded again. "Indirectly, yes. We discovered that an employee did, in fact, send Ms. Davidson the shirt she was wearing when she got into the unfortunate accident. On behalf of PennCo, I'd like to apologize for what might have seemed like a serious, if inadvertent, marketing misstep. We're thankful that Ms. Davidson has fully recovered from her injuries, and we're hopeful that under our new manage-ment, nothing like this will happen again. I'm confident in Jensen's leadership."

As agreed, Chris moved on without asking me to name Layla directly. We spoke for a few more minutes about our partnerships with Apex, Sierra Outfitters, and Zen Activewear before wrapping up the interview. Once the cameras and microphones were off, Chris reached out to shake my hand again and thank me for the opportunity. "Congratulations on your new relationship. Reagan's a good man."

I took a deep breath and reminded myself Chris was also a good man. "He is. And thank you."

Reagan approached hesitantly. "What... the fuck... was that?"

Chris laughed as I leaned in to wrap an arm around Reagan's waist and yank him in close for a kiss that left no doubt exactly what Reagan was to me. The room was still full of other people, but I didn't care. When I finally let him up for air, his eyes were clouded with want.

"I repeat," he said breathily, looking between me and Chris. "What. The. Fuck."

Chris put up both hands and backed away. "I think that's my cue to go help pack up."

After he walked away, I leaned in and pressed a tender kiss to Reagan's cheek. "You're mine," I told him softly. "And I need you to know I'm not keeping you a secret. Ever."

Reagan's body deflated like the weight of the world fell off of him. "Really? But... Thatcher, you hate people knowing your private business."

"You're not my private business. You're my partner. You're *important*. We're going to be seen together in public and at work. Word will get out because I don't plan to keep my hands off you if I can help it. Assuming that's okay with you."

He nodded. A shy smile quirked the corners of his mouth. "Yeah. It's definitely okay with me."

"And baby, next time you're worried about something, talk to me. I know it's early days and we're still figuring each other out, but you need to come to me when you have concerns. Check in with me and tell me how you're feeling."

"I was going to," he insisted. "After things calmed down at PennCo, and Brant was settled, and—"

"And nothing. *You* are my priority," I told him. "First place, always. And I'll remind you as often as I need to until you really believe it."

Reagan's smile spread until it creased his face. "I'll remember," he promised.

His pocket began to vibrate with the familiar buzz of his phone, and when he took it out, his eyes widened at whatever he saw on the screen.

"Everything okay?" I asked.

"My parents heard about my promotion," he said. He lifted his gaze to mine. "My mother wonders if this means I was serious about quitting the campaign and staying in New York."

I wasn't sure which of us began laughing first, but I knew that even after it subsided, neither of us could stop smiling.

Chris came over and took his leave with a handshake for each of us. "Thank you again for the interview, Thatcher. And good luck to both of you. Stay in touch."

I watched him follow his crew to the door, but before he could leave, McGee grabbed his elbow and yanked him into a nearby bedroom before slamming the door closed.

Reagan and I stared at the closed door. "What was that?" Reagan murmured. "Do you think McGee still blames Chris for the bloody nose in Honeybridge? Should we rescue him?"

I shook my head as I remembered McGee's curious comments back in the emergency room. "I... don't think he's angry," I said carefully.

Reagan's confusion cleared to shock and then absolute glee. "Oh my god. Love smacked McGee in the face, just like I told him it would. I am going to give him so much shit about this. But first..."

He drew me over to the sofa and sat down, one leg drawn up so he could face me fully. He looked almost hesitant. "Thatcher. You know how, just a minute ago, you told me that I should come to you if I need something? If I have... concerns?"

I frowned. "Yes, of course. What's wrong, baby?"

"Well." He licked his lips and met my eyes. The fact that his were dancing should have been my first clue. "I'm *concerned* that my boyfriend and I haven't had sex in fucking ages, even though I've told him I'm fine, so I wanted to check in—"

I pushed Reagan down into the cushions with a growl, and he shrieked with laughter until I levered myself over him. "Is that so?"

"It is." He smoothed his hands up my chest and wrapped them around my neck. "So, Thatcher Pennington, how are you feeling right now?"

I leaned down and kissed him lightly on the lips. "I'm feeling lucky as fuck, Reagan Wellbridge. And how are *you* feeling?"

His lips turned up, and in his aquamarine eyes, I saw my future. "I feel loved. Cherished. And like I'm finally Mr. Important."

I moved my hands up to hold his face. "I meant what I

said during the interview, Reagan. As soon as you're ready for more, I'm going to marry you without any hesitation. Do you understand?"

His answering grin was wild, free, and unhesitating, the way it was meant to be.

"*Yes, sir.*"

Epilogue

Reagan

The following New Year's Eve

"MASK STAYS ON. CLOTHES COME OFF," a deep, male voice rumbled in my ear. "You're going to be good for me tonight, aren't you?"

The man's indecent proposal sent a trail of goose bumps washing over my skin, and I froze in surprise. Before he'd spoken, I'd been watching various couples twirl across the floor at the masked charity ball, wondering where the hell my husband was. I'd sent him to get me a vodka soda twenty minutes ago.

"Pardon me?" My words came out husky and flirtatious. "Do I know you?"

A familiar black brow lifted over the top of the man's Roman warrior mask, and his plush lips set in a firm, unsmiling line that made my pulse race with arousal... and then with a sudden wave of affection as he handed me my favorite drink.

"I'm very interested in games," he murmured, leaning

closer. "Especially the kind where my sexy husband teases me by wearing absolutely nothing under his tuxedo." His hand snuck down to brush across my ass, reminding me I'd had to toss my ruined boxer briefs in the trash after Thatcher had made me come in my pants like a teenager in our private elevator earlier.

I let out a laugh. "Yes, I'm a naughty, naughty boy."

"Mm, thought so." His hand brushed my pants again, only this time, it was the fabric over my half-hard cock.

I sucked in a breath. "You're playing with fire," I warned softly, glancing around at the throngs of high-profile people surrounding us in the ballroom.

"Room 5316, thirty minutes," he said roughly, ignoring my warning. With two long, sure fingers, he slid a key card into the breast pocket of my tuxedo jacket, then leaned forward until I was wrapped in the scent of his cologne— smoky and deliciously familiar. "If you're late, I'll find another plaything."

"Liar," I breathed against the side of his face. The rumble of his laugh filled my chest with warmth.

"Maybe. But I have plans for you tonight. This time last year, I didn't get to do everything I wanted."

I closed my eyes and inhaled his presence, suddenly not giving a shit what anyone around us thought. I'd been at public events like this with Thatcher often enough in the past year to know he didn't have a shred of modesty when it came to being affectionate with me in front of others. It never failed to make me feel valued and adored.

His arm wrapped around my waist. "I love you," he murmured before pressing a firm kiss to my temple. "I need to say goodbye to Brant, but after that, I expect you to meet me in the room and let me do dirty, dirty things to your sexy body for hours on end."

"Y-yes, sir," I whispered.

Those two magic words seemed to seal the deal. The beautiful man in the Roman warrior mask nodded once, turned, and disappeared into the crowd.

I shuddered out a breath and pushed up my mask in an attempt to provide my lungs with oxygen. Thirty minutes, he'd said? My phone showed it was 11:02 p.m., less than an hour until the champagne corks popped, and suddenly, I was even more excited with my plans for ringing in the New Year.

I opened my phone, adjusted the settings, pulled my mask down, and posted a quick, unedited selfie—wild grin, skewed bow tie, and all. *Remember, NYE sets the tone for the year!* I captioned as my body tingled with anxious anticipation. *Don't waste time being polite.* *champagne emoji*

I'd barely hit Post when a cloud of Chanel No. 5 swirled around me, and before I could adequately brace myself, Patricia Wellbridge appeared before me like the ghost of New Year's Past, fanning herself with her mask.

"Reagan, my darling! Where is that handsome husband of yours?" My mother's eyes scanned the room. "I could have sworn he was right here."

I squeezed my eyes shut for an instant, but when I opened them, she was very much still there, in full jeweled-and-feathered regalia, blocking my escape yet again, *damn it*, proving that no matter how much some things might change, other things never would.

"He had to go find Brantleigh. He's flying back to LA first thing in the morning to start his new job."

She waved a delicate hand in the air, her large diamond ring catching the light in a blaze of sparkles. "At least he's finally settling down. I think you're a good influence on him."

I bit back a laugh. "More like he's finally gotten his own shit together after realizing how nice he had it on his parents' dime." The truth was, I was happy for Brant. He was still a complete asshole, but at least he was beginning to take some responsibility for his own life, and he'd been generous enough to fly to New York to spend some holiday time with his father. As long as he treated Thatcher with respect, I was content.

"I was hoping Thatcher would offer to dance with me since your father has two left feet," my mother continued, still peering around the room in search of my trophy husband. She'd gotten too used to using his high profile to her advantage this past year, and it grated on me. Thatcher himself was gracious as hell, but I was tired of feeling like my parents valued the man on my arm more than their own son.

"He sprained his ankle," I lied. "No dancing." At least not the vertical kind. I planned to pirouette the fuck out of him in bed later.

"Hm. Shame. He's a lovely dancer. That Willow Honeycutt never misses an opportunity to brag about dancing with him at your wedding reception, and what she fails to recall is that I danced with him *twice*. Of course, that was before Alden and his brother—"

I blocked out her continued complaints about "those Honeycutts" until something in her tirade caught my attention.

"—with that PJ Honeycutt! *That* was quite the surprise, wasn't it?"

"What was a surprise?"

"The man he's with. The..." She looked around as if making sure no one could hear her before she lowered her voice. "The construction worker."

I couldn't stop the laugh that bubbled up. "He's not really a construction worker. You know that, right?"

Mom's eyes narrowed. "That's the *thing* with those Honeycutts, though. You just never know, darling. Maybe he's not who he says he is. I ask you, why would the man come to Honeybridge last summer under false pretenses? That's what I want to know."

I thought back to the whirlwind of last summer in Honeybridge when Thatcher couldn't keep from blurting out a marriage proposal while we were out on the water in my brother's catboat. My mother had catapulted into action as if planning a large society wedding for one of her offspring was her life's greatest dream... probably because it was.

It had taken JT's firm insistence on letting Thatcher and me plan it the way we wanted to finally pull her away from her high expectations. In the meantime, I wasn't the only Honeybridger who'd found love in an unexpected place. PJ Honeycutt, still wallowing in his strange depression after leaving art school, had fallen head over heels despite every attempt to keep the newcomer at arm's length.

"Sometimes the right person shows up at the right time," I said vaguely, though I was mostly focused on how *I* was going to show up in my husband's hotel room at the right time tonight. I glanced at my phone.

11:28 p.m. Damn it. I had two minutes to get upstairs and lose the tuxedo. Just thinking about hotel sex with my husband made my heart race.

"Gotta go, Mother," I said, leaning in to buss her on the cheek. "Happy New Year."

I left her sputtering her disapproval at my back as I hurried through the crowded ballroom to the copper-colored elevator doors. Even the sound of the faint ding as the doors slid open lit me up and sent blood rushing south.

As soon as I found the right room, I paused outside the door and took a deep breath, closing my eyes and resting my forehead against the cool painted wood.

"You're late," he said, stepping up behind me and sliding his arms around my front.

"I've been standing here trying to talk my dick down from the ledge," I admitted.

"Is that so?" His firm mouth twitched at the corner. "You going to come in your pants again, baby?"

"Possibly." I fumbled in my breast pocket for the key card and let myself in the room. He trailed me, following closely enough for me to get another hit of his woodsy scent. As soon as the door closed behind us and I slipped the key card back into my pocket, he moved even closer until his nose brushed the back of my ear and his warm breath hit the skin below.

"I expected you to be waiting for me, naked," he murmured before running the tip of his tongue along the edge of my ear. "But you know what they say. If you want something done right..." My heart hammered as his large hands slid down my shoulders to my lapels and yanked my tuxedo jacket off.

I made a breathless sound of approval as he dropped the jacket and began untying my bow tie. "Mmm. Do you have any idea how hot it makes me watching you across a crowded ballroom, knowing I tied this on you earlier this evening?" He tugged one end, loosening the knot, then kept pulling until the tie slid away from my collar. All the while, his lips continued to tease the skin on the back of my neck with hot, open-mouthed kisses that sent electric shivers all the way to my toes.

I was so lost to sensation already that I barely noticed when he pushed me up against the door and began removing my shirt with excruciating slowness, one stud at a time.

He didn't speak but made deep noises of approval in his throat as he pulled my shirt open and leaned in to kiss my chest. The sensation of my shirt being pulled out of my pants by his sure hands was enough to send blood flowing just as surely into my dick. His confidence was sexy as fuck, and I found myself relaxing into it, letting myself surrender to him—to this thing between us—in a way that was both familiar and exciting.

When he turned me around again so his mouth could begin a trail of hungry kisses down the center of my back, I sucked in a breath and reached for my cock.

He quickly grabbed my wrist and pulled it away before holding it hostage against the small of my back. "Mine," he murmured, biting my shoulder. I squeezed my eyes closed and tilted my head back against him with a groan. His fingers came up to clasp the front of my throat before his lips moved behind my ear, licking and sucking.

It was both too much and not enough. I shook off his grip and reached back with both hands to grasp the back of his head, needing to anchor myself. Needing to remind myself he was mine forever. So when I reached down to pull his face up to me and felt the edge of his mask biting into my wrist, I yanked it off and sent it sailing across the room along with my own before tugging his face closer and slamming my mouth on his.

The kiss was like a flash-bang. It shocked and disoriented me the way kissing Thatcher always seemed to. His lips were warm and soft, but his response to my kiss was aggressive and all-consuming. He clasped the sides of my head and held me in place, caught between the door and the firm press of his lips until even the very air I breathed seemed to come only from him.

It was always like this. The best kiss in a lifetime of kisses. The reality of being with him was better than any daydream I'd ever had.

By the time he moved one hand down to brush my desperate cock through my pants, I was so dizzy and starved for more that an embarrassingly high-pitched "Please" escaped me.

"I've got you, baby," he growled, pressing his forehead against my neck.

I opened my eyes and tilted my head back against the door, suddenly needing to see him. Needing to know this was really happening. Needing to know he was as lust-drowned and wrecked as I was.

When a pair of warm, brown eyes met mine, I sucked in a breath.

I knew those eyes.

I knew that beautiful face. The one I woke up to every morning and fell asleep next to every night.

Thatcher Pennington.

My father's friend.

The CEO of the Pennington Industries.

My boss.

My husband.

The absolute love of my life.

And my Mr. Important.

———

Want more Honeybridge? Check out our FREE bonus story

Mr. Important

*The Crush to see what happens with Chris and McGee after
the interview! Available here →
www.subscribepage.com/the-crush*

*And make sure you've read JT and Flynn's story,
Firecracker, available now!*

A Letter from Lucy & May

Dear Reader,

Thank you for reading *Mr. Important*! We are excited to bring you more adventures in Honeybridge. Which character are you most excited to see next? Get in touch and let us know!

If this is your first book by one of us and you'd like to read more, we suggest you start with *Fakers*, book one in the Licking Thicket series, or Lucy's *Borrowing Blue* and May's *The Date*.

We would love it if you would take a few minutes to review *Mr. Important* on Amazon, GoodReads, or BookBub. Reader reviews really do make a difference and we appreciate every single one of them.

Be sure to follow Lucy and May on Amazon to be notified of new releases, and look for us on Facebook for sneak peeks of upcoming stories.

Feel free to sign up for our newsletters, stop by www.Lucy-Lennox.com, www.MayArcher.com, or visit Lucy's Lair and Club May on Facebook to stay in touch.

To see fun inspiration photos for this book, check out the Pinterest board for Mr. Important → https://www.pinterest.com/lucy_lennox/mr-important/

And, finally, if you missed the offer of a *Mr. Important* bonus story, go back a page or two to find the link. We couldn't help but write McGee and Chris Acton's story in a short bonus.

Happy reading!
Lucy & May

More From Lucy and May

Licking Thicket

<u>Flakes</u>

<u>Fakers</u>

<u>Liars</u>

<u>Fools</u>

<u>Turkeys</u>

Peacocks

Champion Security

<u>Hijacked</u>

Hitched

<u>Hacked</u>

Honeybridge

<u>Firecracker</u>

Mr. Important

About Lucy Lennox

Lucy Lennox is the USA Today bestselling author of over fifty gay romance titles including the GoodReads Hall of Fame winner Wilde Love. Born and raised in the southeast USA, she is finally putting good use to that English Lit degree she earned before the turn of the century.

Lucy enjoys naps, pizza, and procrastinating. She stays up way too late each night reading romance because it's simply the best.

For more information and to stay updated about future releases, sales and audio news and to grab some free and bonus reads, please sign up for Lucy's author newsletter on her website at LucyLennox.com or to stay in the know, join her exciting reader group, Lucy's Lair on Facebook.

facebook.com/lucylennoxmm

instagram.com/lucylennoxmm

amazon.com/Lucy-Lennox/e/B01N0IOYPT

bookbub.com/authors/lucy-lennox

patreon.com/lucylennox

pinterest.com/lucy_lennox

Also by Lucy Lennox

Find me online → https://linktr.ee/LucyLennox

Read my books:

Made Marian Series

Forever Wilde Series

Aster Valley Series

The Billionaire Brotherhood Series

After Oscar Series (with Molly Maddox)

Twist of Fate Series (with Sloane Kennedy)

Licking Thicket Series (with May Archer)

Champion Security Series (with May Archer)

Honeybridge Series (with May Archer)

Find a complete list of my stand alone romances and novellas at www.LucyLennox.com along with audio samples, freebies, suggested reading order, and more!

About May Archer

May is an M/M author who lives in Boston. She spends her days planning vacations, mainlining diet soda, avoiding the gym, reading M/M romance, and when all other forms of procrastination fail, writing it.

Visit her website at <u>mayarcher.com</u> to sign up for her <u>newsletter</u> to hear about sales and upcoming releases, freebies and behind the scenes info and more! Or join her Facebook group, <u>Club May</u>!

facebook.com/may.archer.author

instagram.com/mayarcherauthor

amazon.com/May-Archer/e/B075JQVGLX

patreon.com/MayArcherRomance

bookbub.com/authors/may-archer

Also by May Archer

Find me online → https://linktr.ee/mayarcherauthor

Love in O'Leary Series

Whispering Key Series

The Sunday Brothers Series

Copper County Series

The Way Home Series

Licking Thicket Series

(cowritten with Lucy Lennox)

Champion Security Series

(cowritten with Lucy Lennox)

Honeybridge Series

(cowritten with Lucy Lennox)

For a comprehensive list of titles, audio samples, freebies, suggested reading order, and more, visit my website at www. MayArcher.com!